SHARK BAIT

This book is a work of fiction. Names, characters, places, and incidents either are products of the author's imagination or are used fictitiously. Any resemblance to actual persons, living or dead, events, or locales is entirely coincidental.

Printed in Australia
First Printing: February 2025

Cover design by Jess Chaplin
Typeset by Jess Chaplin

Paperback ISBN 978-1-7638695-0-9
Hardback ISBN 978-1-7638695-2-3
eBook ISBN 978-1-7638695-1-6

Angry Cat designed by Freepik.com

A catalogue record for this work is available from the National Library of Australia

SHARK BAIT

ROBERT M. SMITH

The storyline and characters in this work are entirely fictional. While its setting is based on the Victorian coastal town of Port Fairy, some locations, landmarks, organisations, events, and buildings have been modified or contrived for the benefit of the story.

For the readers who enjoy the adventures of Greg Bowker.

PROLOGUE

It was difficult to keep people back from the edge once news flashed around town about what had washed up among the bluestone rocks lining the shore. But at least the growing crowd respected the exclusion tape that Constable Farrell had hastily rolled out to prevent onlookers descending from the grassed area beside the road and onto the rocky outcrop below.

'If there's a positive side, I s'pose it explains the disappearance,' Senior Sergeant Megan Wilkins said as she crouched on her haunches, using a gloved hand to scrape away sand from a half-buried left foot. 'Saves expanding the search.' She stood up and snapped off her latex gloves. 'Not a great way to leave this world, though, is it? Bloody shark bait.'

Farrell shrugged. 'Worms or fish, once you're dead there's not a lot of difference, I suppose.'

'Once you're dead, yeah,' Wilkins replied, not looking at the older but junior officer. 'Getting to the dead stage is where I'd prefer a shark not to be involved.'

CHAPTER 1

The Port Fairy Birdwatchers Club had followed the course of many hobby-based groups over recent years. Membership was now down to a middle-aged president and six greying individuals who met once a month to plan twitcher excursions and catch up on local gossip. Its clubhouse also showed its age and was in dire need of maintenance. Its fibro cement shell had been stripped of paint by the fierce Bass Strait southerlies, with rough patches now evident where asbestos fibres were breaking free from the surface.

The building had been erected many years before the port's transition from a fishing village to one of the hottest tourist destinations in the state. It clung to a once-unwanted site facing the ocean where no sensible resident would have built a house in an age when shelter from the sea was a priority. As a result, the clubhouse now stood as an anachronistic eyesore wedged between the McMansions overlooking East Beach. Being an unincorporated body, the Birdwatchers Club had no ability to own, buy or sell property, so the structure's long-term future remained unclear, with its title held in a trust overseen by the honorary treasurer elected each year.

With the death of a long-time member the previous Christmas, numbers in the club had dropped to critical levels and an extensive campaign of posters and newspaper advertisements had been undertaken to encourage new blood. The success of their membership drive would be revealed tonight, at the club's annual meeting. The weather did not portend well, a cold easterly wind bringing sleety showers that hammered against the clubhouse door. Even the squawking seagulls that normally coerced visiting humans for the tiniest real or imagined morsel thought better of leaving their shelter on a night like this.

Early signs of new blood to invigorate the club were not promising, with only six existing members in attendance. The table near the door, with its stack of new member enrolment forms, was looking increasingly like a monument to misplaced optimism. But spirits were lifted five minutes before the meeting's scheduled start when a middle-aged couple entered the room and cast a cursory eye around the gallery of dusty bird photos adorning the cobweb-framed walls. The tall man wore casual trousers and a shirt matched with a tweed sports coat, his female partner sporting jeans and a brown vinyl jacket. They made their way to the enrolment table, where they were fervently greeted by Dot Moran, a grey-haired stalwart of the Birdwatchers. Within minutes, optimism had turned to joy when a further three conservatively dressed couples and two younger single women joined the throng and were enthusiastically enrolled. In the space of fifteen minutes, membership had more than doubled.

The meeting was brought to order by outgoing president Simon Levy, a short and balding local potato farmer with a long face and large protruding ears. Much to his annoyance, he had carried the nickname 'Trophy Head' since he was a boy. After thanking everyone for their attendance, he vacated the chair to allow the diminutive Sheila Fells, a non-aspirant for a committee position, to invite nominations for the new executive. Dot Moran nominated

Levy to continue as president, a move quickly seconded by a skeletal woman in the front row. As Mrs Fells was about to declare Levy duly elected, a further nomination came from a red-bearded man leaning against the side wall. 'I nominate Trevor Flynn,' he said, pointing to the first of the new members to sign up earlier in the evening.

'I second the nomination,' one of the new female members called out.

After a quick election where votes were split along old and new member lines, Flynn became the new president much to the chagrin of his predecessor, whose wife soothingly patted his hand. Flynn strode to the chair to conduct the remaining club business. He was a man in his early sixties, tall and in good physical shape for his age. His hair was greying and slicked back, and he sported a salt-and-pepper handlebar moustache. He was handsome in a *Days Of Our Lives* kind of fashion, but his eyes were penetrating and betrayed a latent hostility. He thanked the attendees for bestowing the presidency upon him and promised to honour the club's long history and traditions, confessing that he had viewed it from afar and thought long and hard about how to expand its base and make better use of its facilities. He explained his background as a businessman, and before that, a policeman, most notably serving with the homicide squad in Melbourne. The older members visibly relaxed when this was recounted, although the anger etched on Levy's face intensified as the manner of his dethronement ate deeper into his sense of self-importance.

Following meeting protocol, Flynn in turn called for nominations for secretary, treasurer and three committee members. On each occasion, a nomination was received for an original Birdwatcher, and each time, a second nomination came for a new member, the latter being elected without exception.

Within twenty minutes, the coup d'etat was complete. It was left to a motion from the floor to finalise the takeover. A scrawny woman from the second row of seats stood up, having removed her jacket and gloves to reveal tattoos down both arms and on the back of both hands.

'I move that we have reciprocal club membership with the Barbarians Motorcycle Club,' she stated.

The room was abuzz. Levy stood and stormed from the meeting, kicking a plastic chair across the room as he left. In spite of the brouhaha that followed, the motion was duly seconded and passed.

Flynn smiled at the shocked twitchers in the front row. 'I bet you didn't expect to get a two-for-one deal when you turned up tonight.'

He closed the meeting, thanking attendees for their input. The remnants of the old Birdwatchers Club filed silently out into the rain, vowing never to return, while the new members began removing photographs from the wall.

* * *

Chantel Pickering had struggled with mental illness all her adult life, but in recent years, her bouts of anxiety had subsided both in regularity and severity. She and her husband Craig's purchase of Ocean View Apartments, overlooking East Beach in Port Fairy, had led to a quieter and more relaxed existence, especially when compared to their previous teaching jobs in troubled and under-funded city schools. The fully serviced apartments were popular with older tourists, who caused minimum disturbance and placed few demands on the owners. Many guests were returning travellers who were more like friends to the Pickerings than paying customers. But all this had changed in the three months leading up to her good friend Rachael Bowker's visit.

Four doors up, the once-benign Birdwatchers Club had been commandeered by a threatening and raucous motorcycle gang who used the old fibro hall as their rural headquarters when away from their main compound in Coburg. With the Barbarians now fully entrenched, the once-quiet street was one to avoid. The thundering of Harley Davidsons at all hours of the day and night, the echo of unruly drinking sessions and boisterous arguments, and the not-infrequent rowdy fist fights made life within this area of the town a living nightmare. Bookings for the Pickerings' apartments had plummeted, and several of the glass-fronted mansions in the street were on the market. The one next door to Ocean View had already been purchased by the Barbarians. Bought for a song, according to one of the local real estate agents. Thus, the cancer that had initially taken root at the Birdwatchers Club was quickly metastasising. Despite numerous complaints, the local council and police seemed impotent to limit the damage being wrought on their community, and it appeared to residents that the gang was free to do as they pleased.

Chantel Pickering and Rachael Bowker had met while on the staff of a small Mallee school more than thirty years previously and had maintained a strong friendship since. Often, their families holidayed together, and the two women felt more like sisters than just good friends. This wasn't the first time Craig had called Rachael when Chantel succumbed to the debilitating effects of anxiety, but on this occasion, he felt himself losing control of his own emotions as he witnessed both his wife's health and their business descending into a bottomless chasm.

Luckily, Craig's distressed phone call had come during the term break of the kindergarten where Rachael worked. Her journey down through Colac and the western district was a pleasant one.

The weather was fine and mild, and the paddocks resembled a verdant carpet after early spring rain. For Rachael, the bucolic landscape normally had a de-stressing effect with its natural authenticity and lack of pretension. But not on this occasion. By the time she reached Port Fairy, she was feeling far from relaxed. Chantel had experienced these episodes before, but even over the phone, the tremor in Craig's voice predicted something more sinister.

Port Fairy was a town on Victoria's south-west coast and took its name from the sealing cutter, *The Fairy,* that hunted the nearby waters in the early nineteenth century. In 1835, a settlement named Belfast was established that centred on a whaling station and harbour where the Moyne River flowed into Bass Strait. In 1887, the town officially reverted to its original name of Port Fairy.

Before making her way to the Ocean View Apartments, Rachael parked in the main street, in desperate need of a coffee to settle her nerves. The shopping precinct basically comprised two streets which crossed each other at right angles. Sackville Street was the main shopping strip, with Bank Street intersecting in an east-west direction. The streets maintained their village charm, with the majority of businesses occupying old and sometimes stately buildings. All power lines and services had recently been put underground, adding to the old-world appeal. Today, being in the school holidays, the streets were crowded with tourists, many with uncontrolled children on scooters or skateboards. An inordinate number of designer dogs also made navigation of the footpath unnecessarily difficult. It took Rachael a good fifteen minutes to finally receive her skinny chai latte from Rebecca's Café and another ten minutes before she found a seat on the wharf where she could gather her thoughts while enjoying her beverage and surveying the boats in port.

Rachael was in her mid-fifties but looked twenty years younger. She was tall and slim, and through a lifetime in sport and dance had remained incredibly fit. She had an attractive face and deep green eyes. Her hair had retained its natural dark colour and was kept short in a stylish cut. Today, she wore black jeans matched with a sleeveless grey blouse and white runners.

Like the main street, the wharf was abuzz with tourist activity, the amazing weather drawing people to the water. The beaches would be the same, Rachael assumed. The wharf had changed in character over recent decades. Once, it was a hive of activity as fishermen unloaded their catch at the local co-op housed in indestructible sheds just metres from where the boats tied up. The estuary of the Moyne River was ideal as a sheltered harbour, especially after the river's outflow into Bass Strait was rerouted to the east of Griffith Island, thus avoiding the treacherous exit into the ocean to the south via what was still called the Old Passage. In recent years, much of the fishing fleet had disappeared, replaced by a smorgasbord of pleasure craft ranging from small yachts to large ocean-going luxury vessels to several sight-seeing boats. The co-op had also disappeared, the buildings replaced by a restaurant and take-away seafood shop. At least the nautical theme had been retained.

As Rachael sat sipping her coffee and staring at a luxurious ocean-going launch puzzlingly named *Hippocrates* moored in front of her, she became conscious of a person taking a seat on the bench beside her.

'Didn't realise whores strayed this far from home,' the man said furtively.

Rachael spun around to see the face of her ex-husband from thirty-three years ago. Trevor Flynn. He was the last person she expected to see so far from a big city.

Rachael stood. 'Well, time hasn't taken the edge off that nasty disposition, has it?'

Flynn rose and brought his face up close to hers. 'Not when it comes to sluts like you. I run a business down here, so I'd be careful where you go, just in case we run into each other again in a more private setting.' He feigned a chuckle. 'I might give you a quick reminder of life before you took up with fuckin' Bowker.'

He took a step back and smiled. 'Nice to catch up with you, Rachael,' he said in a louder, more public voice. 'I'm sure our paths will cross again if you're staying down this way for a while.' He nodded and strode off through the crowd.

Rachael slumped back onto her seat and stared at *Hippocrates* rocking in front of her. This trip had suddenly become even more complicated.

* * *

Greg Bowker was finishing his dinner of soup and toast at his Caulfield North home when his mobile rang. A detective inspector with the homicide squad, he was well over six foot, and wide across the shoulders. He was still in good shape despite closing in on sixty. His hair was greying at the sides, but he maintained the handsome looks of his earlier years. As he picked up the phone, he smiled when his wife's name illuminated its screen. He hit the green icon.

'Obviously made it in one piece.'

'Yeah, got down here late afternoon,' Rachael replied. 'Just got back from dinner at the Merrijig Inn.'

'Very fancy,' Bowker replied with a chuckle.

'Craig and Chantel shouted me. Least they could do, they told me.'

'Where are you now?'

'I'm across the road from their apartments watching a couple of wannabe surfers falling off their boards. Still twilight down here, but not much of it left.'

'You out of earshot?'

'Yeah. Craig and Chantel are inside going through their books for the umpteenth time. They're not good. Craig's jumpier than I've ever seen him, and Chantel's a complete mess.'

'Do you think they might be exaggerating the impact of the bikies?'

'I've heard a couple of Harleys roar past, but no big commotion as yet. Every second house on the street is for sale, though, so that says something.'

'Yeah. And I assume the value of the Pickering place has plummeted.'

'They've got it on the market, but apparently, there's no interest. Once a prospective buyer finds out about the Barbarians up the street, it's no deal.'

Bowker was taken aback and thought for a moment before he answered. 'Did you say the Barbarians? Are you sure that's what they're called?'

'Positive,' Rachael answered quickly. 'I strolled up past the old Birdwatchers clubhouse and there's a big sign on the wire fence.'

'Remember the murder investigation Sherlock and I conducted in the Mallee at the end of last year? We crossed paths with the Barbarians as part of that.'

'Skeeta Allender's mob?'

'That's them.' Bowker shook his head. 'Fuck me, if you'll excuse my French, but what are they doing setting up a base in Port Fairy?'

'Sand, beach, sunshine, I guess,' Rachael replied with a laugh. 'I suppose if they want to get away from the city, this is better than most places.'

Bowker wasn't convinced. 'You don't really believe *that*, do you?' There was silence on the line for a few seconds. 'You still there, Rach?'

'Yeah. Just watching those two surfers racing out of the water at a hundred miles an hour. Something's given them a decent scare by the way they're belting through the shallows. Chantel said a shark was spotted by fisherman at the mouth of the river a couple of days ago.'

'Pretty intelligent to go surfing at night, then.'

'Well, they're safe on the beach in one piece now. Both on their hands and knees trying to get their breath back.'

'They're lucky bastards if it *was* a shark. Any other news from down that way?'

Rachael paused long enough for her husband to suspect there was something she wasn't keen to talk about. 'Is there a problem, Rach?' he asked. 'Tell me. Is it Craig and Chantel? The Barbarians?'

'Trevor's moved down here,' Rachael replied hesitantly.

'Trevor Flynn?'

'Yeah.'

'Has he retired or something? Not that he's ever done anything useful to retire from.'

'Craig said he's bought a bit of land on the edge of town and he sees himself as some kind of developer. Apparently, he's also enquired about buying this place. Offered peanuts, so Craig's not interested. The house two doors down is under contract and the rumours say Trevor is the buyer.'

Bowker was dubious. 'Where would he get the money to buy beachfront property?'

'There's no demand for houses on this street now the motorbike gang is here, Greg,' Rachael replied.

'Flynn's no Einstein, but he's as cunning as a shithouse rat.

Why buy property that he can't resell at a profit? And it'll hardly be a relaxing beach house if there's a gang of bikies a few doors up.'

'That's the strange thing,' Rachael replied. 'Apparently, Trevor is the one who led the Barbarians' takeover of the Birdwatchers' clubrooms.'

Bowker was perplexed. 'What? Negotiated the purchase on their behalf?'

Rachael laughed. 'There was no sale. Trevor and a few bikies stacked the Birdwatchers' annual meeting, outvoted the original members and installed a new committee. Trevor is now *el presidente*, and the meeting voted to have reciprocal membership with the Barbarians.'

'Well, stay clear of the bastard. You know what he's like.'

'Too late for that. We ran into each other at the wharf. He hasn't changed much over thirty years. Not in temperament, anyway.'

Bowker was now pacing the kitchen. 'Did he threaten you?'

Rachael chuckled. 'Of course. He'd like to give me a few reminders of our married days, he said. Plus, I got the normal barrage of name-calling. Whore, slut. But that's about the extent of his vocabulary. You know what he's like.'

Bowker was highly agitated. 'I'll be down by lunchtime tomorrow. Don't go anywhere on your own.'

'There's no need, Greg. I'll stay out of his way, and I'll be home in a couple of days. You've got that Dandenong double murder to sort out.'

Bowker was having none of it. 'I'll be down by noon. I'll work the Dandenong case over the weekend.'

CHAPTER 2

A quick search of the internet found what Bowker was after. The office of the pretentiously named Shipwreck Coast Luxury Developments was in Bank Street, Port Fairy. A beaming Trevor Flynn stared out from the webpage, forcing Bowker to resist the strong temptation to punch his computer screen. Flynn was listed as the owner and CEO, and the company's main business was property development. Prime land along the romantically named Belfast Lough, known more commonly as the Moyne Lagoon, had been acquired and was awaiting final council approval for holiday unit construction. Investors were invited to apply for allocations, and a warning was issued that blocks were selling fast.

Bowker picked up his mobile and dialled the private number of his close friend and homicide squad colleague, Darren Holmes. The call was answered after three rings.

'Cracked the Dandenong case, Greg?' Holmes said without seeing the need for pleasantries.

'I wish, Sherlock. I wish,' Bowker replied. 'Just letting you know I won't be in tomorrow.'

'You crook?'

'Nah. I'm taking the day off to go down the coast to Port Fairy. Rachael's there visiting a friend.'

Holmes chuckled. 'So, you fancy a day on the beach with the missus more than working a murder case with me?'

'If it was only that easy, mate. She called last night to say she ran into her first husband on the wharf down there.'

'The former copper, you mean? The bash merchant?'

'Yeah. Trevor fuckin' Flynn.'

'What's he done after all these years to warrant a four-hour trip?'

'He threatened Rachael, the weak prick.' Holmes heard Bowker suck in a deep breath. 'If he even lays a finger on her, I can't guarantee what I'll do to the bastard when I find him.'

'Stay cool, mate,' Holmes advised, not surprised at his friend's response but at the venom in his voice. 'Don't make things worse by putting yourself in the shit.'

Bowker was quiet for a moment before assuring his colleague that he knew where the line was, and he wouldn't cross it. Holmes wasn't so sure. Not when it related to his wife.

* * *

Bowker had just cleared Warrnambool on the Princes Highway when the first of the Harley Davidsons roared past him in the passing lane. He counted twenty-seven bikes with three out of four having a female riding pillion. Each rider wore a leather jacket with the Barbarian name and logo on the back. By the time he hit the eighty-kilometre zone at Tower Hill, he had caught them up again and followed them for the next ten kilometres through potato fields and the tiny hamlet of Killarney. It still puzzled Bowker why this section of one of the country's major interstate highways was so narrow and winding and carried such a slow speed limit. Rumours had circulated for years that a new bypass of Port Fairy was to be built, but there was no evidence anything had reached a practical level, and long lines of slow-moving traffic were the result.

Rather than trailing the Barbarians all the way into Port Fairy, Bowker left the highway a kilometre short of the Rosebrook bridge and entered the town via a back road running parallel to the sand dunes adjacent to Bass Strait. The purpose of his diversion was to inspect Flynn's development on Belfast Lough. Despite stopping his car and walking to the fence skirting the road, he could see no sign of any new activity near the surrounds of the lagoon. On his side of the water, the land was low-lying and prone to flooding when the Moyne River rose little more than a metre. Often, the rough, grassed airstrip that ran close to the road was unusable due to flooding. On the far side, most of the higher ground was already occupied by small farmhouses and outbuildings with paddocks running south towards the lough. There was no evidence of earthworks that would indicate residential blocks were being opened up.

Bowker returned to his Subaru, placed his arms on the roof of the vehicle and absent-mindedly watched a trio of wind-blown golfers play the par 3 hole on the famous links layout on the other side of the road. Trevor Flynn was up to something. Bowker knew that for sure. And if he had acquired land so close to the seaside resort, where did he get the money to make such a purchase?

Bowker quickly reminded himself that he was in Port Fairy to protect his wife, not to investigate shady deals. Maybe the two would merge together when he found Flynn and laid down the law. But first, he needed to check in with Rachael.

His first port of call was to the Ocean View Apartments, where Rachael was staying. Craig Pickering advised that their wives had walked to the main street for coffee then planned to visit the beach for a swim between the flags at the local surf lifesaving club. As expected, the beach was crowded when Bowker arrived, and he was relieved to see several lifeguards on duty and a drone above the area scanning for unwanted visitors. Despite the numbers frolicking in the shallows, he quickly spotted his wife in the breakers twenty-five metres from shore. In thirty seconds, he was standing at the water's edge.

Rachael was wearing her favourite togs, a high-necked clingy blue-and-green-patterned one piece with high-cut shoulders and legs. Bowker felt the urge to throw off his polo shirt and footwear, crash into the surf, clasp his wife around the waist and hold her tightly to him. Before he could plot his next move, Rachael spotted him and stood statuesquely with hands on hips, as though posing for the cover of *Sports Illustrated.* As Bowker flicked off his thongs and waded into the shallows, she pushed through the foamy water in his direction. They met fifteen metres from the shore, Rachael throwing her arms around her husband's shoulders and kissing him on the lips. Bowker's clothes were now saturated as he pushed himself against her, but he couldn't have cared less.

'This water is colder than you'd think,' he said.

'But not too cold, by the feel of it,' she said with a knowing smile before taking him by the hand and leading him back to where she'd left her things on the dry sand. She shook her long beach towel and began drying herself off.

'Where's Chantel?' Bowker asked.

Rachael pointed towards the water. 'In among that crowd somewhere. I was talking to her a minute ago.'

'How's she travelling?'

'Seems to have pepped up since I arrived yesterday. But their financial situation would worry anyone. They borrowed heavily to buy the apartments, and since the bikies moved into their street, their cash flow has basically dried up.'

Bowker closed his eyes as a gust of wind whipped up the fine sand. 'I drove into town the back way. Past the golf course. I didn't see any evidence of the new developments Flynn is advertising.'

Rachael put the towel around her shoulders. 'According to Craig, he's at loggerheads with the local council. Or, more specifically, their chief planning officer. A Mr Ian Petrov, if I've got his name right.'

'What's the sticking point?'

'The land Trevor bought is zoned rural. That's why he was able to buy it on the cheap side, if you believe the rumours about what he paid for it. Plus, it's very low-lying and subject to inundation if there is another once-in-a-hundred-year flood that now happen every ten years or so.'

Bowker laughed. 'Must be below sea level not to get a permit around here nowadays. Have you seen some of the new builds along the river? Three days of rain in the catchment area combined with a king tide and you'd need to tread water to stay in those places!'

'Craig reckons Trevor has plans to build up the level of his blocks so they're not subject to flooding. But it seems the rezoning is the biggest obstacle. Council don't like a developer paying peanuts for land then having its status changed to instantly make it worth a fortune.'

'That hasn't stopped a lot of other councils pulling that trick, especially for one of their mates.'

Rachael hopped on one foot, trying to shift water from inside her ear. 'Well, Petrov is holding firm.'

'There should be more like him.' Bowker surveyed the beach and the carpark above the bluestone retaining wall. 'Have you run into Flynn today?'

'No. And I don't expect to.'

'I'm still going to track him down and have a quiet word.'

Rachael threw her head back and chuckled. 'You? Greg Bowker?

Have a quiet word? Yeah, that's going to happen.'

Bowker smiled. 'I won't provoke anything physical, I promise. But if *he* does, I'll deck the bastard.'

Chantel Pickering seemingly materialised beside them. Bowker was shocked when he compared her to when they'd last met, albeit more than two years prior. Once a short and chubby, happy-go-lucky woman, Chantel looked anorexic. Her face was drawn and her eyes had lost their sparkle. In her swimsuit, she resembled a bag of bones. Obviously, recent events had taken more than just a mental toll. If he hadn't known her backstory, Bowker would have surmised she was in the last throes of a fight against cancer.

After a series of pleasantries, the two women resolved to grab another coffee in the surf club nearby while Bowker visited Trevor Flynn for a chat. Chantel towelled herself off while Rachael finished drying her hair.

'Can you grab the sunscreen from my bag before you go, Greg?' Rachael asked. 'Most of it will have come off on the towel.'

Bowker picked up his wife's beach bag and rifled around until he found the tube of cream. With Chantel nearby, he made no comment on what else he saw in the bag.

* * *

The office of Shipwreck Coast Luxury Developments in Bank Street was more upmarket than Bowker expected. Fresh livery adorned the front window, with an intricate logo featuring a two-storey apartment in the shape of an upward arrow. The display was completed by an aerial photograph of Belfast Lough with blocks of land for sale outlined by red rectangles. To Bowker's untrained eye, all the designated blocks appeared to be in flood-prone areas. Parked in front of the shop were a small yellow Suzuki sedan and a silver-grey Mercedes soft top. *That fits the image*, Bowker thought.

Inside, the office was plush and ultra-modern. A chrome front counter greeted visitors, with a corridor to the left accessing offices to the rear. More maps and aerial photographs decorated the wall behind where a slim, middle-aged woman sat at the counter. She was expensively dressed, with silver jewellery adorning her neck and wrists. Her face was attractive but timeworn and heavily made up. Tiny lines radiating from the corners of her green eyes were still visible. Her platinum-blond hair was dyed, Bowker felt sure. To the detective, she came across as a woman who had once been stunning in looks but had reached her prime early in life and was now desperately hanging onto an image that no longer befitted her age.

'Can I help you, sir?' she said in a girlish voice.

'I'm chasing Trevor Flynn,' Bowker replied, careful not to give too much away.

'He's in his office. I'll give him a call.' She lifted the receiver on her phone. 'Who shall I say wants to see him?'

'Just tell him an old colleague keen to know more about what he's offering,' Bowker replied.

The woman smiled, pushed a button on her phone console and delivered the message to her boss. After a few moments, Flynn appeared from the passage to the side, his cheesy grin disappearing as he recognised his former workmate.

'What do you want, Bowker?' he growled.

'I'm interested in the blocks you have for sale, Trev,' Bowker replied with false cordiality. 'I'm looking to invest in an apartment where I can tie my boat up in the lounge room.'

'Fuck off, arsehole, before I call the cops.'

'The cops are already here, Trevor. Surely you remember our fun times working together.'

The woman behind the counter stared, dumbstruck, as the two

men went at each other.

Flynn was becoming increasingly agitated. 'I said fuck off.'

Bowker was keeping his cool and happy to see Flynn squirming. 'Come on. That's not the type of language a business tycoon should use in front of his PA.'

'She's my fuckin' wife, so she's heard it before.'

Bowker turned to face the woman. 'He belt you too, does he?'

Flynn moved towards Bowker, trying to bundle him out the door. Bowker spun sideways and pinned Flynn against the side wall. 'You just physically assaulted a police officer, shithead,' Bowker said as he held Flynn by the throat. 'I've a good mind to charge you here and now. But that's not what I came here for. I actually came to deliver a piece of simple advice.' He pushed harder against Flynn's windpipe. 'If you threaten Rachael again, or lay a finger on her, it won't be jail you have to worry about, or your dodgy investments. You wouldn't want to end up shark bait, would you, mate?'

As Bowker released Flynn with a last shove against the wall, he caught sight of an expensively suited man standing open-mouthed in the doorway.

'Old friends just catching up,' Bowker said to the man as he pushed past him and left the office.

CHAPTER 3

The Port Fairy police station in Campbell Street was modern by the town's historic standards. An unimaginative flat-roofed white building with blue facias and large aluminium windows, it sat behind a carpark, facing the street. Just inside the wire mesh fence at the front was a flagpole and a small historic bluestone construction that once served as the toilet.

Bowker introduced himself to Constable Grant Farrell, who was seated at the front counter perusing a racing guide. Without undue haste, he folded the newspaper in half when his visitor asked to speak to the officer in charge. Farrell was in his late thirties, of medium height and overweight. The hair on the crown of his head was thinning rapidly, and his pale complexion seemed at odds with a person who lived by the beach. His eyes were a dark brown, his teeth in need of a professional clean, and his flabby cheeks displayed the tiny blood vessels usually associated with a seasoned drinker. Bowker judged him as an officer who spent much of his time sitting at his desk, or in his car when out and about. Given his age and junior rank, Bowker suspected Farrell either was new to the force, was unambitious, or had failed in his efforts at promotion.

Farrell unlocked a door to the side and invited Bowker through to an office at the back, where he introduced Sergeant Megan

Wilkins, the officer in charge of the station. Wilkins was slight in build, with an angular, intelligent face and mousy short hair. She stood to shake hands with Bowker before resuming her seat and inviting him and Farrell to pull up a chair.

'Just a social visit, Greg, or here on business?' Wilkins asked, surveying Bowker's casual attire.

Bowker smiled as he looked down at his shorts and thongs. 'Bit of both, actually. I just dropped in to give you a heads up on a confrontation I had with Trevor Flynn.'

'The property developer?' Farrell asked. 'Seems like a nice enough guy from the little I've had to do with him.'

'Go on, Detective,' Wilkins said without the slightest acknowledgement of her constable's assessment.

'Flynn is my wife's first husband,' Bowker explained. 'They divorced thirty-odd years ago after he treated her abusively. She drove down here yesterday to visit a friend and unwittingly ran into Flynn on the wharf. He physically threatened her, she rang me, and here I am. I've just come from his office, where I warned him to stay away from Rachael or he'd have me to deal with. There was a bit of push and shove. Nothing serious. I think he got the message, but who knows.'

'How long's your wife in town for?' Wilkins asked.

'Only a few days. She's here to support an old friend who's doing it tough right now. She's staying with her at the apartments she and her husband own. The Ocean View, up on the dunes.'

Wilkins folded her arms and leaned back in her chair. 'No wonder she's doing it tough. The arrival of the bikies has put a dampener on that part of town. If you want a cheap beach house, that's the street to check out.'

Bowker nodded. 'Seems that way. Has the gang done anything to give you cause to move them on?'

Farrell shook his head. 'Put up a fence in defiance of council bylaws, but that's for the shire to chase up, not us. The enforcement officer over there thinks it's not worth the angst, I'd imagine. Hard to disagree with him.'

Bowker chuckled half under his breath. 'If it was a little old man who constructed an illegal fence, they'd be all over him like a fat kid on a cream bun.'

Farrell screwed up his face. 'All they can do is issue a fine, which won't be paid anyway, so what's the point?'

Bowker's gut told him the council was taking the easy way out, but he decided not to pursue the matter further. 'What's the word on Flynn?'

'Depends on who you talk to,' Wilkins replied, glancing briefly at Farrell. 'Local tradies reckon he'll be good for business. Others think he's a con artist trying to make a bob out of getting cheap land rezoned.'

Bowker nodded and folded his hands on his lap. 'I'm told he orchestrated the takeover of the Birdwatchers Club. What's his connection with the Barbarians?'

'That's got everyone stumped,' Wilkins replied. 'To our knowledge, he has nothing to do with them socially.' She shrugged. 'Maybe the bikies might return his favour and lean on a councillor or two if he needs a decision to go his way. If it comes to that, then we'll need to get involved.'

Bowker caught Farrell rolling his eyes but didn't comment. 'How long has Flynn been in the district?' he asked instead.

'Came about the same time as me,' Wilkins replied. 'Six months, probably. Just blew in with his missus, bought the land and set up shop in Bank Street.'

'Do you know where he'd get that sort of money?' Bowker asked.

Farrell shrugged. 'We know nothing about his background

except that he was once one of us. Homicide squad, apparently.'

Bowker laughed. 'Yeah, about thirty years ago, when he was given the arse. Besides, you're not going to buy much real estate on a copper's wage.' He smiled. 'But I don't need to tell you guys that, do I?'

'Maybe his wife's brother financed him,' Farrell suggested. 'He's an orthopaedic surgeon. He's got his own medical practice in Warrnambool. Can't be short of a quid. He owns this big ocean-going launch that's moored at the wharf here in Port Fairy. *Hippocrates*, it's called. In honour of the father of modern medicine, I've been told.' He laughed. 'Never heard of the bloke. I thought the name had something to do with African animals.'

'So, Flynn has managed to get himself well connected?' Bowker asked.

'Yeah. The wife's a former beauty queen, according to the locals,' Farrell added. 'Was big in the surf lifesaving club. She's even got its logo tattooed on her ankle if you look closely enough. She still does regular open-water swimming down off East Beach. Usually in the early morning. She has a big red towel and a matching beach bag. If you see that on the sand, you know she's doing a lap of the buoy way out to buggery. She keeps in pretty good trim.'

Wilkins smiled. 'Hasn't stopped Flynn being seen in the company of some young thing in Warrnambool. That's if you believe the rumours.'

'Sounds like the Trevor Flynn I knew,' Bowker replied as his phone buzzed in his pocket. He removed it and checked the screen. 'I might have to take this call. It's my partner at Homicide. We're working on that double murder in Dandenong.'

He stood and shook hands with the local officers. 'Nice to meet you both,' he said before leaving the office and speaking into his mobile.

Once he'd gone, Farrell looked at Wilkins and shook his head. 'The last thing we need is a swinging dick from Melbourne stirring things up down here. While everything's quiet, I say leave it that way. I didn't apply for a rural station to end up in a war against a bikie gang.'

If looks could kill, Farrell would've been a dead man. 'You've had a dream run for twenty years, Constable. It wouldn't hurt for something to get you off your backside.'

Farrell stood and left the room without comment.

* * *

By the time Bowker had reached his car, Holmes was outlining the purpose of his call. 'We've got a breakthrough on the Dandenong murders. A woman has walked into the Portland police station saying her husband has admitted to killing the couple over a financial dispute. Apparently, he's the son of the victims.'

'Shit, that will blow the case wide open. Things will move fast. We can kiss our weekend goodbye.'

'I planned to take Kirsten up to the Mallee. Show her my old stomping ground.'

'If we wrap things up over the weekend, take some time in lieu next week. The Mallee isn't going anywhere.'

'S'pose,' Holmes replied with a hint of dejection. 'Anyway, I thought you being just an hour away from Portland, you might fancy a late-afternoon drive west for a chat.'

'So I'm back on duty even on my day off?'

'It happens,' Holmes replied with a tinge of sarcasm.

'I'm going to look the part, aren't I?' Bowker said, letting Holmes's comment slide. 'Walking into an important interview in shorts and thongs!'

'I'm sure you'll still look professional,' Holmes replied, his tone lightening. 'Especially if you put on a tee-shirt.'

Bowker laughed out loud.

* * *

Portland was a small city of around eleven thousand residents set on a deep-water harbour in far southwestern Victoria. Founded by the Henty brothers travelling across Bass Strait from Tasmania with their sheep, Portland was Victoria's oldest white settlement, having been founded in 1834, a year before Melbourne. Portland was the retail and administrative centre of the Glenelg Shire, and serviced an extensive pastoral region. Its main employer was the aluminium smelter on the southern edge of the city. The police station, a bland brick single-storey building, sat on Glenelg Street opposite Henty Park.

Bowker's interview was with a thirty-three-year-old local woman, the partner of the son of the murdered Dandenong couple. She claimed to be in an abusive relationship which often resulted in her being physically assaulted. According to the woman, her partner had travelled to Melbourne to demand money from his parents. He had built up debts around the district and lost his job after threatening his supervisor at the smelter. On his return from the city, he apparently flew into a rage when asked of his parents' response to his request for funds. In the midst of his fury, he admitted to killing his parents and threatened to do the same to his partner if she breathed a word of what he had said. The woman said she was afraid for her life and had asked for protection at the local police station. Subsequent to the interview, local police arrested the man in question. He was locked in the cells overnight to be transported to Melbourne the following day for interview by Homicide detectives. *If only other murder cases could be solved so simply*, Bowker thought as he walked to his car in semi-darkness.

Once he'd cleared Portland, the drive back to Port Fairy offered little opportunity for Bowker to grab something to eat. Places like Tyrendarra, Codrington and Yambuk were now merely dots on a map, so his first chance for a feed was the servo on the highway back in Port Fairy itself. He was scoffing down the last of his potato cakes when he found Rachael standing on the verandah outside the Ocean View Apartments, staring out over the bay. Instinctively, he knew something was amiss.

When his wife spotted him, she ran quickly to him, throwing her arms around his chest and burying her head into his neck. She sobbed quietly. Bowker dropped his food and took Rachael by the shoulders, gently pushing her away so he could look her in the face.

'What the hell happened here?' he said, staring at the bruising on her left cheek, then touching it lightly with his fingers.

Rachael flinched before hugging her husband tightly again. 'Trevor,' she said into his neck. She felt his carotid artery swell and pulsate.

Again, he softly eased her back so he was able to talk to her directly. Already there was fury in his face. 'Tell me what happened.'

Rachael sniffed, then took a tissue from her shorts pocket. 'This afternoon, I was standing here, looking out over the ocean. Black storm clouds were billowing up above the horizon and I thought it would make a great photo. I grabbed my phone and sprinted down onto the sand so I could get the clouds reflecting off the water.'

'What time was this?'

'Around five, I would say. Trevor must have been inspecting his new purchase just up the street and spotted me on the beach. He came down and started raving on about how you had burst into his office and he'd now lost a potential buyer for one of his developments.' She blew her nose. 'I said the whole thing looked like a big scam anyway. He snapped and whacked me. Then I ran back up here.'

'Well, he just signed his own death warrant,' Bowker replied angrily.

Rachael stared into his eyes. 'Please don't do anything silly. Run him in for assault, by all means. But don't do anything you'll regret.'

'There's nothing I could do to him that I'd regret. Where'd you last see him?'

'On the beach. When I ran off, he just screamed out what a slut and a whore I was. I didn't see where he went. I didn't look back.'

Bowker inhaled loudly. 'You go inside, and don't come out again. I'll be back as soon as I've sorted this out.'

Rachael took a step backwards. 'I'm begging you, Greg. Just leave this to the local police. I planned to head home in the morning, anyway. Chantel seems a lot better, and I have work on Monday. Once I'm back in Melbourne, Trevor will forget about me.'

'Yeah, well, I'm not forgetting about him.' Bowker kissed his wife gently on the forehead and disappeared into the darkness.

* * *

Bowker returned to their apartment two hours later and was met at the door by his wife. He read the look on her face. 'You can relax for now, Rach. I couldn't find the bastard. I went to his house, but his wife said she hadn't seen him since he left work. She could've been lying, of course, but the only car there was the yellow Suzuki, which I presume is hers. He wasn't at his office, either, so I checked out the four pubs and all the restaurants, and cruised around town for a while, but no sign of his silver Merc. Looks like he's either suspected I might be after him and he's decided to get the hell out of Dodge, or he's in Warrnambool visiting the bit of fluff he apparently has over there.'

Rachael was relieved. She put her arms around his neck and kissed him gently on the lips. 'Probably best that you didn't find him. I don't want to live on my own for the rest of my life.'

Bowker put his hands around her waist. 'I'll have another look for him in the morning, but I've cooled off a bit now. I'll arrest him and charge him with aggravated assault. If I can't find him, I'll take you to the police station to make a formal statement.' He touched her gently on the tip of her nose. 'Then we'll put our two-car convoy together, head back to the city, and leave it up to the locals to deal with the prick.'

* * *

At eight o'clock the next morning, the nasty weather that had arrived the night before showed no signs of abating. Near-horizontal, sleety rain was blowing in from the south. The view over the ocean from the Bowker apartment comprised little more than misty cloud, with the windows facing the south a pattern of rivulets making their journey to the decked floor of the verandah outside.

Bowker's quick tour of the town found no sign of Flynn's vehicle, and his office was yet to open. The detective returned to the Ocean View complex, collected his wife and drove to the police station, where a reluctant Constable Farrell took Rachael's formal statement.

'Are you off back to Melbourne this morning?' Farrell asked, sitting at a table opposite Rachael.

'That's right, Constable,' Bowker replied, standing to the side. 'Work awaits both of us. Rachael needs to prepare for her pre-schoolers on Monday, and I'll need to work the weekend to make up for the time I'm wasting on Flynn.'

'So, you're unlikely to cross paths with him again?' Farrell inquired.

'Thankfully, yes,' Rachael replied without looking up from the paperwork in front of her.

'Hardly seems worth going through all this rigmarole and having us chase him up if this thing is a one-off,' Farrell replied. 'Easier to tap him on the shoulder and give him a warning, p'haps.'

Bowker saw red and slapped two palms on the tabletop, raising the level of his voice. 'Trevor Flynn punched my wife in the face, Constable. It's not the first time he's done it to her, and he lost his job with the police force for doing the same thing to another woman. It's his MO.' Bowker tapped the paperwork with the index finger of his right hand, speaking very deliberately but in a lower volume. 'Get that paperwork done properly, then find Flynn and charge the bastard.'

The door of Wilkins's office opened, and she strode across to the group. 'Is there a problem here?'

'Just doing the paperwork for an assault on my wife,' Bowker replied. He pointed to Rachael. 'You can see the bruising coming out on her cheek. Your constable and I were debating whether or not a warning for the perpetrator would suffice.'

'It's Trevor Flynn, one of the bigwigs around town,' Farrell explained, looking up at his sergeant.

Wilkins exhaled loudly and rolled her eyes. 'I don't care if it's the bloody pope! If it's an assault, it's an assault. Understand, Grant?'

'You're the boss,' Farrell replied.

'Glad you remembered,' Wilkins said as she returned to her office.

CHAPTER 4

Following the weekend interrogation of the Portland suspect by the homicide squad in Melbourne, the Dandenong double murder case was quickly wrapped up. The statement by the suspect's partner was corroborated by CCTV footage from various locations, and analysis of forensic samples found in a borrowed car would likely further nail the case shut. In the face of the mounting evidence against him, the accused chose to make full admissions surrounding his parents' murders, pinning his hopes on his violent temper giving strength to a plea of temporary insanity.

Detective Senior Constable Kirsten Larsen was at her desk on Monday when the call for Bowker came through from the Port Fairy police. She took a message and left a note on her senior colleague's desk. Larsen was tall and attractive, her blond hair cascading beyond her shoulders. In her early thirties, she had deep blue eyes, a flawless complexion, perfect teeth, and a friendly, welcoming smile. Today she wore skin-tight jeans, a silky, pale pink blouse and black ankle-high boots. A trendy grey jacket hung on the back of her chair. A recent addition to the homicide squad, she showed outstanding investigative instincts as a detective constable in country Victoria and was already franking that promise in the inquiries she'd been part of since arriving in the big smoke.

Ten minutes later, Bowker and his colleague Darren 'Sherlock' Holmes arrived back from their final interview with the Dandenong suspect. Holmes was in his late forties, slightly shorter than Bowker and not quite as heavily built. He had a totally shaved head, a brown moustache and sparkling green eyes. He put people at ease in his presence, with his happy face and wide smile. He was in a romantic relationship with Larsen after the two had met in an earlier investigation and his twenty-five-year marriage had broken down.

Larsen leaned back in her chair. 'How'd you go with Mr Portland?' she asked over her shoulder.

'Confessed to the whole thing,' Holmes said. 'Didn't even have to beat him with a phone book,' he added cheerily.

'What's a phone book?' Larsen shot back, tongue in cheek.

'When did this come in?' Bowker asked, picking up the note from his desk.

'Ten minutes ago, perhaps fifteen,' Larsen replied.

'Did they say what it was about?'

'Nope.' Larsen shook her head. 'The sergeant just said she needed to talk to you. By her tone, it sounded urgent.'

Bowker picked up his phone and punched in the number on the note. Holmes squeezed Larsen's shoulder. 'Feel like a coffee? My shout.'

Larsen laughed. 'Shout me a free coffee? Last of the big spenders, eh, Detective Sergeant?'

She stood, and the two officers left the room, joking to one another.

'Just letting you know Trevor Flynn still hasn't turned up,' Sergeant Wilkins said on the end of the phone. 'His wife was on our doorstep first thing this morning. He didn't arrive home Friday night and he's been missing all weekend.'

'Flynn is a slimy piece of work, so I wouldn't read too much into that until he hasn't shown his head for a few more days. Probably spent the weekend with his girlfriend in Warrnambool.'

'That was my attitude too, until his car turned up.'

'Where? Three nights ago, I drove down every street in town, and his Merc was nowhere to be seen.'

'It was found bogged in the dunes at Yambuk this morning.'

'That'd have to be twenty k's down the highway towards Portland,' Bowker said. 'I drove through it Friday. Didn't notice any dunes, just a million wind turbines.'

'The dunes are a mile or more to the south. Down beyond the caravan park. The car was driven through the sealed carpark and up a sandy track. Looks like he wanted to take a zip up the beach but bellied out in the loose sand.'

Bowker's brow wrinkled. 'What? Use a hundred-thousand-plus Mercedes as a beach buggy? Sounds like a dickhead thing to do, even for a moron like Flynn. How long has it been there?'

'We're not sure. Yesterday's weather was so diabolical that nobody ventured outside, let alone to an exposed beach like the one at Yambuk. A resident of the caravan park reckons she heard cars go past Friday night, but the weather was closing in, and the sea pretty rough and noisy, so she's not a hundred percent sure.'

'Any sign of Flynn?'

'Nope. But we haven't conducted a full-scale search of the area. Grant is poking around down there now to see what he can find.'

'It's all under control, then,' Bowker replied sarcastically. Wilkins didn't reply. 'So, what's the purpose of your call?'

'Just a courtesy follow-up to the statement your wife gave Saturday morning.' She hesitated for a moment. 'Plus, something tells me we might need Homicide down here in the next few days.'

'Bit early to assume he's dead, Megan. I suggest you involve

Missing Persons at this stage.'

Wilkins hesitated again before she continued. 'And you're sure you didn't come across Flynn on Friday night after your wife was assaulted?'

'What are you implying, Sergeant?' Bowker shot back.

'I'm implying nothing. I'm just asking the questions I need to ask. I'll be in touch if we learn anything new.'

Wilkins hung up. Bowker placed the receiver back in its cradle, leaned back in his chair and stared into space.

His mind was still occupied with Wilkins's call when Holmes and Larsen arrived back with coffees in takeaway cups. The detective constable returned to her desk while Holmes continued across the room to Bowker and placed a coffee in front of him. 'Brought you a present.'

Bowker was shaken from his reverie. 'Thanks, mate.' He picked up the coffee and took a small exploratory sip. 'Bloody hot,' he said as he returned the cup to his desk.

Holmes pulled up a chair. 'What was the Port Fairy call about?' he asked. 'Did they find where you stashed Flynn's body?' he added with a wide grin.

Bowker didn't see the funny side. 'Don't even joke about it, mate. If I *had* found him after he punched Rachael, there's no guarantee I wouldn't have belted the bastard into a lifeless pulp. But despite my best efforts, he was nowhere to be found.'

'So, what was the call about?'

'There's been no sign of the prick, but they found his car bellied out in the dunes at Yambuk.'

Holmes frowned. 'Where the fuck is that?'

'Ten miles the other side of Port Fairy.' Bowker picked up his coffee again and blew over its surface. 'The town, if that's what you'd call it, is on the highway. There's a side road that runs down to where the river flows through a bit of a lake and into the sea. Wilkins mentioned there's a small caravan park there as well. She said it looks as though Flynn tried to follow a sandy track from the carpark to the beach and got the car bogged to the knackers.' Bowker smiled and pointed a thumb at his chest. 'My description, not hers.'

Holmes was puzzled. 'Why would he do that?'

Bowker shook his head. 'No idea. Wilkins suggested he may have planned a drive along the beach. But that's bullshit, as far as I'm concerned. The bloke's as old as me, not some young surfer boy. And he's driving a Mercedes sports car, for fuck's sake.'

'When'd he go down there?'

'Nobody knows. Friday night, when I couldn't find him, p'haps. Saturday was a shit day, weather-wise, so he could have driven down then without being noticed. Or last night, maybe.'

'And there's no sign of the prick himself?'

'Nope. The local constable is down there now, but he's about as handy as sunglasses on a vampire. He's more likely to destroy clues than find anything useful.'

Holmes leaned back in his chair and folded his hands behind his head. 'Perhaps Flynn thought he'd walk home along the beach and was caught out by the incoming tide or something.'

Bowker shook his head. 'He'd have a mobile phone, for sure. Even if he didn't, why not walk a hundred yards back to the caravan park and get someone to ring his missus to come out and get him?' He smiled and took a sip of his coffee. 'But you know what, Sherlock? If the bastard never turns up, that'll be too soon for me. It's not our problem.'

When Holmes didn't respond, Bowker changed the subject. 'What have you and Kirsten got planned for your days in lieu up north?'

'Might spend a night at my brother's place at Murrayville. Or at Carina, a district just out the road, to be more correct.'

Bowker suppressed a loud laugh, knowing Larsen wasn't far out of earshot. 'Shit, that'll be a shock for Kirsten. She ever been to the Mallee?'

Holmes smiled. 'Nope. No further north than Horsham, apparently. That's where her sister lives. We'll stop there for lunch tomorrow on our way up.'

Bowker folded his arms. 'Have you seen the forecast for the next few days?'

Holmes nodded. 'Yeah. Forty-five for Ouyen on Wednesday. Only forty-one tomorrow.'

'Good luck,' Bowker replied with a wide grin.

'I thought we might head back via Mildura and spend a night on a houseboat on the Murray.'

Bowker lowered his voice. 'Gonna be pretty warm up there for shaggin', mate.'

Holmes smiled. 'Never too hot for that, Greg.'

* * *

It was sweltering and windy on Tuesday by the time Holmes and Larsen were on their way north, with Holmes already dreading the predicted weather for his hometown of Murrayville on the southern edge of the Sunset Country. The stiff northerly buffeted Holmes's VW four-wheel drive with fragments of bark and clouds of dust blowing across the bitumen ahead. It was hot outside, but with the vehicle's air con running, the interior was a pleasant twenty degrees. *Thank God for the wonders of modern technology,* Holmes thought, remembering the scorching days of his childhood.

'The weather is turning nasty out there, Darren,' Larsen said, staring out her window.

You have no idea what a furnace it will be in Murrayville, Holmes thought to say but chose to moderate his response instead. 'It'll gradually get a bit worse as we head north. But we won't notice much difference inside the car,' he said. *Until we open the doors and our faces blister*, he decided not to add.

Twenty-five minutes out of Horsham was the tiny settlement of Dadswells Bridge, set on the banks of the Mount William Creek to the eastern edge of the Grampians National Park. A couple of houses, a small caravan park, a gift shop and the Giant Koala were all that comprised what could generously be called a hamlet. The Western Highway, from the speed restrictions signs before the bridge itself to the northern edge of the Grampians bushland, had seen the tragic deaths of more than a few travellers. A combination of blind curves, massive roadside red gums and the ever-present kangaroos had made the stretch a well-known black spot. It was on this length of highway that Holmes first spotted the Harley Davidson among the dust in his mirrors. The motorcycle pulled out to pass on a blind sweeping bend.

'The dickhead behind me has no idea what's coming around this curve,' Holmes said as he planted the foot to avoid being overtaken. The motorcycle pulled back in behind him. On the first stretch of straight road after clearing the restriction signs, the motorbike roared past, its rider giving Holmes the finger. His pillion passenger, a hard-faced middle-aged woman, did likewise. The Harley had swept-back handlebars, Peter Fonda *Easy Rider* style, and on the petrol tank was painted an eagle with an aggravated snake in its beak. A spark of recognition fired somewhere in Holmes's brain but was quickly extinguished by the priority of keeping his mind on the shimmering road that stretched before him.

'I wonder how far it'll be before we find them splattered over the front of a semi or the trunk of a tree?' Larsen asked.

'My guess is that we won't see them again unless there's a patrol car hidden in the bushes somewhere, just waiting for idiots like him.'

As it turned out, the pair didn't have to wait long until they spotted the Harley again. This time, it was pulled in beside a ute in the carpark overlooking Green Lake, a few kilometres from the outskirts of Horsham. A flock of sulphur-crested cockatoos wheeled overhead in the dusty sky.

'Looks like they've found a mate,' Larsen said, pointing towards the two motorcyclists unzipping their leathers, in conversation with a man in shorts and a singlet leaning against a blue Ford ute. 'On a day like this, it's a wonder they don't die in those leathers,' she added.

'Better to cook than come off and leave half your body smeared on the bitumen, I suppose.'

'Probably why they've stopped beside the lake,' Larsen said. 'Hoping to cool off a bit.'

'Perhaps,' Holmes replied with a tone of suspicion.

* * *

By three thirty in the afternoon, following a banquet of cold meats and salad provided by Larsen's sister, the couple were on the Henty Highway midway between Horsham and the turn-off onto the Mallee Highway at Underbool. Fifteen kilometres south of Hopetoun, a brown tourist sign adjacent to the road indicated the Rosebery Sunsets Gallery Café was ahead on their left, which turned out to be a re-purposed small timber church standing alone in the vast landscape. A board out the front advertised coffee and ice creams. However, it was on the other side of the highway that the detectives' interest was piqued.

A pair of concrete silos carried the images of two pioneering farmers. On the left was a woman standing aside a sheep, and on the right, a weathered-beaten faced man had one arm around the neck of his horse and a coiled-up stock whip in his other hand. Holmes slowed to allow a better view of this lofty concrete canvas that formed a small segment of the popular silo art trail that had become a major tourist attraction in country Victoria.

'Remember the painting we saw at Goorambat last year?' Holmes asked. 'We stopped and had lunch at the local pub, remember?'

Larsen smiled and patted Holmes's thigh. 'I remember,' she said quietly, before pointing towards the old church. 'I could go for an ice cream. What about you?'

'Are you sure you want to get out in this heat?'

'There'll be an air con inside, surely.'

'Let's hope,' Holmes replied as he pulled in beside the weatherboard building, narrowly avoiding a blue-tongue lizard that scurried into the bark litter at the base of a sugar gum. An old white Holden Sunbird sat between the road and the front fence, with bird and animal heads hand-painted on it in black. A sign on a tree told visitors the building had been a Presbyterian church between 1920 and 1977. The broad trunk of a large gum nearby held a cluster of fingerboards testifying to Rosebery's history as a larger settlement. Signs pointed in the direction of the cemetery, the memorial park, the *third* football ground 1946–70, the town drive and the 1901–1912 rifle range. Holmes and Larsen surveyed the landscape from their vehicle and, except for the old church, a couple of houses and the silos, saw nothing but open paddocks and stunted Mallee scrub. Certainly nothing to validate the information on the tree.

As Larsen opened the car door, she had visions of her life ending there and then. The temperature was stifling, the hot north wind sucking the moisture from her face. To her relief, the inside of the gallery-cum-café was air conditioned by a reverse-cycle unit poking through a wall at the back. A small, cluttered room was visible through an open door to the side of the main space, and a plastic flyscreen adorned an entrance from the attached residence to the rear. Inside the old church were bookshelves, display cabinets, and plastic-covered tables with painted wooden chairs pushed underneath. Cold drinks were available, along with ice creams and a range of chips and lollies. A coffee machine sat on the counter near the front door.

As Holmes dived into the freezer containing an array of frozen delights, Larsen scanned the ancient photos on the walls, a disparate collection ranging from landscapes to pictures of long-forgotten weddings. After a moment, the flyscreen parted, revealing an elderly woman dressed in black slacks and a swirly purple top. She was stocky in stature, her hair silver-grey. She wore glasses on a friendly face.

'I bet you're not here for a coffee,' she said with a smile.

'Nope. A couple of ice creams will do us fine,' Holmes replied as he put two Streets Magnums into one hand and slid the plastic cover back across the freezer. 'The Cokes inside the fridge look pretty inviting as well.' He collected the drinks and placed them with the ice creams on the counter.

'Where you headed?' the shopkeeper asked as she keyed prices into the till.

'Murrayville,' Holmes replied.

'Be hot up there today.'

Unlike here, Holmes thought but didn't say. 'I was born in Murrayville and lived up there until I moved to Melbourne for work. So I know what to expect.'

The woman nodded towards Larsen. 'Decided to give your

daughter a taste of what you had to put up with in summer there, eh?'

Holmes decided not to correct her assumption. 'Something like that.'

Larsen overheard the exchange and smiled to herself, knowing how conscious Holmes was about their age difference. Holmes checked the amount displayed on the till and pulled his wallet from his back pocket. The prices were a bit steep, but these tiny establishments had none of the buying power of the supermarkets. He doubted the shopkeeper could purchase her items cheaper wholesale than she could buy them retail at the big stores. He wasn't complaining. There had to be some sort of premium for making goods available this far from anywhere.

'How's business?' he asked as he handed over his cash.

'Silos being painted has helped a lot. Get people stopping and taking photos, then wandering over for a coffee and bikkies. Seems the story for a lot of places. Give people a reason to stop and they're happy to spend a few shillings in remote shops or pubs.' She handed him back his change.

'Wouldn't get too many on a day like this, I suppose,' Holmes surmised.

'Nah. You two are the first, to tell you the truth. Hardly worth staying open, really, but I'm in the room next door watching tellie, so I may as well be available. Actually thought I might have had another customer a few hours ago. A couple came into the silo reserve on a motorbike, sat under a tree over there and had a smoke. Not long after, another bloke arrived in a four-wheel drive from the other direction. They had a chinwag out there in the heat, before they both left at the same time.' She laughed. 'Would've been cooler in here for a chat, and maybe I might have sold them something.' She shrugged. 'Everybody's different, I s'pose.'

'Did the four-wheel drive come from Hopetoun way?'

The woman shook her head. 'No, down the dirt road to the side here.'

'Where's that lead to?'

'Nowhere, really. If you follow it through the back blocks, you'll get to Rainbow.'

'And the bloke went the same way back as he came?' Holmes put his wallet back in his pocket and tried to sound as if he was casually interested, rather than conducting a police interrogation.

'Yeah. Back down Windy Ridge Road.' She leaned on the ledge behind her. 'Must have been mates or something. Picked a bad day for a catch-up, though.'

Larsen wandered across with an old-fashioned china gravy boat on an oval saucer. 'I'll take this, please.'

The woman smiled and enthusiastically wrapped the item in tissue paper before dropping it into a brown paper shopping bag. Larsen had made her day.

CHAPTER 5

Despite his apparent disinterest in Flynn's disappearance, Bowker contacted the Port Fairy police station from Vicpol's Spencer Street headquarters first thing that Tuesday morning. Constable Farrell took the call, explaining that his boss was attending a meeting at the council offices. 'I s'pose you're ringing about Trevor Flynn?' Farrell asked.

'That's right, Grant,' Bowker replied, disappointed that Wilkins wasn't around. He had much more confidence in her than the constable.

'No sign of Trevor yet. We searched the area around where his car was bogged but found nothing to indicate where he went.'

'Was the car locked?'

'Nah. Driver's side window was down, so the inside had a fair bit of sand blown in. The upholstery looked like it'd copped a fair bit of rain and sea spray as well. Sort of makes you think he didn't plan to be away from it for very long, don't you reckon?'

Or it wasn't him that drove it there, Bowker thought. 'Were the keys in the ignition?'

'Yeah. But the car was going nowhere.'

'Is it still out in the dunes?'

'The boss got the local towy to drag it out of the sand and pull it onto their tipper tray truck. It's sitting in our carpark here at the moment.'

'Have you printed the inside of the vehicle?'

'Yeah. A crew from Warrnambool came across and did it. Lifted a few decent ones. They've been sent off to the big smoke for comparison with the national database. There are also a couple of dents in the driver's side door panel that we thought were a bit hard to explain. There are no scratches, like you'd expect if the car had made contact with another vehicle or a tree. Just the metal pushed in a bit.' Farrell hesitated before continuing. 'Listen, I know he assaulted your wife, but how come you're so interested in our investigation? I can assure you that when we track him down, we'll charge him and let you know.'

'Flynn and I go back a long way,' Bowker replied, attempting to disguise his annoyance at being asked to explain his motives by a constable he already felt was a lazy waste of space. 'So I've got more than a passing interest in where all this is heading.'

'Yeah, I know that.' Farrell hesitated. 'But it's only fair to tell you that a number of people have told us you were storming into various places on Friday night threatening to knock Flynn's head off if you found him. So I guess you've got some skin in the game.'

'Don't like unfinished business, that's all,' Bowker replied.

'Particularly in this case, I guess, Detective.'

Bowker didn't rise to the bait, but civilly delivered his farewells and asked to be informed if Flynn was located.

* * *

Holmes and Larsen's Mallee sojourn had so far been an enjoyable one. The night spent at the Murrayville farm had been a load of fun despite the brutal weather. Larsen had fitted in well with the Holmes clan. Given her age fell somewhere between her partner's sister-in-law and his oldest niece, she was able to converse confidently on most topics. Except, of course, broad-acre farming. The two brothers chatted for hours about new trends in agriculture, the likely impact of climate change on cropping, and their younger days together in the red sandy country.

Despite the success of the excursion thus far, Holmes and Larsen were both relieved when they finally loaded their gear onto a houseboat in Mildura while watching the blazing sun sink slowly down over the river. They ate Chinese takeaway and consumed a bottle of local wine in the air-conditioned comfort of the houseboat lounge, kicking back as the screeching cockatoos in the giant river red gums farewelled the day.

Even in the centre of the mighty Murray, the heat the next day was ferocious. The searing sun reflected off the water, and the strong northerly wind did its best to push the houseboat to the Victorian banks of the river. The couple took turns navigating the meandering bends in the Murray, avoiding sand bars and the ubiquitous snags. Larsen walked up behind Holmes during his stint as skipper and placed both hands on his shoulders. She saw his face reflected in the boat's windscreen, his eyes staring past the river and into the distance.

'Penny for your thoughts,' she said. 'You're not shagged out after last night, I hope.'

Holmes chuckled. 'Nope.' He hesitated a moment. 'I've just been thinking about Greg and this Trevor Flynn business down at Port Fairy.'

Larsen sat down beside him so they could talk face to face. 'Surely you don't suspect Greg had anything to do with his disappearance?'

'He can get bloody angry, particularly if something threatens his family.' Holmes shook his head. 'But no. I don't think he would have crossed the line with Flynn.' He shrugged. 'But who can be sure about these things? He dealt with the bloke thirty-odd years ago, so I dare say he thought he was rid of the bastard forever. Then, out of the blue, Flynn crosses paths with Rachael and it's back to the future. Violent assault and all.' He took a deep breath as he steered around the end of a sandbar. 'It wouldn't surprise me to hear Greg dotted Flynn, but I can't see him solving the problem permanently.'

'So, what's your worry, then?'

Holmes frowned. 'If Flynn turns up dead, then obviously, Homicide will become involved. At least initially, anyway. The way I see it, Greg would be obliged to sit that one out. He told me that on the night Flynn disappeared, he stormed around town looking for the bastard and advised anyone who would listen that he'd deal with the prick when he found him.'

'I see what you mean. If he wasn't a copper, he'd be the number one suspect if Flynn did meet foul play.'

Holmes stared at Larsen. 'Regardless of being a copper, if he wasn't our *friend*, he'd be the number one suspect.'

Larsen nodded but said nothing.

Holmes relaxed a little and steered the boat away from a large snag blocking half the main channel. He smiled and sighed heavily. 'What did I read somewhere? Nine out of ten things we worry about never happen. Let's hope Flynn turns up and we don't have a problem.'

* * *

But on Wednesday afternoon, Flynn did turn up. Megan Wilkins from the Port Fairy police contacted Bowker with the news that evening.

'The body, or what's left of it, washed up near the lighthouse on Griffith Island, which for all intents and purposes is part of the Port Fairy township. Looks like a shark has had its fill. One leg is gone, and one lower arm is bitten off. There's a shark tooth embedded in the humerus just above where the elbow would have been. His torso is pretty heavily torn apart as well.'

'And you're sure it's Flynn?' Bowker asked.

'Certain. His face is lacerated, but there's no doubt it's him.'

'So what's your theory?'

'Well, stating the bleeding obvious, if you'll excuse the pun, he's somehow ended up in the water,' Wilkins replied. 'Whether he fell or was swept off rocks is anyone's guess at this stage. The remains of street clothes are still on his body, and there is a shoe on the left foot, so he certainly didn't go in for a casual swim. Unless, of course, he'd had enough of the world and just waded into the ocean until he drowned. That would explain his car being abandoned down at Yambuk.' She hesitated. 'But there is a problem with that. Like, how did the body just happen to wash up on the rocks at Port Fairy, twenty-five kilometres of coastline away?'

'Currents, maybe?' Bowker suggested.

'It's possible, but improbable in terms of the hundreds of other places the body could have washed up. It's a hell of a coincidence if he went into the water at Yambuk then reappeared back where he was last seen alive.'

'So you think the abandoned car might be a furphy?'

'Possibly. But it's a bit early to tell.'

'Any guesses on how long he'd been in the water?'

'Hard to say, given the mutilation by the shark. We'll have to wait for a post-mortem. That'll also tell us whether he drowned or was killed in the attack.'

Bowker thought for a moment as he fiddled with pens on his desk. 'Who found the body?'

'A couple of young kids playing chasey through the scrub. Family were out on the island looking for shells once the temp had dropped a bit. Kids followed a wallaby track and there he was in the water.' Wilkins feigned a chuckle. 'Be a while before they go shell-hunting again, I reckon.'

'Besides his car at Yambuk, and without the results of a post-mortem, of course, does anything else grab you as being out of place? Anything that might point to a need for Homicide to become involved?'

Wilkins hesitated again for a moment. 'Only that some hothead was touring the town promising to do harm to the victim the night he disappeared.'

'Well, that hothead didn't find him, did he?' Bowker shot back defensively before softening his tone. 'Is the body on its way to Melbourne?'

'It will be after the Warrnambool crew have bagged and tagged everything. It should all be out at McLeod by tomorrow.'

McLeod was a northern suburb of Melbourne where the Victoria Police Forensic Services Centre was located. Bowker had a close contact there who could normally expedite matters on his request, particularly if that request was accompanied by a bottle of her favourite Johnnie Walker.

'No sign of a mobile phone?' Bowker asked as an afterthought. 'In his business, you'd think he'd have carried one.'

'Nope, no phone. But the way those sharks rip and tear, it's a miracle there's anything left of him.'

Bowker thanked Wilkins for her call and the two promised to keep in touch. After disconnecting, the detective leaned back in his chair and stared into space. Flynn's demise had the potential to become tricky, not least for himself. This wasn't the first time he'd regretted losing his cool over the assault on the Port Fairy beach, but now things had suddenly become much more serious.

Bowker took his mobile from his pocket and searched his

contact list for Erin O'Meara's direct line. O'Meara had slowly worked her way up to a senior position within the police forensic hierarchy in spite of her abrasive and call-a-spade-a-spade nature. She didn't fit the mould of a quiet, subservient and unambitious female scientist, and she had to fight hard to advance through the organisation. She was a lateral thinker who sought and embraced the latest technology, especially from overseas. To Bowker's knowledge, she had never been married and had no children, although he had only got to know her since he joined Homicide. There were rumours she had once been the partner of a Painters and Dockers Union official whose body had been found floating in the bay following a period of unrest on the wharves.

A chain smoker and whisky drinker, O'Meara was a skeleton of a woman known for her rimless glasses, which she somehow balanced on the tip of her long curving nose. Her fingers were heavily nicotine stained, and to those first meeting her, she appeared in the final stages of terminal cancer. But she had looked this way ever since Bowker first met her. Her age was anyone's guess, with various estimates placing her somewhere between fifty and seventy. With her scrawny frame, her bent-forward walking style and protruding nose, she was occasionally called Madam Bin Chicken behind her back, although The Bitch was her most popular moniker. This was out of her hearing, of course.

'How are they hanging, Gregory?' O'Meara asked after seeing Bowker's number come up on her phone.

'Good afternoon to you too, Erin. Still at work, obviously.'

'Always at work, Detective. So, what crime can I solve for you this time? The word on the street is that the Dandenong murders have been wrapped up with a confession.'

O'Meara coughed loudly, and Bowker heard her expectorate, hopefully into a tissue or hanky. With O'Meara, it could have just as easily been directly into her rubbish bin.

'What's on your mind?' she asked. 'You haven't broken up with that lovely wife of yours and are ringing me looking for a bit of replacement cheesecake?' She laughed loudly then broke into another fit of coughing.

Bowker waited for her to regain her breath. 'You'll be receiving a body, or what's left of it, from down Warrnambool way. Shark attack. Can you CC me when you send back the report, please?'

'Any particular shark you're trying to nail?' O'Meara laughed. 'Got him in the lockup, have you?'

Bowker ignored the attempted humour. 'I'd be interested to know if anything suggests foul play.'

'You think a chook may have got at him first?' O'Meara replied. When Bowker didn't immediately respond, she continued. 'Foul play? Chook? Get it?'

'Don't give up your day job, Erin,' Bowker replied. 'The vic's name is Trevor Flynn.'

'Used to be a Trevor Flynn in Homicide decades ago. Clever dick. Up himself. Got the arse, if I remember rightly.'

Bowker smiled to himself, in awe of O'Meara's memory. 'Same bloke.'

'Shark probably didn't like the taste and spat out what's left of him.' O'Meara laughed and coughed loudly again. 'Anything suspicious about his death?'

'He was wearing clothes, for a start,' Bowker replied, 'so he wasn't swimming or surfing.'

'Fell off a jetty, perhaps. Or swept off rocks,' O'Meara suggested. 'We see it all the time. Dumb shits fishing off rocks and they forget waves aren't all the same size or that the tide is coming in. Whooska, and it's all over, red rover.' She paused for a moment. 'What's your interest in this one, Gregory? Where cause of death seems straightforward, it's us that call Homicide if we see something that doesn't fit the narrative. Not the other way around.'

Bowker thought carefully before responding. 'I was in Port Fairy when he went missing from there. He was my wife's ex-husband.'

O'Meara laughed. 'So you want to know if you left prints on the body before you fed him to the fish?'

Bowker didn't smile. 'Something like that.'

* * *

The drive home gave Bowker time to assess the best way to inform his wife of Flynn's demise. It was hard to know how she would react. She had been a victim of his violence during their three-year marriage and had been subjected to ongoing harassment from him after they split and she ultimately married his former friend. Despite all this, at some stage Rachael must have had deep feelings for Flynn, and news of his death would not necessarily fill her with joy or satisfaction. Bowker decided that the best option was to deliver the news in a neutral, matter-of-fact way and let Rachael's reaction guide further discussion.

'I had a call from Sergeant Wilkins at Port Fairy,' Bowker said as he pulled out a chair and took a seat at the kitchen table.

'Yeah?' Rachael replied as she poured milk into a pair of instant coffees. 'Trevor turned up yet?'

Bowker nodded. 'Yeah.'

'Where'd his body wash up?' Rachael asked casually as she placed a mug in front of her husband before sitting down opposite.

Bowker was gobsmacked. 'How'd you know he was dead?'

Rachael shrugged. 'Come on, Greg. The guy has always operated on the edge of the law and lately became an associate of a bikie gang with known criminal links. When you said he'd fallen completely off the radar down there, it seemed obvious, to me anyway, that he was paying the piper somewhere.'

'How did you know his body washed up?' Bowker asked, still perplexed by his wife's insight.

Rachael took a sip of her coffee, then placed the mug on the table in front of her. 'I didn't. But Port Fairy is on the beach. If you want to get rid of a body in a hurry, surely the logical action is to dump it in the surf and hope the tide carries it out of your life forever.' She took a Tim Tam from the tin in the centre of the table. 'They found his car down on the beach at Yambuk, you told me. That's probably where the deed was done.'

'Maybe. But he washed up on the rocks at Port Fairy.'

'That's not all that far from Yambuk, is it?'

'Far enough to pose a few questions.' Bowker looked at his wife in search of a reaction. 'How do you feel about Flynn's death? He *was* your husband for three years. Young love and all that.'

'If he was the Trevor Flynn I went out with in my late teens, then I'd be devastated,' Rachael replied, rotating her coffee mug on the tabletop. 'But the real Trevor Flynn emerged once we were married, and the world is a better place without him.' She stared at the table for a moment or two, sorting her thoughts. 'Where's his body now?'

'On its way to a post-mortem by now. What's left of it, anyway. The local coppers said it's been pretty torn apart by a shark.'

Rachael frowned. 'I wouldn't wish that on anyone, even a bastard like Trevor. At least he wasn't alive to feel anything.'

'What makes you assume he was murdered and not just a victim of a shark attack? Or a simple drowning?'

Rachael shrugged. 'Call it women's intuition.' She smiled. 'To tell you the truth, drowning or a shark attack never crossed my mind. I've always assumed that the treatment Trevor meted out to people would finally catch up with him. It was just a matter of time.

But I may be wrong.'

'We'll have to wait for the post-mortem before we'll know if his death needs further investigation.'

'Let's hope it supports a simple case of drowning,' Rachael said, staring at her husband.

'Yeah,' Bowker replied, holding his wife's stare.

CHAPTER 6

'I didn't expect to see you until tomorrow morning, mate. You have a good break?' Bowker asked when Holmes walked into Homicide headquarters late Thursday afternoon. 'By the grin on your face, I think I know the answer.'

Holmes pulled up a chair beside his colleague's desk. 'Yeah. You and Rachael ought to sneak away on a houseboat some time. Just you and the river, water trickling by, birds singing. Serenity, as they say, mate. Tie up to the bank under the stars and let the boat rock you to sleep.'

Bowker smiled. 'Yeah, and I bet it was rocking for most of the night, too.' Before the chuckling Holmes could respond, Bowker continued. 'What was it like at Murrayville?'

'Bloody hot, mate. And windy as all shit.' Holmes shrugged. 'When you're a kid, you don't notice it, you know. But now, with air conditioning, it's all a big shock to the system. I bet by the end of your stint at Manang, the heat didn't stop you doing anything. Sport. Social events. The lot. You just got on with it.' He chuckled. 'We're becoming too soft in our old age.'

'What did Kirsten think of it?'

'She didn't complain too much. She knew it was my old stomping ground and was pretty keen not to give the impression she thought it was a backwater.'

Bowker laughed. 'Pretty hard to be a backwater at Murrayville when there's no water.'

'There's plenty of fresh stuff under the ground,' Holmes replied defensively. 'That's more than you can say about Manangatang. Bores over there are saltier than the Dead Sea, according to my brother.'

The two men swapped Mallee weather stories for a few minutes before Holmes raised the hot topic. 'I heard on the news that a body was washed up at Port Fairy. Appears like a shark attack, local coppers are saying. Name withheld until rellies are informed. You heard any more than that?'

'Yeah. Local sergeant rang me yesterday. The body has been identified. My mate, Trevor Flynn.'

Holmes leaned back in his chair and folded his hands behind his head. He took a deep breath. 'And they're sure it was a shark attack?'

'Well, half his body is missing and there's a shark tooth wedged in what's left of an arm. So, yeah, there's no doubt a shark's had a piece of him.'

'But you know what I mean, Greg? Do the locals believe he was taken by a shark or that he was dead before the fish found him?'

Bowker upturned his palms. 'I think they're waiting for the forensics before they make any judgement about cause of death.'

'What's your gut feel from what they've told you?'

Bowker shrugged. 'I think it's unlikely he went for a dip and drowned. He's still wearing the remains of his street clothes. Maybe he slipped on a rock, banged his head and was washed out to sea. The post-mortem will answer a lot of those questions.'

This was tricky, and Holmes could feel sweat starting to run down the sides of his chest. He lowered his arms to hide the moistening of his shirt. He was unsure whether to raise his concerns about Bowker's involvement in the case or wait for the forensics to arrive. If the science ruled out foul play, then there'd be no need for an awkward conversation with his colleague and friend. While his conscious brain said wait for more information, his unconscious mind took control.

'If the autopsy suspects foul play, then you can't be involved in that investigation. But you know that better than I do.'

Bowker raised his eyebrows. 'You could look at it that way, I s'pose. But on the other hand, I know Flynn's background and personality.'

Holmes frowned. 'But you were roaming Port Fairy the night he disappeared threatening serious revenge for his attack on Rachael. If the post-mortem shows Flynn was somehow killed before he hit the water, you'd be the number one suspect if you weren't a copper.' Holmes sighed loudly. 'It wouldn't pass the pub test if you were part of the investigating team. But you know this yourself, Greg.'

'Do you think I killed Flynn?'

Holmes threw his head back. 'Of course I bloody don't. But an investigation not only needs to be done right but *seen* to be done right as well.' He exhaled loudly. 'Let's hope it doesn't come to that.'

* * *

The situation was clarified the next morning via a phone call from Erin O'Meara at the McLeod forensic centre.

'Just ringing to say we've finished half the autopsy on Flynn's body,' O'Meara said in her gravelly voice.

Bowker was perplexed. 'Half the autopsy? When are you going to finish it?'

'When they find the other half of his body.' She roared laughing, then coughed until she spat out the issue with a long retching sound.

Although he was alone at his desk, Bowker unconsciously shook his head. 'Shit, Erin, you're a comic genius. So, what did your people find?'

'Massive wounds, as you can imagine. Shark tooth is legit. Sent photos to an expert at Melbourne uni. Without actually examining the thing, he can't be a hundred percent sure, but he reckons his money is on a tiger shark. And a big bastard at that.'

'Must have a pretty savage bite to rip a tooth out,' Bowker replied.

'According to the boffin, sharks regularly lose teeth in attacks. They have several rows of them, and when one is torn out, a new one moves up from the second row to take its place.' She laughed. 'After talking to this bloke, I've vowed to leave my bikini in the bottom drawer.'

The thought of O'Meara in a bikini, or any swimsuit for that matter, left Bowker dumbstruck.

'You still there, Gregory?' she asked after a few moments. 'I can send you pictures if you want.'

'Of the shark tooth?'

'No. Of me in a bikini.' There followed another fit of coughing.

Bowker tried to steer her back on track. 'So, other than confirmation of a shark attack, what else can you tell me?'

'One leg and half an arm missing and most of his internal organs. There were remnants of clothes still on his torso. His left lung and heart were still intact. Major tear wounds over most of his body. His head has extensive lacerations, but no bruising. This would suggest he didn't smack his head on something or get whacked with an object before he hit the water.'

'Have you concluded anything about cause of death?' Bowker asked impatiently.

'I'm getting to that, there's no hurry. He's going nowhere.

The surviving lung contained no water, which indicates he didn't drown and that he was dead before he entered the water. Even if a shark grabbed him and pulled him under, he'd get a lung full of seawater in his death throes.'

'So he didn't bang his head, and he didn't drown, and a shark didn't kill him. What's your theory on cause of death? He have a heart attack and fall into the ocean? What?'

'This is the good bit, Gregory,' O'Meara replied proudly. 'We nearly missed it in among all the torn flesh. There is a small knife wound that penetrated the right ventricle of the heart. The blade must have gone between two ribs. The opening isn't very wide, which would indicate a narrowish blade. And the depth of the penetration suggests it wasn't all that long. Our guess is a pocketknife, or a short kitchen or filleting knife. Perhaps even one of those smaller ones that fishermen carry in their tackle box. Certainly not a Crocodile Dundee "You-call-that-a-knife" type of weapon.'

Bowker didn't respond, just stared into space and rubbed the back of his neck.

'You still there?' O'Meara asked again.

'Yeah, Erin, I'm here,' the detective replied. 'So, in your opinion, he was murdered? And you're pretty sure of that?'

'I'm positive. I've never heard of a bloke topping himself by stabbing himself through the heart, have you?'

'Could he have fallen on the knife and staggered into the ocean?' Bowker asked.

O'Meara laughed. 'You hear talk of people falling on their swords. But falling on a short-bladed knife like that? I don't think so, my friend. Remember Occam's Razor? The simplest explanation is usually the right one. The more conditions you need to impose to explain an event, the further you move from the likely cause.'

'There are exceptions,' Bowker countered quickly.

'Indeed there are, Gregory. But I wouldn't bet my house on this being one of them.'

'Can you give us an estimated time of death?'

'It's difficult, as you can imagine. The body having been in the water and attacked by various organisms, not least the shark, make it hard to put a timeline on it. But our best guess is five or six days.'

'So last Saturday or Sunday?' Bowker asked.

'Yeah. Maybe late Friday at a stretch.' Bowker heard her computer chirp in the background before she spoke again. 'Look, I've got to go. I'll send the full report through when it's ready.'

Bowker thanked her, disconnected the call and leaned back in his chair. A homicide investigation was now inevitable, and things had suddenly become more complex from a personal point of view.

After a few moments, he slapped his palms on his thighs, stood up and walked over to where Holmes was flipping through evidence briefs relating to the Dandenong double murders. Bowker rested his backside on Holmes's desk, folded his arms and looked down at his colleague, who leaned back in his chair.

'Fancy a trip to the beach tomorrow?' Bowker asked.

Holmes tossed his biro gently on top of an open file. 'Why's that?'

'I just had a call from Erin O'Meara over at forensics. Somebody stuck a knife in Trevor Flynn before he was fed to the sharks.'

Holmes hesitated while thinking how best to respond. 'How about Kirsten and I take a run down there and suss things out first? Make a weekend out of the trip. Earn a few more days in lieu. You're a bit too close to all this, Greg. Wouldn't look good. We can keep you updated on what we uncover.'

'If it's my head on the block, I need to be involved in the investigation.'

Holmes exhaled heavily in annoyance. 'So what are you saying? Kirsten and I are incapable of a thorough investigation?' He rolled his eyes. 'Thanks, mate.'

'I'm not saying that at all. But I know Flynn's background, and I know where a lot of people were the night he disappeared.' Bowker stood up straight. 'I'll pick you up at seven in the morning. We can make a weekend out of it.' He smiled. 'But I can't guarantee I'll be more fun than Kirsten.' He walked off before Holmes could respond.

* * *

'Surely you're not conducting the investigation,' Megan Wilkins said when Bowker explained the findings of the autopsy over the phone.

'Absolutely,' Bowker replied.

'From where I stand, you're a suspect,' Wilkins shot back.

'All the more incentive for me to solve the thing, don't you think, Sergeant?'

'Or to manipulate the investigation to your advantage if you *were* involved. In no way am I saying you were, but it wouldn't look good.'

'We can talk about it tomorrow after we arrive. I'll see you then,' he added before quickly disconnecting.

* * *

It was less than half an hour later that Bowker was called to the office of the deputy commissioner in charge of crime, Bronwyn Knight. Knight had steadily advanced through the ranks and was universally respected for her strong work habits and ethical standards. Because she had started as a policewoman on the streets in one of the tougher areas of Melbourne and progressed through the major crime squads, other officers saw her as having paid her dues. As a result, there was no resentment when she was elevated to the higher echelons of the force. Bowker got on well with her and respected her opinions but knew when he was asked to her office that there was a disagreement brewing. And on this occasion, he knew what the difference of opinion would be.

Knight was behind her large desk when Bowker knocked and entered. A woman in her mid-fifties, Knight had kept herself in good physical shape and was always impeccably dressed. In uniform, she was the personification of strength and stability. Her face bore the trials, tribulations and stresses of the career copper. She carried that hardness that comes from learning to trust no one, from not internalising the disappointments seen in human beings, and from insulating the soul from the atrocities that people can inflict on their fellow man.

'Grab a seat, Greg,' she said, indicating the chair on the opposite side of her desk.

Bowker sat down and defensively folded his arms across his chest. 'Is this about the Trevor Flynn murder?'

Knight nodded. 'Yeah. We need to chat about the investigation.'

'You been talking to Holmes?'

Knight shook her head and leaned forward, elbows on her desk, hands folded. 'Nope. Had a call from Sergeant Wilkins at Port Fairy. She's worried your involvement will compromise the investigation. And from what she told me, she's right.'

'So, what *did* she tell you?' Bowker replied quickly.

'That Flynn assaulted your wife on the day he disappeared and that you stormed around town promising to square up. The talk around Port Fairy already has you in the frame, Greg. How would it look if you were down there asking questions and making allegations against others?'

Bowker leaned forward, hands on his knees. 'I can see all that, Bronwyn. But I know Flynn's background. I know how the bastard thinks. Or would have thought. That's a big advantage to throw away.'

'If it makes you feel any better, I would be excusing myself from this case if I still worked in Homicide.'

A puzzled look passed over Bowker's face. 'You knew Flynn?'

'We trained together at the academy. He was all over the female recruits. Pompous, sexist pig, he was. God's gift to women, or so he thought. We crossed paths again when he joined Homicide. Same attitude there, only worse. Believed he was the biggest swinging dick the force had seen. When Jack Moloney nailed him for sexual and physical assault, there were no tears shed, I can assure you of that. Even the blokes were sick of his showboating. And let me tell you, I shed no tears when I heard about his death, either.' She stared straight into Bowker's eyes. 'But we do things right here, Greg, regardless of the victim. You of all people know that.' She leaned back in her chair. 'Holmes and Larsen can handle it. You got something to keep you busy back here?'

Bowker took a deep breath and shrugged his shoulders in resignation. 'Not a lot on. The Dandenong case is sorted. Richardson and Nguyen are working on the shooting at Traralgon. I've got a couple of weeks in lieu owing. Might take them while things are quiet.'

Knight smiled. 'Good idea. Once you've given a statement to Holmes and Larsen, try to get away for a few days. Clear the head. You've worked non-stop for months.'

Bowker nodded, knowing exactly where his getaway would take him.

CHAPTER 7

Bowker provided his statement in one of the interview rooms, feeling strangely under pressure as he sat across the table from his friends Detectives Holmes and Larsen. Holmes led the questioning while Larsen jotted notes.

'Just for the record, Greg, can you tell us your movements on the night Flynn disappeared?'

'I'd been over at Portland conducting an interview in relation to another case. It was after dark when I arrived back in Port Fairy.'

'What time do you reckon that was?'

'Eight fifteen… eight thirty, maybe.'

'Is that when you found your wife and realised she'd been assaulted?' Holmes asked.

'No, a bit before that. I was starving, so I stopped at the servo on the highway and grabbed a couple of potato cakes and an orange juice to tide me over until I found out whether Rachael had already had tea or was waiting for me to get back.'

'I feel stupid asking you this, but you know I have to do this properly,' Holmes said hesitantly.

Bowker shrugged. 'Ask away. The sooner we get this over with, the sooner the proper investigation can start.'

'People in the shop can confirm your visit?' Holmes asked.

Bowker sighed. 'There were two people behind the counter

and half a dozen other customers. I paid with a credit card, so the bank can confirm what time I was there. Plus, the servo has CCTV cameras.'

Larsen looked up from her notes. 'Then you went back to where you were staying?'

Bowker nodded. 'That's right.'

'And that's when you noticed she'd been assaulted?'

'Not straight away. It was dark, with just a sensor light further along the verandah. Rachael was up on the deck crying, and that's when I got a good look at her face.'

'What did she say had happened?'

'She said she'd been standing on the verandah looking at the build-up of the storm clouds in the east,' Bowker explained. 'She thought it would make a good photo, so she took her phone down to the water's edge to get the clouds reflecting off the sea. Flynn must have seen her there and went down to confront her.'

'Why would he have gone down that end of town?' Holmes asked.

Bowker's irritation was starting to surface. 'Stuffed if I know, Sherlock. Rachael assumed he'd been visiting the house he'd bought up the street.' He exhaled loudly. 'The bottom line is, he confronted her, verbally abused her then whacked her in the head.'

Larsen stopped writing and looked up. 'What'd she say happened after that?'

'She ran up to the apartments to get away from him,' Bowker replied.

Holmes nodded. 'She see where Flynn went?'

'I asked her that. She didn't look back. Obviously, her first priority was to get as far away from him as possible. She said maybe he went back along the beach or up to his car if it was outside his new purchase. To be honest, I don't think checking where he ended up was very important to her at that stage.'

Holmes nodded. 'You've already told me the answer to this, but just for the record. What was your reaction to all this?'

'White anger. Desire for vengeance. The way he treated Rachael while they were married has sat in my guts for thirty-odd years. I thought the time had come to do what I should have done decades ago.' He looked at Holmes and then Larsen. 'But I didn't find him, and I didn't kill him.' He held up both palms. 'Don't get me wrong. If I *had* found him, I can't guarantee I wouldn't have punched his ticket.' He paused and sighed quietly. 'Luckily for me, I didn't find him.' He gave a faux chuckle. 'Didn't change much for Flynn, as it turned out.'

Holmes leaned back and folded his arms. 'So, tell us where you went looking for him.'

'I went straight to his office in Bank Street, but that was all locked up like a church. There were no lights on anywhere in the building, and neither of the Flynn cars were out the front. I then drove around to the afterhours address displayed on the office window.'

'And obviously, he wasn't home,' Larsen said.

'No, but his wife was,' Bowker replied. 'She said she hadn't seen him since he'd left the office to go to a meeting at the council chambers. I felt like checking all the rooms just in case, but his car wasn't there, so I assumed she was telling the truth. Plus, there was an angry dog growling its head off somewhere in the house.'

'How did she react to your visit?' Holmes asked.

'Taken aback, I'd say. I was pretty angry. I think I told her she wouldn't have to put up with his abuse anymore if I caught up with him.'

Holmes nodded. 'Where to then?'

'I decided to check the pubs. I looked in at The Commercial.

Well, it used to be called that when I was younger. It's called The Oak and Anchor, or some fancy name like that, now. There was no sign of the bastard in there, but one of the customers said Flynn drank at The Star just down the street. But he wasn't there either. Or at The Stump or The Victoria.'

'So, you went on a pub crawl?' Holmes replied, trying to lighten the mood.

A faint smile crossed Bowker's face. 'Yeah. A pub crawl without a drop being swallowed.'

'Were you still angry at this stage?' Larsen asked.

'Absolutely. Angry, and frustrated at not being able to find him. I stuck my head into every restaurant that was open and drove around for quarter of an hour looking for his car, but no joy. The town was pretty quiet, and the weather had closed in. I saw an old couple walking their dog in the dark and the rain. I asked them whether they'd seen Flynn's Mercedes in their travels. They said they'd noticed a Mercedes sports car parked near the wharf a little while earlier.'

'Presumably, you checked that out?' Holmes asked.

'Wasn't there. I drove around the town again, rechecked the pubs, eateries, Flynn's house and office, but still no sign of him or the car. By this stage, I'd come around to the idea of turning the incident over to the local coppers, so I went back to the apartment and made sure Rachael was OK.'

'Obviously, you'd cooled off a bit by then?'

'Yeah. Next morning, I reported the assault to the local station, Rachael made a statement and we drove back to Melbourne.' Bowker shrugged. 'That's about all I can tell you.'

Holmes and Larsen put follow-up questions, and within fifteen minutes, Bowker had grabbed gear from his desk and was on his way home.

* * *

'Darren Holmes rang and asked that I present for an interview with him and Kirsten at the Caulfield Police Station in the morning,' was the first thing Rachael said when her husband arrived home from work. 'He said there had been some developments in the inquiry into Trevor's death.'

Bowker dropped his briefcase on the kitchen floor, hugged his wife and narrated the events of his day, including the post-mortem findings.

'So he was murdered?'

'Yeah. Stabbed. Blade slipped between a couple of ribs and into his heart. A short blade. Like on a pocketknife or a small kitchen knife.'

Rachael's eyes locked onto her husband's. 'Like the one you caught sight of in my bag when I asked for my sunscreen the other day at Port Fairy?'

'Yeah, but–'

Rachael cut him off. 'Did you see the apple in there as well?'

Bowker shook his head. 'No. I guess I assumed the knife was for self-protection, and that made me even more determined to get Flynn off your back.'

Rachael's eyes dropped and she stared at the floor. 'OK, there might have been a bit of that as well. I grabbed it off Chantel's bench as we left for the beach. More for deterrent value than to actually use.' She looked back at her husband. 'The damn knife will still be in my beach bag. I forgot to put it back. I'll go get it for you, if you like.'

'There's no need to do that, Rach. I know you didn't kill anybody.'

Bowker attempted to grab her arm as she brushed past him and hurried down the passage. She returned seconds later with her floral towelling bag. She placed it on the table and rifled through the items inside before tipping them out on the table. There was no knife. 'It must have fallen out in the car or on the beach.'

Tears welled in her eyes. Bowker put his arms around her and pulled her in close. 'I know you didn't stab him. So don't lose any sleep about the stupid knife.'

Rachael looked up at him. 'Will I be a suspect because I had it in my bag?'

'Nobody saw it other than me. I'm not part of the investigation, so there's no conflict of interest.'

Rachael stepped back, puzzled. 'What do you mean you're not part of the investigation? You're Homicide's top gun. Plus, you know more about Trevor Flynn than anyone else in the force.'

'I'm their chief suspect, Rach. I went gunning for him about the time he was killed. I've been banned from involvement. Directive right from the top. Holmes and Larsen will lead the inquiry.'

Rachael screwed up her face. 'How are you going to handle that? I can't see you sitting in your office twiddling your thumbs while you're drip-fed whatever information Darren is allowed to tell you.'

'There's not a lot on at work, so I've decided to take a couple of weeks in lieu.'

Rachael threw her hands back around her husband's neck. 'Good for you. You've hardly had any time off since August. You should get away for a few days to recharge the batteries. Take the fishing gear and relax. Pity I'm locked into work at the kinder.'

Bowker kissed her on the forehead. 'I've already got it sorted. I rang up an old mate and asked to use his getaway for a few days in return for me cutting the grass and cleaning out the gutters. He said it will be vacant from Sunday, so I'll head off then.'

Rachael smiled. 'You talking about Dave Forrest's place up at Eildon? That'll be nice.'

Bowker shook his head. 'No, Rob and Judi Wikman's cottage at Port Fairy.'

His wife was stunned for a moment. 'Why would you go down there and put yourself in the middle of an inquiry you've been ordered to stay out of?'

'I just want to keep an eye on how things progress,' Bowker replied. 'Sniff around and ask a few questions of my own.'

'Don't you trust Darren and Kirsten to do a thorough job?'

'Of course I do. Sherlock's the best detective I've ever worked with. But a third set of eyes looking from a different perspective won't do any harm.' He smiled. 'Besides, if he needs to do another interview with me, I'll be close handy, won't I?'

'It's going to look like you're interfering with an investigation where both of us have a significant involvement.'

Bowker smiled more broadly this time and stretched his arms out wide. 'I'll be observing, not interfering.'

Rachael began returning the items to her beach bag. 'Yeah, I'd like to see that,' she said sarcastically. She thought for a moment. 'I expect Darren wants to talk to me because I may have been the last person to see him alive.' She looked up at her husband. 'Except for his killer, of course,' she added quickly.

'I could ring Holmes now and tell him to forget the interview tomorrow.' He smiled lecherously. 'We could go upstairs, and I could give you a thorough grilling. Go over you with a fine-toothed comb.'

'I'm not in the mood for jokes, Greg. I worry that Trevor still might have the last laugh and turn our life upside down.'

Bowker hugged her to his chest. 'That won't happen with me on watch.'

* * *

The Caulfield Police Station in Glenferrie Road was a single-storey cream brick building with dark-framed aluminium windows and a black Colourbond pitched roof. The entrance featured a sheltered portico with a heavy prefabbed concrete facade totally out of keeping with the rest of the building's style. Rachael arrived at nine o'clock and was met in the foyer by Darren Holmes, who led her through to an interview room where Kirsten Larsen was seated at a table.

'Thanks for coming in on a weekend, Rach,' Holmes said as he invited her to sit opposite him and his partner. 'This shouldn't keep you too long.'

After quick pleasantries between friends, Holmes got the interview underway. 'Greg no doubt has told you Trevor Flynn was stabbed and killed.'

Rachael nodded. 'Yes. But I've already given a statement to the Port Fairy police about what happened on the beach that day. I'm not sure what I can add.'

'You have to realise that this is now a murder inquiry rather than an assault,' Larsen replied. 'We've probably got questions that the Port Fairy interview didn't cover.'

Rachael folded her arms across her chest, wondering where this was going. 'OK,' she said quietly.

The initial questioning centred around information she had already provided to the local police: why she was on the beach, what Flynn said to her, what the exact nature of his physical assault was, what her reaction was, whether she saw where Flynn went after the attack.

Holmes opened a folder in front of him. 'This is an email copy of the statement you gave at Port Fairy. In it you said that you assumed Flynn was visiting the house he had bought and spotted you on the beach?'

Rachael nodded. 'That's right.'

'Did you see his Mercedes parked near that house?' Holmes asked.

Rachael shook her head. 'No. That was just an assumption I made. Why else would he be in that street?'

Larsen folded her hands on the table. 'Visiting the bikies, maybe. Or stalking you after he realised you were in town.'

'I never thought of him following me. Kinda scary if that was the case.'

'Where had you been prior to going onto the sand to take a photo?' Holmes asked.

'Up on the landing of the apartments.'

'Whereabouts prior to that?'

Rachael thought for a moment. 'Chantel and I walked down to the wharf and had afternoon tea in the restaurant there. We chatted for an hour or so, then walked along the river, over the footbridge and back to the apartments.'

'So, if Flynn was in the wharf area and had caught sight of you, it's possible he could have followed you home?'

Rachael shrugged. 'I guess so.' Her eyes darted between the officers. 'But why would he do that when I was with another person?'

'You'd be surprised by what some sickos do,' Larsen replied. 'Did you go inside when you got home, or stay on the deck until you took the photo?'

Rachael thought for a moment. 'Stayed outside, I think. Chantel went inside to start preparing dinner.'

'If Flynn had followed you home, then, he could have hidden and watched your movements?'

Rachael shrugged again. 'I guess so.'

'You didn't see which way Flynn went after the attack?' Holmes asked.

'No. I just raced back to the apartments and waited for Greg to get back from Portland.'

'What was Greg's reaction when you told him of the attack? When you showed him the bruising on your face?'

Rachael leaned back and exhaled loudly. 'What do you think, Darren? Other than me, you know him better than anyone else on earth.' She took a deep breath. 'Greg exploded, of course. Then he sent me inside and went looking for Trevor.'

Larsen fiddled with a pen on the table. 'How long after Flynn's assault did Greg arrive back from Portland?'

'Fifteen or twenty minutes, I'd say. I know I was still shaking.'

'Did he say where he would go first in pursuit of Flynn?' Holmes followed up.

Rachael shook her head. 'No. But the logical place would be Trevor's home, don't you think?'

After a further quarter hour of questioning, the detectives thanked Rachael for her attendance and told her she could go.

* * *

'You reckon there's any chance Greg did kill Flynn?' Larsen asked as she and Holmes began their journey to South-West Victoria late on Sunday morning. 'You've known him a lot longer than me.'

Holmes dropped one hand off the steering wheel and looked across at his colleague. 'If the victim was anyone but Flynn, I'd say absolutely no chance at all. But two things come into play here. Greg's got a quick temper, which I've only seen erupt a couple of times, and he's super protective of Rachael. He knows the history of her previous marriage and he knows what sort of violence Flynn is capable of. Particularly against women. That's the reason why Flynn got the arse from the force thirty years ago.'

Larsen nodded. 'So, given the right circumstances?'

Holmes shrugged. 'If I was forced to write a script in which Greg committed murder, it would centre around his wife being battered by a bloke he knew had already inflicted pain and suffering, and who had the capacity and motivation to continue doing it.'

'What about using a knife? Doesn't seem like Greg's style.'

Holmes kept his eyes on the road ahead as they slipped by a B-double at the top of the Westgate Bridge. 'No, that doesn't fit with me either. If Flynn had been beaten to death, then maybe you could see Greg doing it in a fit of rage. Particularly if Flynn had bad-mouthed Rachael when he caught up with him.'

Larsen saw a slight wrinkle in Holmes's brow. 'What?'

'It's probably nothing, but I'm pretty sure that Greg took his Subaru to Port Fairy.'

'So?'

Holmes exhaled audibly. 'He keeps his fishing gear in the back.'

'And you're assuming there'd be a knife among it.'

Holmes nodded.

* * *

By the time Holmes and Larsen had reached Camperdown, Bowker was already turning into Regent Street in Port Fairy. His home for the immediate future was Locksley, an historic stone cottage built right on the edge of the footpath. The front was constructed of sandstone blocks with bluestone quoins on the corners and framing the doorway and timber windows. The other original external walls featured higgledy-piggledy laid sandstone rocks of assorted shapes and sizes. Inside, the original backwall of the building was exposed as part of a weatherboard extension, and a number of fossils were revealed among the stone. The home comprised a lounge room and bedroom in the original construction, with a living area-slash-kitchen later added to the rear, along with a second bedroom, a bathroom and laundry. It wasn't an overly large house, but cosy enough, with its wood heater warming the coldest days.

Bowker threw his bag on the floor in the main bedroom then sat down in the kitchen to plan his next move.

* * *

Deciding to begin their investigation on Monday morning, Holmes and Larsen filled in what remained of their Sunday with a long walk on the beach, dinner at the Lemongrass restaurant, and an extended bout of lovemaking in their motel room.

First thing Monday, they drove on to Campbell Street to introduce themselves to the local constabulary.

'How many officers work here?' Larsen asked as she released her seatbelt in the police station carpark.

'Not sure,' Holmes replied. 'Greg said he met two. The sergeant in charge and a slack-arsed middle-aged constable. But I suspect there'd have to be more officers in a town this size, especially at holiday times. The boss's name is Megan Wilkins. I've only heard Greg refer to the connie as Fuckhead Farrell.' He smiled. 'I doubt that's the name his parents gave him.'

Larsen laughed as they got out of the car and walked towards the front door. Holmes wore a charcoal-grey pinstriped suit, white shirt and pale blue tie. Larsen was conservatively dressed in an off-white silk blouse, knee-length pencil skirt and medium-height heels.

'We'll need to be assigned one of the Port Fairy coppers to show us around and answer all our local questions,' Holmes said. He steepled his fingers in front of his chest in mock prayer. 'Please, God, don't let it be Fuckhead Farrell.'

Holmes held the station door open and followed Larsen inside, unconsciously ogling her backside in the tight skirt as he let the door close behind him. A few moments after pressing a button on the customer service bench, a tall, chisel-jawed, blue-eyed and blond-headed young man, a senior constable, appeared and slid open the glass window. Holmes sensed Larsen's breath shorten, and he suddenly felt his age. He introduced himself and his colleague and expressed a wish to speak with the senior sergeant.

The young constable shot out a tanned, muscled arm and strongly shook each detective's hand. 'Dale Small. Pleased to meet you both. Not very often we need Homicide people down here, thank goodness.'

'How long have you been stationed at Port Fairy?' Larsen asked.

Small scratched the stubble on his cheek with his left hand. 'Nearly eighteen months now. I couldn't believe my luck when the transfer came through.' He smiled widely, exposing perfect white teeth. 'I've always been into surfing, so Port Fairy is a perfect spot. Perhaps not quite as good as Torquay, with Bells Beach just up the road. But on the flip side, Torquay is becoming too much like suburbia for me. There's a more laid-back feel down here, which I like.'

He unlocked an entrance to the side of the counter and invited the detectives through to the back, holding the door open while they walked through. A quick glance at the young constable's left hand by both detectives confirmed no wedding ring. Even though Holmes was well over six foot tall, he was still shorter than the senior constable, and although in good physical shape, he lacked the flat abdomen of his younger colleague. He unconsciously sucked in his stomach as Larsen walked between them.

When she saw her visitors, Wilkins rose from her chair and was introduced by Small. The constable excused himself, and the

Homicide detectives were invited to take a seat.

'There's an office next door where you can set up for the duration of the investigation, if you like,' Wilkins said. 'Grant Farrell is using it at present, but he can move back into the main work area.'

'We don't want to put anyone out,' Holmes replied.

'Farrell doesn't need an office,' Wilkins assured her visitors. 'He moved in there when the station was a bit short-staffed a few years ago. It's been on my agenda to move him out anyway, so this gives me a good excuse.'

From Wilkins's tone, Holmes sensed she had a similar opinion of Farrell to Bowker. 'So, what do we know?' Holmes asked. 'Greg Bowker filled us in on the bones of the case, but there are still a lot of unknowns.'

Wilkins smiled sardonically. 'Your chief inspector has an interest in this case in more than one sense,' she said. 'I'm relieved to see you two arrive, to tell you the truth.'

Holmes found himself covering for his friend. 'He was initially keen to be involved, given the history surrounding his wife and Flynn, but in the cooler light of day he realised he needed to stay at arm's length from this inquiry.'

'The cool light of day is a wonderful thing,' Wilkins replied with an edge, causing Holmes to suspect she had been briefed on the assistant commissioner's chat with his colleague. 'Since Chief Inspector Bowker was last in Port Fairy, the body, or what was left of it, has washed up on the rocks near the lighthouse. You've no doubt read the autopsy report. Knife wound through the heart, dead before he hit the water, apparently. His car was found in the dunes at Yambuk, a few k's west of here, with a couple of dents in the driver's side door. There were prints in the car, although exposure to sea spray and rain probably obliterated many, especially those around the steering wheel where the open window was facing the ocean. Of the ones that could be lifted, we've matched most of them to the victim and a few to his wife. There's a couple of other sets that forensics can't match with anyone on the national database. So that's a dead end at the moment. Were the mystery prints left by innocent passengers or people involved in his disappearance? That's one of the sixty-four-thousand-dollar questions.'

'Do you think he could have been killed at Yambuk and currents carried his body across to here?' Larsen asked.

Wilkins shrugged. 'Dunno. But it's a hell of a coincidence that his body would just wash up here, of all places. Might be worth talking to an oceanographer, or maybe one of the older fishermen can give you a heads-up on the local currents.'

'We'd like to take a look at where the body washed up and then where his car was found.'

The senior sergeant slid a few photocopied pages across the desk to Holmes. 'Just for your information, this is a copy of the station log starting on the day Flynn disappeared until today. It'll give you an idea what we've covered so far.'

Holmes nodded his appreciation and picked up the document.

'I've assigned Dale Small to be the local on your team,' Wilkins continued. 'Between you and me, he's my best operator here.'

Be careful what you wish for, Holmes immediately thought. Given the circumstances in which his personal relationship with Larsen had started, he now wished Wilkins had assigned them Fuckhead Farrell.

CHAPTER 8

As an island, Griffith Island was not typical in the sense of being surrounded by stretches of open water in all directions. It was in fact a headland severed from the mainland by the twin discharges of the Moyne River. The area, at the time of white settlement, was a system of multiple islands trapped within the fanlike outflows of the river. Over the last century, major earthworks had taken place both to reroute the main channel of the river to the east and to consolidate Griffith, Rabbit and Goat Islands into a single land mass. Access to the island was via a narrow causeway traversing the link between the old passage and the modern main outflow of the Moyne. On the most southerly tip of the island sat the Port Fairy lighthouse, once manned by a permanent keeper but now run automatically. The lighthouse keeper's cottage was removed several decades ago due to vandalism and for safety reasons, but the island, and more especially the lighthouse itself, was a major drawcard for the many thousands of tourists who visited the town annually.

By the time the detectives met the local officers in the carpark adjoining Griffith Island, they had returned to the motel and changed into clothes more appropriate for walking on gravel paths and sandy stretches. On the track out to the lighthouse, they passed several sightseers and a couple of anglers fishing the bluestone-edged Moyne outlet. Neither had bagged a catch of any sort.

The island was covered in greenery, a combination of native grasses and exotic weeds. Several black wallabies could be seen feeding on the rises in the distance. The ground itself was sandy and pockmarked with tens of thousands of shearwater burrows. Short-tailed shearwaters, or mutton birds, as they were commonly known, spent the southern winter in the Aleutian Islands off Alaska before returning to the island to nest. In a wonder of nature, the shearwaters normally arrived back on Griffith Island on September 22 each year, nested in the same burrow and mated with the same partner. Even more mind-boggling was that the chicks were left behind each year when the adults headed north, and after experiencing hunger, they themselves undertook the fifteen-thousand-kilometre journey to the Aleutians without physical guidance.

A bluestone path ran up to the lighthouse door, protected against big seas from the south by a waist-high stone wall. To the right of the path was a mass of bluestone boulders under constant attack from Bass Strait. To the left, and in the lee of the island, were sandy shallows and rock pools. Today, the surf roared on the exposed side of the island, and the salty air was thickened by the smell of rotting seaweed and decaying mutton birds who'd died of exhaustion after finally reaching home. The quartet gathered on the rise where the lighthouse keeper's house had once stood and took in the 360-degree panorama.

'Is it normal to have shark attacks down this way, Megan?' Holmes asked.

'Not when you consider how many people are in the water. The last attack was over near Portland in 2015, the one before that was at Port Campbell in 2012, and before that in Portland again in 2009.

Going by what the locals have told me, the closest to us was one at Warrnambool in 2007. These were all non-fatal, thank goodness.'

Holmes was intrigued by the rarity of these events. 'What about fatal attacks?'

'Within a bull's roar of Port Fairy?' Wilkins replied. 'That was at Warrnambool in 1849.'

Both detectives were gobsmacked. 'In 1849!' Larsen said. 'A hundred and seventy years ago!'

Wilkins smiled and nodded. 'Yeah. And you'll probably be surprised to hear that the last confirmed fatal shark attack in all of Victoria was way back in 1956 at Portsea on the Mornington Peninsula. Some parties claim that Prime Minister Harold Holt's disappearance at the same location was probably a shark attack too, but even if we count that, we still have to go all the way back to 1967.'

'And yet, thousands of Great Whites past through these waters,' Small explained. 'They roam from Dampier in Western Australia all the way around the coast to Rockhampton in Queensland.' He pointed out to sea in a roughly sou-westerly direction. 'You can only just see it out there about twenty k away. Lady Julia Percy Island. It's one of the largest fur seal breeding areas in Australia. There's also a colony of penguins, and it's visited by sea lions and southern elephant seals. In other words, it's a smorgasbord for sharks. There was a legendary giant Great White out there the locals named Big Ben. Hasn't been seen since the sixties, so it's probably dead now. They're around, but don't attack people very often, thank God.'

If only he had known what the future would bring.

Wilkins led the group down the path towards the lighthouse, then struck off to her left past the shallows and along a rough narrow track through heavy bushes to the water's edge. She pointed to a spot among half-buried bluestone boulders. 'Flynn was found among those rocks. The remains of his shirt were snagged on that sharp piece protruding out of the water. Our best guess is that he floated in on the tide, and as the water receded, he was anchored by his shirt.'

'Who found him?' Holmes asked, hands on hips.

'A young bloke, his wife and a couple of primary school-aged kids,' Wilkins replied. She closed her eyes as if imagining the terror the family must have felt. 'The kids were chasing each other through the bushes. At first, they thought the body was a seal frolicking in the shallows, but a closer look put an end to that theory. It'll probably give them nightmares for the rest of their lives.'

Larsen frowned at the thought. 'Locals?'

Wilkins shook her head. 'No. Croweaters. Naracoorte. They come across fairly often, apparently. They cited the safe beach and the rock pools as ideal for the kids.' She sighed heavily. 'Don't think they'll be back for a while. Not out here, anyway.'

'Poor buggers,' Larsen replied. 'Shades of *Lord of the Flies*, where the marooned boys found the dead pilot's body being blown around in his parachute. They thought it was some kind of beast.'

'Shit, that's a blast from the past,' Holmes said. 'Form Four, I reckon.'

Small wasn't sure what they were talking about so wrapped his ignorance in silence. Wilkins stared across the sheltered bay towards the town. 'You can read the couple's statement, but there was nothing untoward. Just in the wrong place at the wrong time.'

'What hour of the day did they find the body?' Holmes asked.

'Around five-thirty in the afternoon. I took the call,' Small replied. 'We were out here within ten minutes.'

'You spoke of the tides lifting and settling the body,' Larsen said. 'So it could have been here during the night.'

'Hundreds of people run and walk the island track every day, especially during the holidays, but most wouldn't come down here,' Wilkins replied. She turned and pointed to the higher ground behind her. 'You can see the track continues around to the south side of the island, and we had to take this little detour to get down here from the lighthouse.'

Holmes nodded then surveyed the area. 'Forensics find anything else?'

Wilkins shook her head. 'No. But you'd expect that if the body came in on the tide.'

'Nothing came in with it?' Larsen asked.

'Nope. Unless you count seaweed.'

Holmes walked a few paces to view the eastern extremity of the island. 'So, if the body did float down from Yambuk, it would've had to do a U-turn around the lighthouse to finish up here?'

Wilkins nodded. 'Yeah. But that's not impossible if the currents follow the shoreline.' She smiled. 'But I wouldn't be putting any of my hard-earned on it.' She looked at Holmes. 'Seen enough?'

'Yeah, I think so.'

Wilkins led the group back towards the lighthouse path, stepping from one bluestone rock to another. Larsen, who was following her step for step, slipped on one of the boulders but was caught in her fall by Small, who was half a pace behind. With an effortless swing of his arm around her waist, he deposited her back on her feet atop the rock. Larsen smiled broadly and thanked the constable for his quick thinking. Small grinned. 'My pleasure.'

Holmes, who was following, couldn't help wondering if he was watching a replay of the events in Benalla less than a year ago.

* * *

Wilkins turned left off the Princes Highway onto a narrow ribbon of bitumen dubbed Carrolls Road that allowed the officers to bypass the township of Yambuk and take a shorter route to the beach where Flynn's Mercedes was discovered. The pleasant weather had brought people out and about. The carpark was close to full, and the giant slide put Holmes in mind of an ant's nest. Children sprinted up the long flight of steps then rocketed down the steel slide in ones and twos on large pieces of cardboard. Several cars were parked around the boat ramp, their owners now happily fishing in the Eumeralla River or in Lake Yambuk, into which the short waterway flowed. The outflow of the lake into the sea was rarely more than a trickle and provided no viable entrance to Bass Strait for boats of any size. The caravan park looked full, and on a busy day like this, Holmes found it hard to imagine how a top-of-the-range Mercedes sports car could arrive and be abandoned so close by without being noticed. But this was now daytime, the sky clear and sunny. When the Merc had arrived, the weather was diabolical. And it was in the dark of night.

Wilkins parked the car between two four-wheel drive monsters and pointed towards the sound of the ocean crashing on the other side of a line of dunes.

'Up through there,' she said as she headed off in that direction.

The track was barely wide enough to accommodate a normal-sized car, and the sand was loose and deep. *No wonder the Merc didn't make it to the beach*, Holmes thought. A beach buggy with wide, under-inflated tyres had a chance, but not a passenger vehicle on road tyres.

'The car was found bogged in sand just over this rise,' Wilkins advised. 'The towies had to haul it out with a long cable. No hope of getting the truck in here.'

As the group topped the dune, they spotted a tall male in shorts, thongs and a tee-shirt on his haunches in the vegetation adjoining where the car had originally come to rest. Holmes recognised the figure immediately.

'Greg? What the hell are you doing down here? I thought you had taken a few days in lieu?'

Bowker stood up and brushed the sand from his knees. 'I have. The assistant commissioner suggested I get away for a few days and relax.' He smiled. 'What better place to do that than the beautiful Port Fairy?'

Holmes frowned. 'I'm not sure this is a good idea, Greg.'

Bowker upturned his palms. 'I'm not interfering in your investigation.'

Wilkins was clearly annoyed. 'Then what are you doing out here? Looking for something specific? Lost something, perhaps?'

Bowker's eyes narrowed. 'What's that supposed to mean, Senior Sergeant? And remember you are talking to a detective inspector, not one of your constables.'

'A detective inspector who is off duty and not involved in this investigation. And who, at the moment, is interfering with a potential crime scene.'

Bowker feigned a chuckle. 'I don't see any police tape. I don't see any signs prohibiting the public from entry, and right now I am a member of that public just exercising my right to enjoy the beach and its surrounds.'

Holmes was exasperated. 'Come on, Greg, you're not making it easy for us.'

Bowker raised both palms in surrender. 'OK, you've made your point. I was about to leave anyway.' He removed his thongs and trudged away through the deep sand before turning back to face the group. 'I might take advantage of the weather and go for a walk out to the lighthouse on Griffith Island.'

'Who the hell is that?' Small asked when Bowker was out of earshot.

'He's my boss,' Holmes replied.

'And our number one suspect,' Wilkins added quickly.

Small rolled his eyes but said nothing.

* * *

Back at the station, the four officers assembled in the investigation's modest nerve centre. Holmes sat behind the wooden-topped desk, Larsen at its side with pen and paper, and the two local officers on chairs brought in from the staff lunch area next door. Holmes led off the discussion.

'OK, what do we know of the victim's movements after he assaulted Rachael Bowker on the beach?'

'Nothing, unfortunately,' Wilkins replied. 'We've been round to all the pubs and restaurants, spoken to his wife, put out a call for any local who may have seen him that evening.' She shrugged. 'It's like he just fell off the face of the earth.'

'Or into the ocean,' Larsen quipped as she jotted notes.

Holmes folded his arms. 'What about the girlfriend in Warrnambool?'

'We've asked around, but nobody can give us a name,' Small replied. 'His car being found at Yambuk would seem to preclude him driving to Warrnambool that evening. And his body being washed up here points to him not leaving town.'

'Doesn't mean he didn't go there and return later in the evening, or that the girlfriend didn't come across to Port Fairy,' Larsen replied.

'We've given Flynn's photo to the Warrnambool coppers and they're asking around to see if they can turn something up,' Wilkins said.

'What do we know about Flynn himself?' Holmes asked. 'Greg has filled me in on his background, but what's the word on the streets?'

'Depends on who you talk to,' Small replied. 'His drinking mates reckon he's not a bad bloke. But he's not too popular among people who he's done business with.'

'Like who?' Larsen asked with pen poised.

'Ian Petrov, the town planner, for a start. Petrov won't have a bar of rezoning the land Flynn bought, so that kiboshes his big money-making scheme.'

'How serious did that disagreement become?' Holmes asked.

'Flynn threatened to punch Petrov's head in. Petrov is a bit of a hothead himself, so it could have been on for young and old if Grant hadn't sorted it out.'

'Grant?' Holmes asked with a puzzled look.

'Grant Farrell,' Small replied. 'He's one of the constables working here.'

Oh, Fuckhead Farrell, Holmes wanted to say but nodded his head in acknowledgement. 'So, no charges were laid against Flynn for threatening behaviour?'

Small shook his head. 'No. Grant just issued him with a warning when he agreed to back off.'

Wilkins inhaled audibly through pursed lips but said nothing.

'You mentioned business associates,' Larsen said.

'Elizabeth Cronin has been a vocal critic of Flynn. She got sucked into buying one of his blocks after he told her rezoning had already passed through the council. Rohan Parks is in the same boat. Both deals are tied up in legal action at present.'

'What do we know about these two?'

'Elizabeth Cronin is part of the local squattocracy down this way,' Wilkins replied. 'More money than you can poke a stick at but careful about every penny she spends. Parks is a blow-in. But from what we gather, he took a payout when Ford closed down in Geelong and decided to invest it in Flynn's estate on Belfast Lough. He's been in here a few times insisting we charge Flynn with fraud. Bad-tempered bugger. Little bloke, with the attitude of a fox terrier.'

Holmes nodded. 'What's Flynn's connection with the bikies? Greg said that he orchestrated the takeover of the Birdwatchers Club.'

Small shrugged. 'It's hard to know. One story is that he has a cousin in the gang. One of those big hairy bastards, apparently. They might have asked him to front the club's meeting and give their group a bit of respectability.'

Larsen scratched her temple with the end of the biro. 'But what would be in it for Flynn?' she asked.

'Muscle, perhaps,' Wilkins surmised. 'Makes getting your own way a little easier if you can threaten passing a dispute over to a gang of bikies.'

Holmes nodded. 'What about the Birdwatchers? Any ex-fisherman who'd be handy with a filleting knife?'

Wilkins laughed out loud. 'They only had a dozen members, tops. And all bar one are geriatrics. They'd struggle to lift a knife, let alone stick it in someone's heart.'

Holmes smiled. 'Who is the one non-geriatric?'

'Tristan Proctor,' Small replied. 'He runs an animal shelter just out of town. He's the gentlest person you'll ever meet. No way he'd top Flynn.'

Wilkins agreed. 'He came into the station complaining about the bikies' takeover and asking what could be done about it, but that was about it. He had to leave because someone had cleaned up a koala out towards Codrington.'

Small screwed up his face. 'I can't think of anyone else in the district who'd have sufficient motive to kill Flynn.'

'Course, he was such a prick that someone from his past may have bobbed up and topped him,' Holmes replied.

'Someone like Greg Bowker, you mean?' Wilkins said, staring straight at Holmes.

CHAPTER 9

'Well, that added bugger-all to what we knew already,' Holmes said when the local officers left the room. 'I've got a feeling we've got a long row to hoe on this one.'

Larsen moved her chair to the desk so she sat directly opposite her partner. 'Yeah. We're left with a lot of half-maybes but nothing to get too excited about. We've got nobody who was seen with Flynn on the night he disappeared, and nobody making overt physical threats against him…' – she hesitated – '…except Greg.' Her eyes met Holmes's for an instant before she looked away, hoping her words did not imply she doubted Bowker's account.

Holmes didn't respond for a moment. He turned his head and gazed out the window. 'I think we should start with the wife,' he eventually suggested. 'Try to establish who was last to see Flynn before the encounter with Rachael on the beach.'

Larsen nodded. 'Sounds like a plan.' She hesitated for a few seconds. 'I didn't want to raise this in front of the locals, but why the hell is Greg in Port Fairy? It's not helping his cause.'

Holmes leaned back in his chair and put his hands behind his head. 'He believes it's his case to solve, I assume. It's his wife who was assaulted, his head in the frame, and all that.' He hiked one shoulder. 'But I agree, it doesn't look good from a public point of view. And to tell you the truth, I could do without feeling he's looking over our shoulders.'

Larsen stared at the desktop as she thought more about the case. 'What about the car, Darren? Is it being dumped at Yambuk part of the murder narrative or separate from it?'

'Could be either, I guess. A number of scenarios could've played out. Flynn could've driven the car to Yambuk and met his demise down there. Or he could've been driven by someone else, who did him in. But then we have to ask how the killer left the scene when the car got bogged. Or was there more than one person involved, and another car was driven down there? Or did the killer inadvertently bog the Merc and walk back to the main road to hitch a ride, or maybe ring for someone to pick them up?' He shrugged his shoulders. 'Or, as you say, the car could be a complete red herring and the events at Yambuk have nothing to do with Flynn's death.'

Holmes reached down and picked up his briefcase. 'Just remembered something Greg mentioned about that car in his interview on Friday.' He placed the case on the table and snapped open the lid. He flipped through a few papers until he found what he was looking for. 'Here we are,' he said as he started to quote. '"I saw an old couple walking their dog in the dark and the rain. I asked them whether they'd seen Flynn's Mercedes in their travels. They said they'd noticed a Mercedes sports car parked near the wharf a little while earlier."'

Larsen saw the implication. 'That's where Rachael and her friend had afternoon tea that day. But whether the times match up is anyone's guess.'

'I wonder if there's CCTV coverage of that carpark? It might answer a few questions. We'll check it out after we talk to Flynn's missus.'

* * *

Later that morning, the detectives drove to Flynn's home via his office, on the off chance his wife was there tidying up affairs. The shopfront was locked, with a handwritten note informing the public that the office was closed until further notice due to a family bereavement.

The Flynn house was an example of the ubiquitous cement-rendered ugliness of much modern Port Fairy architecture. Two stories tall, with glass walls fronting South Beach across the road, the house was a window cleaner's dream, and its future existence faced the dual threats of rising sea levels and shoddy modern building standards. When the detectives pulled up outside the sterile box in Ocean Drive, Katy Flynn was standing at the salt-streaked floor-to-ceiling windows, staring out over Bass Strait. She glanced down at the car before resuming her gaze over the ocean. An attack dog standing beside her barked incessantly.

The sea roared behind Holmes and Larsen as they approached the Flynn residence. Seagulls squawked, wheeling above. The stiff southerly whined through the steel underbelly of the building and brought the smell of rotting kelp from the boulder-strewn edge of the ocean. It took several minutes before Katy Flynn answered the door and reluctantly asked the officers inside. The dog growled its displeasure, and intermittently glanced at his owner, hoping for the attack signal. She took her visitors through to the lounge room but made no moves to invite them to sit down, leaving the trio standing awkwardly in the centre of the large space facing one another. At least she ushered the dog into a room off to the side, where it continually scratched on the closed door.

Mrs Flynn was wearing jeans, a pale orange short-sleeved blouse and flat white leather shoes. Her dyed-blond hair was pulled back in a bun, and she had a yellowing bruise on her cheek and a welt on her left forearm. She pulled a pair of yellow clip-on earrings from her ears and placed them in an ornamental saucer on a bookshelf beside a large stone fireplace. Larsen noticed another pair of clip-ons in the dish, alongside a single silver earring in the shape of a butterfly designed to be worn by someone with pierced ears.

'Today I've had a long and frustrating discussion with Trevor's solicitors in Warrnambool,' Mrs Flynn said tersely as she stared out over the water. 'Before that, I had a radiation session at the hospital. So on top of Trevor's death, I've just about had enough of things. You better make it quick.'

Holmes hadn't heard she was suffering from cancer and suddenly felt sympathy for her. He explained that he and Larsen were leading the investigation into her husband's death and needed to ask her a few questions. Her retort was swift.

'I would have thought you'd be better off talking to your mate, Bowker. There's not a person in Port Fairy who has the slightest doubt he killed my husband. He came here looking for Trevor and making threats, and he did the same in half the other places in town.'

'That's what we're here to talk to you about, Mrs Flynn,' Larsen explained quietly. 'To piece together a timeline of what occurred the day your husband disappeared.'

Mrs Flynn feigned a chuckle. 'The day Bowker killed him, you mean?'

Holmes ignored the comment. 'When was the last time you saw your husband that day?'

She folded her arms and stared at the floor in thought. 'Late afternoon at the office. He left for a meeting with the local planning officer. From there, he said he had a few errands around town and he wasn't sure when he'd be home.'

'What time was that?' Holmes asked.

'Around four thirty.'

Larsen took a notebook and pencil from her jacket pocket. 'Did you know the agenda for that meeting?' she asked.

Mrs Flynn shrugged. 'It was about rezoning some land Trevor had bought. But as for the exact details, I wouldn't have a clue. He doesn't share company information with me. I'm just the bitch on the switch in the office. Take calls and make appointments for visitors if he's not in.'

'Don't you type up his commercial documents?' Larsen asked as a follow up.

'Can't type. I worked in a dress shop before Trevor cut me from the herd, as he likes to describe it. All his typing is done in Warrnambool by an agency recommended by his solicitor over there. Manley, O'Neil and Schwandt in Timor Street.'

'I thought his planning application had already been denied,' Holmes said.

'Trevor wasn't one to have anything he wants denied. That's why he was back to see Ian Petrov at the council.'

Holmes pointed to her face. 'That why you've got the bruise? Your husband unhappy with something you did, or didn't do? And the mark on your arm?'

Mrs Flynn stared straight at the detective. 'They're from the dog, if you must know. The silly bastard gets all enthusiastic when I arrive home, and one day he jumped up when I was putting shopping on the bench and his head whacked against mine.' She looked at her arm. 'Scratched me in the same motion.'

That's bullshit, Holmes thought. 'Trevor had a history of belting women, did you know that?'

'Yes, but they deserved it, from what I could gather.' Mrs Flynn replied. 'He was always the complete gentleman around me,' she added unconvincingly.

The detectives exchanged dubious glances. *Once a woman basher, always a woman basher*, Holmes thought.

'What happened the day Greg Bowker came here looking for your husband?' Larsen asked.

'He nearly knocked the door down, he belted on it so hard. The dog was growling his head off in the laundry and I was tossing up whether to let him out. When Bowker yelled that he was a policeman, I thought I was safe enough.'

Larsen nodded. 'So what did Detective Bowker say when you opened the door?'

'That he was looking for Trevor. He said Trevor had assaulted his wife. That he was going to put an end to my husband's violence once and for all.'

'And how did you respond to that?' Holmes asked.

Mrs Flynn shrugged. 'I told him my husband wasn't here. I pointed to the empty carport where Trevor's car is parked when he's at home.'

'Did you say where your husband had gone?' Larsen asked.

'I told him Trevor had gone to the municipal offices. But in all honesty, I thought by that time he could have been anywhere.'

Holmes rubbed his chin. 'Did you also tell Bowker that?' he asked.

She nodded. 'I was trying to be as vague as possible once I saw the mood he was in and what he was threatening to do.'

'But you told him about the meeting with the council and your husband later running some errands?' Holmes persisted.

'Yes,' Mrs Flynn replied. 'That was before I realised it was more than just police business, so I threw in the stuff about Trevor being anywhere in town.'

Larsen continued to scribble notes on a pad. 'So let me see if I've got this right. Late afternoon at the office, your husband tells you he's off to run a few errands. What time are we talking here?'

Mrs Flynn's brow wrinkled. 'Four thirty, about. He needed to catch the council before their offices closed. Petrov is only in Port Fairy three days a week. Wednesday and Thursday, he works from the Moyne office in Mortlake.'

'And when *do* those offices close?'

'Four forty-five.'

Larsen was perplexed. 'And he left here at four thirty? Doesn't leave much time for a meeting.'

A smirk came over Mrs Flynn's face. 'That's why Trevor left it that late. To make sure that he would keep Petrov there after knock-off time just to give him the shits. To my husband, that was a win. The longer he kept him, the bigger the victory.'

Larsen raised her eyebrows and wrote on her pad. 'And after that meeting, he planned to run a few errands?'

'Yes.'

'What time did you close the office?'

'Five o'clock.'

'And you went straight home?'

'No, I went via the supermarket and bought a few groceries and a couple bottles of red.'

Larsen nodded as she kept scribbling. 'And what time did Detective Bowker arrive here?'

Mrs Flynn thought for a moment. 'It was dark.' She shrugged. 'Around eight thirty, quarter to nine, I'd guess.'

'What will happen to the business?' Holmes asked.

She rolled her eyes. 'Without council approval, it's worth bugger-all. With court cases pending, it's more likely to be a liability than an asset.'

'Are you going to wind it up, or persevere with his plans for a housing estate on the water?'

Mrs Flynn chuckled sarcastically. 'Not my decision. His will leaves me nothing. This house, the new place he bought up on East Beach and the business all go to his only living blood relation, a cousin on his mother's side. If I can be bothered going to court, I may be able to keep this place.' Her brow wrinkled. 'At this stage, I'm not sure I can put myself through the angst. My brother and I are close, and he's worth a mint. I won't go starving, anyway.'

Again, Larsen had her pen poised. 'What's his cousin's name?'

'Jason McCulloch,' was the reply.

'Where would we find him if we needed a chat?' Holmes asked, then smiled. 'Before you tell me, I bet he lives interstate or overseas.'

'Close,' the woman replied, her face deadpan. 'He's one of those dumb-arse bikies up at the Birdwatchers Club.'

* * *

'She doesn't seem particularly devastated by her husband's demise,' Larsen said as she clicked home her seatbelt and started the car.

'Nope,' Holmes replied. 'Can't blame her, though, if he was abusing her. Especially if she knew he was getting a bit on the side over in Warrnambool and she'd been left out of his will.'

Little more was said as Larsen followed Ocean Drive east until it became Gipps Street at the Martin Point park. A couple of hundred metres on, she flicked on her right indicator and turned into one of the carparks beside the wharf abutting the Moyne River. The wharf structure itself only made contact with dry land for a short distance outside what was now a restaurant and fish shop but was once the fishermen's cooperative. For the remaining sections of its length, the wharf was a walkway set on pylons several metres into the river from its bank and connected to solid ground by a series of short bridges. As a result, the walk along the wharf had water on both sides. Larger vessels, such as fishing trawlers and ocean-going pleasure craft, tended to be moored at the south or ocean end of the structure, with smaller boats berthed further up the river. A pedestrian bridge connected the township with the spit of land that separated the river from the sea for the mile or so before it emptied into the ocean. Road access to the other side of the Moyne required crossing a road bridge further upstream or approaching Port Fairy past the golf course and Belfast Lough. On the other side of the river was a marina, a yacht club, a boat builder, and a ramp for launching pleasure craft.

'Can't see any CCTV cameras,' Holmes said as he climbed from the vehicle and scanned the area. Seagulls squawked as they fought each other for any morsels left at wooden picnic tables near the wharf.

Larsen closed the driver's side door and locked the car remotely. 'Maybe there are some on the other side of the building,' she said, pointing to the restaurant.

A wander down the length of the wharf failed to identify a single camera in the public area, but it was still a nice day for a stroll in the sun, despite the chilly southerly blowing up the river. The detectives were partners in both senses of the word, and Holmes fought the urge to hold Larsen's hand during their promenade. Professionalism precluded flaunting their personal relationship, although they both recognised it was merely a matter of time before the fact that they were sharing a room at the motel became common knowledge.

A group of school-aged kids running along the wharf towards them and pointing into the water between the walkway and the riverbank piqued the officers' interest. Beside the bank, in no more than a metre of water, swam an enormous stingray, gliding its way forward with the simplest movements of its pectoral fins and taking no obvious notice of the humans gazing down from above. Within a few seconds, the creature turned towards the centre of the river and, much to everyone's disappointment, disappeared under a commercial squid fishing boat named the *Isla Anne*. Within a few moments, the spectators had dispersed, leaving Holmes staring at the boat.

'The lights are for attracting squid,' Larsen said as she pointed to the scores of high-powered and boom-mounted light globes adorning the boat's deck and superstructure.

'Yeah, I know,' Holmes replied. He nodded towards a modest rectangular sign screwed to the side of the boat's wheelhouse. 'That's what grabbed my attention.'

This vessel is monitored by CCTV.

Holmes began scanning the boat for the location of its cameras. One was above the wheelhouse door looking aft of the vessel. There was another above the front window, pointing to the bow. But it was a camera located on an upright under the roof of the ship's work area, pointing amidships, that roused his interest. 'That camera covering the middle of the boat may take in parts of the carpark,' he said.

Larsen looked behind her, hands on hips, surveying the general area. 'A lot of things would have to go right for us to get anything useful,' she said, turning back to face her partner. 'Number one, the camera works or was even turned on. Two, it actually takes in any of this area. Three, the boat was in port when anything suspicious happened, and four, it always moors in this spot.'

Holmes nodded. 'Agreed. But it's worth asking a few questions.' He stepped onto the boat and felt it move a little in the calm water.

'Hey, mate? Where the fuck do you think you're going?' came a loud voice from the fishing boat next door.

CHAPTER 10

'You fuckin' tourists think you've got the right to go wherever you please.'

Holmes stepped back off the squid boat and walked to the next vessel along. A man in bib and brace overalls, gumboots and a black beanie sat with another weathered character on the rear deck. In his sixties or early seventies, the sailor had a week's stubble on his burnt and wrinkled face. A half-smoked rollie hung out the corner of his mouth, sticking to his cracked bottom lip and jerking up and down as he spoke.

'Just walk into people's houses uninvited?' the man asked as Holmes approached.

'Who owns the boat next door?' the detective responded.

'What's it to you?'

Holmes took his wallet from his back pocket and showed his police ID. 'Darren Holmes, Homicide.' He nodded towards Larsen, now standing beside him. 'That's my colleague, Detective Sergeant Larsen.'

The fisherman smiled, exposing a gap where one of his front teeth had once been. He steadied the cigarette as it threatened to fall out. He looked Larsen up and down. 'Nice,' he said dryly. His friend, of similar age, attire and appearance, grinned and nodded his agreement.

Holmes used a thumb to point over his shoulder. 'So, who owns the boat?'

'That'd be me,' the fisherman replied.

'And you'd be?' Larsen asked.

'Mick Henderson, if you must know. Why are you interested in my boat?'

'We've got no interest in your boat as such, Mr Henderson,' Holmes replied. 'What does interest us are your security cameras. Or, more specifically, what they may have recorded.'

Henderson scratched his head through his beanie. 'Fishermen are not the brightest, Detective, so you'll have to spell it out for me pretty slowly.'

'We're interested in what may have occurred in this carpark a week or so ago,' Holmes explained. 'We were hoping those cameras on your boat may have picked up something that could be of some help in our investigation.'

'The cameras are focussed on the boat,' Henderson replied. 'Deter people knocking stuff off at night or just fucking around with our equipment when no one is around.'

'There's the possibility of something in the background we can use,' Larsen said.

'The ocean is a hostile environment, especially for electronic stuff. To tell you the truth, I don't even know if they're all still working,' Henderson said, rubbing his stubble. 'Unless something goes missing or is interfered with, I never check what's recorded.'

'But the system is activated when you're in port?' Holmes asked.

Henderson nodded. 'The last thing I do before I lock the wheelhouse is turn on the cameras and security lights.'

'How long is the recorded vision kept for?' Larsen asked.

Henderson shrugged. 'The bloke who installed it said about a month, I think. Then it starts to record over the oldest stuff.

But I'm a simple fisherman, not a techno whiz.'

'Can we take a look at what you've got?' Holmes asked.

'I guess so,' Henderson said, climbing up from his seat. 'What's this all about, anyway?'

'We're investigating the death of Trevor Flynn,' Holmes responded.

Henderson laughed. 'You don't need my security cameras. I can tell you who did the deed. It was one of your detective mates from Melbourne.'

'What makes you think that?' Larsen asked.

'It's all around town, honey,' Henderson replied. 'I was in The Star the night Flynn disappeared, and this detective bloke stormed in looking for him. When he left, he said he had a message for Flynn if he happened to come in. He said to tell him he was a dead man.'

'So, obviously, your boat was moored here on that night?' Holmes said, ignoring the fisherman's accusations.

'Yep. We came in that morning, unloaded and cleaned the boat,' Henderson replied as he led them onto his vessel and into the wheelhouse.

Henderson may have claimed he wasn't a techno whiz, but the wheelhouse on the *Isla Anne* was packed with electronic aids for navigation and fish-finding. He opened a cupboard to the side of the helmsman's chair, exposing a computer system complete with a small monitor. Pulling a set of eyeglasses from a case in the pocket of his bib, he knelt down in front of the unit, put on his glasses and flicked a switch. The unit lit up. After a few moments manipulating a mouse, he brought up a playback menu and selected the date that Flynn had disappeared.

The start of the replay was time-stamped at 17.37, the time the crew had left the boat. The weather that night had been brutal, and the picture on the screen rocked and swayed as the boat was buffeted by the wind and rolled in the rough conditions on the river. The bottom left-hand quarter of the screen was blank, indicating the camera pointing aft was faulty. Luckily, the feed that most interested the detectives was intact, although a little blurry, probably due to the rain and the build-up of grime and salt on the camera's protective plastic bubble. The vision showed sections of the carpark in the background and the movement of rugged-up tourists and tradespeople. What immediately piqued the detectives' interest was the Mercedes sports car parked front and centre among other vehicles, its roof in the closed position. There was no sign of Trevor Flynn.

The number of intrepid passers-by thinned as the daylight began to fade. Within a few minutes of scrolling, the carpark area and the wharf were deserted. By 19.21, the only car in sight was Flynn's Merc, as the wharf lights flickered to life. At 19.33, a Nissan one-tonner with tradie racks supporting a ladder pulled in behind the Mercedes. A well-built man dressed in high-vis attire and a red trade-named beanie climbed from the vehicle and walked with his back towards the wind and the sleety shower that was passing. He surveyed Flynn's car then looked up and down the wharf. After a moment or two, he drove his hand into his jacket pocket and wandered off upriver and out of picture. Several minutes later, he came back into view and repeatedly slammed his boot into the driver's door panel of the Mercedes. He looked around again, undid the fly of his trousers and urinated downwind on the windscreen of the vehicle.

'Fuck me,' the fisherman said, almost to himself. 'Someone's not happy with our Mr Flynn.'

'Stop it there,' Holmes ordered. When the vision froze, he looked at Henderson. 'You recognise that bloke?'

The fisherman shook his head slowly. 'Nope. Never seen the bastard in my life.'

'OK, let it roll again,' Holmes said.

Within a few seconds, the unidentified visitor had returned to his ute and left the carpark at speed. As the rear of the vehicle came into the camera's view, Holmes again asked for the vision to be paused. Henderson did as asked, and both detectives moved closer to the screen.

'The number plate is impossible to read,' Larsen said. 'Perhaps the techs at Forensics can get something from it.'

Holmes asked that the vision be rolled on at a higher speed. After half an hour in real time, a Mini Moke entered the carpark, its canvas top in place, displaying P plates. Four young men, two wearing hoodies and all holding stubbies, climbed from the vehicle. Despite the recording carrying no audio, it wasn't difficult to discern that the quartet was loud and in a raucous mood in spite of the atrocious weather.

'You know these blokes?' Holmes asked the fisherman.

'That's a negative too,' Henderson replied unconvincingly, following a moment of hesitation.

'You sure?' Larsen pressed.

'Yep. I'm sure. Never laid eyes on them.'

The vision showed the four chiacking on the edge of the wharf, before one of the men drunkenly over-armed his empty stubby into the garden of a double-storied apartment that overlooked them. Following a few minutes of scruffing and play-wrestling, the quartet walked back towards their vehicle, perhaps realising for the first time they were getting wet. As he passed the Mercedes, the last of the four tried the driver's door and was pleasantly surprised when he found that it opened. He looked inside, stooped down, collected a set of keys from the driver's side floor and yelled to his mates. Within seconds, Flynn's car was following the Moke out of the carpark, spraying a wall of water and narrowly missing a motorcyclist entering the area. Holmes and Larsen exchanged glances, acknowledging they had both seen the Harley with the swept-back handlebars and extended chrome backrest before.

The bike came to a stop and was parked in the shelter of the restaurant corner overhang. It was impossible to see the face of the rider, who was wearing a helmet and had their head down, avoiding the rain. They disappeared from view around the front of the restaurant. Holmes asked Henderson to scroll slowly forward, and another few minutes of vision rolled by before the motorcyclist reappeared from the side, still wearing the helmet. They started the bike then placed a duffle bag in a storage box behind the seat, climbed aboard, hesitated for a few moments and sped off into the white mist.

Holmes stood up straight after another thirty minutes of vision. 'There's a thumb drive in the glove box of the car, Kirsten. Would you mind grabbing it? We'll take a copy of Mr Henderson's footage.'

As Larsen left the boat, Holmes turned to the fisherman. 'Thanks for your help, mate. You've gone a long way towards solving this thing.' He reached into his pocket and retrieved a business card. 'If you have any second thoughts about recognising those young blokes, I can be contacted on this number.'

Henderson put the card on the dashboard above the helm. 'I'll leave it up here, but I can assure you I don't know anyone we've seen on that tape.' He folded his glasses and returned them to their case, which he slipped into his bib pocket.

Larsen returned with the memory stick, and as she was about to slot it into the computer, a shadowy figure crossed the screen in front of her. She looked up at Holmes, and the two exchanged glances without saying a word.

'Who's that?' Henderson asked as he bent down to take a closer look before shuffling in his pocket, chasing his glasses.

'No idea, mate,' Holmes replied.

By the time Henderson had retrieved and donned his glasses, the figure had retraced their steps and passed out of view, with Larsen in the process of saving the day's vision to her memory stick.

* * *

'So, Greg was on the wharf that night,' Larsen said as she started their car.

'Yep,' Holmes replied, fastening his seatbelt. 'There are a number of things that camera captured that ask more questions than they answer.'

'The bloke who kicked in the car door needs to be found, for a start.'

'Correct. And my gut says the Mercedes being abandoned at Yambuk has nothing to do with Flynn's death.'

'Opportunist joyriders, you reckon?'

Holmes nodded. 'I reckon. I'll bet they've driven that Moke along the beach at Yambuk a hundred times and thought it'd be a lark to do the same with the Mercedes. Except wrong night and wrong car to try that trick. Bellied out Flynn's car in the sand, pissing off and leaving it there.'

'If we put a line through Yambuk, then the odds pretty much favour Flynn being topped somewhere closer to where his body was found.'

'Yep.' Holmes suddenly clicked off his seatbelt. 'Let's have a closer look at this wharf.'

Larsen turned off the car. 'What are we looking for?'

'Dunno yet,' Holmes replied with a smile before leaning over the seat and retrieving gloves and evidence bags. 'For a start, I'd like to find the stubby that was heaved into that garden. Hopefully, it hasn't been cleaned up.'

It was Larsen who found the bottle lodged in a waist-high hedge that separated the grounds of the high-end apartments from the wharf's boardwalk. With a gloved hand, she removed the stubby by the neck and placed it in a plastic ziplock bag that was then deposited in the rear of their vehicle.

'Where to now?' she asked.

'A walk along the wharf.'

'We looking for bloodstains?'

'And anything else that might catch our eye,' Holmes replied.

Larsen stopped and looked at her partner, hands on hips. 'It's a fishermen's wharf, Darren. There'll be bloodstains everywhere.'

'Agreed,' Holmes replied, nodding. 'But what the commercial fishermen bring in won't still be bleeding, and the amateurs and kids won't catch anything that leaves more than a few splotches of blood. On the other hand, if a six-foot-something human gets stabbed directly in the heart, I reckon there'd be a pretty big loss of blood before he even hit the ground.'

Larsen wasn't convinced. 'It was pissing rain the night he disappeared. Any traces would be long gone.'

'Probably. But the video showed there were squalls rather than heavy rain. Squalls from the southwest. You never know our luck – we might find something in the lee of the building. Or if Flynn was killed somewhere around here, perhaps it happened between storms and the blood dried enough to survive being completely washed away.'

Larsen remained far from convinced but acquiesced to her senior partner's plan. There was nothing to lose except a few minutes of their time.

Their walk along the wharf found nothing that piqued their interest. Holmes was now ready to concede that their efforts had been wasted. As they headed back towards their vehicle, Larsen stopped and stared at the ground in thought.

'What?'

'We've been slagging off that night's weather as hindering progress on this investigation. Maybe we should look at it as our friend.'

Holmes was intrigued. 'Go on.'

'Flynn's car was left in the carpark here, so we have to assume he was on the wharf at some stage. Given the weather, it's most likely he would have sought somewhere sheltered.'

Holmes looked around. 'The only spot that fits that bill is in the lee of the restaurant.'

'That's my best guess too,' Larsen replied with a grin.

Along the wharf side of the restaurant, and out of the wind that night, was a series of picnic tables with bench seats either side. During most days, they were occupied by groups, often families, consuming fish and chips purchased at the takeaway shop on the northern end of the restaurant.

Today, two of the tables were in use. Holmes wondered how to best examine the area without causing angst and creating more gossip around the town. It was Larsen who came up with the solution. After unsuccessfully examining the area around the vacant tables, she approached one of the occupied.

'I wonder if you could excuse the intrusion of my friend and I for a few moments,' Larsen said to a woman she assumed was the mother of the children who sat next to her, scoffing down handfuls of chips. 'This morning, I was fiddling with my engagement ring while we were having coffee at this table, and I suspect I might have dropped it without realising.'

A quick inspection between the occupied table and the one adjacent revealed what they were really looking for. In the join between the paving and the restaurant wall was what both believed to be dried blood. Barely visible smears could also be detected by a trained eye on the weatherboards above.

A glance between Holmes and Larsen confirmed their agreement. The detectives thanked the family for their patience and casually wandered away, Larsen ringing the Port Fairy police station and asking that a forensic team be called from Warrnambool. She also requested a uniformed officer guard the area until the testing was completed. The moment the family had vacated the table and moved on, Holmes ran blue and white exclusion tape around the area.

The detectives sat at another vacant table to discuss possible scenarios. 'For the sake of the exercise, let's assume that's Flynn's blood,' Holmes said. 'Henderson's CCTV captured the Mercedes parked here at around five thirty. How long it had been here before that, we don't know. Rachael estimates she was attacked at about five o'clock. So did he take the car up to East Beach to look at his new house, or did he leave it here and follow Rachael on foot to where he assaulted her?'

'That's one of the nine thousand unknowns in this case.'

'If Flynn was killed here, the most logical thing is for his body to be dumped in the river. It ended up in the water at some stage, that's one thing we do know.'

'If you dropped him over the edge of the wharf here, there's no guarantee he wouldn't have become snagged among the boats. He could have been taken somewhere else and dumped in the sea.'

'At least we know that Piss Man didn't take the body. Well, not at the time we saw him drive away on the video. If it is Flynn's blood, we'll need to call in police divers to check if there's anything under the water that may help us.'

The pair were silent for a few moments.

'What about Greg?' Larsen asked tentatively.

Holmes shrugged. 'We didn't see his vehicle. However, there's another carpark on the north side of the restaurant. He'll need to explain his presence down here that night, that's for sure.'

Larsen nodded but didn't respond.

Holmes folded his arms and stared absently across the river. 'I think when things are under control here, we might pay a visit to the planning officer at the council. He was one of the last people to see the victim alive.'

'If Flynn pushed him hard enough, he may have been *the* last to see him alive.'

'Possibly. That's why we need to talk to him today.'

The detectives' theorising was interrupted by the arrival of Senior Constable Small in a campervan with surfboards on a roof rack. Wearing a wetsuit and thongs, he walked to where they were sitting.

Holmes grinned and pointed at his attire. 'Formal uniform for down this way, is it?'

Small smiled. 'Just finished my shift. Grant Farrell is coming here to look after what you found. But he wanted to grab a burger from the servo on his way, so I said I'd cover for him until he arrives.'

Holmes rolled his eyes. 'Fuck me!' he said, just loud enough for Small to overhear.

A smirk crossed Larsen's face. 'That area inside the police tape is what we want protected until Forensics arrive.'

Small walked closer to the tape as a seagull swooped low over the restaurant roof. Several passers-by had gathered, along with Mick Henderson the fisherman, curious as to what the police tape was protecting. 'What's the go?' Small asked.

'We found blood in the crack where the wall meets the paving,' Holmes replied quietly. 'And if you look closely, there are faint stains on the weatherboards above.'

Small leaned over the tape and squinted. 'I'll take your word for it.'

'Do you always go surfing after work?' Larsen asked.

'Depends on the surf,' Small replied. 'Got a text from a mate that there are good waves rolling into the old passage.'

'Is that where most people surf?' Larsen asked.

'Only if you're pretty seasoned. You wouldn't want learners out there on the Passage Break.'

'Surfing's one sport I've never tried,' Larsen mused. 'I've had a go at just about everything else along the way.'

'I could teach you,' Small responded enthusiastically. 'We'd have to start down on East Beach until you got the hang of it.'

Holmes scratched his cheek. 'The closest thing I've done to surfing is riding a body board when I was a kid.'

Small screwed up his face. 'It's hard to teach an old dog new tricks, unfortunately,' he replied.

Before Holmes found the words to respond, the divi van arrived and Farrell parked it on the wharf itself. *Fuckhead Farrell is big-noting himself*, Holmes thought but didn't say in the presence of Small. The senior constable said his goodbyes and trotted to his van. Holmes noticed Larsen's eyes follow him all the way.

'What's the go?' Farrell asked, clasping a hamburger in one hand and a takeaway milkshake in the other.

'We've found what we believe might be bloodstains on the ground against the wall,' Larsen replied.

'Doubt it,' Farrell said as he took a bite of his burger. 'I checked right around this area the day after Trev went missing.'

Holmes looked at Larsen and rolled his eyes.

'Still, little things can get by the best of us,' Farrell said as he took another bite and sent tomato sauce and fat sliding down the front of his uniform, slowing as it negotiated his pot gut. 'Fuck me!' Farrell yelled. 'This is only the second day I've worn this shirt!'

Holmes tried to ignore the constable's antics. 'If you could keep people away from here until the forensic team arrive, that would be great.'

'Easy-peasy,' Farrell mumbled through a mouthful of food. As the detectives turned to leave, he held up the remains of his burger. 'Hey, before you head off, the boss wants you to drop into the station. She says she's got something important to show you.'

'Like what?' Holmes asked.

'Buggered if I know, mate. She tells me nothin'. But apparently, it's something a kid found on the beach and handed in.'

Holmes turned to Larsen. 'Can you do the planning officer interview on your own? I'll see what the senior sergeant has got for us. When we get a chance, we'll need to track down our friend on the Harley as well.'

Larsen nodded as they climbed into their vehicle.

CHAPTER 11

The main offices of Moyne Shire Council were housed in an historic double-storey building in Cox Street with access via a modern glass façade on Princess Street to the side. The entrance door opened onto a large foyer with a long service counter traversing the wall opposite. Larsen was greeted by a neatly dressed middle-aged woman who initially informed her that without an appointment, the town planner was unavailable. A flash of identification prompted a quick call, and within a few seconds, the receptionist was showing Larsen through to an office at the back, where they found Ian Petrov standing in front of his large desk, primed to greet his visitor.

Petrov wasn't overly tall but was in good physical shape. His bare forearms below his rolled-up shirt sleeves were muscular, with large blood vessels like lengths of cord just beneath his tanned skin. He wore navy-blue trousers, a white cotton business shirt and a blue silk tie. His face was thin, his hair brown, and his cheekbones protruded like those often seen on people who follow Pritikin diets or the like. His dark eyes were well set back, and his mouth was little more than a line beneath his sharp nose.

The receptionist politely introduced Larsen and left the two to their business. Petrov motioned for his visitor to be seated then returned to the plush swivel chair behind his desk.

'So, what can I do for you, Detective?' Petrov asked.

'Trevor Flynn. We believe you may have been one of the last people to see him alive.'

'He did come here on the afternoon he apparently went missing. I've already told your local colleague everything I remember about his visit.'

Larsen took out a notebook and pencil then crossed her legs and leaned the book on her thigh. 'Well, I'd like to hear it again, please. Before anything else, let's establish a timeline. When did he arrive that afternoon?'

Petrov closed his eyes and exhaled heavily, as though his precious time was being wasted. 'Around five minutes before knock-off time. Roughly four forty.'

Larsen smiled. 'He did well to get past your receptionist at that stage of the day.'

Petrov chuckled ingenuously. 'Didn't go through the front desk, did he? Bowled straight into my office and started coming the heavy.'

'So, he'd obviously been here before?'

'Around five times,' Petrov replied, holding up the fingers of his left hand. 'Each time getting more and more aggressive.'

'He wanted his land rezoned as residential?'

'Of course. He'd been left holding the baby, hadn't he? Bought the land then thought he could buy me off as well.'

Larsen raised her eyebrows. 'He tried to bribe you?'

'Yeah. But I can't be bought.' He chuckled. 'Bit old-fashioned, I know, but my parents brought me up to do the right thing.'

'How'd Flynn react to that?'

'He said everyone had a price. He asked me to name mine.'

'And what did you say?'

'Told him to get the fuck out of my office, if you'll excuse my language. His plan wouldn't have passed the council anyway, unless he had a few people in his pocket that I don't know about.'

'Could the council have rezoned the land without your imprimatur?'

Petrov leaned back in his chair. 'Probably, but I've never heard of a paid officer's advice being overridden in these sorts of applications. The council would have known I'd play merry hell in the community if that happened. And in the press as well.'

'Did you inform the police about the attempted bribery?'

'Yeah. Told Grant Farrell, but nothing seems to have come out of it.'

With Fuckhead Farrell, I'm not surprised, Larsen thought. 'So then Flynn came the heavy?'

'Tried to, anyway.' Petrov's eyes half-closed in anger, and his face contorted. 'But I'd bloody had enough. He started making threats concerning my wife and kids, so I got out of this chair, walked to his side of the desk and shoved him up against the wall. I may not have been as big as the prick, but I wiped that arrogant smirk off his face, that's for sure.'

Larsen folded her hands on her lap. 'How'd he react to you pushing back?'

Petrov's fists clenched. 'The way all bullies react. He stormed off, making threats as he left.'

'What time did he leave?'

Petrov shrugged. 'Ten to five, maybe a bit after. He wasn't here for very long.'

Larsen recorded the times on her notepad. 'Was anyone else in the building at that time? I know the office closes at four forty-five.'

'Might have been a few people at their desks who left after me.' Petrov thought for a moment. 'I think Dianne was still shutting down computers at the front counter.'

'How long after Flynn stormed out did you leave?'

'I wasn't in the mood for work, so it was probably five minutes or so.'

'Where'd you go?'

Petrov leaned back in his chair and knitted his fingers behind his head. 'Home,' he said matter-of-factly. 'I wanted to ensure Flynn hadn't decided to make good on his threats. My wife works part-time at the supermarket, so she would have been home, and school was well finished for the kids.'

'The wharf is a block away. You didn't go home via there?'

Petrov shook his head. 'Why would I? I live on the other side of the highway, in Villiers Street. A few doors across from the hospital.'

'So you didn't follow Flynn?'

'Nope. Didn't see him leave.'

'You didn't trail him and make sure the threats weren't repeated?'

Petrov leaned forward in his chair, forearms on his desktop, hands folded. 'I'll level with you, Detective. I didn't feel the least bit sad when I heard the bastard had been eaten by a shark, and even less when I heard he'd been done in first. Good luck to that copper who knifed him, I say. Despite all that, I had no part in his death.'

'How'd you know he'd been knifed?' Larsen asked.

'It's all around Port Fairy,' Petrov replied with a smile. 'Small town, and all that. I think it was Grant Farrell who told me in the pub.'

Larsen shook her head as she tucked her notebook and pencil into her jacket pocket. She stood and thanked Petrov for his time, then left the office. The reception area was deserted except for two staff working behind the long service counter. Larsen wandered across to the woman who she'd spoken to earlier, checked her name badge and confirmed she was the one Petrov said was still in the office when Flynn stormed out.

'Sorry to bother you again, but I wonder if I could have a quiet word about the last time Trevor Flynn visited these offices?'

Dianne glanced across at her colleague, who took the subtle hint, picked up a handful of documents and disappeared down a corridor. 'What can I help you with, officer?'

'Mr Petrov mentioned you were still behind the counter when Flynn left that afternoon?' Larsen asked.

'Yes,' Dianne replied. 'We'd closed the office, but that gentleman was still in with Mr Petrov.'

'And what time did he leave?'

Dianne thought for a few moments. 'I'd say around five, at a guess. Maybe a touch earlier. He wasn't with Mr Petrov very long.'

'Did he say anything to you as he left?'

'Yes,' she replied, her face reddening. 'But it wasn't really towards me. It was more a message for Ian – er, Mr Petrov. And loud enough for Mr Petrov to hear from his office.'

'And the message was?'

Dianne was a little embarrassed. 'You'll have to excuse my language here, Detective. I don't normally use these types of words.'

Larsen smiled. 'In my line of work, I'm sure I've come across them before.'

Dianne looked around the area to double check that no one was in earshot then leaned forward as far as the counter would allow. 'He said to tell fucking Petrov that his time was up. If he didn't value his own neck, he should worry about his fucking wife and kids.' She shuffled around among her papers until she found a handwritten note. 'I wrote down what he said as soon as he left the building.' She smiled conspiratorially at the detective. 'I tidied up his grammar as I wrote it down. He has a tendency to drop the g off some of his adjectives.' She handed the note to Larsen.

The detective smiled. Fuck*ing* just didn't roll off the tongue quite as easily as fuck*in*. 'How come you didn't give this note to the local police when they came here asking questions?'

'Nobody spoke to me,' Dianne said. 'He just had a five-minute talk with Ian, and that was it.'

'Which officer did the interview?'

'Constable Farrell. He's been here for as long as I can remember. Everyone around town just calls him Grant. He's pretty well liked. Doesn't book the locals if he can help it.'

Larsen didn't react. 'Did you see Mr Petrov leave that day?'

Dianne nodded. 'Yes. Only a minute or so after Mr Flynn's outburst.'

'Did he say anything?'

'Not really. He just asked me in which direction Mr Flynn went after he headed out the doors.'

* * *

While Larsen interviewed Petrov, Holmes was little more than a block away in a briefing with Senior Sergeant Wilkins. A photograph sat atop her desk.

'Where was it found?'

'In among bluestone rocks beside one of the concrete ramps leading down onto East Beach,' Wilkins replied. 'Kids were playing cricket on the sand and the tennis ball was hit into the rocks. One of the boys fossicked around searching for it, and bingo.'

'Whereabouts on East Beach?

'Up near the Ocean View Apartments.'

Holmes picked up the photograph of the short filleting knife for a closer look. 'You suspect that's a trace of blood where the blade attaches to the handle?'

Wilkins shrugged. 'Dunno. That's why I bagged it up and sent it away to Forensics.'

Holmes nodded. 'The kid's prints will be all over it, unfortunately.'

'Actually, they aren't,' Wilkins replied. 'As soon as the boy saw what it was, he wrapped it in a towel before a group of them brought it in here to us. They wanted to know if there was a reward for solving a murder.'

'The knife being hammered by salt water wouldn't help in the preservation of fingerprints anyway.'

'I don't think the surf gets that high up unless there's a king tide and a big stormy swell,' Wilkins said. 'The weather was terrible the night Flynn went missing, but it was more squalls than a big rolling sea. That's why we dusted it for prints.'

Holmes was suddenly more interested. 'Get anything readable?'

'Lots of smears, but there was a good one that we photographed and emailed to McLeod. And guess what, we got a match.'

Holmes grinned and leaned back in his chair. 'That national database is a bloody marvel.'

Wilkins remained stony-faced. 'The match came from personnel records, Darren.' She took a deep breath. 'The print belongs to Greg Bowker.'

* * *

Bowker was dressed in shorts, a tee-shirt and thongs as he wandered East Beach beside the long pile of rocks deposited many years prior to inhibit the erosion of the beach and dunes. To anyone watching, he was just another visitor searching for seaborne detritus. The few shells and pieces of cuttlebone he carried in a plastic shopping bag added to that perception – but what he really sought carried much more value than any flotsam he might find.

CHAPTER 12

Holmes found Larsen leaning against the bonnet of their vehicle in the police station carpark. He listened carefully as she recounted her interviews with Petrov and the Moyne receptionist, at the same time privately ruminating on the implications of Bowker's prints being lifted off the knife.

'I'm not sure Petrov was totally forthcoming,' Larsen said. 'He swears he didn't follow Flynn after he stormed out of the council offices, and he claims he left five minutes after Flynn had gone. But the receptionist recalls Petrov being only a minute behind him and asking which direction Flynn had gone. Unless I'm too hung up on small details, something just doesn't add up.'

'Where'd Petrov say he went after he left work?'

'Home. To make sure his wife and kids weren't being harassed.'

'We'll need to talk to his missus.'

Larsen nodded. 'That was my next stop after I checked what you were up to.'

Holmes leaned against the car beside his partner, arms folded, and detailed his discussion with Wilkins. When he reached the part about Bowker's fingerprints, Larsen stood up straight and turned to face him.

'Greg's prints were on the knife?' she asked, open-mouthed.

Holmes nodded. 'And there could be small traces of blood

where the blade is screwed to the handle.'

Larsen looked at the ground, shaking her head and kicking at a small stone. 'How would the blood on the wharf marry up with blood on a knife up on East Beach?'

Holmes slipped his hands into his pockets. 'Too many assumptions involved to spend a lot of time thinking about that, I reckon.' He hiked his shoulders. 'Is it even blood at the wharf and on the knife? Is it human blood? Is there any match with Flynn?'

Larsen stared into the distance. 'If it's Flynn's blood on the wharf and the knife, then you could make a case that he was stabbed on the wharf and the knife was later discarded in the rocks on East Beach.'

Holmes met her eyes. 'On East Beach, near the flats where Greg was staying that night, you're saying.'

Larsen looked away. 'Or near the bikies' clubrooms, perhaps.'

'If Flynn was knifed on the wharf, surely the easiest way for his killer to dispose of the knife would have been heaving it into the middle of the river.'

Larsen shrugged. 'Unless he was worried that if the blood was found on the wharf, we'd send divers searching for the weapon. Hell, if it *is* Flynn's blood there, we'll definitely send divers down.'

Holmes turned and placed his forearms on the roof of their car. 'Forensics will give us a clearer picture on where to head next.' He thought pensively. 'But Greg's print on the knife worries me.'

Larsen turned and mirrored her partner's stance. 'So, what's our plan?'

'You catch up with Petrov's wife, and I'll track down Bowker for a heart to heart.'

Larsen frowned. 'You don't want me there when you front Greg?'

'He and I go back a long way. I'd like our chat to be informal. See where he's at and if there's anything he'd like to talk about.

If we're both there, it'll seem like a formal interview. At this stage, I don't think that's the way to go. Maybe in a few days that'll be required, but not right now.'

Larsen shrugged, not totally convinced. 'Your call. I'll grab a car from here and meet you back at the motel. It's a pity Small has knocked off for the day, otherwise he could have driven me around to the Petrovs' and grabbed a few pointers on how detectives run an interview.'

Holmes exhaled loudly. 'Don't talk to me about Senior Constable Small. Can't teach old dogs new tricks! Smart-arsed wanker.'

'I don't think he meant any harm,' Larsen said with a laugh as she walked towards the station door. 'See you a bit later.'

Holmes called after her. 'You could ask Fuckhead Farrell to drive you!'

Larsen turned, smiling, and shushing him with a finger to her lips.

Holmes removed his mobile from his pocket and rang Bowker. It was answered almost immediately.

'Sherlock. You still in Port Fairy, or have you solved Flynn's murder and you're back at Spencer Street filling out the paperwork?'

Holmes chuckled. 'Very funny. Look, I wonder if we could catch up and compare notes.'

'I've got no notes, mate. I'm off the case, remember?'

'That's bullshit, Greg,' Holmes replied without venom. 'You've been out to Yambuk, plus you threw us the teaser that you planned on visiting the lighthouse where Flynn's body washed up.'

'Just filling in the time before you crack the case. I'm working out which sights I should try and see in the meantime.'

Holmes cut straight to the point. 'You home now?'

'Yeah, just got back from the beach.'

'Do you mind if I come around for a chat?'

'On your own or with Larsen? Just wondering how official this chat will be.'

'Only me. Kirsten is conducting an interview.'

Holmes heard Bowker inhale loudly. 'Eighty-Nine Regent Street. You'll see my Subaru parked out the front.'

'I'll be there in five.'

* * *

Fortunately for Larsen, it was a non-workday for Petrov's wife, and the detective found her at home hanging out washing in her backyard. A mouse of a woman both in stature and nature, Maree Petrov was hesitant and unsure in relation to her husband's movements the afternoon Flynn had disappeared. She did confirm that Petrov was concerned about their family's safety but had trouble recalling the exact time he had arrived home.

Larsen left the property none the wiser as to whether the town planner had told his wife the whole truth about going straight home that afternoon. She consoled herself with the knowledge that a firm confirmation from Maree wouldn't have been a solid alibi anyway, since the history of law enforcement was riddled with examples of spouses supporting even the most heinous of criminals.

* * *

Holmes knocked on both the front and side doors of the Regent Street residence but gained no response. He opened the garden gate to the side of the house and followed the red brick path around to the rear of the building, where he found Greg Bowker sitting at an outdoor table in the shade of an ancient, heavily laden peach tree.

'Grab a peach off the tree,' Bowker said by way of introduction. 'Old-fashioned fruit. Actually has a taste and is full of juice. Bit different to the sponge-rubber shit you buy in the supermarkets.'

Holmes pulled a fully ripe peach off the tree, sending a pair of wattlebirds scurrying to higher branches. He dragged an aluminium-framed chair out from under the table and plonked himself down. 'Nice quiet spot,' he said as he sank his teeth into the fruit.

'Yeah,' Bowker replied. 'When you're sitting here in the shade, it makes you question why you waste your life chasing shitheads who couldn't give a fuck about the welfare of anyone else.'

'What have you found out?' Holmes asked with peach juice running down his chin.

'About what? I'm off duty.'

'Cut the crap,' Holmes replied, wiping the juice away with the back of his hand. 'We go back too far together to piss each other around.'

Bowker thought for a moment, fiddling with one of the peach stones on the table. 'Look, Sherlock, I'll level with you. I've checked out Yambuk and the lighthouse and found nothing that would help. I've searched the beach where Rachael last saw Flynn and found zilch there either. The coppers here won't talk to me, and every time I try to start a conversation with a local, they either know who I am and clamp up, or they don't know me and tell me to mind my own business.'

'Have you shown anyone your badge?' Holmes asked as he threw his peach stone into the tangle of Hardenbergia hanging from a side wall.

'What do you reckon? I'd be suspended and likely lose my job if the brass found out I was conducting an investigation that I'd been specifically removed from.'

Holmes nodded, then hesitated as he plotted his next move, knowing he was close to crossing a line. 'If you promise not to get involved and cloud the investigation, I'll tell you what we've got. I'd value your opinion. Then I've got a question I'd like to ask you.'

Bowker was intrigued. 'OK. You've got my word I won't shit in your nest.'

Holmes got up from his seat and used a garden tap to rinse the sticky juice off his hands. He wandered back to the table, shaking the excess water from his fingers, and sat down opposite his senior colleague. 'We've established that on the day Flynn was killed, he left his office at around four forty and visited Ian Petrov, the town planner, at the Moyne offices. There was a big blue, and Flynn left threatening harm to Petrov and his family if his rezoning request was refused. There is some suspicion that Petrov may have followed Flynn when he stormed out. Kirsten is chasing that up as we speak.'

'So he's your number one suspect? After me, that is,' Bowker said with a smile.

Holmes ignored the comment. 'We gained access to CCTV vision of the wharf area the night Flynn disappeared.'

Bowker seemed surprised. 'There's no cameras down there. I checked.'

'One of the squid boats moored there had cameras running. In the background, we can see part of the wharf and the carpark on the southern side of the restaurant.'

'Did it show anything of interest?' Bowker asked, placing his forearms on the table and folding his hands.

'Yeah. It cleared up one mystery and muddied the waters in another.' Holmes kept an eye on Bowker's face, looking for any reaction.

Bowker forced a smile. 'You've got my attention.'

'The vision starts when the fishermen leave the boat at the end of the day. Nothing unusual happens until the carpark empties, leaving just Flynn's Mercedes. Unfortunately, we don't see Flynn. What we do see, though, is a bloke in a tradie's ute roaring in and parking behind the Merc. He then disappears to the north of our picture before returning to kick in Flynn's car door and piss on his windscreen before hightailing it out of the carpark.'

'Shit.'

'Nope. Just piss,' Holmes said with a grin.

'Yeah, yeah. Good one. Anything else?'

'Half an hour after the urinator drives off, four blokes in a Mini Moke turn up half tanked. They piss-fart around on the wharf for a few minutes, then as they're about to leave, they find that Flynn has left the keys in the Merc. Two blokes jump in, start the car then follow the Moke out of vision.'

'Joyriders, you reckon?' Bowker asked.

'Yeah. Kirsten and I think they probably planned to take the Merc for a spin on the beach at Yambuk but bogged the vehicle in the process.'

'So Yambuk is a red herring in terms of the murder?'

'That's our view at the moment. As the Moke leaves, someone on a Harley Davidson turns up, and the rider disappears out of view of the camera. A short time later, they returned to their bike carrying a duffle bag and shot through.'

Bowker closed his eyes and thought for a moment. 'You need to identify the tradie and the bikie, then.'

Holmes nodded. 'And nail the blokes in the Moke. It'll be theft of a motor vehicle at least, but we'll need to talk to them to make sure there's not some link to Flynn we haven't thought of yet.' He hesitated. 'There was someone else on that vision, Greg.' He looked straight at his friend. 'You, mate. After all this other stuff had occurred, you walked along the wharf.'

Bowker didn't miss a beat. 'Yeah, that'd be right. I told you I talked to an old couple walking their dog who said they'd seen a Mercedes soft-top parked at the wharf. I took a look along the river to see if it was still there. It was dark, and the weather was shithouse. There wasn't a soul or a vehicle in sight.'

Holmes nodded slowly, taking in Bowker's explanation. 'You didn't see blood on the wharf anywhere?'

'It was pissing rain, mate. Any blood would have washed away in two minutes.'

'We found some on the ground below the eaves of the restaurant. On the side facing the river. The techs have taken samples. They'll go to McLeod for analysis.'

'I'm sorry I can't help you with that one,' Bowker replied. 'It was wet, and the areas close to the walls of the buildings down there would have been as black as pitch. The lights along the river are designed to illuminate the wharf and the boats.'

A flock of white cockatoos landed in the Norfolk pine in front of the house and began screeching. But Holmes's gaze was on the ground as he unconsciously watched a line of ants carry unknown quarry into a sand-cratered hole between the pavers. Bowker sensed his old friend's hesitancy.

'If there's something else, you better tell me,' he said.

Holmes looked up at his colleague. 'Some kids found a knife in among the bluestone rocks on East Beach. Looks to have traces of blood on it.'

Bowker's eyes never left Holmes's. 'Whereabouts on East Beach?'

'Beside a concrete ramp near the Ocean View Apartments.'

Bowker leaned back in his chair and stared up into the peach tree, where a blackbird flitted around, oblivious to the whirlwind that had sequestered the detective's mind.

'What type of knife?' Bowker finally asked.

'Small filleting knife,' Holmes replied before a slight hesitation.

'But, of course, you knew that already.'

Bowker remained poker faced. 'Why so?'

Holmes pursed his lips. 'Your prints are on it.'

'Has to be a mistake.'

'I doubt it, mate,' Holmes replied. 'The knife's gone to Melbourne and will be retested there.'

Bowker spread his arms and upturned both palms. 'I've got no explanation, Sherlock. I really don't.'

'Well, if McLeod confirms that they're your prints, you're going to have to find one. Especially if it's Flynn's blood on the thing.'

Bowker stared out into space as Holmes stood and placed his chair back under the table. 'Any other prints on the knife?'

'Yes, but none that match anything on the database. Catch you next time, eh?' Holmes plucked another peach from the tree and made to leave.

Bowker stayed seated. 'Thanks for coming round.' He feigned a chuckle. 'I suppose the upside of this is that you and Kirsten have been able to get away to the beach for a few days together.'

'That's what I thought until Wilkins assigned this Adonis to be our local team member. Late-twenties, six-foot-four, blond-haired surfer boy. He and Kirsten get on like a house on fire.'

Bowker forced a smile. 'You're worried it might be déjà vu all over again?'

'Yeah. I haven't been game to look in a mirror since I met him.' Holmes walked around the corner and was gone.

CHAPTER 13

Larsen had showered and was sitting on the side of the bed in a satin robe towelling her wet hair when Holmes arrived back at the motel. 'How'd you go with Greg?' she asked quickly.

'He's hiding something, I reckon. When I mentioned his print on the knife, he couldn't, or wouldn't, give me an explanation. Just said he can't explain it.'

Larsen stopped drying for a moment. 'That's got to be bullshit, surely. Who handles a knife and can't remember doing it? Especially when you're the chief suspect for sticking a blade into someone.'

'Totally agree,' Holmes said as he removed his jacket and laid it on the round table in the bay window. 'If the forensic report comes back saying it's Flynn's blood, then he's in more shit than a Werribee duck.' He took his keys and ID out of his trouser pocket and threw them on the bed. 'How'd you go with Mrs Petrov?'

'Very vague about her husband's movements that evening.' Larsen picked up a brush from her bedside table and began running it through her long hair. 'I'm not sure if she's hiding something or just doesn't remember anything as being out of the ordinary. But *unforthcoming* would be the term I'd use.'

'You happy with The Stump for dinner?' Holmes asked, then grinned. 'We have to have a meal at Victoria's oldest licenced pub at some stage in our lives.'

'No arguments here.'

'Over the next two days, I'd like to talk to the bikies. Other than that, there's not much else we can do until the forensics come back.'

Larsen stood up and flicked her hair back with the turn of her head. 'If there's a few spare hours, it will be great. Dale Small rang and asked me to go surfing with him down on East Beach tomorrow afternoon. Teach me the basics. The weather's supposed to be hot, so it should be fun.'

'Doesn't the guy ever work?' Holmes said, not trying to hide his annoyance.

'He's not rostered till late, apparently.' She placed her hands on Holmes's shoulders. 'You'll come for a swim, won't you?'

Holmes didn't smile. 'That'd be the best I could manage. You can't teach old dogs new tricks, remember?'

Larsen undid her dressing gown, let it drop to the floor and climbed naked between the sheets. 'It's your old tricks that I'm interested in, Detective,' she said seductively as she patted the bed beside her.

* * *

The Caledonian Inn, or The Stump, as it was often called by locals, was situated on the corner of Bank and James Streets. It was a colonial-style white limestone structure built right on the footpath with a red roof and dormer windows on the second floor. It had no verandah but provided outdoor seating under umbrellas along the Bank Street side. Established in 1844, it was in operation before the Victorian goldrushes and the major pastoral expansion into the western district.

Holmes led Larsen into the dining room without any display of affection, keen to protect their professionalism as police officers despite the fact that it was probably common knowledge around the town that they were sharing a room at the motel. A waitress dressed entirely in black showed them to a table towards the rear of the room and took their orders for drinks. They had been seated less than ten minutes before Greg Bowker entered the restaurant and spotted his friends.

Bowker made his way through the crowded dining room to the detectives' table. Both Holmes and Larsen noticed the glances and whispers from fellow diners as the new arrival passed. *There's the killer*, Holmes knew most of them were thinking.

After five minutes of chit-chat, Bowker retired to his own table, keen not to give locals more grist for the mill of a compromised investigation. Bowker's presence in the town already had tongues wagging that the fix was on. After a cursory glance of the menu, he walked to a counter separating the dining room from the main bar to order drinks. From that position, he could see an off-duty and casually dressed Constable Farrell talking to a trio of men he assumed were locals. The barman wandered across from his conversation with a couple of barflies and took his order for a schooner of diet Coke and ice.

As he turned to leave the counter, he heard his name mentioned above the hubbub. He moved slightly to be out of view of Farrell's group but still within earshot of their conversation.

Farrell was holding court, happy for anyone to hear his pronouncements. 'We've just about nailed the bastard. A bloodied knife was handed in to the station with Bowker's prints all over it. It's been a busy day. We also found blood down on the wharf. You might have seen me there today making sure everything was done right.'

'I saw the police tape,' a ruddy-faced man wearing a beanie replied. 'Didn't see you among the crowd.'

'I was there, alright,' Farrell pontificated. 'The boss sent me down to give the techs a heads-up on what we'd found.'

A jockey-sized character wearing a cap on backwards frowned. 'Blood on the wharf could be anything, Granto. Fish, squid. A gull, even.'

'That's what I need to find out. If the blood belongs to Trev, then it's all over for bighead Bowker.'

Beanie-Head smiled as he took a sip of his beer. 'Who's the hot chick following the other copper around? His secretary, or something?'

'Careful. That's a bit sexist, mate,' Farrell replied with a smirk and a waggle of his finger. 'That hot chick is Detective Senior Constable Kirsten Larsen of the homicide squad, so watch your Ps and Qs, otherwise she might put the long arm of the law around you.'

'He wishes,' a fat, red-faced middle-aged man in a blue singlet and red shorts said with a laugh.

'If she did, I'd slip one into her real smart,' Beanie Head replied. 'Kawoompa!' he added, thrusting his hips forward.

They all laughed.

'She bangin' the old bastard she's workin' with, do ya reckon?' Beanie Head asked seriously after a few moments.

'They're sharing the same room, according to Pauline at the motel,' Farrell replied. 'Taxpayers paying for a bed that's not even slept in.'

Reverse Cap shook his head. 'He's old enough to be her bloody father.'

'Yeah, but if she's in the same room, you have to root her, don't you?' Farrell replied.

The quartet laughed. Fat Guts held up his drink. 'Hear, hear to that!' he said, and the four men clinked glasses.

Bowker had heard enough and made a beeline straight for Holmes. He leaned on his colleagues' table and quietly explained what he had just overheard, omitting the parts about Holmes and Larsen. 'My first reaction is to walk in there and punch the fucker's head in then haul him down to the station and book him on every charge I can think of. But unfortunately, I'm on leave, so I might have to give you the pleasure of handling this, Sherlock.'

Holmes walked into the public bar and approached Farrell from behind. His friends' facial contortions tried to warn him of the impending confrontation, but Farrell missed the cues in his eagerness to remain the centre of attention. 'It'll be hard to keep the smile off my dial if the local flatfoots wrap the case up before that big swinging dick from Melbourne and his piece of young pussy have even got to first base.'

Holmes tapped Farrell on the shoulder hard enough for the constable to suspect major swelling would result. 'Got a minute outside, Grant? There's a new development in the Flynn case I'd like your advice on.'

Farrell frowned, then downed the dregs of his beer. 'Shouldn't be long, fellas.' He gave his empty glass to Fat Guts. 'Grab us another one of those, will you, mate?' he asked as he left to follow Holmes through the side door onto Bank Street.

Outside, a few patrons sat at the wooden tables under umbrellas, so Holmes indicated that they should talk in the yard behind the hotel. On its perimeter sat the pub's ancient colonial accommodation, upgraded over the years to meet modern expectations. Holmes looked around to make sure their conversation wouldn't be overheard then invited Farrell to join him under a large peppercorn tree in the corner of the yard. 'I want to talk police business, so it's important that we're not overheard. Get my drift?'

Farrell nodded. 'Of course,' he said as he walked across to his colleague.

The moment Farrell was close enough, Holmes grabbed him by the lapels of his open-neck Hawaiian shirt and slammed him against the trunk of the tree. 'If I ever hear you talk about Detective Senior Constable Larsen in that way again, I'll snap you in half, alright? You're one of those useless bastards that give the rest of us coppers a bad name. At your age, you should be at least a senior sergeant instead of the fuckin' constable you were when you left the academy as a twenty-year-old. So you're either the most incompetent officer I've ever encountered, or you're just an unambitious, lazy piece of shit. I suspect both.' Holmes released his grip but held Farrell against the tree with a hand on his chest.

The blood had drained from the constable's face, but he managed to choke out a few words. 'You'll do your job for this, Detective. This is assault of a fellow officer.'

'You're not a fellow officer, Farrell. You're just a turd who dresses up in a uniform and spends all day pretending to be a policeman. Before you start threatening me with a breach of professional services, perhaps I should note down what I've seen and heard tonight while I was getting drinks at the counter in there. An officer leaking sensitive information concerning important evidence, making public claims about the outcome of an investigation before a thorough inquiry has occurred, providing crucial information to potential witnesses and possibly the perpetrator themselves, compromising an investigation with sloppy handling of evidence. The list goes on and on. By all means, report me for roughing you up a bit, but be prepared to suffer the consequences if you do. I'll deny I even laid a hand on you, and with your shit reputation, you'll be laughed out of the force.' Holmes brushed Farrell's chest as if removing dirt from his shirt. 'Are we clear on this, Constable?'

Farrell pushed Holmes's hand away. 'Fuck off,' was all he could find to say as he hurried off.

When Holmes re-entered the dining room, Bowker was at the counter ordering his meal. Holmes winked as he walked past. In the bar, Bowker glimpsed Farrell returning to his mates. The detective moved out of view, but his ears honed in on their conversation.

Fat Guts handed Farrell his beer. 'The Homicide dude needing your help, Granto?'

Farrell was coy. 'Nah. Just wanted to ask how long the forensic team were at the wharf today.'

'So when does the report on the blood come back?' Beanie Head asked, rubbing his hands together excitedly. 'This is like CSI, but it's real.'

Farrell stared into his beer. 'Can't tell you much. I've probably told you more than I should already.' He looked up with a feigned smile. 'Sorry.'

Beanie Head frowned. 'That swinging dick put a clamper on you?'

Farrell shook his head. 'No. But he asked me to keep a couple of things to myself. That made me realise that maybe I'd let a few things slip that I shouldn't have. So keep what I've told you under your hat, OK?'

Reverse Cap nodded seriously. 'Yeah, no worries. Don't want to get a mate into trouble, do we, boys?'

They all agreed, and the topic moved to the Australian cricket team selections for the upcoming test. Bowker smiled and returned to his table. As he passed Holmes, he leaned down and whispered, 'Touché.'

CHAPTER 14

The weather was pleasantly warm and the ocean at their back inviting, but a growling American pit bull and screeching gulls overhead delivered a feeling of foreboding to Holmes and Larsen when they arrived at the Barbarians' rural headquarters on Tuesday morning. Adjoining the former Birdwatchers Club building was a long skillion roof, under which a line of chrome-plated Harley Davidsons was parked. The bike closest to them created the most interest with its long, set-back *Easy Rider* handlebars and its fuel tank featuring an eagle holding an angry snake in its beak.

'I've seen that bike on our trip to the Mallee,' Larsen said. 'It roared past us on the Horsham side of the Grampians, remember? We then spotted it a couple of times later when it stopped in remote rest areas, seemingly for prearranged meetings.' She looked through the wire netting that provided the compound's first line of defence. 'It's starting to smell like a drug running operation, don't you reckon?'

The dog made a dive at the fence, snarling. Holmes took a step back, fighting the instinct to lay a boot into the netting. 'Might answer the question as to why this mob set up shop here in the first place. Port town, boats coming and going all the time. Centralising the operation makes sense. Pick up the gear from a boat and distribute it directly to customers.'

'If we're right, it poses some new questions concerning Flynn's murder. We know he's had dealings with this mob.'

Holmes nodded. 'Yeah. Maybe his involvement is more than just a one-off favour for his bikie cousin to arsehole the Birdwatchers.'

The dog kept snarling, but neither detective paid him much attention, until he spun around with his ears pricked as an overweight, leather-clad, late-middle-aged man appeared through the side door of the clubhouse. He sported long, scraggy hair, a beard and faded tatts on his forearms.

'This will be fun. Here comes Cement Head,' Holmes said, gesturing towards the lumbering figure.

'Cement Head?' Larsen asked quizzically.

'Greg and I crossed swords with this mob last year. A murder case up in the Mallee. This bloke's their receptionist.'

When the bikie reached the fence, Holmes flashed his ID.

'I know who you are, arsehole,' Cement Head growled in a low, guttural voice. 'Why are you harassing us this time?'

Holmes didn't overreact but spoke sternly. 'We'd like to have a chat with a couple of your mates.' The dog snarled. 'How about you call off the bloody dog before I ring the ranger and have him taken away? He looks like a prohibited breed to me.'

Cement Head laughed. 'I'd like to see the ranger try and tackle this bastard. He'd get his throat torn out.'

'Well, shut the mongrel up before I put a bullet between his eyes,' Holmes replied.

'Fuck me!' Cement Head said half under his breath before kicking the animal in the ribs. 'Shut the fuck up, Satan!' he screamed. The hound yelped then stopped barking and stood at attention, yearning for an attack command.

Holmes nodded his appreciation. 'We'd like a quick chat with a bloke named Jason McCulloch.'

Cement Head looked puzzled. 'Jason? Is that Chainsaw's real name?'

'He's the cousin of Trevor Flynn,' Larsen said.

'Yeah, that's him,' Cement Head replied. 'But he's not going to want to talk to this bastard,' he added, using a thumb to indicate Holmes. 'It's his mate that topped Flynn.' He then addressed Holmes. 'Can't remember the arsehole's name. Tall prick, full of himself. Was with you when you hassled us at our Northcote headquarters last year.'

'Whatever,' Holmes replied dismissively. 'Just get McCulloch.'

'Chainsaw ain't gonna be too happy being woken up at this hour.'

Larsen looked at her watch. 'Nine forty-five. Yeah, it is a bit early,' she said sarcastically.

'Tell you what,' Cement Head said, 'when he wakes up, I'll tell him you called, and he can decide if he wants to talk to you. I s'pose you can be contacted at the local cop shop.'

Holmes had heard enough. 'You've got thirty seconds to go get McCulloch before I ring for a search warrant to go over this place for illegal drugs and any other contraband you're hiding in there.'

Cement Head exhaled loudly. 'Alright, alright, don't get your knackers in a fuckin' tangle.' He trudged back towards the side door of the building.

Holmes looked at Larsen. 'I can't see why the drug squad haven't raided this place already.'

Larsen smiled. 'Bit too far from home base, perhaps?'

Holmes didn't respond. After a couple of minutes, a tall and skinny man in his forties or fifties came through the clubhouse door, hitching up a pair of leather trousers and tucking in the waist of a dirty white tee-shirt displaying a picture of Ned Kelly with the caption *Such is Life*. A pair of unzipped leather boots flopped on his feet. He hid a drawn face behind a spindly red beard, his eyes a piercing blue and his greying red hair long and unkempt.

'This better be fuckin' good,' he said as he approached the officers.

Holmes was debating whether to continue the absurdity of an interview through a chain wire fence or order McCulloch to the police station for more formal questioning. Given this was more a fact-finding mission than the pursuit of a specific lead, he opted to keep it informal. For now. An official interview was an option he still had up his sleeve.

'Jason McCulloch?'

'What the fuck is all this about?' McCulloch replied. 'It's bloody early, if you haven't noticed.'

'You're Trevor Flynn's cousin?' Larsen asked.

'I *was*, until some copper blew him away!' McCulloch replied angrily. 'They had history, you know. Fuckin' Bowker stole Trev's wife years ago. I warned Trev she was a conniving bitch, but he said he'd slap her into shape. She pissed off with fuckin' Bowker before he had the chance to break her in. And it was Bowker who cost him his job in the homicide squad, too. Bit fuckin' ironic, don't you think, that the bastard now works there himself. But all that wasn't enough for your mate, was it? Took Trev's wife, then his career. What was left? Just his life, and Bowker took that too.'

Holmes didn't speak until McCulloch had got what he had to say off his chest. 'Well, that's what we're investigating now,' Holmes said. 'Trevor Flynn's death.'

McCulloch let out a fake laugh. 'You lot investigating one of your own? That'll give everyone peace of fuckin' mind.'

'Was your cousin part of this organisation?' Larsen asked.

'No. And this isn't an organisation, it's a club,' McCulloch replied with a straight face. 'Just a group of people with a common interest.'

'What? Standing over people and dealing drugs and firearms?' Holmes replied aggressively.

'No. Feeling the fresh air on our faces as we travel around on our bikes, smart-arse,' McCulloch said, grabbing the wire and rattling the fence. The dog came to life and snarled.

Holmes raised both palms. 'OK, if you want to play it this way, I'll ask you to come down to the station and we'll take a formal statement.'

'I'm not going anywhere unless you want to charge me with something.'

Larsen tried to take some heat out of the situation by speaking quietly. 'If your cousin wasn't a member of the Barbarians, how come he fronted your takeover of the Birdwatchers Club?'

'Because I asked him to,' McCulloch replied. 'We had another third party approach the fuckin' geriatrics about us buying this hall, since they only had half a dozen members and it was dead in the arse anyway. But they wouldn't come to the party, so Trevor suggested we should all buy memberships and take it over legally.'

'You spoke to Flynn prior to the plan?' Larsen asked.

'Yeah, he's my fuckin' cousin! Our mothers are sisters. When we both ended up in Port Fairy following our own interests, it was obvious we'd catch up. We played together as kids, got pissed together as teenagers, attended each other's weddings.'

Holmes scratched the side of his head. 'And Flynn was happy to head up the plan to stack the meeting even though he wasn't a member of your merry band?'

'We needed someone who the locals would see as legitimate,' McCulloch replied. 'Imagine if me or Cement Head fronted the meeting with our plans to put the club back on the rails.'

'Does the motorcycle club have any involvement in the developments Flynn had out on Belfast Lough?' Larsen asked.

McCulloch looked at her as if she'd lost her mind. 'Where would we get the money to do that?'

'Where would you have got the money to buy this building?' Holmes asked with a smirk. 'Prime ocean-front property.'

'We thought we'd get it for bugger-all.' McCulloch turned and pointed at the fibro cement structure. 'Look at it. The next big wind would have blown the place down if we hadn't reinforced it.'

'Did you see Flynn on the day he went missing?' Larsen asked.

McCulloch shook his head. 'Nope, hadn't seen him for a few days, actually. We tend to keep pretty much to ourselves up here.'

Holmes gestured towards the line of motorcycles. 'Who belongs to the bike with the eagle on the tank?'

'Rooter Allender,' McCulloch replied.

'Rooter?' Larsen asked with a smirk.

'He comes from a one-horse town up in the Mallee somewhere. When he joined the club, people just christened him Rooter because everyone has heard of Mallee roots.'

Holmes stared at Rooter's motorbike, deep in thought. Allender was involved in the case they had investigated a year earlier, and here he was popping his head up again. 'Can you send Allender out for a chat, please, mate?'

Before McCulloch could reply, a short and fat, balding man with a greying beard exited the clubhouse, followed by a podgy female sporting dyed-red hair and dressed in full leathers. The male carried his bike helmet in one hand and a kit bag in the other. The moment he threw his bag over the back of the eagle-painted Harley, Holmes recognised him as Daryl Allender, or Skeeta, as Bowker always called him from their dealings many decades ago in the Mallee town of Manangatang. Holmes knew from their previous year's meeting that Allender was happy with his new nickname and resented the Skeeta sobriquet being mentioned.

Holmes placed two fingers between his lips and whistled loudly. Allender looked around and saw the detectives at the compound gate.

'Hey, Skeeta, got a minute? Holmes yelled.

Allender pretended not to hear and proceeded to pack his kit into the saddle bags on his bike.

'What's with the *Skeeta* business?' McCulloch asked.

Holmes grinned. 'That's what he was called since he was a little kid growing up in the bush, I've been told. He was like a mosquito, always hanging around giving everyone the shits.'

For the first time in their conversation, McCulloch smiled, exposing stubby, nicotine-stained teeth. 'Skeeta suits him, actually. He's still inclined to hang around and give everyone the fuckin' shits.' He started to walk back towards the clubhouse, Holmes feeling his level of antagonism had abated. But that feeling was fleeting, as McCulloch yelled across to Allender, 'Rooter, the pigs want a word with you.'

Allender reluctantly wandered across to the fence, his moll following a few metres behind. He looked Holmes in the face. 'Not you again.' He then gave Larsen the once-over. 'At least your partner's better looking than fuckin' Bowker.'

'I should formally introduce you two, eh, Skeeta?' Holmes said as he gestured towards Larsen. 'This is Detective Senior Constable Larsen. Detective, this is Skeeta Allender and his girlfriend Jolene.'

'It's Janine, not bloody Jolene,' Allender said aggressively. 'And nobody's called me Skeeta for the last thirty years. The name's Rooter. Or Daryl if I'm doing something official.'

'Like a police interview?' Holmes asked sarcastically.

'No, like Centrelink, smart-arse!' Allender shot back.

'You and Janine off somewhere?' Larsen asked. 'Seems like you were loading the bike for a trip.'

'Yeah. I originally come from up the Mallee, so we thought we might go for a run up there and see a few old mates,' Allender explained. 'It's been a while since we visited.'

'Last week, wasn't it?' Holmes asked, stony-faced.

'No way. It'd have to be a year,' Allender replied. He then turned to Janine. 'November last year, wasn't it, Jan? When I took you up to see the family farm.'

Janine was caught off guard, her drug-induced stare interrupted. 'Yeah. I always lose track of time, but it would've been a fair while ago.'

Larsen smiled and shook her head. 'I'm afraid we saw you both last Tuesday. Ironically, we were also heading north to see our families. You passed us going like a bat out of hell between Stawell and Horsham. Then we saw you meet with a bloke in a ute at Green Lake and later on heard of you rendezvousing with someone in a four-wheel drive at a whistle stop called Rosebery, just south of Hopetoun.'

Allender shook his head vigorously. 'You've got the wrong bloke, Detective. Easy mistake to make when riders all wear the same leathers and helmets.'

'Not all Harleys have got the *Easy Rider* handlebars and a snake in an eagle's mouth painted on the fuel tank,' Holmes said coolly. 'Plus, I was sure I recognised the face when you passed us and gave me the finger at Dadswells Bridge. Just couldn't put a name to it. Now I have. Skeeta bloody Allender and the lovely Jolene.'

'It's Janine!' Allender bit back, not recognising that Holmes was purposely provoking him. 'Look, you might have seen us on the road last week, but we didn't get far enough north to see our friends. It was bloody hot, so when we got to Hopetoun, we made the decision to head back before the real heat rolled in. That's why we've decided to give it another go today.'

'Who'd you meet at Green Lake and Roseberry?' Larsen asked.

'We didn't meet anyone. We pulled up for a smoke and the other blokes just happened to be there.'

'Just pulled up for a ciggie?' Holmes pressed.

'Yeah. Ever tried smokin' on a motorbike?'

Larsen decided to fly a kite. 'If you turned back at Hopetoun, how come we saw you again in Mildura?'

Allender sensed the trap and laughed. 'Where'd you see us in Mildura, then?'

Larsen took a punt on Mildura's main thoroughfare into the city. 'You passed us in Langtree Avenue near that line of motels.'

Before Allender could respond, Janine jumped in. 'You couldn't have seen us in Mildura, because we turned off at Irymple,' she said proudly. Allender dropped his head.

Holmes smirked and replied quickly. 'The same Irymple that's on the outskirts of Mildura?'

'She always gets Hopetoun and Irymple mixed up,' Allender said, trying to repair the damage.

'I can understand that,' Holmes said sarcastically. 'Hopetoun, in the middle of semi-desert wheat country, and Irymple, surrounded by irrigated citrus trees and grape vines. Shit, their names are nearly identical.'

Allender folded his arms across his chest. 'What does it matter if we did travel up that way, anyway? It's a free world.'

'We reckon you were making a drug run, Skeeta,' Holmes replied. 'Dropping supplies off to the little towns along the way. You've got form on this. Bowker nailed you for distributing weed thirty-odd years ago when he was the copper at Manangatang. Looks like you haven't changed.'

'What was in the bag you loaded onto your bike Friday week ago at the wharf?' Larsen asked, trying to keep him off balance.

'I don't remember being anywhere near the fuckin' wharf,' Allender replied angrily.

Holmes raised his eyebrows. 'Of course you remember, Skeeta. It was pissing rain. We've got you on video. Lovely images of you arriving on your painted Harley and then leaving with a package which you stowed on the back of your bike.'

'Who brings the drugs in, Daryl?' Larsen asked.

Allender shook his head. 'I dunno nothing about drugs.'

'You've got a problem here,' Holmes said. 'We think that Trevor Flynn was killed that night on the wharf, and we've got you on video in the right place and at the right time. Drug deal go wrong, did it?'

Allender pointed straight at Holmes. 'You're not going to pin that on me. Grant Farrell said you blokes would likely set someone up to take the rap for Bowker.'

Holmes looked at Larsen and rolled his eyes. 'Been talking to Big Mouth Farrell, have you? He keep you up to date with what's in the wind on the police front?'

'Every now and then, he cruises past here to make sure things are quiet up this end of town,' Allender replied. 'He only said what the rest of the town are thinking.'

'Do you mind if we come in and check what you just put in your saddle bags?' Larsen asked.

'No chance without a warrant,' Allender retorted quickly. 'I can spot a setup a mile away.' He looked at Holmes. 'Got the drugs in your pocket ready, have you?'

'Who's the boss of the drug racket, Skeeta?' Holmes asked aggressively. 'Jason McCulloch? Cement Head? Trevor Flynn, before someone topped him?'

'Dunno what you're on about,' Allender replied. 'We're a motorcycle club and nothing more.' He took Janine by the hand.

'Come on, Jan. This conversation has stirred my guts. Might need a few minutes' rest and a quick drink before we head off.'

'Good move, Skeeta,' Holmes said. 'Don't want to bring that bike through this gate with us here. We'd likely pull you over for a search. But you can't hide forever, and we're not leaving town.'

He nodded at Larsen, and the two detectives returned to their car.

CHAPTER 15

The weather had warmed further by the time the off-duty detectives found a sheltered spot on the hot sand on East Beach, among the bluestone rocks. Holmes threw down a multicoloured drawstring bag and dragged out two large beach towels. By the time he had laid these carefully on the sand, Larsen had removed an oversized cotton top to reveal her hot-pink string bikini. Holmes's first glimpse took his breath away.

'I haven't seen that before,' he managed to blurt out.

Larsen smiled. 'It's new. I bought it on the way back from interviewing Petrov's wife.' She spun around, arms stretched above her head. 'What do you reckon? I'm not too old for it, am I?'

Holmes shook his head, open-mouthed. 'Absolutely not. And you're barely thirty, for God's sake.' *Not pushing fifty like myself,* he thought but didn't say, not wanting to remind Larsen of what he hoped she'd forgotten about.

'You two hiding up here?' came a voice from behind them. The couple turned to see Dale Small approaching from the shallows, dripping with water. The senior constable cut an impressive figure, not just because of his imposing height, but stripped down, he was a ball of muscle with a washing-board set of abs. Complimenting his golden tan was a pair of skimpy pale-yellow speedos that left nothing to the imagination and quashed any theory that a man could be defined by his surname.

Holmes was removing his tee-shirt but aborted the action when he spotted Small. Never in his life had he felt so old and inadequate. Never in the time he'd known Larsen had their age difference seemed such a yawning chasm.

'It's a pity we'll have to cover all that up with a wetsuit,' Small said candidly as he looked Larsen up and down.

'Likewise,' Larsen replied with a smile. 'It's warm enough to surf without one, surely.'

'We wear them to prevent getting a rash from the board, and they eradicate the need for sunscreen except on the face,' Small said. He gestured towards Larsen's bikini with a wide grin. 'Plus, if you get dumped, you'll be searching for that all summer.'

The sooner they both get wetsuits on, the better, Holmes thought, feeling like a third wheel – or, even worse, the adult sent to supervise the kids. Deep down, he asked himself whether Kirsten had bought the bikini because Small had arranged to give her surfing lessons today.

'What are you going to do while we try out a few waves, Darren?' Small asked.

Holmes shrugged. 'Probably go for a swim. The salt water will do me good.'

'Make sure you stay between the flags,' Small said, as if he was talking to a child. 'This beach is pretty safe, but there are still traps out there. I've seen even young fit blokes get into trouble, so you be careful. I'll just get the gear out of the van.' He trotted off up the beach.

Holmes looked at Larsen. 'I better head back to the car too. Get my floaties,' he said without the hint of a smile.

Larsen could see he was a bit peeved and put her arms around him, kissing him on the lips. 'Relax, Darren. This is all just a bit of fun in our time off.'

A fat, hirsute man in his sixties walked past with an overweight woman trudging behind dragging a heavy bag and a beach umbrella. He saw Holmes and Larsen in their embrace. 'Is there a phone number to ring to get me a secretary like that, mate?' he said with a grin as he trudged on. Holmes closed his eyes and allowed the anger to settle.

* * *

Larsen was true to her word that she picked up new sports quickly. After a few early spills, she became proficient at kneeling on the board to catch a wave, and within an hour, she was able to stand and ride a breaker to the shallows, albeit in a straight line. Holmes decided to make the best of the situation and cool off in the surf. But his eyes and his mind never left Larsen and Small, and he found trouble discerning whether this feeling in his gut stemmed from jealousy or straight-out apprehension that Larsen would finally see him for the middle-aged man he was.

He looked down at his midriff as the salt water drained over his chest. He wasn't in bad shape for a bloke his age. He had a slight paunch, but no bulging gut like many of his contemporaries. Still, he was no match for a senior constable with abs of steel. When they'd left the motel for the beach, Holmes thought he looked pretty good in his coloured board shorts, but alongside Small's speedos he'd fallen short. If he'd worn speedos himself, he would have fallen even shorter.

After nearly two hours of tuition, Small and Larsen dragged their boards up to where Holmes was sitting on a towel, tee-shirt safely back on. They both collapsed onto the sand, laughing.

'I can see why that gets addictive, Dale,' Larsen said. She looked at Holmes. 'It's incredible. The power under the waves just lifts you up like you weigh nothing.'

'She's a good student, mate,' Small said. 'A couple more lessons and she'll be hanging five.'

We need to crack this case open in the next twenty-four hours and get the fuck out of here, Holmes thought but nodded towards Small. 'Yeah, she looked to be picking it up pretty quickly.'

Small checked his expensive waterproof watch. 'Shit, time flies when you're having fun.' He stood up. 'I'm on duty in an hour, so I better head.' He picked up his board and reached for the one Larsen had been using.

'I'll carry it back to your van,' Larsen said, climbing to her feet and grabbing her board. 'I'll shower up on the lawn before I take the wetsuit off. Best do that at your vehicle so I don't cover it with sand again.'

'Being a newbie, you'll need help getting out of that thing anyway,' Small suggested.

Holmes started gathering their belongings and putting them in the beach bag. 'No need for you to pack up yet, Darren,' Larsen said. 'I'll be back as soon as I help Dale load his gear.'

Holmes didn't reply. He folded his towel in half and sat back down.

It was more than fifteen minutes before Larsen returned. She spread her towel on the warm sand. 'What do you wanna do now?'

'I thought we could go for a splash around in the surf.'

'You go for it, Darren. I'm happy enough to lie here in the sun.' She stretched out on her back and shielded her eyes with her hands.

'Fair enough,' Holmes said disappointedly, wondering if Small would have received that response if he had made the same suggestion. He spread out his own towel and lay down, mentally punishing himself for his teenage reactions.

* * *

The call from Erin O'Meara came through to Bowker on Wednesday morning as he sat sipping coffee at the Regent Street cottage. After a warm and sunny few days, the weather had turned foul. A cold southerly blew in from Bass Strait, delivering fast-moving silky black clouds and sleety showers. The air was salty and smelt of fish and rotting seaweed.

'This discussion is totally off the record, and I'll deny it if ever I'm asked,' O'Meara stated by way of introduction. 'You happy with that, Greg?'

It took Bowker a few moments to realise it was O'Meara. He didn't recognise the mobile number and her tone was less strident than normal. It was her rasping cough that finally convinced him the call was genuine. 'You got a new phone, Erin?'

'I'm working from home,' O'Meara replied. 'Have I got your word that this is off the record?'

A shiver of apprehension ran down the detective's spine. 'Of course. What's the go?'

'I'm just finishing up the forensic report around items that were sent to us as part of the Port Fairy investigation. I'll email a copy to the locals down there and to Darren Holmes soon. I know you've got yourself tangled up in this case, so as a courtesy to a friend, I thought I'd give you a heads up. Nothing in writing, just a few results, OK?'

'Thanks, I appreciate it.' He heard O'Meara's cigarette lighter snap open then closed, and he imagined the satisfied look on her face as she drew in the smoke despite knowing she was hastening her death with every puff. 'What have you got?'

'The knife they sent down with your thumb print on it. There *were* traces of blood at the base of the blade.' She hesitated for a moment, and Bowker sucked in a deep breath. 'Bovine blood.'

Bowker exhaled with relief. 'OK.'

'Obviously, the knife had been used to cut beef at some stage and hadn't been properly washed. Once the blood hardened, it could have survived later washes, provided they weren't too harsh. Probably hadn't been through a dishwasher, but you'd expect that. Manufacturers advise against using dishwashers for their specialist knives as they blunt the edge. Anyway, the blood's been there for a while, so I'd imagine it was already on the knife when you handled it. Whether it's one you brought from home or picked up from where you were staying is obviously impossible for us to determine.' O'Meara wheezed then coughed. 'Take your pick on which scenario fits best.'

Bowker didn't address the implied question. 'What else did you find?

'The blood on the wharf belongs to Flynn. Not super old and seems to fit with the time we estimate he was killed.' She coughed into the phone, and Bowker instinctively moved his mobile away from his ear before smiling when he realised his reaction. *These iPhones are good*, he thought, *but not* that *good*. 'So, your report will say he was killed on the wharf?'

'Our report will say he *bled* on the wharf,' O'Meara corrected, 'but whether he cashed his chips there is impossible to tell from what we were sent.'

'But highly likely, from what else we know?'

'You're the detective, Greg. We just solve the cases for you,' O'Meara fired back before coughing loudly and expectorating into who knew what. 'Pity you can't buy that old-fashioned cough mixture. It used to be good for these fits.'

'You could give up smoking.'

'That shop has long closed. Besides, all the specialists told me I'd be dead by forty, and here I am still going strong.' She spat out another mouthful of what Bowker knew would be brown slime.

'The other thing we've found which might help is the rego on that tradie's ute. Our video enhancement team worked on the boat CCTV vision for hours, came up with ten possibilities of what the numberplate read. They cross-checked them with the type of vehicle the plates were on, and bingo.'

She read out the registration details, which Bowker copied onto the margin of the newspaper in front of him.

'Who's it belong to?' he asked.

'It's registered to a proprietary limited company called Warrnambool Handyman Services. The owner of that company is Graeme Connolly of Koroit Street, Warrnambool. Of course, Connolly may have other people working for him.'

'Yeah. But at least that's a good start.'

'They were also able to enhance other parts of the vision from that night,' O'Meara said. 'Got a nice still frame of you on the wharf in the rain.'

'I was there looking for Flynn,' Bowker replied.

'You find him?'

'Of course not. Do you think I'm a murderer, Erin?' Bowker fired back.

'I didn't ask if you killed him, Greg. I asked if you found him,' O'Meara shot back just as fast.

'No. I didn't see him.'

'OK, I believe you. We also were able to produce a pretty good photo of one of the idiots who drove the Mini Moke into the carpark. But no luck enhancing the plates on that car. Looks like it carries plastic plate protectors, and there's sand between them and the number plates. No Mokes registered down Port Fairy way, and none in the state to drivers still on their Ps.'

'Can you send me the photo with the written report?'

'Nope. I'm not sending you anything, Bowker,' O'Meara replied quickly. 'I'm already holding my arse over a fire by telling you what I have so far. Shit. Disclosing information to an officer banned from investigating the case? An officer who's the prime bloody suspect? If this discussion gets out, not even my good looks will save me.' She laughed out loud then coughed for what seemed to Bowker several minutes. 'I'll send the full report through to Holmes. If he wants to discuss it with you, that's his own risk. But for God's sake, don't let on you know already.'

'Appreciate the call, Erin, and I know the risks you're taking by ringing me,' Bowker said sincerely.

'Just watch your back. The big dogs are always the easiest targets,' O'Meara said before disconnecting the call.

Bowker leaned back in his aluminium chair, wondering what to make of O'Meara's information. He'd known all along that the knife that the kids found and handed to police was the one Rachael had borrowed from the Pickerings' kitchen and taken to the beach. It had to be. He hadn't handled another knife of that kind, and surmised he'd left a print when he'd rifled through Rachael's bag searching for sunscreen. But the blood had worried him. Although he found it impossible to imagine Rachael stabbing Flynn, he was taking no chances, finding it judicious to suppress any connection between his wife and the knife. With the blood deemed bovine, he could now concentrate on clearing his own name.

It was thus with some relief that Bowker moved to Flynn's blood on the wharf. What did that tell the investigation? He bled there, but it was impossible to say whether he was stabbed there, or if he died there. Flynn could have been bleeding when he arrived under the shelter, or he could have left that spot and died somewhere else. It was pissing rain, so any blood trails would have been washed away. Hell, they didn't even know whether he'd left the blood that night or at some time previous.

Identifying the tradie's ute was perhaps the biggest lead Forensics had provided, but to protect O'Meara, he was forced to wait until Holmes received her official report and trust his colleague would follow the same lines on the investigation that he himself would.

CHAPTER 16

The police carpark was spotted with puddles, the rain forcing Holmes and Larsen to sprint from their vehicle to the station entrance. A few adventurous gulls squawked and wheeled overhead, struggling not to be blown off a course to who knew where.

The forensic report was discussed around a table in an interview room after the full transcript had been printed and duplicated at the station. Each of the four officers had a copy in front of them, although Holmes and Larsen had read the digital version prior to the meeting.

'It's highly likely the killing took place at the wharf,' Wilkins said. 'Not a certainty, but that's where my money would be.'

Holmes raised his eyebrows. 'There's a chance he was already bleeding when he took shelter there. Maybe he was stabbed elsewhere and struggled back towards his car. Or, on the flip side, he may have been stabbed on the wharf then dragged himself off somewhere else before he died or was heaved into the water.'

'Well, we know he wasn't bleeding when he drove the Mercedes into the carpark,' Small said. 'Not a sign of blood in the vehicle.'

'So, obviously, the stabbing took place after he drove the car to the wharf,' Holmes replied. 'That's a start, I suppose. If we knew his exact movements after he parked the Merc, it would focus things a bit more. Did he hang around the wharf, or did he walk to the beach, where he assaulted Rachael Bowker, and then walk back? Maybe that assault occurred before he even drove to the wharf. We have the approximate time he attacked Rachael, but no idea when the Merc was parked beside the restaurant. If we can somehow establish that timeline, then we're halfway there, I reckon.'

There was a nod of approval from his colleagues.

'When we're finished here, I'll put a call in for police divers,' Holmes continued. 'Maybe they'll find something on the bottom of the river that helps sort the sequence of events.'

Larsen flipped the page of the forensic report. 'Blood on the knife came up negative in relation to Flynn. Do we write it off as irrelevant to the murder investigation?'

'The victim was stabbed, and a suspect's prints were on the knife,' Wilkins replied quickly. 'He could have wiped the blade, leaving only the old cow's blood.'

Holmes shook his head. 'If an experienced detective like Greg Bowker had decided the blade needed wiping, then gone to the trouble of hiding the knife among the rocks, it makes no sense that he'd leave his prints on the handle.'

'I presume you've interviewed him,' Wilkins replied. 'How does he explain his prints on the knife?'

'He can't. Says he has no idea how they got there.'

Wilkins frowned. 'Don't you find that strange, Detective?'

Holmes nodded reluctantly. 'Yeah, I do. But I still don't believe that knife was used to kill Flynn. If Greg did commit murder, he wouldn't be that sloppy.'

Larsen could see this had the potential to go around in circles, so she moved the conversation on as the rain outside became heavier and spattered against the office window. 'The good news is that we now have the rego of the mystery work vehicle.' She rustled through some pages. 'The ute is registered to Warrnambool Handyman Services, which is a company owned by a Graeme Connolly of Koroit Street.'

'We'll zip across this afternoon,' Holmes added. 'See if Connolly is our man with the uncontrolled bladder, or someone else who uses his ute. One thing we know, the driver of that vehicle didn't have much love for Flynn.'

'The other good news is that we have a picture of one of the yobbos in the Mini Moke who stole Flynn's car,' Larsen said. As she pulled the picture from her pile of paper, Constable Farrell entered carrying a tray supporting four mugs of coffee and a plate of biscuits.

'Drinks as ordered, ladies and gentlemen. Courtesy of the police station's office boy.'

Wilkins glared at her constable, who looked away, attempting to conceal a smirk.

'Before you go, Grant. You've lived in this area for years. Take a look at this photo and tell me if you recognise the face.'

Farrell took the picture from Larsen and perused it. His eyes revealed a spark of recognition, but he shook his head slowly. 'Not someone I know.' He laid the picture back on the table and turned to leave. As he did, Small picked up the photo and immediately identified the subject.

'Come on, Granto,' Small said, looking up at his colleague. 'This is Jamie Henderson. Hangs around the cricket club. Lives out at Toolong.'

Farrell again took the picture and made a big show of looking at it more closely. 'Shit, it could be too, you know. He looks different without the beard.' He threw the photo back on the table. 'Haven't seen him since last cricket season.'

'Fuck me!' Holmes uttered quietly in frustration as Farrell left the room. He looked at Small. 'What do we know about Henderson?'

'Prize dickhead, but pretty harmless. He hangs around the cricket club where Grant plays C-Grade. Just sits and watches, and drinks a heap of grog. Been done a few times for minor stuff. Vandalism, drinking in a public place, DUI.'

Larsen's brow furrowed. 'Henderson? Any relation to Mick Henderson, who owns the squid boat?'

'Son,' Wilkins replied. 'But Mick won't have him on the boat. More worry than he's worth, apparently.'

'Well, our young Jamie must have a totally forgettable face,' Holmes said sarcastically. 'Even his father didn't recognise him when he came up on the boat's CCTV.'

'Do you want us to bring in Jamie?' Wilkins asked.

'Can we put that on hold until Kirsten and I get back from Warrnambool? I'd like to be there to hit him cold. But our first priority is the tradie.'

* * *

Before leaving for Warrnambool, Holmes and Larsen visited the harbour, hoping to find Mick Henderson's squid boat in port. The berth where *Isla Anne* had been moored was empty, and a tour boat operator further up the wharf yelled that Henderson was due back later in the afternoon. Rather than wait, the detectives set off on the twenty-five-minute journey east to Warrnambool. As they passed the spectacular Tower Hill nature reserve with its crater lake, Larsen again raised the puzzle of Bowker's thumb print on the knife found on East Beach.

'Darren, you know Greg better than anyone except his wife. What's your take on that knife?'

Holmes overtook a car and caravan shrouded in white spray before answering. 'Well, I'll tell you one thing. In the unlikely event that Greg did top Flynn, that knife wasn't the weapon he used. There is no way he would have left his prints on it, and there's no way he would have done such a half-arsed job of disposing of it. As I said back there, he's an experienced homicide cop. He knows how the game works.'

Larsen looked at her partner. 'Then why the bullshit about not knowing how his prints got there?'

'He's covering arse,' Holmes replied. 'My guess is the knife came from the Ocean View apartment where he and Rachael were staying. It's just twenty metres up from where the knife was found in the rocks.'

Larsen was puzzled. 'Then why doesn't he say the knife came from the kitchen of their accommodation and he'd handled it while preparing food?' Before Holmes could reply, the answer struck home. Larsen threw her head back, closing her eyes. 'Because we would then ask why the knife was out of the kitchen. And what reason could he give? He couldn't claim it was used for fishing, because he stormed into Port Fairy the morning after Rachael rang about Flynn's threats and they were back in Melbourne the day after that. Not much time to drop a line even if he had the inclination to. Which, given the circumstances, would have been a long way down his list.'

Holmes nodded as he snapped on his blinker and passed a slow-moving tractor towing an old-fashioned hay press that had at least moved off the bitumen. Its flashing orange light was difficult to see in the spray spinning off its large rear tyres, but the detective didn't comment. His mind was elsewhere. 'And he was in Portland on the Dandenong case for much of the only full day he spent down this way.' When the road was clear in front of him, he looked back at Larsen. 'So, who else might have had that knife outside the apartment, do you reckon?'

Larsen's jaw dropped. 'Are you saying Rachael?' After a moment, she chuckled. 'Come on, Darren. Rachael Bowker? Carrying a knife? Really?'

'Think about the chronology of all this, Kirsten,' Holmes replied. 'Rachael is threatened with violence on the wharf. She's worried enough to ring Greg, who races down here the next morning. The thing that really sets him off is Rachael reporting she's been physically assaulted on the beach shortly before he arrived back from Portland. Greg goes ape shit and takes off looking for Flynn, who he swears he never found.' Holmes shrugged. 'From what we know, Rachael is the last person to see him alive.'

'But under that scenario, Rachael has stabbed him on East Beach. That's a good ten-minute walk to the wharf where his blood was found. And we know he didn't drive back, because there's no blood in his car.'

'The bastard could have been bleeding badly and only made it back to the wharf where he left the vehicle. He died there and toppled into the water, or his body was thrown in by a person or persons unknown.'

Larsen clasped the top of her seatbelt and exhaled loudly. 'Surely you don't believe Rachael Bowker stabbed her ex-husband?'

Holmes shook his head. 'No, I don't. But I reckon she had that knife with her. And I reckon Greg's put together the same possible scenario as I just have. He's acting dumb to prevent Rachael being implicated, just in case that's how Flynn's death really went down.'

'But surely Greg would know if Rachael had stabbed Flynn,' Larsen replied strenuously. 'I've never seen a closer couple.'

'There are all sorts of dynamics at play here, Kirsten. If Rachael did kill Flynn, she may not want to place Greg in an impossible position by confessing to that. She'd know he'd protect her, and that would go against everything he's stood for in a lifetime of policing.'

'But wouldn't Greg ask her if she'd done it?'

'Not necessarily. To even ask that question would imply he believed her capable of sticking a knife into someone's chest. That's as bad as accusing her straight out.'

Larsen shook her head. 'That doesn't make much sense to me. Rather than an accusation, I'd see it as just getting the facts on the table.'

Holmes thought for a long moment, considering the wisdom of his next move. 'It's the same as if I asked you whether you'd checked out Dale Small's speedos.' He smiled weakly. 'To ask would imply I think you'd be interested in taking a peek. That's why I'd never ask.'

By the look on Larsen's face, Holmes knew he'd chosen an unwise example but tried to make the best of the trouble he was in. 'See what I mean?'

Luckily, they hit the speed restriction signs on the outskirts of town and the conversation switched to finding the address of the handyman. But Holmes knew he had just kicked a hornets' nest.

CHAPTER 17

A regional city of around thirty-five thousand people, Warrnambool sat on the coast adjacent to the estuary of the Hopkins River. Koroit Street was a major carriageway slicing through the city centre, but the detectives found the address they were looking for to the west of the shopping precinct in an area lined with Norfolk pines and comprising mainly mid-twentieth-century homes.

A small sign attached to the front fence of a modest weatherboard house advertised Warrnambool Handyman Services. Grass grew from the gutters, the lawn needed cutting and the flywire window screens needed replacing. Either the owner wasn't much of a handyman or was so busy that his own house had to wait for his services. A shed sat at the end of a driveway to the side of the house, its roller door up, revealing tools and machinery inside. There was a small passenger sedan parked beside the house, but no sign of the ute they were looking for.

Larsen climbed from the police vehicle and quickly made her way through a passing squall to the front door. The wind roared in the Norfolk pines and rain hammered the tin roof of the verandah along the front of the house. She pushed a doorbell button to the side of the entrance, but when nobody came, she suspected it was non-operational and knocked heavily on the glass pane in the top of the door. After a moment, she heard footsteps approaching and took a step back, allowing the flywire screen door to slowly close.

The main door opened to reveal a woman of pension age. Larsen flashed her badge and explained they were looking for a vehicle registered to the address. The woman said the company owned two vehicles, but the one the detective was seeking was usually driven by a Damien Norton, her husband's employee. Both men were working on a paving job in Dennington, a suburb on the western outskirts of the city. She didn't have the actual address but gave clear instructions on how the worksite could be found.

Unfortunately, those clear instructions proved opaque at best and forced the detectives to drive the streets of Dennington until they spotted the vehicle they were after. It was parked on the muddy nature strip of a new but nondescript home on the rather grandiosely named Boulevard, a street that roughly followed the course of the Merri River.

It was Graeme Connolly himself who met the detectives as they walked up the partly paved drive, dodging a second ute loaded with sand, and stacks of pavers placed at intervals beside where substrate was laid out. Connolly looked in his late sixties or early seventies, with a weatherworn face and a wiry frame. In spite of the freezing weather, he wore only shorts and elastic-sided work boots, his bare torso heavily tanned and his skin like buffalo hide. His face carried a happy countenance, and his blue eyes twinkled with life. Before Holmes could display his identification, Connolly raised his palm.

'I know who you are, mate,' he said. 'The missus just rang. Sounds like you're chasing Damo. He's the only one who drives the Nissan.' He put his hands in the pockets of his shorts. 'What's he been up to?'

Holmes ignored the question. 'So you never drive it yourself?' he asked.

Connolly shook his head. 'Only if we're out on a job and it's the closest vehicle. For all intents and purposes, the Nissan belongs to Damo, except that I pay the rego, insurance, petrol and servicing.' He smiled. 'Pretty good deal, eh?'

'Does he use it out-of-hours?' Larsen asked.

'Only vehicle he's got to use,' Connolly replied. 'His bitch of a wife has a nice VW, but she won't let him drive it.' He unconsciously flattened a small patch of sand with the sole of his work boot. 'I dunno why he stays with her, to be honest. She's fifteen years younger than he is, and she'd give an alley cat a bad rap.'

'What's the wife's name?' Larsen asked casually, wanting to avoid any discussion of age difference that could metastasise in her partner's mind.

'Bethany Symons.' Connolly smiled. 'There used to be a joke around Warrnambool. What's the difference between Bethany Symons and Tower Hill? Not every bloke's been up Tower Hill.' He chuckled.

A strongly built man of medium height appeared from the back of the building. The detectives immediately recognised him as the man caught by CCTV urinating on Trevor Flynn's car.

Holmes gestured towards Norton. 'That Damien there?'

Connolly turned and nodded. 'Yeah, that's him. Poor bastard's been shitting himself since I told him you were on your way.'

'He tell you what he's worried about?' Larsen asked.

'Nope. None of my business, so I didn't ask.' Connolly beckoned to Norton. 'I'll leave you to it. Go easy on him. He's not a bad bloke. If he's stuffed up somewhere, there'll be a good reason for it.' He grabbed a rake leaning against the side wall of the house and made his way to the back end of the drive.

Norton was younger than Connolly by a few years and in good physical shape. His hair was receding from the front, and he tried to compensate with thick black sideburns. Like his boss, his skin was weather-beaten, but at least he had the sense to wear a shirt. Whether this was the case on warmer days was hard to tell. His face was round and a little podgy given his apparent fitness. His nose was flattened like a prize fighter's, and he sported two small scars on his chin. His brown eyes darted between Holmes and Larsen as he approached.

'I heard you're looking for me,' he said tentatively.

'If you normally drive that Nissan over there, then we are,' Holmes replied, pointing to the vehicle on the nature strip. He pocketed his ID.

'Sometimes the boss takes it at work to grab stuff, but normally I drive it, yeah.' Norton scanned Holmes's face. 'Is there a problem?'

'You drive the vehicle to Port Fairy the Friday before last?' Larsen asked.

Norton shook his head, then looked away. 'Haven't been down there for months,' he replied.

'Are you sure?' Holmes asked, giving him a chance to change his story.

'Dead certain. We haven't had a job down there since early April. And there's nothing you can get over there that we don't have here in Warrnambool.' He put his hands on his hips. 'Most of the Port Fairy locals come here to do business and leave the place to the tourists.'

'I need to show you something, mate,' Holmes said, before scanning the darkening sky and jogging back to the police car. He returned with a manilla folder. He flipped through the contents before retrieving a photo of the Nissan taken from *Isla Anne's*

CCTV. 'Recognise the vehicle?' he said, handing the picture to Norton. 'Taken at the Port Fairy harbour Friday week ago.'

Norton feigned a puzzled look. 'That's my vehicle, but I can't explain why it would be in Port Fairy. Unless the boss borrowed it that day. I know he was having trouble with his Triton about that time.'

Holmes pulled another photo from the folder as a squall closed in from the west. 'Let's adjourn to the front verandah before this shower hits.' The trio scurried under cover. Holmes handed the picture to Norton. 'There's not much doubt about who that bloke is.'

Norton ran a hand across his head. He inhaled deeply then held up a finger as if a bolt of enlightenment had just hit him. 'Sorry, I forgot about the evening I went to Port Fairy to look at an old car I saw for sale on eBay. The seller was supposed to meet me in the wharf carpark, but he was a no-show. Either the car had been sold, or the bloke thought the weather was too shitty to leave home for an eight-hundred-dollar car. Whatever the reason, my trip was for nothing.'

Holmes pulled out another photo. 'So why urinate on the Mercedes you were parked behind?'

'Can't remember that, really,' Norton replied hesitantly. 'I was obviously busting for a leak.'

'Why do it on the car?' Larsen asked.

'I assume so nobody would see me. Plus, it was out of the wind, I s'pose.'

Larsen looked him in the eye. 'But you're not just urinating in between cars. You're going out of your way to piss all over the windscreen. This appears to us a very deliberate and personal gesture, Mr Norton.'

'Well, it wasn't,' Norton replied without conviction.

'But it was a deliberate and personal gesture when you kicked in the driver's side panel,' Holmes said.

'I was kicking the mud off my boots,' Norton replied feebly.

'Bullshit,' Holmes said, moving closer to the handyman.

'We have you on CCTV disappearing down the wharf in front of the restaurant,' Larsen said. 'Then you come back into view a minute or so later. What happened in that time, Damien?'

Norton shrugged. 'I guess I must have walked down the wharf looking for the bloke who was selling the car. I didn't find him. Obviously. So then I returned to the Nissan and relieved myself on the way back.'

'What sort of car were you hoping to buy?' Larsen asked.

Norton again hesitated before answering. 'It was a 2003 Camry. Had a lot of miles on the clock.'

'From eBay, you say?' Larsen said, taking out her phone. Her fingers danced over the screen. 'A 2003 Camry… eight hundred dollars… Port Fairy.'

'It's bound to be gone by now,' Norton retorted urgently.

'Still should be in their history,' Larsen said as she continued entering information. 'If it's not, we'll just get your login details and check whether you viewed such a car or made contact with its owner.'

Norton leaned against a verandah post, suddenly needing physical support.

'Have you heard of a bloke called Trevor Flynn?' Holmes asked, keen to keep him off balance.

'Everybody in the district has heard of him,' Norton replied. 'He was murdered in Port Fairy a week or so ago. It's been in the local rag every day.'

'Have you ever met him?' Holmes asked.

'No.'

'Did you know he was the owner of the Mercedes that you pissed all over that night?'

'Of course not. How would I?'

'Does your partner have a paid job, Mr Norton?' Larsen asked.

Norton appeared flummoxed. 'What's that got to do with anything?'

'It's a simple question, Mr Norton. Has she got a job?'

'She's thrown some casual work by a solicitor in town. Mostly typing.'

Larsen flipped through her notebook. 'Manley, O'Neil and Schwandt?'

'Yeah, that's right,' Norton replied aggressively. 'So what?'

'Did you know Manley, O'Neil and Schwandt handled Trevor Flynn's legal affairs?' Holmes asked.

'How would I?' Norton replied quickly.

'Because your wife typed up his business documents, and the two would have met to tidy up drafts, I'd imagine,' Larsen replied, keeping the pressure on.

'So?'

'Seems a bit of a coincidence that the vehicle you urinated on belonged to Flynn,' Holmes said.

'What are you saying? That I pissed on the car because my wife did some typing for Flynn?' Norton feigned a chuckle. 'If that was the case, I'd be pissing on half the cars in Warrnambool, probably.'

Yeah, and if you did the same to the blokes who were banging your missus, you'd still be pissing on half the cars, Holmes thought. 'We heard that Flynn was involved with a woman in Warrnambool,' he said instead. 'By your actions at the wharf and the evasive answers you've given us today, I'm inclined to think that woman might be your partner.'

'You see, Mr Norton,' Larsen added, 'Trevor Flynn was killed on the night you were at the wharf. The video captured you walking towards the river side of the restaurant, and that's where we've found Flynn's blood. The time you were out of picture was sufficient for you to knife Flynn and push him into the water. The river's current and the outgoing tide would have taken his body out into the bay, where he ultimately became shark food.'

Norton's jaw dropped, and he shook his head vigorously. 'No way! I didn't even see Flynn on the wharf that night!'

'So you knew what he looked like?' Larsen asked quickly.

'No!' Norton said. 'What I meant was I didn't see *anyone* that night, so obviously I didn't see him.'

Holmes folded his arms across his chest. The trio moved closer to the front wall of the house as misty rain blew in under the verandah. 'Time to tell us the truth, Mr Norton. We have proof you were in Port Fairy that night, and I think we'll be able to establish that your story about buying the Camry is pure bullshit.' Holmes shrugged. 'To be honest with you, mate, you now head our list of suspects. You can run us over all the jumps and put us through all the hoops of investigating your eBay story, and establishing Bethany was on with Flynn, but you know that will only bring us back to the same point we're at now.'

Norton stared at the ground. 'Alright, I admit I was in Port Fairy looking for Flynn, but I didn't find him. Only his car.'

Holmes unfolded his arms and slid his hands into his trouser pockets. 'Now we're getting somewhere. Let's start at the beginning. Your wife and Flynn were having an affair, right?'

'Not sure you'd call it an affair, but the bastard was banging her, yeah,' Norton responded, his eyes moistening. 'He's not the first, and I dare say he won't be the last. Most of the others I've been able to scare off.'

'You're an ex-pug, right?' Holmes asked. 'Spent a bit of time in the ring?'

Norton looked into the detective's eyes, puzzled. 'How'd you know that?'

Holmes touched the end of his own nose. 'The old snoz looks to have copped a few too many whacks. And your jaw's been opened up a few times, by the scars on your chin.'

'Did you just go to Port Fairy on spec?' Larsen asked. 'You know, hoping to run into him somewhere around town?'

Norton shook his head. 'No. I knew where he'd be, because I found Bethany's phone on the floor of the carport when I arrived home from work fairly late. It must have dropped out of her bag as she got into her car. I read her messages, and one was from Flynn inviting her to Port Fairy for a root while his wife was working at the office.'

'Were they his exact words?' Holmes asked. 'To come to Port Fairy for a root?'

Norton shrugged. 'That's what he meant. He said to come to Port Fairy while his wife was at work. They needed to talk. All code. He wasn't going to put it down in print that he was wanting a fuck, was he?' He chuckled sadly. 'In all the time I've known Bethany, I've never met a bloke who's just been interested in talking to her. And that includes a couple of pricks in Port Fairy too.'

'Was her phone turned on when you found it?' Larsen asked.

Norton nodded. 'Yes.'

'How'd you know the text was from Flynn?' Holmes asked.

'Because his name was at the bottom of the message.'

Holmes looked puzzled. 'We've already checked Flynn's phone records for the day he was killed. He only made three calls, and two were to his office. The other was to the local council.'

Norton shrugged again. 'Well, his name was in that SMS.'

Larsen raised her eyebrows at Holmes. She flipped open her notebook and handed it plus a pencil to the handyman. 'Can you write her mobile number down as well as your own, please?'

Norton did as requested, then passed the book and pencil back.

'So, when you saw the text, you followed her to Port Fairy?' Holmes asked.

'Didn't follow her,' Norton replied sharply. 'She could have left hours before I found the phone. I drove down there and searched the town looking for either her VW or his Mercedes. Had no luck finding Bethany's car, but as you know, I found Flynn's at the wharf.' He held up both palms. 'But I didn't find the bastard, right?'

'If you say so, Damien,' Holmes replied.

'What *would* you have done if you had tracked him down?' Larsen asked.

'Belted the shit out of him,' Norton replied angrily. 'But no way would I have murdered the prick. I'm not going to jail because of that bitch.'

'On your way to Port Fairy, you didn't pass your wife heading back to Warrnambool by any chance, did you?' Holmes asked.

'It was dark and pissing rain,' Norton replied. 'I could have passed the Batmobile and not known it.'

Holmes smiled. 'I'd like you to accompany us to the local station and make a formal statement.'

The wind howled and a new squall blew in as Norton gathered his gear.

CHAPTER 18

After taking Norton's statement, the detectives drove to his residential address, hoping to speak to Bethany Symons, who he said normally worked from home. The house was in a newish estate on the eastern side of Warrnambool adjacent to the Hopkins River and abutting the local campus of Deakin University. A fresh squall that seemed to follow the river swept in, sending a pair of screeching sulphur-crested cockatoos heading for cover in the ancient pines that grew in the university next door.

With the car windows fogged inside and droplets running down the outside, it was difficult to see house numbers in Dunvegan Court, but luckily a VW sedan parked in a driveway provided the best clue to the residence they were chasing. The house was a chocolate-coloured brick veneer, with faux marble columns supporting a tiled roof portico sheltering the front door. It was more upmarket than the detectives expected for a handyman and a casual typist, but how much did they owe the bank, and how close to the brink were they if interest rates increased from their record low?

Larsen rang the doorbell as she brushed raindrops off her clothes. Within a few moments, a plain-faced woman opened the front door. Larsen introduced herself and her colleague before confirming the woman as Bethany Symons. She was of medium height with short auburn hair and brown eyes. She was slim without being athletic and dressed in brown trousers, an off-white cotton top and cheap home-brand sneakers. She wore gold studs in her earlobes. She certainly didn't fit the image of the town bike, but who knew what talents were concealed behind her underwhelming appearance.

Symons looked puzzled by the detectives' presence, but invited them into a large lounge area, where they sat in easy chairs overlooking the Hopkins. Clouds hung low and leaden over the river, and the misty rain made seeing the steep banks on the opposite side difficult. Symons sat on a couch and leaned forward, tidying a few items on the coffee table that separated them. After establishing that she was the wife of Damien Norton and worked casually as a typist for a local solicitor, the conversation moved to her relationship with the murder victim.

'Does the name Trevor Flynn mean anything to you?' Larsen asked.

The expression on Symons's face didn't change. 'Yes. On several occasions, I typed up documents relating to his land development down the coast at Port Fairy. Unfortunately, he was murdered a week or so ago, which I presume is the reason for your visit today.'

Holmes nodded. 'What were your impressions of Mr Flynn?' he asked. 'We're trying to build a picture of his business network.'

Symons shrugged. 'I didn't know him very well, as you can imagine,' she replied, straight-faced. 'But he appeared a nice enough fellow. Friendly, didn't get overly annoyed if I misspelt a word like some other clients do.'

Holmes decided to cut to the chase. 'He rang you on the day he disappeared, we believe.'

Symons showed her first modicum of emotion. 'Obviously you've been talking to Damien,' she said before exhaling loudly.

'He has this stupid obsession that I'm on with every male I have any dealings with. Something to do with me being a fair bit younger, I suspect. He accused me of going to Port Fairy to have sex with Mr Flynn.'

Holmes wasn't to be side-tracked. 'But he did ring you on the day he disappeared?'

Symons hesitated slightly. 'Yes. Asked me to go to Port Fairy. There was a document he needed retyping. That's why Damien got his knickers in a knot.'

Larsen feigned confusion. 'Surely he could have emailed the paperwork to you. Or faxed it through.'

Symons didn't flinch. 'He has this thing about privacy. I don't have a fax, and he's worried that anything emailed can be hacked. He had a meeting with the council in the afternoon, so he couldn't get to Warrnambool to meet personally. He said he'd pay my petrol and throw me a few dollars for travelling if I zipped down to Port to sort out the wording of his new proposal to the Shire.'

That sounded like bullshit to Holmes since Flynn's meeting at the council was apparently no more than an attempt at intimidation. And Petrov had made no mention of any new proposals in his interview with Larsen.

'What time did Flynn ring?' Holmes asked.

'About two in the afternoon.'

'And you went straight to Port Fairy?'

'Yes. He wanted me there as soon as possible.'

I bet he did, Holmes thought.

'And his wife can verify what time you arrived?' Larsen asked.

'I didn't see his wife.'

'She's the receptionist for the business, is she not?' Larsen persisted.

Symons's eyes didn't meet Larsen's. 'I didn't go to the office.

Mr Flynn was working from home.' She looked away into the gloom outside the window.

Holmes winked at Larsen. 'What time did you head back to Warrnambool?'

Symons shrugged. 'Probably around four or four fifteen.'

'So you spent nearly two hours doing paperwork?' Holmes asked.

'What else would I be doing?' Symons responded aggressively.

'You tell us,' Holmes shot back. 'The rumour around Port Fairy is that Flynn had a girlfriend in Warrnambool. The general consensus is that it was you,' he added, even though that consensus was little more than her husband's suspicions and his boss's description of Symons as promiscuous in the extreme.

Symons rolled her eyes. 'Once you're judged, you're just like Sergio the Fisherman.' Larsen looked at Holmes, bewildered. 'I admit I was a wild child in my younger days and pushed the boundaries, but that's all behind me now. That doesn't stop people jumping to conclusions every time I have even the slightest contact with a man.' She exhaled loudly. 'I can assure you my trip was all business. I took my laptop to Port Fairy, and Mr Flynn edited a document that I put on a memory stick for him to print off at his office.'

'What time did you arrive back in Warrnambool?' Holmes asked.

Symons shrugged. 'Five, maybe quarter to.'

'Where'd you go when you arrived back?'

'Here. I went on with the work I'd been doing before I received Trevor's call.'

'You take the phone with you to Port Fairy?' Holmes asked.

'Of course. I'm a casual typist. I rely on my phone to get jobs.'

Holmes folded his arms and leaned back in his chair. 'I've got a problem with that, Ms Symons, because your husband told us that he was very late getting home from work and your car wasn't here. He found your phone on the carport floor.'

Symons was flummoxed for a moment before feigning a smile. She tapped her forehead with the palm of her right hand. 'He would have arrived home and gone out again while I'd slipped out to buy a few things for dinner. I must have dropped my phone when I took that trip to the supermarket. I found it on the kitchen table when I arrived home. Obviously, Damien must have put it there.'

Larsen leaned forward. 'Would I be able to have a look at your phone, please, Bethany? I'd like to view the number on which Mr Flynn contacted you. It certainly wasn't on his registered mobile.'

'Do I have to show it to you?' Symons replied. 'Don't you need a search warrant or something?'

'We can get a warrant if that's the way you want to play it. But it will avoid a lot of stuffing around if you just give me a look.'

Symons hesitated momentarily. She then stood, retrieved her phone from a kitchen bench, unlocked it and handed it to Larsen. Larsen opened the contacts list and retrieved the number on which Flynn had called.

'I'll warn you, Ms Symons, that we will obtain your phone records to review other calls to and from this phone. And no doubt you'll be keen for us to confirm that your phone pinged the tower at Port Fairy, thus confirming you arrived home prior to Mr Norton finding the mobile in your carport.'

Symons was silent for a moment before looking at Holmes. 'Why are you treating me like a suspect in Mr Flynn's death?'

Holmes kept his tone matter-of-fact. 'At this stage, we are checking the movements of all people Flynn had contact with on the day he was killed. The more people we can exclude from our investigation, the easier the case becomes to solve. If everything you have told us checks out, then yours is another name we can cross off our list.'

'What time did Damien arrive home that night?' Larsen asked.

Symons screwed up her face, chasing a memory. 'It was dark, so it must have been at least eight thirty.'

'Did he say why he was late?'

Symons's face soured. 'He said he'd been home earlier, found my phone and read my messages.' She rolled her eyes. 'Of course, he jumped to his usual conclusion that I was on with someone, so he went down to the pub. He said if I was going to keep rooting, he would keep drinking. Bloody baby's brain inside a man's body.'

Holmes and Larsen exchanged glances. 'Nice house you have here,' Holmes said, changing the subject. 'You've done well to purchase a place like this on your and your husband's wages. Inherit a few bob from somewhere?'

'The bank owns ninety-five percent of it. We both work flat-out to service the mortgage and have little time to enjoy it.' Symons chuckled to herself. 'Has to be something wrong with the logic, don't you think?'

After a few follow-up questions, the detectives thanked Symons for her time and braved the weather back to their car.

'You reckon she's telling the truth?' Larsen asked.

'Hard to know with some people. She seems open enough, but maybe twisting the truth is how she's made her way through life. I reckon her going to Port Fairy to tidy up some typing sounds like bullshit, but the more you do this job, the more your assumptions get tested.'

'If she's truthful about Norton claiming he went to the pub after he found her message, then obviously there's not a lot of honesty between the two of them. If he'd already accused her of meeting Flynn for sex, why not go the whole hog and tell her he went to Port Fairy to catch her out?'

'If he topped Flynn while he was down there, that'd be a pretty good reason to keep the trip to himself, though,' Holmes replied.

'Yeah, good point.' Larsen thought for a moment. 'Getting back to Symons. Her whereabouts at the time Norton found her phone seems crucial to validating her explanation of her movements that day. She says she went straight home after departing Port Fairy around four or four fifteen. That should put her at home at four forty-five, or five o'clock at the very latest. That's way earlier than Norton said he'd arrived home and found the phone in an empty carport. She's either lying about the time she left Port Fairy or about where she went after she met Flynn.'

Holmes nodded. 'And when we made that point, she conveniently remembered that she'd gone out again, this time to the supermarket, and that's when she must have dropped the phone.' He exhaled loudly. 'If her phone didn't ping the tower at Port Fairy that day, then we can assume it never left Warrnambool and was still sitting on the carport floor until Norton found it after dark. She'll need to do more explaining about her whereabouts if that was the case.'

'If she's smart, she'll claim her phone was turned off when she went to meet Flynn,' Larsen surmised.

'If the records show it was pinging the Warrnambool tower all afternoon, then that'll shoot a big hole through that one.'

Larsen nodded but didn't reply.

Holmes pulled into the McDonalds drive-thru on the corner of Raglan Parade and Liebig Street. 'Feel like a coffee?'

'Yeah. Skinny chai latte.'

Within five minutes, they were back on the Princes Highway. Larsen sipped her steaming coffee and looked across at her partner. 'Who's Sergio the Fisherman?'

'What do you mean?' Holmes replied as he pulled to the right lane to pass an empty log truck on its way back to the South Australian pine plantations.

'In the interview with Symons, she said that once you're judged, you're like Sergio the Fisherman. You never batted an eyelid, and here I am wondering what the hell she's talking about.'

Holmes pulled back into the left lane and smiled at her. 'I thought everyone had heard the story of Sergio the Fisherman?'

Larsen shook her head as she took another sip of her latte. 'Not me.'

'Apparently, this tourist was walking through a fishing village in Italy when he took a photo of an elderly man sitting on a wooden box mending a fishing net in between two boats. The tourist introduced himself and asked the man his name so he could attach it to his photo. The old bloke introduced himself as Sergio and explained he was the fifth generation of his family to fish the local waters and had done so since he was a small child. "So, you are Sergio the Fisherman?" the tourist asked. The old man shook his head. "No," he replied disappointedly. "I am not known as Sergio the Fisherman." He then stood and became animated. "See all these nets along the shore? I made all those nets, but do they call me Sergio the Net Maker? No way!" He pointed across the bay. "See all the boats tied up to the jetty? I built all those boats, but do they call me Sergio the Boat Builder? No way! But you fuck one goat…"'

Larsen spurted a mouthful of coffee all over herself and the dashboard.

'Where to from here, do you reckon?' she asked when she had finished wiping herself down.

'We need the phone records for that number Flynn used to ring Symons,' Holmes replied as they crossed the Merri River. 'We'll also get a printout for Symons and Norton's phones as well.

And I'd like Mick Henderson to explain why he didn't identify his son knocking off the Merc from the wharf.'

'Father protecting his boy, he'll tell us. That he hoped we wouldn't show the vision to anyone who could ID his son.'

'If he thought that, he's not too smart,' Holmes replied as another squall hit, rocking the car and causing him to nudge the wipers up to maximum. 'Surely he'd assume we'd show the vision to the local coppers.'

'Maybe he hoped Farrell would cover for the son.'

'Well, he did, didn't he? If it hadn't been for your mate Small, he probably would have got away with it. Wilkins is new, so she may not have known the dickhead.'

Larsen's face tightened, and she thought carefully before she spoke. 'Senior Constable Small is no more my mate than he is yours, Darren.'

Holmes stared straight ahead. 'I'm sure he doesn't want to shag *me*,' he said half under his breath.

'Stop with the suspicion crap, alright?' Larsen shot back. 'Dale seems like a really nice guy who was good enough to teach me a little about surfing. End of story.'

Holmes decided to let the matter drop, and nothing was said for a few minutes as they drove past expanses of green pastures blurred by the swirling mist. Dairy cows crowded into the corners of paddocks, seeking warmth in numbers.

'We need to talk with all the idiots who stole Flynn's car, not just Henderson's son,' Larsen finally suggested to break the silence.

Holmes nodded. 'The only thing that interests me with that lot is what they might have seen at the wharf. The locals can sort out the theft of a motor vehicle charges.'

* * *

Larsen was spot-on with Mick Henderson's response to not identifying his son driving away Flynn's Mercedes.

'He's my bloody boy, isn't he?' the fisherman replied angrily when Holmes questioned him upon his boat's arrival in port late that afternoon. 'He may be a useless piece of shit, but he's my flesh and blood.'

'Surely you knew someone would recognise him when we showed the vision to other people?' Holmes persisted.

'Probably, but I wasn't going to be the one to put him in,' Henderson shot back. 'Friends and family. You look after them. You of all people should know that, Detective. You're doing everything in your power to protect your mate when everyone in the town knows he killed the bloke they found in the water.'

'We follow the evidence, Mr Henderson,' Holmes replied with annoyance. 'Right now, I'm considering whether to charge you with obstructing an investigation, so I'd watch what I was saying if I was you.'

Henderson held up both palms in submission. 'I'm not telling you anything you don't know already, mate. That's all I'll say. I'm sorry that I lied to you, but my first instinct was to protect my son.' He dropped his hands and shrugged his shoulders. 'Besides, there's no harm done. He went to the local copshop and turned himself in. Spent most of the afternoon there being grilled.'

CHAPTER 19

Farrell appeared within a few moments of Holmes pushing the visitors' button on the police station reception desk. Before the constable could open his mouth, Holmes showed his irritation. 'Let us through, please, Grant. I need to speak to Senior Sergeant Wilkins.'

'She shot through to a meeting in Hamilton at lunchtime,' Farrell replied. He looked at the clock on the wall. 'She won't be back to the station tonight, I wouldn't think. She'll go straight home.'

'Then we'll talk with Senior Constable Small.'

'He's rostered off every second Wednesday, so he hasn't shown his face today.'

'Then who conducted the interview with Jamie Henderson?' Holmes asked, already knowing the answer.

'You're looking at him, mate,' Farrell replied with a smirk. 'He came in and confessed to taking Flynn's Merc for a joyride.'

A suspicious expression crossed Larsen's face. 'You tip him off we had his photo knocking off the car?'

'Why would I do that?'

'Because you're a mate and you knew we were onto him,' Holmes suggested, leaning across the counter. 'And you knew I'd asked that Henderson not be brought in until Detective Senior Constable Larsen and myself could talk to him. We wanted to hit him cold before he had got wind of why we were after him.'

Farrell shook his head. 'When did you issue that order?'

'In the meeting this morning. You were there.'

Farrell smiled. 'I was just the tea boy, remember. I was only in the room for two minutes.' He shrugged. 'Sorry, Detective, but I missed your decree.'

Holmes leaned back from the counter and realised Farrell was probably right. But he still had no doubts that the constable had tipped off Henderson. He decided to get what information he could from Farrell and take up the matter of his behaviour with Wilkins when she returned.

'So, Henderson admitted to stealing the car?' he asked.

'He admitted to taking it, but he said he didn't steal it. Apparently, he was pissed and not thinking too clearly. He said he intended to bring it back after they'd gone for a burn up the beach at Yambuk. But they bogged the bloody thing by accident and had to leave it there.'

'Still theft of a motor vehicle,' Larsen explained.

Farrell frowned. 'I'm sure under common law, joyriding is not considered theft, because most people don't intend to keep the car after they've finished their fun.'

'Statutes override common law, but you know that,' Holmes replied tersely. 'Or you *should* bloody know.' He inhaled deeply. 'Where's Henderson now?'

'I sent him home. I said I'd be in touch after I'd spoken to the boss to see if it was worth pressing charges.'

'He'll be charged, alright,' Holmes said, angrily tapping an index finger on the countertop. 'He stole a car, pure and simple.'

'Who were the men with him?' Larsen asked.

'Didn't ask. He said he was the only one who drove the car. The others just tagged along in the Moke.'

Larsen could see Holmes was about to explode. 'Where's Henderson live?' she asked. 'I recall Toolong being mentioned.'

'Toolong's just a district,' Farrell explained. 'He lives in an old farmhouse on one of the backroads.' He took a piece of paper from under the counter and drew a rough map indicating how to reach Henderson's abode.

Holmes's ire receded marginally as the map was drawn. 'Did Henderson say whether he saw anyone else on the wharf that night?'

'I asked him that, but he said it was deserted, so he won't be of much help to you there, I'm afraid. He said the weather was shithouse and the wind was so strong one of those fancy big rich man's boats was having trouble manoeuvring into its mooring.'

Holmes rolled his eyes. 'And you didn't think that was worth telling us?' he asked angrily.

'Whose boat was that?' Larsen asked.

'Dunno. Didn't ask him.'

'Fuck me,' Holmes said as he snatched the map and hurried out the station door with Larsen a metre behind.

* * *

The weather had cleared a little as Greg Bowker wandered down the concrete path above East Beach. A few rays of sunlight were breaking through the overcast sky to the west, but everything was still dripping water, and the cool wind kept most sensible people indoors. A black Toyota Land Cruiser was parked overlooking the lonely beach, a family eating fish and chips behind fogged-up windows inside. As if by magic, a dozen seagulls circled the vehicle, squawking their demand for easy tucker. Two birds patrolled the car's bonnet and made the occasional sojourn to the windscreen to check the progress of the meal and remind the occupants they were ready and waiting if any leftovers were to be jettisoned.

Bowker wasn't looking for anything or anyone in particular but was keen to resurvey the scene of Flynn's assault on his wife and search for any clues the police may have missed. He wandered up past the Ocean View Apartments and was about to make his way back when a motorcycle thundered past, splashing water on his shoes and trousers. Neither the rider nor his pillion passenger seemed to notice, much less care.

Bowker turned on his heels and briskly followed the Harley back towards the Barbarian Club compound. He caught up just as the rider was punching buttons and springing the large combination lock on the double gates. Bowker kicked at a large puddle on the footpath, showering water over the leather-clad pair, who had either failed to notice his presence or ignored it.

'What the fuck?' the rider grumbled as he turned, opening his helmet. His mouth dropped as he instantly recognised his long-term nemesis. 'Fuckin' Bowker. What are you doing down here?'

'I was about to ask you the same thing, Skeeta,' Bowker replied with a half-smile. 'You're like a turd that won't flush. You keep popping up to stink out wherever I go. Running drugs, I hear. Nothing much has changed since our early days at Manang, eh?'

'Bit rich coming from a bloke who's wanted for murder,' Allender shot back. 'Lucky you've got Holmes and his dolly-bird covering your arse. If it wasn't for them, you'd already be inside.'

Bowker didn't take the bait. 'Working for Flynn, were you? You and the rest of these toy soldiers? He procures the drugs, and your pretend army distributes it. Suddenly, he gets too greedy, or you blokes do, and Flynn's taken out of the picture. As they say, there's no honour among thieves.'

Allender feigned a laugh. 'You can invent as many stories as you like, Bowker, but everyone knows you killed Flynn because he was hassling your missus. I've seen her, mate, and even in her prime she wasn't worth the trouble.'

Bowker's fist perfectly bisected the distance between the sides of Allender's helmet, making contact with the rider's nose. Allender's moll heard the dull crack and saw blood instantly cover the bottom of his face. She jumped clear of the heavy bike as it fell to the ground after Allender released the handlebars to put both hands over his injury. She pushed open the gate and rushed through towards the clubhouse.

Bowker rubbed his knuckles but felt no pain. 'Apparently, I killed Flynn because he abused my wife. Watch your mouth, Skeeta, otherwise there could be a trend developing here.'

Allender didn't reply, just whimpered as he watched Bowker walk away down the footpath. By the time other bikies had spilt from the clubhouse, Bowker was around the corner and out of sight.

* * *

It was a short trip to where Toolong Road split to the west and to the north. The detectives followed the latter and eventually found a tumbled-down house where Farrell's map indicated Jamie Henderson lived. The building seemed barely habitable, its once proud sandstone walls covered in algae, its front door closed over with sheets of old corrugated iron and its rusty gutters buckling under the weight of green vegetation. The detectives dodged puddles in the driveway and found Henderson working on his car at the back of the house, his head under the bonnet.

'Jamie Henderson?' Holmes asked, placing his hand on the wet roof of the old Commodore.

Henderson lifted his head quickly, smacking his skull on the underside of the hood and sending drops of water flying into the air. 'Yeah, that's me,' he replied, rubbing the back of his head.

'Who's asking?'

Both detectives displayed their IDs. 'We're from Homicide,' Larsen said. 'We'd like a few minutes of your time.'

Henderson took an oily rag from atop the radiator, wiped his hands and feigned a smile. 'Flat bloody battery. Left the lights on when the rain stopped, didn't I?' When his smile wasn't reciprocated, a serious look crossed his face. 'Homicide? So, you're not here to talk about me borrowing the Mercedes?'

'You stole that car, Jamie,' Holmes responded quickly, 'but Senior Sergeant Wilkins will handle that.'

Henderson suddenly looked worried. 'Granto told me *he'd* deal with it. Probably get a fine or maybe a bond. It's not as though I was going to keep the bloody thing. Just having a bit of fun, that was all.'

'Makes no difference, mate,' Holmes replied. 'You took someone else's property without permission. That's the definition of theft. A luxury car – you'll be lucky to stay out of jail.'

'But I was pissed!' Henderson protested loudly, arms outstretched.

'Your decision to drink, Jamie,' Larsen said, stepping sideways to avoid rainwater dropping from the tree above every time the wind gusted. 'They might tack DUI onto the theft charge as well.'

Holmes folded his arms across his chest. 'Constable Farrell said you saw a boat returning to port that night.'

Henderson frowned at the change of tack. 'Yeah. Not a fishing boat, though. One of those fancy ones the rich people have parties on.'

'Who owns it?'

Henderson shrugged. 'Wouldn't have a clue. Don't go down to the wharf much.'

Larsen looked up as an arrowhead of black swans flew overhead, taking advantage of the tailing wind. 'Your father runs a squid boat from there, doesn't he?'

Henderson squeezed out a weak chuckle. 'That's *why* I don't go down there. I stay as far away from the bloody slave driver as I can. Six months I worked for him, but he never got off my back. In the end, I told him he could shove his squid up his arse.'

'Do you remember the name of the boat?' Holmes asked.

'Didn't take any notice, really. Plus, it was pissing rain and blowing a gale. I just remember how much trouble the boat was having trying to line up with its dock.'

'What colour was it?' Larsen asked.

Henderson thought for a moment. 'Mainly white, I think. Had a bit of blue trim. One of those ones with above-deck accommodation and a cockpit on top for when the weather's fine. Had a deck area at the back where wankers can sit around and sip wine. I'm surprised it was even at sea. Most of those boats are in port a lot of the time so guests can sit aboard and flaunt their money in front of the rest of us shit-kickers.'

Larsen privately agreed. She'd travelled to France three years before and visited Saint Tropez. Billionaires' mega-yachts were backed up to the main pedestrian thoroughfare, where open-mouthed peasant tourists walked by and watched tuxedo-clad waiters serving wine and caviar to the rich and famous on the rear decks. She wondered whether these pampered pups ever mistook the disgust on the little people's faces for envy. Her reverie was broken by Holmes demanding the names of the other three who had been involved in the car theft.

'I was the only one who drove the car,' Henderson replied.

Holmes was having nothing of that. 'They were willing participants in your joyriding scheme. But that's up to Senior Sergeant Wilkins to sort out. Detective Larsen and I want to learn more about that boat you saw. So, names, please, otherwise you'll also be charged with obstructing a homicide investigation.'

Henderson mulled his options before relenting. 'Dan Cavanagh, Matt Tyrell and Sam Voogt.'

Larsen removed a notebook from her jacket pocket and scribbled down the names. 'Who owns the Mini Moke?'

'Sammy Voogt's older brother. He lives in Lakes Entrance. Sammy's been using it since he totalled his Monaro.'

'Better tell him to clean the shit off the number plates,' Holmes said. 'It's an offence to have an unreadable rego.'

* * *

The weather was clearing quickly by the time the detectives joined the Princes Highway a few kilometres east of Port Fairy. The sky was the colour of blood on the horizon, and lines of thin grey clouds crossed a yellow background.

'Long day,' Holmes said, looking at Larsen, who was driving.

'Yeah,' she replied, without taking her eyes off the road ahead. 'I'll sleep well tonight.'

'How about dinner at the Merrijig Inn?' Holmes hesitated before adding, 'Then I might drop around and see Greg if he's at home.'

Larsen's face tightened. 'Aren't I invited?' she asked with a hint of annoyance. 'Secret men's business or something?'

Holmes tried not to react to her accusation of being left out. 'No, nothing like that, Kirsten,' he replied matter-of-factly. 'Like I've said, if Greg and I meet up, it's just two old mates catching up for a beer. If we both turn up to his place, then to some people it will have collusion with a suspect written all over it.'

Larsen didn't reply.

* * *

The Merrijig Inn was one of the oldest establishments not only in Port Fairy but Victoria in general. The restaurant sat on the east side of an old coach residential inn and faced the wharf across Gipps Street. The doors at the corner opened onto a small reception room that gave access to the two dining areas to the side.

Few words had been exchanged as the two officers showered separately and dressed before snaring the last unbooked table at the restaurant. Holmes wore bone-coloured trousers teamed with a navy polo shirt. Larsen's blond hair was out, and she sported a pink silk top above black skin-tight wet-look leggings and pink stilettos. The look caused Holmes's heart to flutter, and he had suggested skipping dinner. He received a half-smile in return.

Walking back to their car following a meal that matched the restaurant's reputation, the couple encountered a casually dressed Dale Small strolling up the footpath, a long thin bag in hand. His face lit up when he saw the detectives. Holmes was shocked when he was addressed first.

'Darren, just the bloke I need. The coppers have a team in the pub's pool competition on Wednesday nights. Me, Grant and Chad Simpson, a senior constable who comes over from Warrnambool. Chad's just rung me to say he's crook as a dog. Fancy filling in for us? Only take an hour and a half or so.'

Holmes was genuinely chuffed by the offer but explained in vague terms that he had an interview scheduled.

'I'll play,' Larsen said enthusiastically. 'I'll be rusty, but I was a bit of a shark at uni.'

Small's face lit up. 'Fantastic. It'll give our team a bit of class.'

This was Holmes's worst nightmare. He could imagine the heart rates in the pub, especially Small's, when Larsen was bent over the table in her tight shiny leggings.

'I'll drop you out at the motel after we've finished,' Small added.

'You're not in a car,' Holmes said, almost in protest.

'I live just around the corner in Gipps Street. We can walk back and get my car after the game.'

Great! Walk back to your place after the game and a few drinks! What could go wrong there? Holmes thought but didn't say.

CHAPTER 20

'Thanks for your text,' Bowker said as he invited his long-time Homicide partner and friend into the kitchen. 'Gave me a chance to grab a six pack at the IGA.' He smiled. 'I try to keep out of the pubs these days. I'm not flavour of the month down here.'

Holmes took a seat at the table as Bowker retrieved a pair of stubbies from the fridge.

'How's the case going?' he asked as he sat down opposite Holmes. 'Any breakthroughs?'

Holmes snapped the cap off a stubby. 'We've identified the tradie who kicked and pissed on Flynn's car. A bloke by the name of Damien Norton, a handyman from Warrnambool. His partner is a bird named Bethany Symons with a scarlet reputation across the area. He found her phone that she'd accidentally dropped on the floor of their carport on the day Flynn disappeared. There was a text from Flynn asking her to come to Port Fairy and retype some work she'd done for him. Norton assumed she went there for a root, so he spat the dummy and came over to track her down. Said he had no luck with that but found Flynn's car on the wharf. No sign of Flynn himself, so he made a statement with the Merc and pissed off back to Warrnambool.'

'You believe him?'

Holmes shrugged. 'Not sure. On the squid boat CCTV, we see him disappear out of frame for a minute or so. Time to kill Flynn and shove him in the river if he did find him. I'm not convinced that happened, but there's certainly an opportunity and a motive there.'

Bowker took a long draw on his beer and wiped his mouth with the back of his hand. 'What does his missus say?'

'Played it straight. Says she had no relationship with Flynn and her trip over here was purely for typing. Says she returned to Warrnambool after a couple of hours, but that doesn't fit with Norton finding her phone later that same day. When I pointed that out, she appeared to invent a story about having dropped it when heading out again, this time to the supermarket.'

'So what's your plan there?'

Holmes took a swig before replying. 'Phone records. See if her mobile pinged the tower over here. If it didn't, it was likely on the carport floor in Warrnambool until it was found by Norton. That then raises the question of where Symons was for the rest of the afternoon.' He took another short swig. 'And the number Flynn rang her on was not his normal mobile number. The records for that phone should tell us where it's been and what other numbers it has called.'

Bowker nodded. 'You've been busy. Any leads on the clowns who stole the Mercedes?'

'Yeah. Believe it or not, the actual thief is the son of the bloke whose CCTV captured vision of him. Jamie Henderson is his name.'

'The old man didn't ID him, I bet.'

'Nope. One of the local coppers did. Your mate Constable Farrell tipped him off that we were after him, so he came into the station and confessed.'

Bowker shook his head. 'How do fuckheads like Farrell survive in the force?' He went to the fridge and brought back two more stubbies. 'The theft have anything to do with Flynn's disappearance, do you reckon?'

'Don't think so. Simple case of four drunken idiots pinching a car to take joyriding at Yambuk. But Henderson did say something that piqued my interest. He saw a large pleasure craft docking at the time they were fart-arsing around on the wharf.' He drained the dregs of his bottle. 'You didn't see it when you walked the wharf that night?'

Bowker shook his head. 'Nothing docking, no. But there were some swanky boats moored there.' He frowned. 'Who would take one of those boats out on a night like that?'

'My thinking exactly. Whatever their reason, I wouldn't mind a chat about what they might have seen as they docked.'

Bowker snapped the cap of his second beer. 'Do you reckon there's a connection between the boat and the bikie who collected a backpack?'

Holmes nodded. 'It's a possibility.' He rubbed his chin. 'If drugs are involved, and if Flynn had a connection to that trade, then we have motives for murder coming out our ears.'

'You'll need to interview whoever runs the show up at the Barbarians' compound.'

'Yeah, it's on the list.' Holmes thought for a moment before continuing. 'We're pretty sure your old mate Skeeta Allender did a pickup that night on the wharf.'

Bowker didn't seem surprised. 'I ran into Skeeta on my walk today. We had a chat, and I ended up rearranging his face.'

Holmes lurched back in surprise. 'What brought that on?'

'He insulted Rachael, and before I knew it, I'd broken his nose.'

'You'll be in more trouble if he goes to the locals.'

'He won't go to the police, because he knows I'll accuse him of running drugs. That's a hassle he doesn't need.'

'I'd watch my back. His mates won't be happy when they find out you belted him.'

Bowker nodded and chuckled weakly. 'Yeah. That possibility did cross my mind.' He leaned back in his chair and folded his arms across his chest, still holding his beer in one hand. 'So, who are your main suspects? Besides me, I mean?' he added with a forced laugh.

Holmes ignored the last question. 'I'm not sure you'd call them suspects, but there's a few people we can't eliminate at this stage.' Holmes placed his stubby on the table and used the index finger on his right hand to tap the thumb on his left. 'Number one. Flynn's wife would have to be high on the list. Physically abused, cheated on. She was one of the last to see him alive and knew his movements after he left the office.' He tapped his left index finger. 'Two. If Flynn was in league with the bikies, then you couldn't rule them out. Especially if drugs were involved.' He tapped his middle finger. 'Three. Damien Norton certainly had an axe to grind, and he was in the right place at the right time to take out Flynn. And we can see on the CCTV vision that he has a temper.' He tapped his ring finger. 'Four. The movements of Norton's partner Bethany Symons are still in question. Whether she had a motive to kill him is another matter. Maybe he knocked her around like he did with all women, but surely a better way to handle that is just to piss off and refuse to meet the prick. Unless he had some hold over her we don't know about.' He tapped his pinkie. 'Five. As far as we can ascertain, the last person to see him alive was the council planning officer. He possibly followed Flynn after their animated meeting, but it's hard to see him getting sufficiently stirred up over a council matter to commit murder.'

'Didn't Flynn threaten violence on Petrov's family if he didn't push the planning application?'

'Yeah, that's a point.'

Bowker took another pull on his beer. 'Anyone at the old Birdwatchers Club capable of sticking a knife into Flynn?'

'They're all as old as Mount Buller except for a bloke called Proctor. The locals describe him as an animal-loving tree-hugger. According to Dale Small at the station, there's no way he'd be involved.'

'Don't write him off until you're sure. Have you spoken to Proctor?'

'We've more or less ignored the Birdwatchers because of their age and interests. It's hard to imagine someone invested in protecting birds sticking a knife in another human being.'

Bowker upturned his palms. 'Stranger things have happened.'

'Yeah, probably worth a yarn to Proctor anyway,' Holmes replied.

The two men chatted about the case in general before Kirsten Larsen's name came up. 'I presume you didn't bring Kirsten so you could explain this is a social visit.'

Holmes cracked the top of a new stubby and flashed Bowker a dejected look. 'Spot on. But now I wish I had invited her.' He explained the chance meeting with Small in the street. 'I can imagine she'll be a big hit at the pub among blokes her own age.'

'Don't sell her short, mate,' Bowker replied, lifting his stubby in salute.

* * *

The thought of Small walking Larsen back to his own house to collect a car was too much for Holmes. He decided to circumvent that plan by visiting the pub rather than returning to his motel.

The bar of The Victoria was virtually deserted, with most of the clientele squeezed into the room next door where the police team were playing a group of fishermen at the pool table. At centre stage was Kirsten Larsen potting ball after ball, stretching over the table, her shiny black leggings reflecting the lights in the room. Holmes looked at the faces of the men jammed into the small space. Not a single eye was focussed on the pool balls as they ricocheted around the table. After each successive ball was pocketed, Larsen and Small high-fived.

A patron in his fifties flashed a lecherous grin at Holmes. 'Warms the cockles for blokes our age, don't you reckon?' he whispered.

Holmes didn't answer, just turned and left the room as cheers broke out with the sinking of yet another ball.

* * *

When Holmes returned to his motel room, he was still wondering how to play this. He already felt he was punching well above his weight with Larsen, and playing the jealous lover at his age might risk her cutting her losses and looking for a more appropriate mate. Someone like Dale Small. Young, fit, good-looking, and with a promising future in the force.

Holmes opened his briefcase and spread files across the room's round table. When Kirsten returned, he would be playing it cool, re-examining the files they had compiled. That's if she did return. Staying with Small was a possibility he couldn't erase from his mind. With that scene dominating his thoughts, he lay on the bed, hands behind his head, wondering how long his wait would be.

To his surprise, it was less than fifteen minutes before lights brightened the curtains in the bay window. He jumped to his feet and pulled up a chair to the table as he heard a car door open and indistinct chatter outside before the door slammed closed. A key was inserted in the lock, and Larsen entered the room with

Holmes hunched over paperwork, deep in thought. He looked up with a forced smile.

'Did you win?' he asked.

'Yeah. Five matches to four. I won my three, Dale won two and Grant Farrell lost all of his.'

'Big crowd?'

Larsen shrugged. 'A few of the regulars.'

Holmes kept a straight face. 'You're home earlier than I expected.'

'Dale said it'd only take an hour and a half or so,' Larsen replied, throwing her leather handbag on the dresser.

'I thought by the time you walked back to get Small's car, you'd be away a bit longer.'

'When we left the pub, Grant Farrell noticed we had no car, so he insisted he run me home. Save putting Dale out.'

Holmes felt like jumping to his feet and boisterously recommending Farrell for promotion. He played a straight bat instead. 'That was nice of him.'

'Yeah,' Larsen said quietly.

'I've been going through the file of this case again,' Holmes said, pointing at the pages on the table.

'It's a bit late to get my head around police work,' Larsen replied. 'Might feel a bit more like it in the morning, hopefully.'

Holmes climbed to his feet and put his arms around his partner. He let them drop until his hands were on her backside, his fingertips stroking the slinky material. 'You're right. Let's forget about work.' He took a deep breath. 'What about a roll in the hay instead?'

Larsen pecked him on the lips then pulled away. 'Sorry, Darren, it's been a long day. I just need some sleep.'

Holmes was left standing empty-handed as he watched Larsen kick off her stilettos, grab her nightie and disappear into the bathroom.

* * *

With police divers to arrive around lunchtime, the detectives used the morning to tick a few boxes. At eight o'clock, with the blazing sun prickling any exposed skin, Holmes and Larsen entered the rundown property of Tristan Proctor, an unemployed twenty-something-year-old whose days were filled with birdwatching and animal rescue. Holmes saw this interview as one of elimination, and had it not been for his chat with Bowker, he probably would have put a line through Proctor's name without a formal interview. Proctor's motive was weak and his opportunity to kill Flynn on the day he died non-existent. As far as they knew, anyway.

Proctor's house was set in a patch of bush along Hamilton Road. There was no formal garden, and the building was more a hut than a residential dwelling. On the southern side, a rough skillion roof constructed of unsawn timber support poles gave cover to an old Falcon ute. Scrawled on both sides of the vehicle in what looked like house paint was *Southern Wildlife Rescue*. There was no obvious front entrance, so the detectives made their way to the rear of the dwelling via the bespoke carport. Holmes stopped as he passed the tray of the old Ford, looked at Larsen and pointed to an open wooden box among an assortment of cages. In the box were a variety of tools used in wildlife rescue, including wire cutters, pliers, scissors, heavy leather gloves and an assortment of knives.

The backyard resembled an old-fashioned zoo. Cages of various sizes housed a menagerie of creatures, from small birds to reptiles to larger animals, including two kangaroos, an emu and a wombat. They eventually found Proctor in a small shed feeding a joey with an eyedropper. He was no taller than five six in the old and skinny as a reed. His greasy hair was tied back, and he sported a wispy, patchy beard. His face was pale and drawn, his eyes set well back in his skull. On first appearances, Holmes doubted he could lift a knife, let alone fatally stab a man of Flynn's stature.

'Mother hit by a truck at Codrington a week or so ago,' he said without any apparent surprise at having visitors or need for introductions. 'What have you got for me? A wombat in your car, I bet.' He pointed to a cage. 'That poor bugger got cleaned up the other day. I've bandaged his leg and been hoping for the best. The vet wanted to put him down, but I offered to at least give him a chance.'

'No injured animals with us, mate, thank goodness.' Holmes flashed his badge. 'Wonder if we can ask you a few questions?'

'Fire away,' a surprised Proctor said. 'I'm listening.'

'You're a member of the local Birdwatchers Club, we've been told?' Larsen asked.

Proctor smiled. 'One of the mighty dozen. The only member under sixty by about twenty-five years.'

'And we've heard you complained to the local police about the motorcycle gang taking over your clubhouse. Is that right?'

Proctor's face tightened. 'Bloody oath it's right. They stacked a meeting and just took everything. Our clubhouse, our bank account, the whole lot.' He shook his head. 'I told our members a thousand times to incorporate the club so it couldn't be taken over and re-purposed. But they wouldn't listen, even when I mentioned legal liability. I told them about the president of a country tennis club in South Australia who had lost his farm when a player sued for injuries incurred on the local courts. Get the club at arm's length from its members, I'd been advised by a solicitor. But no way were the oldies interested in doing anything different from what had happened for a hundred years prior.' He shook his head and stared up at the blue sky.

'According to Senior Sergeant Wilkins, you blamed Trevor Flynn for orchestrating the takeover?' Holmes asked.

'Absolutely,' Proctor replied. 'Smart-arsed blow-in trying to force a dodgy development out beside Belfast Lough that would have destroyed habitat for dozens of different waterbirds. Then he teams up with a pack of thugs to orchestrate stealing our clubhouse. To tell you the truth, officers, I wasn't the slightest bit sad when his body washed up at the lighthouse. When the rumour circulated he'd been murdered, I was tempted to nominate his killer for a knighthood. Services to humanity.'

'You didn't let your anger boil over and take him out?' Holmes asked.

Proctor feigned a chuckle. 'I approached him once as he entered his office. He grabbed me by the throat and lifted me up like a rag doll. At that point, I decided to let sleeping dogs lie. I wasn't going to get the clubhouse back, so I asked myself why I should get killed fighting a lost cause.'

'Smart decision, I'd say,' Larsen replied.

'One thing I did want, though, was the telescopic lens I used for photographing wildlife. It was stored in the clubhouse, so one afternoon I went back there to get it.'

Holmes smiled, anticipating the reception he'd received from the Barbarians. 'How'd that go?'

Proctor stopped feeding the joey and looked at the detective. 'There were more bikes there than usual, so something was on the go, and the compound gate was ajar. I just waltzed in and straight through the side door of the building. Flynn was in a screaming match with a skinny red-headed turkey. There was a fair bit of push and shove.'

Holmes looked at Larsen. 'That sounds like Jason McCulloch.'

'When they saw me, all hell broke loose,' Proctor continued. 'Flynn grabbed me by the collar, dragged me out through the gate and pushed me down onto the road. I tried to explain that I'd just come to collect my camera lens.'

'How'd Flynn respond?' Larsen asked.

'Told me if I ever came near that place again, he'd shove the camera lens so far up my arse I'd be able to take pictures through my mouth. If I went to the cops, he said he'd have me done for trespass.' He shook his head and inhaled deeply. 'I've never hated a human being more in all my life.'

'Where were you on the day he went missing, Mr Proctor?' Holmes asked.

Proctor burst out laughing. 'You think I was involved in his stabbing?' He held both arms apart at full stretch. 'Look at me, Detective. A decent wind would knock me over. I struggle to overpower the smallest animals I rescue. A big prick like Flynn is way out of my league. If he'd been shot, I could see how you could suspect me – although I don't own a gun, mind you. But knifed? Get real, mate.'

'We noticed an array of knives on the tray of your ute,' Holmes said. 'Should we take those and run them by Forensics?'

'Be my guest,' Proctor replied defiantly. 'But those tools are used exclusively for disentangling animals from wire, traps, nets or fishing line. You'll be wasting your own time as well as mine.'

Larsen leaned against the empty bird cage beside her. 'You still haven't told us where you were a fortnight ago this Friday.'

'All days are the same for me. I look after the animals here or pick up injured ones if I get called. I go into town occasionally to stock up on food, and once a month I attend the Birdwatchers meeting at the library.'

'You'd remember this day,' Holmes replied. 'It was a shocker, weather-wise. Wild winds, heavy rain, big seas.'

Proctor's eyes widened. 'Oh, that day. That's when the truck hit the roos. Didn't stop. A motorist who was following called the police, and they called me. By the time I got out there, both animals had died.' He pointed to the joey he was feeding. 'The female had this bloke in her pouch. I brought him back here. Not sure what time it was, but it was pitch black and the rain was hammering down.'

'And the police would confirm they rang you to go check the injured roos?'

'Yeah. Ask Grant Farrell. He made the call.'

Holmes rolled his eyes, looked at Larsen and shook his head. Farrell's slack police work, this time neglecting to record his call to Proctor in the station log, had cost the detectives more time and effort.

CHAPTER 21

Holmes was forced to rattle the steel gates at the Barbarians' compound and yell loudly to gain attention from the bikies sheltering inside the clubhouse. The heat was now stifling, the normal sea breeze non-existent, and on the other side of the road the ocean was flat, its cool water appealing. Finally, an overweight thirty-something-year-old stumbled from the side door wearing just boxer shorts, his lily-white skin reflecting a dazzling glare.

'Hold me back,' Larsen said with a straight face.

Holmes laughed. 'I'm gonna need stronger sunglasses.'

The bikie hobbled towards the detectives, hopping and swearing as he stood on stones and the surface heat penetrated the virginal skin on the soles of his feet. 'What the fuck do you two want?' he growled through stubby, rotted teeth.

Holmes flipped open his badge. 'We'd like to have a word with Jason McCulloch.'

'He's not here,' the fat man replied as sweat beaded on his pale skin.

'We'll just come in and check for ourselves, if you don't mind, mate.'

'No, stay here. I'll go get him,' the bikie replied without the slightest guilt about having lied.

Larsen pointed at the clubhouse. 'It might be easier if we go in there, out of the heat.'

'No non-members allowed,' the man replied quickly. 'Even coppers, unless they've got a warrant.'

'Just send out McCulloch,' Holmes replied wearily.

The bikie turned and hopped his way back to the clubhouse, swearing as he went.

When McCulloch appeared, he at least had the common sense to wear a tee-shirt above his boxers and motorbike boots on his feet.

'What's so fuckin' important that I have to come out in this fuckin' weather?' he demanded, rubbing sleep from his eyes.

Larsen looked at her watch. 'Nine thirty. Sorry to wake you so early,' she said with a smirk.

A spur-winged plover swooped low overhead, screeching rat-a-tat instructions at the trio below. McCulloch didn't notice. 'You play your cards right, darlin', and I'll keep you in the sack way past nine thirty.'

Holmes was in no mood for bullshit. 'What was your run-in with Trevor Flynn all about?'

'We don't have run-ins. We were fuckin' close. Grew up together. Cousins.'

'Trouble over money, was it?' Holmes persisted.

'You're talkin' shit, mate. Trevor and I got on like a house on fire, not that we had a lot to do with each other on a day-to-day basis. He ran his property development company, and I spend the odd day down here dodging the fuckin' rat race in Melbourne. Since he helped us acquire these headquarters, we'd have been lucky to cross paths more than once, I reckon.'

'So he wasn't a visitor here?' Larsen asked, setting a trap.

'Why would he be? Not sure he'd ever ridden a motorcycle.'

'Drug trafficking creates strange bedfellows,' Holmes replied.

McCulloch feigned indignation. 'What the fuck are you on about? It's one of our rules that we won't have drugs in the place down here. To my knowledge, Trevor would have stayed well clear of them too.'

Holmes looked at Larsen with a smile. 'Perhaps you can tell your favourite fairy story as well, Detective Senior Constable. But it'll have to be good to beat Mr McCulloch's.'

McCulloch looked up towards the sun and squinted. 'It's too fuckin' hot to be standing out here talking bullshit,' he said, wiping his brow with a sweaty forearm.

'Perhaps we could continue this inside, Jason?' Holmes suggested. 'In the shade and out of the sun?'

'Get to the fuckin' point of your visit.'

'We have a witness who saw you and Flynn in a heated physical encounter a few days before Flynn was murdered. Pushing and shoving, the witness said. We're thinking there's not a big step from pushing a finger into Flynn's chest to sticking a knife in there. Especially for a violent man like you.'

'Is that what that poofter birdwatcher told you happened?' McCulloch asked heatedly.

Larsen slipped her hands into her pockets. 'So you remember the incident, do you?'

'I remember Proctor visiting while we were fart-arsing around. It was the only time Trev had been to the clubhouse, and we were taking the mickey out of him for being our absent El Presidente.'

Holmes laughed out loud. He could feel sweat running down the inside of his shirt, not only the result of the weather but also his growing annoyance with McCulloch's evasiveness. 'This is the way we see it, Jason. Your mob have been importing illegal drugs through the port here and distributing them across the state and possibly into New South Wales and South Australia. I also think Flynn was up to his knackers in it as well, as evidenced by his role in acquiring this building and the financing of real estate purchases and their development. I reckon there's been a big blow-up between him and you blokes, probably over the profit split, or future plans, or who knows what. Something had to give, and Flynn was taken out to solve the disagreement.'

McCulloch shook his head. 'The lengths you fuckers will go to protect your own is beyond belief.' He hesitated for a moment before issuing a challenge. 'If you've got evidence that I killed Trevor, then arrest me now.' He held out his wrists, daring Holmes to slap on a set of cuffs. When the detective made no move, he dropped his hands. 'If you reckon we're dealing drugs, then bring in the drug squad and raid us. And if you want to look inside our clubhouse, come back with a search warrant. Until then, it's too hot to be standing out here talking fucking bullshit.' He turned and made his way back to the building.

The detectives stood for a moment in the blazing sun, Holmes's hands clenched into fists.

* * *

The police divers arrived at the wharf late morning, where they were met by Holmes and Larsen. Henderson's squid boat was at sea, making the area that was cordoned off with police ribbon more accessible for the search. Within minutes, two officers were submerged in the cool below the surface of the estuary. All the detectives could do was shelter in the shade of the restaurant and wait.

The first half hour of the search netted little of value to the investigation. A rusted tricycle, a dozen corroded soft drink cans and innumerable stubby bottles were thrown up on the wharf.

Both divers lamented the difficulty of searching the river bottom through the weed that waved with the tide. Just when a sweat-soaked Holmes was about to suggest calling an end to the exercise, a diver surfaced and heaved a rolled-up fabric parcel at Holmes's feet. He lifted his face mask. 'Nearly missed it. It was in a tussock of sea grass. Hasn't been there for all that long, by the absence of silt covering it and the way it was lodged in the weeds.'

Holmes dropped to his haunches for a closer look. The parcel was a rolled-up navy-blue parka, the sleeves loosely knotted together to form an improvised binding. Holmes photographed the find before slipping on a pair of rubber gloves and undoing the knots. He unrolled the parka to reveal a stainless-steel kitchen knife and a chunk of bluestone that he assumed was included as a weight. He picked up the knife in two fingers and inspected it closely. It was of medium size and composed entirely of metal, its handle embossed in a wavy pattern.

'Whereabouts did you find it?' he asked. 'Near the wharf here, or further out?'

'Further out. Towards the centre of the river,' the diver replied. 'I'm no bloody detective, but my money would be on someone heaving it as far into the river as they could.'

Holmes thought the same thing and nodded.

After a further forty minutes, the consensus was that the search had found all there was to find, and the divers packed their gear to begin their long journey back to their Williamstown base. Holmes photographed the knife, the parka, the bluestone and the section of river where the parcel was found. He placed each item in a plastic evidence bag for shipment to Forensics before transferring them to the rear of the police vehicle. As he slammed the rear door closed, he turned to Larsen. 'Fancy a stroll down the wharf to suss out the boats?'

'Got a particular one in mind? Something white with blue trim, perhaps?'

'Yeah. One with cabins at deck level, with a cockpit on top of that.'

'And capable of surviving at sea in foul weather?'

Holmes chuckled and instinctively moved to take Larsen's hand before remembering they were at work. 'You read my mind.'

A saunter down both sides of the river revealed only one vessel matching all their prerequisites. *Hippocrates* was moored among the fishing fleet, its sides protected from contact with the wooden wharf by sausage-shaped cushions. Strong nylon rope secured the bow and stern to bollards, and a striped synthetic tarpaulin protected the socialising area on the rear lower deck.

Holmes stood beside the boat, arms folded, as a middle-aged fisherman wearing bib and brace overalls over a bare chest climbed to the deck of the vessel next door and poured a bucket of soapy water over the side and into the river. 'This vessel seems to fit the bill,' Holmes said to Larsen. 'Wonder which millionaire owns the bloody thing?'

He walked to the boat next door, where the fisherman was now throwing craypots into a heap. He pointed towards *Hippocrates.* 'Who owns that baby moored next door?'

The fisherman didn't look up. 'Who wants to know?' he mumbled.

Holmes took his ID from his pocket and waved it in the direction of the fisherman, who looked up for less than a nanosecond.

'It's owned by a bloke named Gareth Matheson. He's an orthopaedic surgeon from Warrnambool. If you're looking to buy it, it's way above your pay grade, mate.' He smirked, still looking at his work.

Larsen wandered over to join her partner. 'How often does he use it?'

The fisherman glanced up when he heard the new voice. The statuesque Larsen standing above him demanded more of his attention than Holmes did. He straightened, one hand in the small of his back. 'Not all that often. It sits here most of the time as a monument to his wealth. Every now and then, he'll have a party on board, or he'll take it out for a run in the open sea.' He gave Larsen his best smile. 'My name's Jerry. Jerry Machkevitch. Not married, by the way. Just thought I'd put that out there.'

'Why doesn't he keep it at Warrnambool if that's where he lives?' Holmes asked, attempting to move the fisherman's attention away from his partner.

'You can't keep a boat like that in Warrnambool,' Machkevitch scoffed. 'There's no marina. A few fishing boats are anchored in the lee of the pier, but that's about it.' He laughed. 'Besides, there's bugger-all pedestrian traffic on the Warrnambool pier to ooh and aah at the boat. Not like here, where every bastard walks along this wharf and gets an eyeful of his prized possession.' He pushed up the peak of his Nike-branded cap. 'What's the point of being rich if other people don't know you are?'

'Yeah, you do get people like that,' Holmes replied.

'I've been told he's also got a decent boat on a trailer that he keeps at his place in Warrnambool,' Machkevitch added. 'More for fishing with his mates than showing off, apparently. But he's got all the gear. The big rods, illegal craypots, the lot.'

'How long's this boat been here?' Larsen asked, pointing at *Hippocrates*.

The fisherman shrugged as a pair of black cormorants shrieked overhead. A woman and two young boys walked past, all eating multiple-flavoured ice creams. Machkevitch waited till they passed before answering the question. 'A year. Eighteen months, perhaps. He owned a smaller vessel before upgrading to that big bugger. Must have a hell of a business, is all I can say.' He feigned a chuckle. 'Course, when you get paid a fortune even if you fuck up, doesn't take all that long to put a few shackles together. I busted my shoulder playing footy, and Matheson guaranteed he could make it as good as new.' He lifted his elbow and rolled his shoulder. 'It's bloody worse now than it was before the operation, but I still paid through the nose.'

'If he lives in Warrnambool, who looks after the boat?' Holmes asked.

Machkevitch waved away a fly burrowing into his eye socket. 'His sister lives down here, so I suspect she keeps a weather eye on it.'

Holmes and Larsen exchanged glances. 'What's his sister's name?'

The fisherman took off his cap and fanned his forehead. 'Shit, mate, it's too hot to give you the family history of the friggin' town.' He exhaled loudly then returned his cap to his head. 'Don't know her name, but she was married to the bloke the Homicide cop stuck a knife into a week or so ago. The bloke who was trying to develop those water-logged blocks out on the lagoon.'

Further up the wharf, where the level dropped via two steps, one of the ice cream boys lost a rainbow-coloured scoop that hit the wooden walkway with a splat. His mother thwarted his efforts to pick it up in his fingers and dragged him by the arm towards a Kia people mover in the carpark. A fisherman hosing the deck of the vessel moored adjacent shook his head and squirted a jet of water onto the wharf, washing the ice cream away in coloured streaks.

Holmes shook Machkevitch's hand. 'Thanks, mate,' he said with a polite smile. 'Don't want to keep you out here in the heat any more than necessary.'

Machkevitch nodded then looked up at Larsen. 'Before you go, and I don't want to be rude, honey, but you must be the bird Dale Small is squiring around. The boys in the pub said he had a young white-hot detective on his arm.'

Before Larsen could answer, Holmes set the record straight. 'Well, you tell them they've got it wrong.'

He walked away, leaving his partner following a few steps behind. His mental picture of her and Small together continued to fester, and he knew it was clouding both his private and professional decision-making. Personal experience and examples he'd encountered within his job taught him that road-blocking affairs of the heart, or wishing them away, at best delayed the inevitable moment of truth and at worst fermented further resentment. If Larsen had a physical attraction to Small, then no amount of his manipulation would erase that.

At times like these, he missed Greg Bowker's counsel. So many personal issues were discussed and resolved in the course of an investigation. Before he bared his soul to Kirsten, he decided to run his quandary past his old friend to seek a second opinion.

'What's the big hurry?' Larsen called from behind.

Holmes looked over his shoulder. 'No hurry. Sorry, I was thinking about something else.'

At that moment, Larsen saw her partner miss the first step onto the lower level of the wharf, try to regain his balance, then slip on the wet timber where the fisherman had washed away the ice cream. She broke into a trot as Holmes fell heavily, clasping his knee in two hands and rolling on his back.

'Are you alright, Darren?' Larsen asked as she dropped to her haunches and placed a gentle hand on Holmes's shoulder.

'Twisted my knee, but other than that, nothing's broken, I don't think,' he said through gritted teeth. 'I'll have a sore bum in the morning, though.' He grasped the wooden railing and, with the help of his partner, clambered to his feet. He attempted to place weight on his left leg, but grimaced in pain. Larsen wrapped his arm around her neck and he hopped his way back to their vehicle.

'You drive,' Holmes said before awkwardly manoeuvring himself into the passenger seat.

CHAPTER 22

Over the next hour, Holmes's knee swelled and became increasingly painful despite a poultice of ice wrapped in a motel tea towel. After an uncomfortable lap of the motel room, he was forced to accept the inadvisability of his planned trip to Warrnambool to interview Matheson. And, much to his chagrin, he conceded the need to see a doctor, if for nothing other than pain relief. The Matheson interview was important to maintain the new momentum they had established with the case, so Holmes suggested Larsen still make the trip. It didn't surprise him when she proposed taking Dale Small in his lieu. It was logical that someone accompany her, and it would have been churlish and immature for him to fight her plan. Feeling like an elderly father, he instead assured her he would make a doctor's appointment and call a taxi when he needed transport to the clinic. From there, he would visit the police station to brief Wilkins and obtain any information she may have received that could help solve the case.

When Larsen departed in a white sleeveless top and a dark blue knee-length pencil skirt with matching stilettos, Holmes felt his heart drop, knowing that Small would feel the same flutter he did when Larsen dressed to kill. He watched her disappear into the bright sunshine outside and open the police vehicle door, dragging up her skirt and pulling her long legs into the car. He continued to stare out through the door until the vehicle had left the carpark and turned onto the highway. He closed his eyes, fearing Kirsten was slipping away.

After thirty seconds, he exhaled loudly and retrieved his mobile from his bedside table. He had two calls to make. The first secured a four o'clock appointment at the medical clinic, thanks to a cancellation. The second had Bowker on his doorstep five minutes later.

Holmes had the kettle boiling when Bowker arrived and made two mugs of coffee as his old partner took a seat at the round table in the bay window. It wasn't until after Holmes had outlined the latest developments in the Flynn case, including the push and shove between the victim and McCulloch, the arrival of Matheson's boat at the wharf, and the discovery of the submerged parka and knife, that he brought up his relationship with Larsen.

'So, you're worried that Kirsten and the senior constable may be hitting it off a bit too well?' Bowker asked, taking a quick sip from his mug. 'And now, all of a sudden, you're feeling vulnerable to losing her. You look in the mirror and don't like what you see.'

'That's probably it in a nutshell, yeah.'

'What do you want Kirsten to do? Stop acting naturally? Stop acting the way that attracted you to her in the first place?'

Holmes shook his head. 'No. I love her bubbly, outgoing personality.' He scratched his cheek. 'I just don't like it when other blokes are attracted to that too. Especially handsome six-foot-six blokes less than half my age.'

Bowker shrugged. 'You can't have it both ways, mate. If you start dictating how Kirsten should act or dress, it's all over.'

Holmes screwed up his face. 'So I just let things play out and hope for the best? Is that what you're suggesting?'

'What will be will be, Sherlock. Up until now, your relationship has been rock-solid. You need to trust that. Trying to engineer an outcome will blow up big time.'

Holmes nodded but didn't answer. He took a long gulp of his coffee.

Bowker drained his mug, gathering his thoughts before continuing. 'I realise my entanglement in this case has thrown you and Kirsten together as lead investigators. So far, I've got no complaints about the job you're doing, but I won't let it happen again. It creates too many distractions.'

'Apologies about that, mate,' Holmes said after a moment's contemplation. 'Your job shouldn't be made more complex by a jealous forty-nine-year-old schoolboy.'

'I know it's hard, Sherlock, but my advice is to put your efforts into the investigation, and everything else will take care of itself.'

Holmes held up two sets of crossed fingers.

* * *

Gareth Matheson was already running behind on his day's appointments and showed his annoyance when Larsen and Small arrived and demanded an interview. A small group of patients in his waiting room flashed them a glance and feigned disinterest as the surgeon attempted to negotiate a time later in the afternoon. Larsen was having nothing of it.

'We can have a ten-minute chat in your room now, or we can go down to the station and work through the protocols there,' she advised.

Matheson rolled his eyes at his middle-aged, heavily-made-up receptionist before exhaling loudly and leading the detectives into his consulting suite. His rooms had once been a stately house, and his spacious office featured high ceilings, ornate cornices and floor-to-ceiling double-hung windows partly hidden by long white tulle curtains. Matheson slumped down into an expensive leather chair behind his enormous desk and with the wave of his hand suggested the officers take a seat in more modest but period-appropriate chairs opposite. The surgeon was shorter than both Small and Larsen, but broad across the shoulders and overweight, the buttons on his white business shirt straining to contain his bulk when he leaned back in his chair. He sported a ginger goatee and trendy shoulder-length auburn hair that seemed unsuited to a man of his age and build. His green eyes were intense, the corners of his mouth perpetually turned down in a frown. Larsen saw only a slight resemblance to his sister, Katy Flynn.

'Can you explain what's so important that I need to keep patients waiting?' the surgeon asked tersely.

'We're investigating a murder, Doctor Matheson,' Larsen replied with a steely stare.

'It's *Mr* Matheson. Surgeons have skills beyond doctors.'

Small smiled at Larsen, flashing his perfect teeth. 'I didn't realise my dad was a surgeon. Everyone called him *Mister* too. I always thought he was only a butcher.'

Matheson remained stony-faced as he looked the senior constable up and down with disdain. Small was dressed in his civvies, with an open-necked white linen shirt, navy slacks and black leather slip-on shoes. 'How come the police assigned Ken and Barbie to a murder investigation?' he said sarcastically.

'You own a boat called *Hippocrates*, Mr Matheson?' Larsen asked, not taking the bait.

Matheson looked puzzled. 'What's that got to do with anything?'

'So the boat's yours?'

'Yes,' Matheson replied, his eyes darting between the two officers. 'I don't see why that would interest you.'

'Do you own it outright? No bank loans or credit arrangements? We can check.'

Matheson folded his arms, still confused by Larsen's questions. 'I own it outright. It's my pride and joy.'

'You also own one of the most expensive houses in Warrnambool, from what we've been told,' Small added. 'Plus this place.'

Larsen eyed Matheson with a smile. 'Orthopaedic surgery must pay well,' she said.

Matheson's annoyance was growing. 'We have two incomes. My wife is a GP, and she does some anaesthetic work for the hospital as well.' He eyeballed Larsen. 'What's all this about, Detective? Wealth envy by low-paid public servants, is it?'

Again, Larsen ploughed on, undeterred by the barbs. 'The Port Fairy fishermen tell us you owned a more modest vessel before you upgraded to *Hippocrates*.'

'That's right. Once my practice was established, I was able to afford a vessel like I'd always dreamed of. One that I could take ocean cruising and hold parties on for friends and business associates.'

'Also allowed you to show off your wealth, I s'pose,' Small said.

Matheson leaned forward and folded his hands on his desk. 'I won't deny that I like nice things. My parents didn't have two bob to rub together, so I don't mind flaunting the fact that I'm a poor boy made good.'

'No inheritance to set you up?' Larsen asked.

Matheson missed the implication. 'Nope,' he answered proudly. 'Self-made man. The only asset our parents passed on to my sister and I was the broken-down bush shack we were brought up in.' He laughed nervously. 'At a place called Nowhere Creek, would you believe? Up near Ararat and not worth the trouble of cleaning up to put on the market.'

'Who else captains *Hippocrates*?' Larsen asked.

Matheson shook his head. 'Nobody touches the wheel of that vessel except yours truly,' he said vehemently, driving the index finger of his right hand into the top of his desk to make his point.

Larsen smiled. 'So you were the skipper the night Trevor Flynn was killed on the Port Fairy wharf?'

Matheson frowned. 'You'll have to remind me of the date when that happened.'

Larsen raised her eyebrows. 'You don't remember the day your brother-in-law was killed? And the weather that night would be hard to forget.' She looked Matheson in the eyes. 'From all accounts, you had trouble manoeuvring the vessel into her moorings because of the rain and wind.' She leaned forward in her chair. 'Why were you at sea in that weather, Doctor Matheson?'

Matheson shrugged. '*Hippocrates* hadn't had a run for a good fortnight. When I left port, the weather looked OK. And it's *Mister!*'

'Did you meet someone at sea?' Larsen asked casually. 'Perhaps bring a package back to port on their behalf?'

Matheson stood up angrily, hands on hips. 'Are you accusing me of smuggling contraband, Detective?'

Larsen shrugged and smiled. 'I'm just trying to explain why Trevor Flynn would be on the wharf in that sort of weather. And why a member of the Barbarians motorcycle club arrived in the pouring rain and collected a rucksack full of something shortly after you berthed your boat.'

'I didn't see a bikie on the wharf,' Matheson replied, sitting back down and avoiding eye contact. 'I did see Trevor, but he was back towards the footbridge talking to a bloke I didn't recognise.'

Larsen raised her eyebrows. 'Can you describe this other man?' she asked.

Matheson looked up at the ceiling as if scanning his memory.

'Tall, about the same height as my brother-in-law,' he replied after a few moments. 'But as you say, the weather was atrocious by the time I returned to port, so it was hard to see much through the squall.'

'Who helped you crew the boat that night?' Small asked.

'I took it out on my own,' Matheson replied without conviction.

'A big boat like that? When you got back to port, you'd need someone on deck to secure the lines while you manoeuvred the vessel into her berth.'

'I was using the lower wheelhouse. Once I got her close to the wharf, I only had to walk a few metres aft to secure the stern line, and the current of the river just pushed the boat in against the wharf. Securing the bow line was easy after that.'

Small raised his eyebrows. 'A manoeuvre like that in shit weather is a hell of an ask even for a professional skipper, let alone an amateur working on his own.'

'Well, that's what happened, officer.' Matheson forced a smile. 'Maybe I was lucky it worked out. But if it makes you feel better, I'll check the weather forecast before I attempt anything like that again.'

Larsen rolled her eyes at Small and then stood up, hands on hips. 'We might leave it at that, Mr Matheson, but I've got a feeling we'll be in touch again soon.'

As the officers left the room, the smile disappeared from Matheson's face and his head dropped slowly into his hands.

* * *

Bowker dropped Holmes in the street outside the police station, where he limped past three young men, their faces solemn, their discussion muffled. The little Holmes overheard piqued his interest: a reference to the theft of a motor vehicle. The Mini Moke parked in the shade on the other side of the road was enough to confirm their identity.

Holmes entered the station and hobbled straight through into Wilkins's office unannounced. The senior sergeant stood behind her desk, chatting sternly to Constable Farrell, who sat opposite, arms folded defensively across his chest.

'I saw three young blokes outside,' Holmes said, bypassing normal pleasantries. 'Were they Henderson's mates?'

'Yes,' Wilkins replied through gritted teeth as she dropped into her swivel chair. 'I was just speaking to Constable Farrell about them. Enquiring why he didn't make me aware he was interviewing them and why he didn't follow orders and wait for you or Detective Larsen to be present.'

Holmes looked down at Farrell, who was staring at the floor, his hands now knitted together between his knees. 'And what was your answer to those questions, Constable?'

'It was routine stuff,' Farrell replied without looking up. 'They admitted they'd been with Jamie Henderson when he borrowed the Mercedes. That was all we wanted to know, wasn't it?'

Holmes was clearly annoyed. 'What did you charge them with?'

Farrell looked up. 'I didn't charge them with anything,' he replied, puzzled. 'It was Jamie who took the car, not them. They were just his mates.'

Holmes put his hands on his hips and stared at the ceiling in frustration. If it hadn't been for the presence of Wilkins, he would have exploded. He took a deep breath and looked down at Farrell. 'I want them back here, pronto,' he demanded, pointing at the ground. 'Can you track me down a contact?'

Farrell removed the mobile phone from his pocket and scrolled through his contact list.

'Fuck me,' Holmes said out loud, then apologised to Wilkins for his language.

Wilkins raised her eyebrows and leaned forward, forearms on

her desk. 'Why do you have their numbers in your phone, Grant?'

'I'm in the cricket club with them,' Farrell replied. 'Lucky, eh?'

Holmes couldn't make up his mind about Farrell. Was he as dumb as dog shit, or just a conniving prick? A bit of both, he suspected. 'They should still be together if they all came in the Moke. Call one and we should get them all.'

Farrell stood up and moved towards the door. 'I'll give Sammy Voogt a ring. He won't be the one driving.'

Holmes stepped into the doorway to block Farrell's exit. 'I'll make that call, thanks, Constable.'

Farrell seemed surprised. 'OK. Grab your pen and I'll give you his number.'

Holmes smiled and held out his hand. 'No need for that, mate. I'll use your phone.'

Farrell reluctantly handed over his mobile.

'Besides, there's no need to write the number down,' Holmes said, suspecting another breach of procedures. 'It'll be in the record of interview.'

Wilkins leaned back in her chair. 'That was another thing we were chatting about, Detective.'

Holmes eyeballed Farrell. 'So, no record of interview either, Constable?' He again exhaled loudly and shook his head. Farrell's days as a police officer were numbered, and he'd make sure of that the moment this investigation was over. He looked over at Wilkins. 'I'll be back in a tick.'

In the privacy of the interview room, he punched in the number displayed on the screen of Farrell's mobile. It was answered almost immediately.

'Granto, mate. Can't thank you enough. Hopefully that's the last we'll hear about that night, unless that fuckin' detective gets his balls in a knot again.'

Holmes wished he could shove his hand down the line and grab Voogt by the throat. But instead, he smiled to himself as he saw the humour in the situation. 'Actually, Mr Voogt, you're talking to that fuckin' detective right now, and his balls *are* most definitely in a knot. You and your mates get your arses back to the police station now.'

Holmes heard muffled discussion for a few seconds before Voogt responded. 'Can it wait till tomorrow? We're off to the Warrnambool races. We're halfway there already.'

Holmes wasn't in the mood for negotiation. 'You've got twenty-five minutes before I send the van out to pick you up.' He disconnected the call, wandered back into Wilkins's office and handed the phone back to Farrell without saying a word.

Farrell put the mobile in his pocket. 'Thanks, Sarge. Can't do without the old phone. Got the afternoon off in lieu. Might head to the races at Warrnambool. Great day for it, weatherwise.' He chuckled nervously. 'See if I can pick a winner.'

Holmes rolled his eyes at Wilkins as Farrell left the room. 'He's got to go, Megan. Guess where Voogt and his mates were headed?'

'Warrnambool races?' Wilkins replied quickly. 'I've started the paperwork, but I have to be careful. Dismissal of a serving officer is not easy. Police Association and all that. Strongest union in the state, even though they refuse to call themselves a union.'

Holmes nodded. 'It should have been done long before you took over here. The last bloke was obviously just kicking the can down the road.'

'Yeah,' Wilkins replied as she pushed a stapled document across her desk. 'This telecommunications report for you arrived this morning. Contains data on the phone numbers you requested.'

Holmes pulled a chair up to the table and was reading the report before his backside hit the seat.

CHAPTER 23

When the knock came on the side door of his temporary home, Bowker was lying on the couch reading *The Age*. He half expected a visit from Holmes and was surprised to see Kirsten Larsen on the doorstep. The two detectives exchanged pleasantries before Larsen introduced Dale Small. The two men shook hands, and Bowker instantly appreciated Holmes's anxiety concerning the senior constable and Larsen. Bowker assumed his friend had exaggerated Small's attributes because of his unease about his own age and declining physical attributes, but now he saw what Holmes feared. Together, Small and Larsen looked like a Hollywood couple, both blond, physically striking and dressed to kill.

'Can we have a word, please, Greg?' Larsen asked.

'Yeah, come in,' Bowker replied. He indicated they sit at the pine kitchen table and offered hot drinks, but Larsen explained they had stopped for a coffee before leaving Warrnambool. Bowker nodded and sat at the table, wondering what was to come.

Larsen was first to speak. 'We just interviewed the owner of a luxury boat that's moored down here at the wharf. A Gareth Matheson. He's an orthopaedic surgeon based in Warrnambool.'

'He's also the brother of Katy Flynn, wife of the deceased,' Small added.

Bowker raised his eyebrows. 'OK,' he said, a little puzzled. 'So why were you talking to him, other than the family relationship?'

'On the night Flynn went missing, he took his boat out to sea,' Small replied.

Bowker frowned. 'On a shit night like that?'

'He said the weather wasn't as bad when he left port,' Larsen replied. 'Turned ugly when he was off the coast, so he headed back in. Had a lot of trouble berthing the boat in the wind and rain.'

'So you're chasing a motive for someone to take a boat out on a night like that, and a reason for a bikie with a haversack to be on the wharf in that type of weather?'

Larsen nodded. It was obvious to her that Holmes was keeping him well abreast of the investigation. Small was left to wonder how a leading suspect would know these details but thought it not his place to ask. Deep down, he knew the answer anyway.

Bowker fiddled with the salt shaker in the centre of the table, suspecting there was more to come. 'I appreciate you dropping in and telling me the latest.'

Larsen nervously scratched her chin with an index finger. 'Matheson told us something else too, Greg. Something we need to ask you about.'

Bowker spread his arms. 'Shoot.'

'He said he saw someone talking to Flynn as he manoeuvred his boat towards the wharf,' Larsen explained, looking Bowker in the eye, watching for a tell. 'His description of the bloke sounded a bit like you. Similar build to Flynn. Up the footbridge end of the wharf.'

Bowker's face didn't change. Larsen paused for a moment.

'We know you were out and about that night. And you were gunning for Flynn.'

Bowker leaned back in his chair and folded his arms defensively.

'That's right. But if there *was* a bloke talking to Flynn, it wasn't me. I didn't find the bastard, end of story.'

'But you *were* looking for him?' Small asked tentatively, acutely aware of his junior status compared with the detective inspector.

Bowker leaned forward quickly and eyeballed Small. 'Of course I was looking for him, Senior Constable. I've never denied that. And I've never denied that, in the mood I was in, I could have killed the bastard. But I didn't find him, and I didn't kill him.' He knocked the salt shaker over with the back of his hand in a show of frustration.

Small looked away without replying. To him, Bowker killing Flynn seemed infinitely more believable than assuming drug deals, corrupt doctors and bikie gangs.

* * *

Holmes explained to Wilkins that the report contained three parts. The first two were rundowns of the mobile phone activity of Flynn's typist Bethany Symons and her handyman partner Damien Norton. The third related to the new number on which Flynn had contacted Symons the day he died.

Holmes checked the activity report for Norton's phone first. There were two calls received from a number registered to his boss, Graeme Connolly. His only outgoing call was to the Bunnings Hardware trade desk. His phone pinged the Warrnambool, Tower Hill, and Port Fairy towers late that afternoon at times that matched his explanation of his movements that day. Holmes saw nothing that gave him cause to doubt the handyman's honesty.

Bethany Symons was a different story. Her phone records clearly proved her a liar. Holmes explained to Wilkins that Symons had claimed she took her mobile to Port Fairy on the day she met up with Flynn. To explain why it was found by Norton in her carport that afternoon, she surmised she must have dropped it after she returned home, on her way out to a supermarket. But the phone records showed her phone was turned on all day and pinged only the Warrnambool tower. Obviously, it hadn't made the trip to Port Fairy, and this raised questions concerning her whereabouts between leaving her session with Flynn and arriving home. She would need to be interviewed again, and Holmes decided it wouldn't hurt to peruse her bank records either.

The most intriguing aspect of the report was on page three and surrounded the mobile number that Flynn had used to summon Symons to Port Fairy. It was an anonymous pay-as-you-go phone, or a burner, as it was known in police circles. Other than the call to Symons, its only traffic involved two numbers. Both also belonged to pay-as-you-go phones. If Holmes hadn't already been suspicious that Flynn was involved in underhand dealings, he certainly was the moment he read these records. Burner phones were notorious for their use by criminals because of their anonymity, and their low cost allowed them to be easily discarded and replaced by others of their ilk.

The new challenge was to find the owners of the two mystery numbers. Holmes was sure this would close a circle surrounding Flynn's murder. But identifying who held the burner phones would be easier said than done.

* * *

It was less than half an hour before Henderson's mates returned to the station. Holmes interviewed each separately, but received the same account from all three except for a small detail dropped as a casual afterthought by Matt Tyrell. When Holmes enquired about other people on the wharf the night they stole Flynn's car, like his mates, Tyrell mentioned the expensive boat that was finding docking difficult. But unlike the others, he recalled seeing a yellow Suzuki enter the carpark as they left.

The wharf carpark was accessible via two entrances. Only one was captured by the camera on Mick Henderson's squid boat, leaving the other entry and the northern section of the carpark invisible to the investigation. While Henderson's camera had recorded visits to the wharf by Damien Norton, Skeeta Allender, Greg Bowker and the car thieves, Holmes had always worried there were other actors involved that night who had escaped being accidentally logged on the squid boat's security system.

'Who was driving the Suzuki?' Holmes asked, already anticipating the likely response.

Tyrell shrugged. 'No bloody idea. It was dark and pissing with rain.'

'Do you know anyone in town who owns a car like that?'

Tyrell upturned his palms. 'I've seen one around, but I don't know who owns it. It's often parked in Bank Street. Stands out like dog's balls, that colour.'

Holmes nodded. He'd seen it in Bank Street too, outside Trevor Flynn's office. And he'd also seen it parked under Flynn's house on South Beach. He assumed it belonged to Katy Flynn. He rubbed the back of his neck, pondering what she was doing at the wharf that day and at that time of night.

'Anything else you remember, Matthew? See any other cars?'

Tyrell shook his head. 'I've told you everything I know.' When Holmes didn't respond, he assumed the interview was over. 'Can we go now?'

'Not quite yet. I'll send in Senior Sergeant Wilkins. She'll charge you and your mates with theft of a motor vehicle.'

Tyrell sprang to his feet. 'Granto said we'd be OK! Jamie was the one who drove the car.'

Holmes smiled. 'Well, Constable Farrell gave you dodgy information. My advice is to engage a decent solicitor.'

He stood up and left the room, leaving Tyrell staring into space.

Once outside, Holmes rang both Katy Flynn's home and the office where she worked, but was unable to make contact. Ascertaining why she had been at the wharf that night, and what she had seen, had suddenly become a priority. A forensic search of her car would also need to be scheduled.

* * *

At the same time, Larsen and Small were hunting Katy Flynn. But for a different reason. Their interview with Gareth Matheson had raised more questions than it had answered, and they felt his sister may help clarify a few issues. Flynn's office was closed when they checked, and there were no cars at her residence on South Beach. Opposite, the tide was out, exposing algae- and seaweed-covered bluestone and creating numerous rock pools where children gathered in groups, pointing at the strange lifeforms in the water below them. Seabirds skipped from rock to rock, feasting on the newly exposed marine manna. The wind was no more than a zephyr but still carried the twin aromas of salt and rotting seaweed.

The sun was warm on their backs as they walked to the front door of the Flynn home. Larsen knocked loudly, but there was no sign of life from inside. She knocked again, with the same negative result. She walked to the rear of the building and checked the high-fenced backyard.

'Her car's not here, so we have to assume she's not home,' Small suggested.

Larsen nodded. 'I agree. But at the moment, I'm looking for her dog. She owns this big angry Rottweiler-cross. There's no way it would allow us to prowl around without making us aware of its presence.'

Small shrugged. 'Probably with her.'

Larsen nodded. 'Not the sort of dog you take down the street when you do your shopping. My guess is that she's away for a few days and she's taken the dog with her. Saves finding someone with enough guts to feed the thing in her absence.'

'So what now?'

'I'll call her mobile.' Larsen removed a small notebook from her handbag and flipped through the pages until she found what she was after. She copied a number into her phone and hit the call icon. She drummed the fingers of her free hand on her thigh as the phone dialled. After thirty seconds, the call was transferred to voicemail, where she left a message requesting Katy Flynn call back.

Larsen again consulted her notes and rang another number. This time, it was answered quickly by Matheson's receptionist, who transferred the call through to the office of her boss. He was in no mood to resume their earlier discussion.

'I'm not sure you appreciate that I'm trying to run a medical practice here,' the surgeon stated gruffly. 'It's only pure luck that I haven't got a patient with me at present.'

Larsen was terse and straight to the point. 'I'm attempting to locate your sister, Mr Matheson. I've checked her office and her home, but no luck. I thought if she'd gone away for a few days, you might know where she is.'

'What do you want her for? Surely she's been through enough without you people harassing her.'

'We're not harassing her,' Larsen shot back. 'We were hoping to confirm some of the information you gave us this morning. Especially that relating to your personal finances and your acquisition of the boat.'

Matheson was clearly annoyed. 'Katy wouldn't know the first thing about my finances or the bloody boat. Just as I know nothing about her monetary situation.'

'But she'd be able to confirm any inheritances or lack of such,' Larsen said. 'To be honest, we're still struggling to understand the source of your recent wealth. A lucrative practice plus your wife's income would not explain the assets you own outright.'

Matheson exhaled heavily and hesitated before responding. 'Look, Detective, I don't want to advertise this, but I've had several big collects on the horses in recent times. Over the years, I've put a few broken jockeys back together again, and they give me good information. Anyway, I have no idea where Katy would be. But I suspect she won't be too far from home.'

Larsen thought the gambling explanation was bullshit but let the matter slide. Little more was gleaned from the conversation, and she disconnected. She shook her head at Small. 'Well, that was a waste of time. He's now claiming he's had a few big wins on the neddies.' She looked at her watch then back at the senior constable. 'I'll run you back to the station. Thanks for your help this morning.'

Small scratched his cheek. 'My place is in the first street back from here, if you fancy a late lunch,' he said a little tentatively. 'I can offer you a sandwich and a homemade ice coffee.'

'Why not?' Larsen replied after a moment of indecision.

Small smiled widely and led the way back to their vehicle on the other side of the road. 'After lunch, I've got something to show you,' he called back over his shoulder.

* * *

The young doctor at the Port Fairy Medical Centre jotted notes as Holmes explained how he'd injured his knee and the main area of pain. She manipulated the joint and suggested the most likely issue was a torn meniscus. She was reluctant to prescribe medications or recommend a therapy until Holmes had consulted a specialist. With this escalation in medical intervention, he now wished he had skipped the appointment. He was sure the knee would get better by itself, and all he really wanted was pain relief and a set of crutches.

'Gareth Matheson from Warrnambool visits this surgery every second Friday and sees his local patients here,' the doctor explained. 'With a bit of luck, we can get you in to see him tomorrow. I suspect he'll suggest an MRI scan or an arthroscope over in Warrnambool to get a proper handle on what damage you've done.'

With the mention of Matheson, the doctor now had Holmes's full and undivided attention. 'It's only twenty minutes to Warrnambool,' he said as casually as possible. 'Unusual for specialists to run clinics so close to their home base.'

The doctor smiled. 'There's method in his madness, Mr Holmes. He owns a fancy boat that he keeps at Port Fairy. He kills two birds with the one stone. Sees his local patients on Friday and sails his boat on the weekend. Lives on board, the lucky bugger.'

Within fifteen minutes, Holmes left the medical clinic on crutches with an appointment to see the Warrnambool orthopod on the coming Friday.

CHAPTER 24

Holmes's arms and shoulders felt like red hot pokers by the time he turned the corner from Bank Street into Sackville Street, the main drag of the seaside town. His plan of using his crutches to make the walk from the medical clinic back to the police station had initially seemed achievable to a man who prided himself on his fitness despite approaching his half century in years. But the main roundabout was as far as he got before he conceded the journey would need to be broken into two halves. The Hub, a restaurant on the corner, seemed as good a place as anywhere to take a breather. After all, he told himself, he hadn't had lunch, and a cold drink would help rehydrate an aching body. He slumped into a vinyl couch just inside the door, feeling guilty but relieved when a young waitress took pity on his situation and traversed the room to take his order. Never had he felt so old and useless.

That feeling was easily superseded later in the afternoon when he finally dragged himself into the police station, throwing his crutches against the wall and dropping onto a padded bench in the public reception area. His biceps ached, his armpits too tender to touch. When Small and Larsen bounded through the door, laughing and joking, his humiliation was complete.

Small saw him first. 'Shit, are you alright?' he said as he hurried across and dropped to his haunches.

Holmes's ego ordered him to stand. Small tried to help, grabbing the detective under the armpit in a vain attempt to haul him up. Holmes silently winced in pain as he gently pushed away Small's hand. 'I'm OK, mate. Just a bit further from the medical centre than I thought. Especially on one leg.'

Small was genuinely impressed. 'That's gotta be a good couple of k's. It'd be a hell of an effort even for a bloke my age.'

Larsen suppressed a grin, collected the crutches, placed them under Holmes's arms and led him into the office that had been set aside for their investigation. Small followed them through and closed the door behind him. Holmes sat down behind the desk, propping his crutches against the filing cabinet to the side.

'How'd you go with Matheson?' Holmes asked before Larsen and Small could take their seats.

'Tell me about your knee first, Darren. You look in more pain now than you did when I left.'

Holmes was desperate not to appear an invalid. 'My knee hurts less, but using these bloody crutches has wrecked the rest of my body.' He smiled awkwardly. 'Now, Matheson. How'd you go?'

Larsen sat down and folded her hands together on the desktop. 'He's a pompous bastard who drinks his own bathwater. Happy to glory in his affluence. But he painted himself into a corner when he skited about coming from modest roots and being a self-made man. The logical next question was the source of his apparent wealth.'

Holmes leaned back in his chair, hands behind his head, exposing large patches of sweat-stained shirt under his arms and down his sides. 'That boat has to be worth at least a mill on its own.'

Small remained standing, his back against the wall. 'He boasted that he owns it outright. No credit. His house in Warrnambool is a mansion, and he owns the stately old home where his practice is based as well.'

'Did he explain where he gets his money?'

'Successful practice in a highly profitable speciality,' Larsen replied. 'And when we started digging, he was quick to add that his wife is a GP and does anaesthetics at the hospital.'

'Still love to see his tax records,' Holmes said with a grin. 'You reckon he's got another source of income, don't you?'

'Yeah, I do,' Larsen replied. 'I kept pushing him about that, and then out of the blue, he remembered he'd had a few big wins on the ponies. I reckon that's rubbish. He's worried about us digging into the real reason he took his boat out that night in such shitty weather.'

'I'm booked in to see him tomorrow about this bloody knee.' Holmes smiled. 'Total coincidence, but I'll use it as a chance to suss him out.'

'Are you going to tell him you're a detective?' Small asked.

Holmes's smile widened. 'Not unless I need to.'

* * *

After Small had left for other duties, Holmes updated Larsen concerning Katy Flynn's appearance at the wharf, or at least the presence of her car on that fateful night. He then passed across the phone records he had perused earlier in the day. After carefully reading the first two pages, Larsen looked up at her partner.

'Norton seems legit, but Symons has been telling porkies.'

'Absolutely. She's hiding something.'

Larsen nodded and turned to page three. 'Burners,' she said without looking up.

'Yeah. Three of them.'

Larsen took out her mobile.

Holmes leaned forward urgently. 'Don't ring them until we get this sorted,' he said.

'I'm not ringing anyone. I need a calendar.'

Holmes was intrigued but said nothing as Larsen used a biro to notate calls on the printout in front of her. Attention to detail was Larsen's strength. She'd broken open a case in Benalla by finding inconsistencies in documents that he and Bowker had both missed. After five or six minutes, Larsen put down her pen and phone. She turned the printout 180 degrees so Holmes could read it.

'There is no overall pattern in the timing of the calls between the burners,' Larsen explained. 'Random days of the week and random times of the day. However, there are some days when there is a concentration of calls between all three phones.' She pointed to the printout, where she had circled these clusters. 'I've checked these busy dates against my calendar, and guess what? They're all Fridays.'

Holmes looked at her, puzzled. 'Every Friday?'

Larsen shook her head. 'Nope. At first, they look random. But that's not totally accurate. There's a pattern. For a start, there are never two consecutive Fridays.'

'So where's the pattern?'

Larsen picked up her pen and pointed to a circle she'd drawn towards the top of the page. 'The printout goes back about six months. Let's call this circled Friday number one. We'll then number each successive Friday two, three, four, five and so on until we get to the present. If we check which Fridays the hives of phone activity happened on, we find they are on weeks one, five, eleven, fifteen, nineteen, twenty-three, twenty-seven. Then, for the last week or so, there has been a flurry of calls between the two burners whose owners remain unknown to us.' Larsen looked up at Holmes. 'What do you see in these patterns?'

Holmes was the first to admit that he lagged a mile behind Larsen in all things mathematical. She was a whiz in these subjects at school and had used her high grades to study medicine at Melbourne University before deciding to change careers in her fifth year.

He looked at the numbers in front of him. 'Well, for a start, Friday number twenty-seven was the date Flynn was murdered. I suspect the flurry of calls in the time since relate to the events that night and the investigation we're conducting. And, obviously, the reason only two phones are now involved is because the burner on which Flynn called Symons is in the guts of a shark somewhere.'

Larsen nodded. 'Spot on. But what other pattern do you see in the Fridays where the peak activity took place?'

'They're all odd numbers, obviously,' Holmes replied. 'Never an even number.' He smiled, knowing he was defeated. 'OK, Einstein, tell me.'

Larsen was determined Holmes find the answer himself, even if she had to give him clues. 'Who are you seeing about your knee this Friday? Which, of course, will be our Friday number twenty-nine?'

'Matheson, the orthopod.' Holmes smiled as the light bulb came on. 'And he was in Port Fairy on Friday number twenty-seven, when his boat went out in the wild weather.' He smiled even wider. 'And since he only comes over from Warrnambool every second Friday, all his visits would have been on the odd-numbered Fridays.'

Larsen's eyes sparkled. 'Exactly. He would have been in Port Fairy on every one of those Fridays when that little burner network exploded into life, and his boat would have been available for extracurricular activities.'

The grin left Holmes's face as he began to think through the possibilities. 'Could be a coincidence. Correlation doesn't prove causation. Just because he was in town doesn't prove he was part of whatever clandestine schemes were afoot. It doesn't prove his boat was being used for any illegal activity. Doesn't prove he even put to sea.'

Larsen was having none of it. 'Come on, Darren. The pattern is too neat.'

Holmes tapped the printout with his index finger. 'We don't even know who owns these two burners. They may have nothing to do with Matheson.'

Larsen sat back in her chair as a plan formulated in her brain. 'What time is your appointment with Matheson on Friday?'

'Two forty. Why?'

'How about I call each of the burners while you're in with him? I'll ring twice. The first will be very short so there's no time to answer. Then I'll ring again. If you hear that pattern, you'll know he owns one of those mobiles.'

Holmes mulled the idea for a moment. 'Even if he owns one, he may not carry it with him.'

Larsen shrugged. 'Then we've lost nothing, have we?'

Holmes beamed, and for the moment, he forgot his suspicions regarding Kirsten and Constable Small. 'You're more than just a pretty face,' he said.

* * *

Dinner that night at the Lemongrass Thai restaurant in Bank Street was a tasty feast in friendly surrounds. Holmes took his time before mentioning Dale Small. 'How'd the young constable go with Matheson?'

Larsen remained straight-faced. 'Good. Asked intelligent questions and didn't get in the way when I was following a particular line of inquiry. He's got a good career in front of him,

I think. It's early days, of course, but he has a detective's instinct.'

As long as it's not in Homicide, Holmes thought. 'That's good to hear. Sort of balances out Farrell,' he said with a laugh. 'What did you do for lunch?' he added as casually as he could.

Larsen hesitated for a moment, knowing this had the potential to ruffle feathers. 'Katy Flynn's house is just a few streets from Dale's place, so he suggested we go there, where he made me a sandwich and iced coffee.'

Holmes nodded, remaining po-faced but with his stomach churning. He feigned a chuckle. 'I had a toastie with black tea at The Hub as I limped back from the hospital.'

Nothing was said for a good minute as they both scanned the dessert menu without reading a word. Finally, Holmes broke the silence. 'It'll be good to have a few days back in Melbourne over the weekend. A bit of distance between us and the case might give us a clearer view of where we're at with the investigation.'

Larsen looked up from her menu, puzzled. 'This weekend in Melbourne?' she asked, wracking her brain for what she'd forgotten.

'It's my ex-mother-in-law's seventieth,' Holmes replied quickly. 'Remember? When I mentioned it, you said it sounded like a good night to check out the latest movies.'

Larsen nodded slowly. 'Yeah, I remember that, but I didn't realise it was this weekend.' She hesitated. 'I assumed we'd still be down here. Dale has asked me to go surfing with him on Saturday afternoon. Before lunch today, he showed me what the locals call the Passage Break, where most of the serious surfers go.'

Holmes nodded. Several moments of tense silence passed before he overrode his jealousy and opted to follow Bowker's advice. Demanding she stay away from Small would end their relationship, while skipping his Melbourne event would be equally damaging. *Go with the flow*, he told himself.

He looked into Larsen's eyes and smiled weakly. 'Well, that works out for both of us,' he said unconvincingly. 'It would be silly for you to go all that way only to be left on your own. And it saves me feeling guilty about you having done that for me. I'm sure developing your surfing skills will be more fun than sitting on your own in a cinema.' He was quiet for a moment. 'You're still welcome to come with me to the party, if you want,' he added, it sounding almost like a plea.

Larsen shook her head vigorously. 'The scarlet woman who took the golden-haired boy from the daughter? I don't think so.'

Holmes knew that was fair enough, so he took a deep breath and looked down at his menu. 'What do you fancy for dessert?'

Larsen reached across the table and took Holmes's hands in hers. 'How about we skip dessert and have an early night?' She winked. 'What do you reckon?'

Holmes smiled. 'I'm a bit of a cripple these days.'

'There's more than one way of skinning a cat,' Larsen replied, rubbing her foot against his calf.

Holmes's smile widened, but deep down, he questioned whether her suggestion was a way of assuring him that he was still her man, or merely a means of temporarily diffusing a tricky situation they would eventually need to confront.

CHAPTER 25

The calm and sunny weather of the day before was nowhere to be seen on Friday morning. The sky was overcast, with misty rain carried in on the southerly breeze. Gulls screeched, jumping in and out of the motel's open rubbish skip as Holmes threw his crutches on the back seat of their vehicle and clambered into the passenger seat. Yesterday's struggle with the crutches convinced him to dispense with his suit in favour of more casual attire. A navy-blue tracksuit over a tee-shirt and a pair of cross trainers still gave him an air of respectability. Larsen wore her shiny black leggings, a pink blouse and a charcoal-grey overcoat that matched her stilettos. Holmes's heart fluttered as he watched her climb behind the steering wheel, at the same time praying that Small was not on duty today.

Holmes had read the latest forensic report received by email around seven thirty that morning but waited until they were at the station and both had a hard copy in front of them before analysing its contents.

'So, they found minute traces of Flynn's blood on the knife,' Larsen said, thinking aloud as she read.

Holmes smiled and nodded. 'By the lengths someone took to get rid of it, I say we've identified the murder weapon.'

'Agreed. The size of the bloodstain on the parka suggests more than just a flesh wound, that's for sure.'

'No prints on the knife, unfortunately. Fast-flowing salty water is perhaps the worst environment to preserve fingerprints, but you'd expect something, given the weapon was wrapped up in the parka.'

Larsen leaned back in her chair. 'My bet is that it was wiped clean of prints before it was heaved in the river.'

The rest of the report was technical data and provided nothing that would progress their investigation. The bluestone used as a weight was analysed and assessed as common to the area. It was of no help.

'Where to from here?' Larsen asked.

Holmes folded his arms across his chest and thought for a moment. 'To tell you the truth, Kirsten, I'm sick of piss-farting around the edges of this case. I think we need to stir the pot a bit. See what rats we can shake from the nest.'

Larsen smiled. 'Go on.'

Holmes unfolded his arms and picked up the document in front of him. 'This report, plus the movement of Matheson's boat that night, plus our suspicions about drug running, give us enough reason to come down heavy on some of these bastards.' He thought for a moment as he replaced the report on the desk. 'I'm requesting a full forensic search of the *Hippocrates* boat plus a drug squad raid on the Barbarians' compound.'

'That'll send a few sparks flying,' Larsen said with a grin.

'And hopefully some arses will catch fire in the process.'

The grin left Larsen's face. 'As long as they're not ours.'

* * *

That afternoon, Larsen watched Holmes limp across the footpath and into the medical clinic for his appointment with Gareth

Matheson. The plan was simple. After confirming his attendance with the receptionist, Holmes would take a seat in the waiting room near the window, where Larsen could see him from their vehicle outside. When called for his appointment, Holmes would stand and pause for a moment or two as a signal that he was about to enter Matheson's consulting room. Larsen would wait five minutes to allow Holmes time to settle in, before calling one of the burner numbers she had written in the notebook on her knee. She would hang up quickly, then call again and let the phone ring out. That same process would be followed with the second number. With an ounce of luck, the detectives would confirm Matheson as the owner of one of the phones, and with a ton of good fortune, the owner of the other phone might identify themselves as well.

At two fifty, Holmes hadn't moved, and it was obvious that Matheson was running late. *Thank God our plan wasn't based on the clock*, Larsen thought.

Precisely at three o'clock, Matheson appeared from a corridor and called Darren Holmes for his appointment. The surgeon made no attempt to introduce himself and led Holmes into a windowless room in the centre of the building. The detective placed his crutches on the floor beside a chair, where he sat down. He looked Matheson up and down and mentally complimented Larsen on her description of the man. A stocky but overweight, up-himself wanker summed him up perfectly.

Inwardly, Holmes was smiling. Outwardly, he was the very model of a nervous patient.

Matheson consulted the details on his computer screen. 'Mr Darren Holmes, forty-nine years old, injured your knee in a fall. Correct, Mr Holmes?'

Holmes nodded. 'Yeah. Slipped on a child's ice cream.'

Matheson raised his eyebrows with an air of disinterest. 'I assume the injury will impact your work and you'll require a certificate as well as a remedy? What do you do for a living?'

'Humble public servant, Doctor,' Holmes replied, stretching the truth to breaking point. 'Just got into Port Fairy with the family on our annual holiday.'

'Unfortunate timing,' Matheson said dispassionately. 'And I'm a surgeon, so my title is Mister, not Doctor.'

More like Wanker, Holmes thought. 'Sorry. I didn't know that,' he said quietly.

'Well, you'll know next time, then,' Matheson replied. He looked down at Holmes's leg. 'Pull up your tracksuit and indicate where you feel the most pain.'

Holmes did as requested and indicated a spot on the inside of his knee. Matheson asked him to flex his leg and identify when it hurt most. Again, Holmes complied.

Matheson turned back towards his desk and began typing. 'You more than likely have a torn meniscus on the inside of your knee,' he said. 'We'll do an arthroscope in Warrnambool to assess the injury, and it's likely I can repair any damage while I'm in there. Usually, it only involves trimming the torn bits of cartilage. At your age, I wouldn't expect you play any top-grade sport, so anything more than a tidy-up won't be necessary.' He stopped typing, ticked a few boxes on an A5 sheet and handed it to Holmes. 'Take this to reception, and they'll make an appointment for you in Warrnambool. Just day surgery, but you will be given a light general anaesthetic. You'll need to have someone drive you home after your scope.' He nodded at Holmes, assuming he would stand and leave.

Holmes looked at the clock on the far wall and realised barely five minutes had passed since he'd left the waiting room. He needed to stall until he could be sure the burner phone didn't belong to Matheson, or at least that it wasn't with him.

'I don't need an MRI?' Holmes asked. 'A mate of mine said his son needed one after he hurt his knee playing football.'

'He probably had ligament damage, which you haven't got.' Matheson looked at his screen. 'Your GP said the knee is stable, so I think we can be fairly sure it's just a cartilage. But to put your mind at rest, I do check the ligaments with the scope, so I won't miss anything.' He stood to move things along.

'Just one last thing,' Holmes said, without a question readily in mind. He managed to continue after a hesitation. 'If you remove my cartilage, will I end up with bone on bone and suffer from arthritis in my older years?'

As Matheson was about to answer, a mobile phone sounded but stopped after a few seconds before ringing again. Holmes feigned searching his pockets until he pulled out his own mobile. 'Not mine,' he said before nodding at Matheson's iPhone sitting on his desk. 'It's not yours, either.' He pointed to a coat stand in the corner of the room. 'Is it in your jacket over there?'

Matheson was clearly flustered and tried feebly to explain. 'That's my private phone. I don't want patients interfering with leisure time by ringing my practice number.'

Holmes stood up and limped to the coat. He removed the still-ringing mobile and put it to his ear.

Matheson was in a panic. 'What the hell are you doing?' He stood up and stormed towards the detective but was stopped in his tracks by Holmes holding up his ID.

'Senior Constable Larsen?' Holmes asked theatrically into the phone. He then laughed out loud as Matheson slumped back into his chair. 'How the hell did you get me on this number?' he continued, his tongue firmly planted in his cheek.

Holmes heard a self-satisfied chuckle on the other end of the call. 'I rang the other burner first with no answer,' Larsen explained. 'But looks like we hit the jackpot with this one.'

'Yeah. Be out in a couple of minutes.' Holmes hit the disconnect button and slipped the phone into his tracksuit pocket.

Matheson decided attack was the best form of defence. 'This is a gross invasion of my privacy.'

'Invasion of privacy should be the least of your worries, *Mister* Matheson,' Holmes said as he crossed the room and resumed his seat. 'Your biggest worry should be explaining why you own a pay-as-you-go phone that has documented contacts with only two other phones, one of which belonged to Trevor Flynn.'

'He was my brother-in-law, for God's sake,' Matheson replied nervously. 'And I used it occasionally to contact my sister.'

Holmes feigned a chuckle. 'You don't expect me to believe that bullshit, surely?'

'Well, it's the truth.'

'Who's the other burner belong to?'

Matheson looked puzzled. 'Burner?' he asked.

'The other pay-as-you-go mobile that you ring and receive calls from, particularly on certain Fridays.'

'I really don't know what you're on about here, Detective,' Matheson replied before attempting to change tack. 'Have you really injured your knee, or is this just some sort of sting? Some sort of entrapment when your investigations have come up short?'

Holmes smiled. 'Unfortunately, I *have* done my knee, and I thank you for your diagnosis.' He laughed. 'Nothing personal, but at this stage I don't think I'll take advantage of your professional services, especially if your wife administers the anaesthetic.'

Matheson didn't reply.

'This is what will happen from here, Mr Matheson. Your

orthopaedic work is probably done for today. You'll be taken down to the station to be formally interviewed.'

'Formally interviewed about what?' Matheson spat back. 'The fact that I carry a second mobile phone that can be linked to my brother-in-law?' He rolled his eyes. 'High-powered stuff.'

Holmes stood up and put his hands on his hips. 'We have several witnesses who place your boat at the murder scene around the time we suspect Flynn was killed. We also have a member of the Barbarians Motorcycle Club collecting a haversack and departing the same scene. When all this is happening, the weather is diabolical, and the wharf is the last place any sensible person would choose to be. And yet, here we have your boat going to sea in conditions that made docking almost impossible when you returned, and we have a motorcyclist attending that location and collecting some sort of consignment. Something valuable, one would suspect, given the circumstances faced.'

Matheson remained po-faced but increasingly aggressive. 'So, besides my second phone, all you have is that I took my boat out for a run that night. Somehow, in your tiny mind, this adds up to some sort of major crime.'

Holmes leaned over so he was in Matheson's face. 'If something walks like a fucking duck and quacks like a fucking duck, it usually is a fucking duck.' He stood up straight again. 'My theory is that on certain Fridays, you take your boat out to sea, meet a drug supplier and bring the gear back to be distributed by your bikie friends. I reckon your brother-in-law was one of the kingpins in the operation, judging by the cash he threw around buying land and flash cars. And while being a surgeon is probably a lucrative profession, it doesn't buy you one of the most expensive houses in Warrnambool, the building where your practice is situated, and a boat like *Hippocrates.* All that must add up to millions. And you boasted to my officers that you owned everything outright and received no inheritance. Stand up, please, *Mister* Matheson, and kindly accompany me to the local police station to make a statement. You can tell the receptionist to put your patients on hold until we decide when, or if, you'll be back today.'

'This is all just a fairy tale you have made up, Detective,' Matheson said as he climbed to his feet. 'Just one big fabrication to deflect attention away from your police mate killing Trevor in a fit of rage.'

Holmes bent down and picked up his crutches before placing them under his armpits. He eyeballed the surgeon. 'Flynn was killed on the wharf while all this action was occurring around your boat. And to give you a little incentive to tell us the truth when we sit down at the station, I should inform you that a forensic team is already going over your boat with a fine-tooth comb. Providing them with a key to access its internal spaces would save them splintering a door to gain access.'

Matheson exhaled loudly as he picked up a bunch of keys from his desk and removed the one for his boat. 'They won't find anything untoward, I'll guarantee that. Just tell them to be careful not to damage anything.' He handed the key to Holmes.

The detective nodded as he pocketed it. 'Oh, and another thing that might convince you to tell us the whole truth.' He stared into Matheson's face, looking for a tell. 'Police divers recovered a kitchen knife wrapped in a parka and weighted down with a rock. Blood on the knife and the parka was matched to your brother-in-law. And the neat little parcel was found right under where your boat is moored.'

Matheson tried hard to act cool, but a detective of Holmes's experience clearly spotted a tiny flinch in the left corner of his mouth.

CHAPTER 26

A long and exhaustive interview with Matheson gleaned little more than what Holmes had uncovered in their discussion at the clinic. Opting for consistency above believability, Matheson wasn't budging on his earlier explanations around the source of his wealth, the purpose of the burner phone, or his use of his boat on the night Flynn was killed. But the detectives were certain that Matheson and his brother-in-law were in league with the Barbarians in the importation and distribution of illicit drugs. At present, they had insufficient evidence to charge the surgeon but hoped the forensic sweep of his vessel might provide something concrete to support their suspicions. Matheson was fingerprinted, for elimination purposes with regard to his boat, he was told. He was subsequently released, pending further investigation. Constable Farrell volunteered to ferry him back.

In terms of solving Flynn's murder, they were no closer to identifying the killer. Was it Matheson himself, or Skeeta Allender, who picked up the haversack, or maybe even Flynn's wife, who they now believed had attended the wharf around the time Matheson's boat had berthed?

By the time the detectives visited the wharf in the late afternoon, the cloud had cleared. The wind was still cool, but the sun made conditions pleasant by the river. Sparkling ripplets danced on the surface of the Moyne with the tide on the turn. Various species of sea bird adorned the bollards, a pelican taking pride of place in front of the restaurant. The whole area was teeming with pedestrians, the odd family dipping lines at various points along the wooden wharf, with none having much luck, judging by the empty buckets sitting by their seats. Holmes smiled as he recalled fishing in the Murray with his father, the exercise being more about expectation and hours of relaxation with his dad than it was about actually hooking a fish. Those were simpler days.

The forensic team were in the process of packing up among a crowd of rubberneckers. Holmes discarded his crutches and stepped aboard *Hippocrates*, flashing his ID to a pair of technicians in white Tyvek coveralls, complete with hood and boots. He was impressed. It had been a fortnight since the murder, and much of the boat had been exposed to the weather in that time. It was hardly a pristine crime scene, but the team was treating the job with their normal professionalism.

'The boss is below deck if you're chasing her,' the younger of the techs volunteered as he packed gear into a metal box.

Holmes nodded. 'Do we need to don gloves and shoe covers?'

'Not anymore. We've been over the vessel inside and out, and we're about finished. Carolyn is just doing a final check.'

The second technician stood up, preparing to tote an evidence case back to their van. 'You missed all the action. A bloody big tiger shark came cruising up the river. Bold as brass. Had to be four or five metres long.'

His mate laughed. 'Gave the tourists something to talk about other than us screening the boat.'

'So is the shark still in the river?' Holmes asked.

The younger tech shook his head. 'Nah. Turned around and

headed back towards the sea. Apparently, cops in the divi van cleared the beach until they were sure he wasn't heading that way.'

I hope he's still around tomorrow so Kirsten's surfing date gets called off, Holmes thought.

'I wonder if he's the same one that savaged Trevor Flynn's body?' Larsen asked without expecting an answer.

Hippocrates was such a large vessel that it hardly moved when the detectives walked into an expansive glassed dining and lounge room. The area was lavishly furnished with a large table and an array of comfortable chairs. The main cockpit at the front overlooked the foredeck and the bow of the vessel. Above this room was a sundeck and a second cockpit used for piloting the vessel in fair weather. Below were sleeping quarters.

Carolyn Walters, the forensic team leader, sat in the captain's swivel chair scribbling notes on a series of proformas. Her hood was down, revealing an attractive woman in her thirties, so unlike the stereotypical female scientists portrayed in movies. For a start, she didn't wear thick lens glasses, and there was no sign of a Marie Curie bun in the back of her hair.

'Can we have a word, skipper?' Holmes said with a grin as he held out his ID.

Walters smiled. 'I wish I *was* the skipper, Detective.' She mimed rotating the boat's steering wheel. 'I could go for one of these.'

'Couldn't we all,' Larsen replied before introducing herself.

'Have you found anything useful?' Holmes asked.

Walters leaned back in the swivel chair and placed her pen atop the paperwork. 'Well, for a start, everything seems to have been washed clean with a bleach solution. Especially outside on the rear deck. Even after all the shitty weather since the murder, there are still traces of bleach. And there's hardly a fingerprint to be found on the entire vessel.'

'So we've either got a boat owner with an obsessive cleanliness disorder or one who is going to great lengths to hide something.'

'I'd say the latter.' Walters smiled smugly. 'But they missed something. Under a little moulded fibreglass flange on the deck outside, we found a bloodied fingerprint. It would appear someone placed a hand on the flange and one of their fingers curled underneath. It wasn't visible unless you got down on your hands and knees, which obviously the cleaner didn't.'

'Two clues, then,' Larsen said. 'The blood and the print.'

'Yep. Could be from the same person, or the print could belong to someone who contacted another person's blood. We took some high-res digital images of the print before scraping the blood off for DNA testing.' She shrugged. 'Can't get too excited yet, though. The blood may belong to a fish.'

'The boat hasn't left its moorings since the night of the killing,' Larsen advised, 'so I doubt there'd be too many fish hauled aboard.'

'How old was the blood?' Holmes asked.

Walters shrugged again. 'Bit hard to tell with the gear we have here and the small sample size, but by the ease of its removal, I suspect it wouldn't be much older than a week or two.'

'Was there anything else that piqued your interest?' Holmes asked.

Walters shook her head. 'Nothing as obvious as the bloodied fingerprint. But until we return to the lab, we won't know for sure. We wiped as many of the surfaces as we could and vacuumed the fabric cushions around this room and out on deck. Something useful might come up under the microscope.'

Holmes scratched his cheek. 'Can I suggest you keep an eye out for evidence tying the vessel to illicit drugs?'

'I don't do the analysis,' Walters replied. 'But the protocols include testing for illicit substances.'

Holmes thanked Walters for her summary and wished her team a safe journey home. Larsen followed him aft towards the exit door. As they passed a series of photographs screwed to the pillars between the glass windows, Larsen stopped suddenly. She grabbed Holmes by the arm and dragged him back. She tapped a photo featuring Matheson and his sister Katy Flynn.

'Recognise the parka Matheson is wearing?' she asked.

Holmes smiled. 'Too right I do.'

* * *

Stepping off *Hippocrates,* Holmes spotted a familiar face twenty metres away sitting on one of the low fences that divided a line of million-dollar houses from the wharf itself.

'What's the go?' Holmes asked as he approached on his crutches.

'Just squeezing in a bit of sightseeing while I'm in town,' Bowker replied with a half-smile. 'What'd you do to yourself?'

'Slipped on a kid's bloody ice cream. Torn meniscus, according to the doc.'

Bowker and Larsen exchanged nods. 'Left for you to carry things, Kirsten,' he said with a grin.

'As always,' she replied, smiling.

Bowker stood up, put his hands in his pockets and looked at Holmes. 'Forensics find much?'

'A bloodied fingerprint was the main thing. The whole vessel has been scrubbed clean, which says something in itself.'

'You put that together with Matheson taking the boat out that night and Skeeta picking up a bag, and you get what? A drug deal gone wrong?'

'That's the theory at the moment. We've recently discovered that Flynn's missus was there as well, which adds another dimension.'

Bowker looked at Larsen but waited for a young couple to pass before speaking. 'You agree with Sherlock?'

Larsen put her hands on her hips, conscious that their discussion with Bowker was not kosher in terms of police procedure. 'We're a team, Greg,' she replied with a half-smile. 'We walk in lock step.' She looked at Holmes. 'Fancy a piece of fish and a few chips? I'm starving.'

Holmes endorsed the plan and watched Larsen walk back towards the restaurant. Bowker suspected she was uncomfortable with their conversation, particularly in public view, but said nothing of that to his old partner. 'What's on for the weekend?' he asked instead.

'Heading back to Melbourne. It's my ex-mother-in-law's seventieth birthday. We always got on well, and she wanted me to share in the celebrations, especially when my kids will be there.'

Bowker waved away a fly. 'Should be a nice distraction from the case.'

'I don't really want to go, but I'm trapped between a rock and a hard place. Kirsten's staying down here to go surfing with Dale Small. How does a bloke relax when all he can think about is his girlfriend in a string bikini frolicking in the surf with a bloke who puts Mr Universe to shame? I could always pull the pin on the reunion, say I can't drive because of my knee, but Kirsten would claim I don't trust her.'

'*Do* you trust her?' Bowker shot back quickly.

'Yeah, I do. But unexpected things happen, you know. Do I think Kirsten is planning to get it on with Small? No I don't. Do I think that one thing can lead to another? Yes I do.'

Bowker took his hands from his pockets. 'Kirsten is putting her trust in you. I presume Cassie will be at her mother's party.'

'Different thing altogether, mate,' Holmes replied, brushing off any possibility of a reunion with his former wife.

'And if you decide to stay in Port Fairy, what are you going to do? Sneak down to the beach with a set of binoculars?'

Holmes could see Bowker's point and decided to let the matter drop. 'What about you? Heading back to the city?'

'No, staying here. Rachael's coming down for the weekend, so it should be fun.' He patted Holmes on the arm. 'Well, I might grab some fish and chips myself and head home. I've had my excitement for the day.'

Holmes smiled. 'The real excitement will happen tonight at the Barbarians' compound. Drug squad. Full-scale raid.'

* * *

Stars shone like diamonds in the clear black sky. Small waves lapped the sand on East Beach. At two o'clock, the town was peaceful as the three police vans moved quietly down the ocean-side street, lights turned off and engines barely idling. They parked outside the Barbarians clubhouse before each vehicle disgorged officers in black protective gear, one carrying bolt cutters and another a battering ram. Two sniffer dogs quietly jumped from the third van and followed their handlers in a purposeful and disciplined fashion.

The bikie compound was in complete darkness as an officer used heavy-duty bolt cutters to remove the large padlock securing the main gate. With the enclosure now open, drug squad officers slipped inside, passing the line of motorcycles parked under the skillion shelter. Both sniffer dogs became silently animated and zeroed in on the Harley Davidson with the eagle painted on the fuel tank. As the team approached the main entry door of the clubhouse, security lights snapped on, illuminating the compound. Inside the building, an angry dog barked and growled, and within seconds, windows lit up as the occupants roused from their sleep.

'Open the door!' the team commander yelled. 'This is the police! There are eighteen armed officers surrounding the building.'

There was no response from inside, except from the dog, now in a fit of uncontrolled fury, and the general hubbub of voices as the gang tried to assess their options while still half asleep.

'You've got thirty seconds to open the door before we break it down!' the lead officer yelled. 'And secure that dog, otherwise it will be shot dead.'

He signalled for an officer to bring forward the battering ram, a solid metal cylinder with looped handles welded along one side. He also removed a pistol from a side holster and checked it was ready to fire. 'You have fifteen seconds before we splinter this door!'

'Hold your fuckin' horses,' came a voice from inside.

The sound of locks being released preceded the door being slowly opened. The guard dog was snarling, its teeth exposed, but held securely on a leash. Inside were a dozen scruffy, mostly overweight males in various states of undress, along with an equal number of women similarly attired.

Jason McCulloch confronted the officer in charge. 'What the fuck's this all about?'

The officer showed his ID. 'I'm Senior Sergeant Gerard Drummond of the drug squad.' He then removed a document from his trouser pocket, unfolded it and held it where McCulloch could see. 'This is authorisation for this raid to be conducted. We have reason to believe that drugs are being trafficked through this building and distributed throughout Victoria and interstate by this club.'

McCulloch feigned a laugh. 'Drugs!' he exclaimed loudly. 'Be our guest and search the premises, Sergeant, but you won't find anything illegal here.'

By this stage, the sniffer dogs were spinning in circles, eager to be released. Drummond ordered the occupants to one end of the large hall while his officers went to work. Once set free, the sniffer dogs guided their handlers from one area to another, and although no caches of drugs were found, the officers held no doubt that they had passed through the building. Every site that excited the dogs was wiped with a sterile swab to sample any residues.

'Who owns the Peter Fonda Harley with the eagle and snake on the fuel tank?' Drummond asked McCulloch as the gang huddled together, wondering how much they would get away with.

'Rooter!' McCulloch yelled. 'Elliot Ness would like a word with you.'

Allender made his way to Drummond, who asked if he was the owner of the Harley.

Allender nodded. 'Yeah, so what?' he replied. 'It's not for sale,' he added in a failed attempt at humour.

'Just advising you that our dogs were all over that motorcycle. Is there anything you'd like to disclose before our guys examine it?'

'I brought back an order of burgers from the servo tonight,' Allender replied unconvincingly. 'They probably smelt that.'

Drummond walked away, shaking his head, but with a big smile on his face.

CHAPTER 27

Saturday dawned warm and sunny, the exact opposite of the weather Holmes was praying for. A cold, wet and windy day would have made surfing almost impossible and deemed a bikini inappropriate, even if a wetsuit was to be worn over the top. On the other hand, if Kirsten and Small had something in mind, being forced indoors was likely a worse outcome than a romp in the surf.

Holmes departed Port Fairy, leaving himself ample time to reach the Richmond pub by the start of the birthday festivities. But the drive east accelerated the fermentation of his suspicions. Just short of Colac, his jealousy finally subsumed his common sense. A semitrailer narrowly avoiding his sudden U-turn across the busy highway was the first indication he was not thinking clearly. His oft-quoted level-headedness was not in play today.

A quick drive through the Old Passage carpark failed to locate Small's van. The sky was cobalt blue, the sea turquoise as monster waves boomed beyond the bluestone shoreline. A dozen surfers were in action, but even to the detective's untrained eye, the conditions seemed too treacherous for a learner like Kirsten.

His next stop was East Beach, where the shallower waters would temper the ferocity of the surf. He spotted Small's van at the end of the crowded carpark, and unable to find a vacant space, he took a chance and parked in the driveway of one of the adjacent multimillion-dollar mansions. *It'd be best if the owners are away, but what the hell, I'm a policeman*, he thought, *and this is an emergency.* He walked to the edge of the bouldered retaining wall and surveyed the beach below. It seemed like a thousand people were in the water, a few in wetsuits but mainly kids in the early stages of their surfing journey. He saw no sign of the blond locks of either Small or Kirsten. He limped down the ramp to the sand and wandered along the beach, surveying those sitting on towels or playing cricket, oblivious to how silly he looked in his formal clothes.

After ten minutes, he abandoned his search, even more agitated than when he arrived in town. As he passed by Small's van, he glanced through a side window to where a bikini-clad Kirsten was lying on the carpeted floor in an urgent, groping embrace with the golden-speedoed Small. In a fit of jealous rage, the detective thumped his fists against the window.

Larsen sat bolt upright in bed, torn from her heavy sleep by Holmes's hands flailing against her. 'Wake up, Darren,' she said, putting a hand on her partner's shoulder, shaking him from his nightmare.

* * *

Bowker's wife arrived earlier than expected on Saturday morning and caught him with eyes closed, half asleep on a banana lounge in the shade of the peach tree. She approached him quietly, removed the open Jane Harper novel from his chest, and kissed him lightly on the lips. He awoke from his slumber with a smile on his face and threw his arms around her, pulling her down on top of him and hugging her tightly.

'How did you know it was me?' Rachael asked as she kissed him again.

'Who else is going to pash this ugly face?'

'For all I know, you may have found another squeeze down here,' Rachael replied jokingly as she climbed to her feet.

Bowker sat up and swung his legs to the side, leaving room for his wife to sit beside him on the lounge. Following a few snippets of hometown news from Melbourne, Bowker brought Rachael up to date with the Flynn case, or what he knew of it, anyway. At the end of his spiel, Rachael shuffled sideways so she could look directly into his eyes.

'It's time to come home, Greg. You've accomplished what you set out to do down here.'

Bowker was surprised by her directness. 'I'm just protecting my arse. I'm still a persona non grata to most of the locals. Ask anyone in town and they'll tell you I killed Trevor. That's in spite of any evidence to the contrary. Until Sherlock nails the real killer, I'd like to be close enough to make my own observations and put out my side of things if it looks like I'm in the gun.'

'From what you've just said, Darren has dismissed you as a suspect and has a couple of others in his sights.' She put her hands on her husband's shoulders and took a deep breath. 'Besides, you're not really down here to protect yourself from prosecution, are you? You're down here to protect me.'

Bowker feigned surprise. 'Sorry, I'm not with you, Rach.'

'You didn't kill Trevor, and as a senior detective, you knew the circumstantial evidence linking you to his death would never support a charge. And we both know Darren is too good a cop to let that happen, anyway. You're camped down here ready to take the rap if it was me who knifed Trevor.' She stared at him for a few long seconds. 'Why didn't you just ask me if I'd done it and avoid all of this bullshit? And just for the record, I didn't attack anybody.'

With her palms still on his shoulders, Bowker gently placed his hands around her wrists. 'Also for the record,' he said, 'I've never believed you killed him. But to ask you for confirmation would have implied I thought you capable of doing something like that.'

Rachael frowned. 'But despite all that, you still came down here to cover that possibility. Remember your case involving the young policeman who hid his family's involvement in a murder? At the time, I asked if you'd ever break your police ethics to do something similar, and you said you'd do it in a heartbeat to protect me.'

Bowker lifted both her hands off his shoulders and held them in his own. 'There's one thing we need to get straight here, Rach. In no way could I ever conceive you killing someone in cold blood. But I've seen good women terrorised and frightened to the point where they lash out in self-defence and someone dies as a result. I couldn't dismiss the remote possibility that when Flynn grabbed you on the beach, you stuck him with the knife you carried in your bag and he later bled to death on the wharf.' His face contorted. 'There was no way that piece of shit was going to take you down on his way out. Better me in prison than you if there was no other choice.'

They stared into each other's eyes for a few moments before Bowker continued hesitantly. 'How come you've never asked me if *I* killed Trevor?'

Rachael blinked away tears. 'Because I was afraid of what the answer may be. You're the noblest man I've ever met, Greg. But when it comes to me and the kids, there is no limit to where things could lead if you became angry enough.' She sucked in a deep breath. 'And the night you went looking for Trevor… I've never seen you so enraged.'

Bowker rested his forehead against his wife's. 'Well, everything's fine now. As you say, the investigation has moved past us both. I'm only hanging around in case Sherlock needs a sounding board.

Particularly with his personal life.'

Rachael again kissed him gently then sat and listened as her husband explained Holmes's fears concerning his relationship with Larsen.

* * *

When Holmes reached the spot where he had made the U-turn in his early-morning dream, he was strangely tempted to repeat the manoeuvre in real life. But, fearing the same outcome, he ploughed on, hoping ignorance was indeed bliss. He grabbed lunch via the McDonalds drive-thru, convincing himself that a Big Mac was no different than a pub meal of rissoles, salad, chips and a dinner roll. Plus, a diet Coke with his lunch was better for him than the beer he would have ordered at a hotel.

His mind was in three different places as he ate lunch at a table on the foreshore of Lake Colac. His thoughts jumped between Flynn's murder, Kirsten and the young constable, and the upcoming party he wished he could avoid. His ex-mother-in-law had asked him to make a short speech, but he was now forced to concede he would end up winging it, given his scrambled thinking and mind obsessed with young and tanned bodies, pink string bikinis and yellow speedos.

* * *

Larsen spotted Small's van at the far end of the East Beach carpark with two surfboards leaning against its side. The back doors were open, the young officer sitting on the rear bumper sunning himself, today opting for skimpy black speedos. His eyes lit up and he unconsciously licked his lips when he saw Larsen. He smiled widely and climbed to his feet as she walked towards him wearing a tee-shirt with quarter-length sleeves, long baggy shorts and trendy sandals that laced up around her lower calf. She wore a floral-patterned sun hat and carried a multicoloured towelling beach bag with circular cane handles.

'Where's your mate?' Small asked, dispensing with the usual pleasantries.

'He's got a commitment in Melbourne tonight. He'll drive back here tomorrow.'

Small tried desperately to suppress his glee but couldn't disguise the glint in his eye. Larsen spotted it.

Small grabbed the wetsuit folded beside him. 'Well, come on, girl. Get your gear off,' he said, waving his index finger up and down Larsen's shorts and top. 'That surf waits for no one.'

Larsen undid the laces on her sandals and threw them in the back of the van. Small's bottom lip dropped when she removed her shorts and top to reveal a rash vest and bike shorts. 'Where's the pink bikini?' Small asked, the disappointment scrawled on his face.

'Not very practical under a wetsuit,' Larsen replied.

'I thought we might go for a swim after we finished surfing.'

Larsen pointed to the gear she was wearing. 'Perfectly good for a splash around. Besides, you warned me that the bikini wasn't ideal for the surf. There was a danger I could lose part of it in the waves. Remember?'

Small reluctantly agreed, inwardly kicking himself for the smart-arsed, throwaway comment that had now come back to bite him.

* * *

The heavy swell in Bass Strait made surfing conditions along the Victorian coast ideal for both learners and experts depending on the break chosen. East Beach, with its shallow water, normally boasted benign surfing conditions, but today, sets of booming waves broke further out in the deeper water. Most of the experienced surfers were near South Beach battling the monster waves hammering the Old Passage. Small conceded that this break was far too dangerous for a surfer of Larsen's experience, and while her skills were developing at an astonishing rate, he knew tackling the Old Passage was out of the question. Had he been on his own, he would have been there in a flash, but his main mission today didn't involve a surfboard.

After an hour and a half in the surf, Larsen had mastered controlling her balance and found riding a wave into the shallows quite routine. She now experimented with manoeuvring the board and changing direction, albeit with a few wipe-outs along the way. Following two runs where she managed successful cutbacks, Larsen rode a wave until she ran aground in ankle-deep water. She picked up the board, tucked it under one arm and carried it back to where she had left her bag and towel. By the time she had guzzled down a drink, spread out her long beach towel and lain down on her back, Small was towering above her, rivulets of seawater running over his chest and down the front of his wetsuit.

'You had enough already?' he asked. 'Just when you were moving like a real pro out there.'

'Just taking a breather,' Larsen replied, looking up at the young officer's face silhouetted against the bright sun. 'I needed a drink. Might go back out in a few minutes.'

Small picked up his towel, walked downwind and shook away the sand that had accumulated with the freshening breeze. He placed it so that its edge overlapped Larsen's. He lay down on his side, propping his head on his hand and elbow so he was looking straight at Larsen no more than a foot away.

'Nice view from here,' he said with a grin. 'Bikini rather than a wetsuit would make it perfection.'

Larsen didn't react, just closing her eyes and feeling her face cool as a cloud passed over the sun.

'What time is Darren due back tomorrow?' Small asked.

Larsen opened her eyes. 'Sometime in the afternoon, I suspect. Why?'

'No particular reason,' Small replied unconvincingly. 'Do you have any plans for the rest of the afternoon?' he added after a few moments.

The sun came out again, prompting Larsen to knit her fingers and cover her eyes with the backs of her hands. 'Probably just lie here for a while. Then I might go for another surf or have a swim. I'm playing it by ear at the moment. My plan was to spend the evening going through notes on the Flynn case.'

Small laughed. 'All work and no play makes Kirsten a dull girl. Forget work for the weekend and freshen up your mind. The more you mull over telephone calls and knives and parkas, the more confusing it all gets. Best give it a rest for a while and do something to take your mind off the mundane things in life.'

Larsen suspected what Small had in mind but played a straight bat, her hands still covering her eyes. 'That's what I'm doing out there in the surf.'

'Come on, you know what I mean. We're both young and fit and unattached.'

'I'm in a relationship with Darren. End of story.' A cloud passed over the sun and she removed her hands from her face, folding them across her waist.

Small was bewildered by her loyalty to Holmes. 'He's old enough to be your father, Kirsten. Don't waste the best years of your life. You should put your energies into someone more your own age.'

'Someone like you, presumably,' Larsen shot back. 'And when this case wraps up, I'd have lost Darren and be living on my own in Melbourne. And you'll still be back here on the beach, plying your charms on another girl in a bikini.'

'I could always transfer to the city,' Small replied. 'Plenty of beaches close by, and I'm getting a taste for this detective caper.'

Larsen again shielded her eyes as the sun broke from behind the cloud. 'Look, I appreciate the surfing lessons, and you're good company, but–'

Before she could finish, Small leaned over to kiss her on the lips.

* * *

The function room in the Richmond pub was decorated in a style befitting the seventieth birthday milestone. Streamers adorned the walls, and phalanxes of helium balloons reached towards the ceiling from each table. Photos of the guest of honour were posted on a pinboard inside the entrance door, chronicling the life of a woman who had been sent to the educational outpost of Murrayville and had followed the destiny of so many new bloods by marrying a local farmer. Now, nearly fifty years later, and after the death of her husband, she was back in her city birthplace.

Holmes gazed at the face of the pretty twenty-one-year-old who had packed all her belongings and courageously boarded a train to a location and a lifestyle she knew nothing about. He could see where his ex-wife obtained her looks, her eyes, her determination, and her spirit of adventure. His mind wandered as he stood perusing the photographs. The years he and Cassie had spent together, from kindergarten to their marriage, to the birth of their kids, to their separation nearly a year ago, spooled before his eyes in bright technicolour. So much had changed in a few short months.

His reverie was broken by a familiar voice. 'Remembering old times, Daz?'

Holmes turned and saw his ex-wife gazing into his face. She was shorter than him but slim and athletic. Her face was friendly, her eyes sparkling. She wore what women called 'a little black dress', black stockings and high-heeled shoes. His heart missed a beat, but he was unsure whether it was an unconscious sign of attraction, or just an old neuron firing from when things had been good between them.

'You look good, Cass,' he said honestly.

She smiled. 'You too.'

'Still thriving across the ditch?'

'The business is going well, but I miss home, of course.'

Holmes knew his next question was loaded, but he needed to ask it anyway. 'Your boss treating you well? Living up to everything he promised?'

'He's OK. Got himself engaged to a young Kiwi girl who works in the office.' She feigned a smile. 'You know the story.'

Holmes scanned his ex-wife's face, looking for a tell, but didn't see one. Was it just a throwaway line, or a barb aimed at his relationship with Kirsten? He decided to play it straight. 'You plan to keep working over there?'

'The way things stand at the moment, the answer is yes. It's an interesting job, and the pay's good. New Zealand is a cruisy place to live.' She chuckled. 'After you master the accent, that is. Once you realise that when they ask for sex, they're not talking about a roll in the hay.'

Holmes smiled and was about to respond when she continued. 'If there was something here worth coming back to, I'd happily chuck in the job.' She paused for a moment, checking his reaction. 'Don't get me wrong, I love seeing the kids. But they've got their own lives now and don't want me living in their pockets.' She stared into Holmes's eyes then touched him gently on the forearm.

'Anyway. Great to see you again, Daz. No doubt we'll cross paths during the evening.'

She turned and walked away, knowing that her ex-husband was watching her every step.

CHAPTER 28

Larsen threw her arms around Holmes when he arrived back from Melbourne on Sunday just before lunch. Her presence was a bonus for Holmes, who'd worried that she would be off somewhere with Dale Small – in a worse-case scenario, after having spent the night in his bed.

'How'd the birthday party go?' Larsen asked as she led him by the hand from his vehicle and through the door of their motel room.

'Good,' Holmes replied without hesitation. 'My speech went down a treat, and the old girl seemed happy with what I said about her. Obviously, catching up with the kids was great as well.'

'You talk to Cassie?' Larsen asked without a hint of an agenda.

'Of course,' Holmes replied. 'We chatted about what we've both been up to since the separation.' He was careful not to disclose the hints his ex-wife had dropped about a possible reconciliation, hints that had become more transparent with each conversation they had during the course of the party. And there was no way he would reveal the flicker of attraction he still felt for Cass. 'She's flying back to New Zealand tomorrow.'

'Family occasions can often be difficult, so I'm glad it all worked out,' Larsen said, kissing him gently on the cheek. 'Long trip, but well worth the trouble, by the sounds of it.'

Holmes nodded and took Larsen's hand. He sat on the bed and

pulled her down beside him. 'Tell me about your weekend?' he asked, churning inside but keeping his tone as literal as possible.

Larsen smiled and nodded, knowing what her partner's real question was but skirting around the issue. 'It was good. I think my surfing has improved.'

May as well go straight to the nub of my fears, Holmes thought, before choosing a throwaway line as his mode of approach. 'Did you get through the day without Constable Small putting the moves on you?' he asked jovially.

'He wouldn't dare.' Larsen replied, po-faced.

'Really?'

'You seem surprised.'

'He's a man, isn't he? I couldn't blame any bloke for trying it on, really. You in that pink bikini does something to the male psyche.'

'I didn't wear it,' Larsen replied quickly. 'I wore a plain rash jacket with bike shorts.'

Holmes was puzzled. 'How come?'

'Because when I left here, I was determined Dale not get the wrong idea about our afternoon on the beach. Especially when he found out you were in Melbourne.'

Holmes pulled her close and hugged her tightly, now ashamed of his lack of trust and his jealous insecurities.

'So, tell me about the party,' Larsen suggested. 'Who'd you talk to, and what's the goss?'

Holmes shrugged. 'Not much to tell, really. Caught up with a few people. Had a good chat with the kids.' He smiled. 'What about you? Tell me how you filled in the weekend.'

'Nothing to tell. Except for actually riding the waves, it was boring, boring, boring. I was counting down the minutes until you'd be back.'

As Holmes was about to reply, she pointed out the window.

'Look outside. It's a great day for a swim, and the salt water will be good for your knee.'

She walked quickly to her bedside table and removed her pink bikini from the top drawer.

* * *

At seven thirty on Monday morning, Bowker knew O'Meara would be at work and already suffering withdrawal symptoms, having not had a cigarette since she left her car fifteen minutes earlier. He was spot on. O'Meara was at her desk in MacLeod reviewing the weekend's analysis of various cases when her mobile phone rang.

She leaned back in her swivel chair, smiling as she saw Bowker's name displayed on her screen. She had always liked this particular detective. He was a no-nonsense, cut-the-bullshit type of person, like herself. Plus, he was good-looking and built like an AFL footballer. Given different circumstances, she would have been happy to get it on with him, although that thought usually departed quickly when she caught sight of herself in a mirror. Always a picture of ill health and no oil painting even in her younger years, she realised Bowker was out of her league and was happily married to boot. In her quieter moments, she gave thanks for the decades she had spent with her former Painters and Dockers Union partner, who loved her for her intellect and sense of humour. Sadly, he met his death violently in an industrial dispute, but was on his way out anyway, thanks to the cancer sticks she knew would take her down the same path in the not-too-distant future.

'Gregory Bowker,' O'Meara said cheerfully. 'What are you doing up at this time of morning when I believe you're still on leave?'

Bowker chuckled. 'Rachael's been down at Port Fairy with me for the weekend. Just waved her off back to Melbourne.'

'It's a wonder you've got the strength left to make this call.'

'Come on, Erin, I'm getting a bit long in the tooth for that sort of thing.' Bowker chuckled again. 'All weekend, anyway.'

'And now you're looking for the forensic results from Port Fairy, right?'

'Yeah, I am.'

O'Meara took a deep breath then coughed incessantly for thirty or forty seconds. She spat the product into a tissue and wiped her mouth with the back of a hand. 'Gregory. You know I can't give you those results when you've been ordered not to touch this case.'

Bowker had expected this response but hoped for a compromise. 'I know you can't give me your written report, but–'

O'Meara cut him off. 'You're right there on two counts. First, it won't be available till lunchtime, and second, the boss would have my tits if I gave it to you. That's if I had tits, of course.' She laughed, followed by another bout of coughing.

'How about a rough summary?' Bowker suggested. 'Nothing official or technical. Our little secret. I won't tell if you don't.'

O'Meara shook her head, knowing she was being played. 'Hold on a minute while I get the file up on my screen. I'll see what's come out in the wash and what I can tell you without putting my head in a meat grinder.'

'You're a champion, Erin,' Bowker replied with a quiet sigh of relief. He heard the keys clacking at the other end of the phone line, and after another bout of coughing, O'Meara was ready to respond.

'I've got two reports here, Greg,' she said. 'One a forensic search of a vessel and the other a raid of a motorcycle clubhouse. Pages and pages of technical data and details of search locations and testing processes used.'

'I'm only interested in the bottom line. Anything catch your eye that might interest me?'

O'Meara was quiet for a few moments. 'I'll give you one sentence on each, and that's it. No minutia, no detailed shit, OK?'

'Yeah, OK,' Bowker replied with a wide grin that O'Meara obviously couldn't see. 'You always drive a hard bargain, Erin. Too good for me. The boat first.'

'There was a bloodied fingerprint which belongs to a Gareth Matheson imprinted in blood belonging to the victim, Trevor Flynn.' She hesitated for a moment. 'I'll be generous and give you another half sentence. There were traces of cocaine and methamphetamines in swabs they took on the boat.'

Bowker knew this was the breakthrough Holmes and Larsen were chasing but tried not to sound too enthusiastic over the phone. 'And the Barbarians' clubhouse?'

'Traces of the same two drugs right through the building, plus on the motorcycles outside. Firearms were found in the ceiling with prints all over them.'

* * *

As Bowker disconnected his call to O'Meara, Holmes and Larsen sat down with Senior Sergeant Wilkins and brought her up to date with developments in the Flynn case. At the end of their spiel, Holmes raised the absence of Constable Small. Larsen wasn't sure where her partner was heading, and she held her breath. Small's name hadn't been mentioned since her short account of Saturday's surfing expedition, and she was in no hurry to provide further details.

'Dale not rostered on today?' Holmes asked casually. 'He should know the things we've talked about here, seeing he's been directly involved with the case.'

'It's one of his RDOs,' Wilkins replied. 'It's worked out alright for him, actually. His sister is a nurse in Geelong. She's wangled a bit of time in lieu and is heading down for a few days. A real stunner, according to Grant Farrell, who will no doubt spend the next few days making a fool of himself trying to impress her.'

Holmes and Larsen exchanged glances but said nothing.

* * *

The Barbarians' compound was alive with activity when Bowker arrived. A furniture van, sans livery, was being loaded with items from the clubhouse. Obviously, the bikies' mission control was being evacuated in the wake of Friday night's full-scale raid. Bowker spotted Allender struggling to carry a cardboard box to the rear of the truck. The lovely Janine was sitting in the shade chewing her fingernails.

'Hey, Skeeta,' Bowker yelled through the locked gate.

Allender looked up and feigned not hearing.

'Come on, I know you can see me.'

Allender placed the box on the ground and wandered across. 'What do you want, Bowker? And the name's Rooter. Nobody calls me Skeeta anymore.'

Bowker smiled. 'You'll always be Skeeta to me, mate.'

'And you'll always be Shithead Bowker to me.'

Bowker laughed out loud before his face turned to steel and he stared into Allender's eyes. 'I've just got off the phone with Forensics in Melbourne. The results of the raid are back. Traces of coke and ice all over your building. Same thing on your bikes. You lot are going down in a big way.'

Allender shrugged. 'If you say so.' He smiled. 'But knowing you, that's probably bullshit, especially when you're not working on this case and you're only down here to save your own arse.'

'Illegal firearms found in the roof will be traced back to previous crimes, I'd imagine, so the raid is a bonus for law enforcement across a lot of areas.'

Allender's face tightened and he kicked at the ground as the realisation dawned that Bowker really did have access to the results of the raid. He decided that silence was probably his best option.

Bowker pointed towards the men loading the truck. 'But you're in more trouble than any of those other pricks, aren't you, Skeeta? You're going down for murdering Trevor Flynn.'

Allender immediately abandoned his commitment to silence and arced up. 'I didn't kill anybody, and there's no evidence to prove I did.'

'Come on,' Bowker replied calmly. 'We go back a long way, and I'm trying to do you a favour here. You hand yourself in and that'll go in your favour in sentencing.'

Allender was having none of it. 'No way! I'm not taking the rap for something I didn't do.'

Bowker chuckled. 'Look at it from the court's point of view, mate. You're on the wharf that night picking up drugs. There is drug residue all over your bike, and it was found on the boat that delivered cargo to you. The police know Flynn was killed at the collection point, and at this stage, the only other people the detectives can place there are you and the good doctor. He's a man who is very rich and influential. When push comes to shove, who do you think he'll claim killed Flynn?' Bowker pointed through the wire at Allender's chest. 'You, mate. So are you going to take the rap, or are you going to get in first and shop Matheson?'

Allender thought for a moment then stared at Bowker with impotent eyes. 'Look, Bowker, I honestly don't know who killed Flynn, but he was alive on the wharf when I left.' Before Bowker could call his bluff and pressure him further, Allender went on. 'But I *will* tell you this. As I left, Flynn's missus arrived from around the other side of the restaurant. She was bloody angry and had one of those sharp kitchen knives in her hand.'

* * *

Allender was still standing at the compound gate five minutes after Bowker had departed when Jason McCulloch wandered across. 'What was all that about?'

'Just a cop who's been on my case for the last thirty years.'

McCulloch folded his arms. 'What'd he want?'

'Accused me of killing Trevor. Said it was either me or Matheson, and I'd get blamed because I'm a bikie dealing drugs.'

McCulloch inhaled loudly, worried at what Allender may have told the detective. 'What'd you say?'

'Said it wasn't one of us,' Allender replied confidently. 'Told him I saw Flynn's missus turn up with a knife just before I left.'

McCulloch thumped Allender on the shoulder with the heel of his hand. 'Shit, Rooter! Why tell him anything? Get Matheson offside and he'll trade anything to save his own arse.'

Allender stared at McCulloch. 'We saw them find the guns, and Bowker said they found traces of coke and ice. We're all going down, mate. Pissin' off out of here won't change that. But murder is a different thing altogether.'

'Fuck off and load the bloody truck,' McCulloch said angrily as he removed his pay-as-you-go phone from his pocket. He dialled Matheson's burner, but after a short ring, he disconnected, suspecting Matheson didn't have the phone with him. He then took a calculated risk, rang Matheson's office and spoke to the surgeon. He passed on what Allender had told Bowker, especially the bit about his sister turning up at the wharf with the knife. The orthopod hung up quickly, knowing things were spiralling out of control.

CHAPTER 29

Larsen and Holmes assessed the value of another interview with Craig Matheson as they stretched out on the lush grass of the Village Green, slowly consuming salad rolls and coffee. Across the roundabout further down Sackville Street, a flock of cockatoos rose noisily from a Norfolk pine as a garbage truck passed beneath. Holmes looked up as the birds circled above before landing on branches in the same tree they had left. *Going around in circles, just like we are on this case,* he thought, before being shaken from his reverie by his mobile phone. He checked the screen and looked at Larsen. 'Greg,' he said before accepting the call.

'Have the forensics on the boat and the bikies' clubhouse reached you yet?' Bowker asked after the friendly bullshit had subsided.

'Not yet, mate,' Holmes replied, placing his roll on the grass and waving away a fly.

'I thought you'd have it by now.'

'Why so?'

Bowker was hesitant before continuing. 'I was talking to Erin O'Meara this morning and she said you'd have the full results by lunchtime.'

Holmes knew Bowker would have weaselled something out of his old friend at the forensic centre. 'What else did she tell you?'

'All she'd give me was two sentences. Crystal meth and cocaine traces on the boat and at the bikie clubhouse. Boat cleaned with bleach, but the bloodied fingerprint on the boat belongs to Gareth Matheson. The blood is Trevor Flynn's.'

'That's three sentences.'

'Two and a half, rounded back to two.'

Holmes was delighted in the findings but a little annoyed they came via Bowker. 'How come you were talking to Erin?'

Bowker sensed his angst. 'I'm invested in this case as much as you, Sherlock. So, obviously, I was keen to know if they'd turned up anything. It's *my* head everyone is wanting to see lopped off. I've left it till now to call you because I assumed you'd have the full report and not have to hear things second-hand from me.'

Holmes and Bowker had been partners for long enough not to play games or harbour jealousies. 'Yeah, righto. I can see where you're coming from, but as yet I haven't seen the report. Sounds like we're getting pretty close to busting this thing wide open. The hole Matheson's dug for himself just gets deeper and deeper.'

Larsen raised her eyebrows at Holmes, struggling to patch together the conversation but knowing something important was on the go.

'I took a run up by the Barbarians' compound,' Bowker continued. 'They're packing up their gear. They know it's all over, red rover as far as drug importation down here is concerned. My bet is most of them will see jail time when everything comes out in the wash.'

Holmes waved away another fly. 'I'll leave that to the drug squad, but they can all rot in prison as far as I'm concerned. Parasitic pack of pricks.'

Bowker anticipated his next admission would rankle his old partner but also push him closer to solving the case. 'I spoke to

Skeeta Allender while I was there. He said Katy Flynn arrived at the wharf that night. She was angry and wielding a kitchen knife.'

'Fuck me, Greg!' Holmes said loudly before recognising other park users were staring in his direction. He lowered his voice. 'You've been banned from this case, mate. You're still on leave, for shit's sake. Any decent lawyer will have a field day constructing a defence around a major suspect interfering with the course of an investigation and deflecting blame upon other parties.'

'It wasn't a formal interview, Sherlock. Allender and I go back over thirty years to when he was a skinny kid rooting a local schoolgirl and I was the copper in a one-horse town. I just gave him some free legal advice. I said that there were now only two viable suspects for Flynn's murder. Him and the good doctor. I advised him that in my experience, rich men didn't go down for murder when there's another poor bastard to take the rap. I expected him to put in Matheson, but instead he tells me about Katy Flynn and the knife.' Bowker hesitated and exhaled loudly. 'If I was running the case, I know where I'd be heading this afternoon.'

'Warrnambool,' Holmes replied. 'See if he can explain his fingerprint in Flynn's blood and why his vessel carries traces of drugs.'

'You betcha.'

'I'd like to catch up with his sister before we front him. And I'd still like to see inside her car, if it really was there on the night. Problem is, she hasn't been seen for a few days, so I'm doubting we'll find her at home.'

* * *

Holmes's prediction proved accurate. Katy Flynn was not at home, nor was her yellow Suzuki or her guard dog. Flynn's office in Bank Street was still closed, and a circuit of the town failed to locate Mrs Flynn's distinctive sedan. Accepting that she was not in Port Fairy, the detectives changed tack and within thirty-five minutes were in the Warrnambool consulting room of an aggressive Gareth Matheson. Among the items on the orthopod's desk was a plastic model of a human knee that caused Holmes to consciously acknowledge the pain emanating from his own joint. He resisted the urge to rub his leg and possibly weaken the impact they had made by striding into the clinic full of purpose.

'This is bloody police harassment,' Matheson said loudly without offering the officers a seat. 'You bowl into my practice as if you run the place, keep my patients waiting, waste my time, all because you won't arrest the real killer of my brother-in-law. It seems you'll go to any lengths to protect one of your own, including deflecting blame onto innocent people.' He exhaled loudly. 'Are you still on about my boat being in the vicinity of where Trevor was murdered that night, or have you dreamt up another angle to come from?'

Holmes was happy to let the surgeon blabber on. His experience told him that often, this could result in a slip of the tongue that could lead to a breakthrough. When Matheson had finished his tirade, the detective suggested they all sit down, citing the possibility that their discussion may become lengthy. After Matheson had reluctantly dropped into the leather chair, Holmes laid out their new evidence.

'We have the report on the forensic search of your boat,' Holmes began, massaging the truth a little. The email with the full statement attached had reached his phone, but as yet, he hadn't opened it to read the details. For now, Bowker's summary would suffice.

'Good,' Matheson replied confidently. 'Perhaps now you can get off my back. Didn't I tell you the boat was clean? You blokes certainly know how to waste the taxpayers' money.'

'It was *too* clean, actually, Mr Matheson,' Larsen replied. 'The vessel has been washed down with a bleach solution.'

Matheson struggled to disguise a smirk. 'I like *Hippocrates* to be spotless and sterile. I pay well to have it kept that way.'

'You might have to ask for a refund,' Holmes replied. 'Traces of illegal drugs were found inside the cabin. How do you explain that?'

Matheson seemed taken by surprise but didn't refute that such a finding was possible. 'The only reason I can think of is that some of my party guests may have brought some illicit substances on board.' He forced a smile. 'Don't they say that cocaine is the choice of the rich and famous? I usually have the odd wanker or two at my shebangs.'

'Nobody mentioned cocaine, Mr Matheson,' Holmes shot back.

'I just assumed that…' Matheson's response dropped away.

'They found crystal meth as well,' Larsen added quickly. 'You need syringes or pipes for that. Can't see high-flyers getting down and dirty with that shit.'

Matheson shrugged his shoulders, trying to appear casual, but the arrogant smirk had disappeared. 'Maybe someone had traces on them when they boarded my boat and it's just a simple case of transfer.'

Holmes leaned back in his chair and folded his arms across his chest. 'Forensics found a fingerprint near the rear of your boat. They were able to match it to you.'

Matheson laughed out loud. 'Big deal. It's my fuckin' boat.'

'It certainly is. So perhaps you'll be able to explain why the fingerprint was preserved in blood belonging to Trevor Flynn.'

'This is more bullshit,' Matheson replied confidently. 'The boat was pristine.'

'Except for under a flange in the fibreglass gunwales,' Larsen replied.

Matheson was suddenly deflated and struggled for an answer. 'Could have been there for months,' he said finally.

'Except that the blood was fresh, according to the lab techs,' Holmes shot back. 'No more than a few weeks, tops,' he added, hoping the laboratory tests matched the onsite appraisal he had been given.

Matheson stared down at his desk, fiddling with a pen set. After a few moments, he looked up at Holmes. 'OK, I'll admit Trevor was there that night. He came with me when I took the boat for a run.'

Holmes raised his eyebrows. 'So why lie to us?'

For the first time, the doctor's confidence had evaporated and genuine fear filled his eyes. 'I was afraid you'd use it to frame me for his murder.'

'We don't do that sort of thing, Mr Matheson. How do you explain the bloodied fingerprint?'

'It was a shit of a night, as you say. As I got the boat close to the wharf, Trevor tried to secure the aft line, and the wind lifted the vessel and jammed his finger against the timber. He bled like a stuck pig. I grabbed a handful of tissues from inside and tried to wrap it up. I remember getting his blood on my hands, but I don't recall touching the side of the boat.'

'What happened after you secured the vessel?' Larsen asked.

'Trevor jumped in his car and went home to deal with his injury,' Matheson replied.

'His car had been stolen earlier in the night, so I'm not sure how that could have happened,' Holmes fired back.

Matheson shrugged. 'Well, he headed off in that direction. I'd parked the Porsche on the other side of the restaurant building, so I didn't actually see him go to his car. I just assumed that's what happened.'

Holmes rolled his eyes at Larsen. 'So how does the bikie fit in?'

'What bikie?'

'The one we believe collected drugs from your boat,' Larsen said.

Matheson threw up his hands melodramatically. 'How many times do I have to tell you? That theory is all bullshit. There were no bloody drugs. And if there was a motorcyclist there that night, he had nothing to do with Trevor and me.'

'Why did your sister storm onto the wharf wielding a knife?' Holmes asked, keen to keep Matheson off balance.

'What?' the surgeon asked, arms now outstretched. 'Where'd you hear that horseshit?'

'We've got witnesses who saw Katy drive her Suzuki into the carpark. And we've got a separate witness who saw her on the wharf with a kitchen knife. The knife I suggest was hidden in your parka and sent to the bottom of the Moyne.'

'What parka was that?' Matheson asked quickly.

'The one you're wearing in a framed photo hanging on the inside wall of your boat,' Larsen replied.

Matheson climbed to his feet and strode to a coat locker in the corner of the room. He removed a parka on a hanger. 'This parka, you mean?' he said sarcastically.

Larsen glanced at Holmes, acknowledging that the garment did match the one in the photograph.

It was only a minor setback, and Holmes wasn't about to lose momentum because of it. He stood up and walked over to where Matheson was returning the parka to the cupboard. 'Right now, I have enough to arrest you for obstructing a police investigation and being an accomplice in the murder of Trevor Flynn. We have you and Flynn on the boat together that night, we have the victim's blood on your hand, and we have a likely drug deal going down with a bikie gang whose headquarters contain traces of drugs identical to those found on your boat. We also have your sister arriving with a knife, its description fitting both the knife found in the river and the shape of the wound in Flynn's chest. By anyone's reckoning, you and your sister are in deep shit.'

'And why would I kill my brother-in-law?' Matheson asked defiantly. 'Why would my sister kill her husband?'

'There's no honour among thieves, Mr Matheson,' Holmes replied. 'Expect to see us back here fairly soon. If you've got anything you need to tell us, now's the time.'

Matheson looked at the floor and didn't answer.

'It's on your head, mate,' Holmes said as he indicated to Larsen that it was time to leave. As he reached the door, he turned back. 'Be prepared to walk home. I'm impounding your Porsche for forensic examination.'

* * *

As the detectives reached their vehicle, Holmes phoned Forensics and arranged the appraisal of Matheson's car. When he disconnected the call, his mobile pinged. He checked his messages, leaned against their police vehicle, and smiled at his partner. 'Megan Wilkins has sent through the bank details for Bethany Symons. In summary, her mortgage account has been the beneficiary of several large repayments.'

'From Trevor Flynn?' Larsen asked.

'Cash. So they could be from anyone. But the amounts seem way beyond the earnings of a part-time legal typist.'

Larsen checked her watch. 'While we're in Warrnambool, how about we slip around and see if she's home? Question her about the help she's been getting with her mortgage? We already know she lied about her movements the day Flynn went missing, and we haven't quizzed her yet about her phone records. She's got a few questions that need answering.'

Holmes screwed up his face. 'I'm not sure it's worth the trouble, is it? In the light of what we now know about the victim being on Matheson's boat and his missus arriving with a knife, I can't see Symons being involved in the murder. Not directly, anyway. The timing is all wrong. She was back home by the time we believe Flynn was knifed.'

Larsen put her hand on her partner's shoulder and smiled. '*Tie up the loose ends* was one of the first pieces of advice you and Greg gave me when I transferred to Homicide. The loose ends often plait together and lead to the final answer, you said.'

CHAPTER 30

The wind gusted from the north, buffeting the young trees on the nature strip as the detectives pulled into the driveway behind Bethany Symons's car. Their knock on the door was answered quickly, and a puzzled Symons invited her visitors into the loungeroom overlooking the Hopkins River. Today, the steep bank on the opposite side was clearly visible. A number of small fishing craft making use of the sunny day were anchored in the main channel of the river with their tethered bows straining against the steady current.

'Done a fetlock?' Symons asked the limping Holmes.

'Slipped over and twisted a knee. Ripped a cartilage, according to the specialist.'

'Who'd you see?'

'Gareth Matheson. Knows his stuff, according to the locals.'

Symons nodded. 'I was sent to him when I rolled an ankle pretty badly. Didn't need surgery, but it took months to come good. Hope you have better luck.'

'Unfortunately, it looks like I'll need to go under the knife, but I'm delaying that until this investigation is sorted out.'

Symons pointed to the couch, inviting the officers to take a seat. After a few moments of small talk about the weather and how much more impressive the view was on a fine day, a nervous

Symons was keen to discern the purpose of the detectives' visit. It was almost a week since they had last called, and she'd become increasingly confident that any interest they had in her had waned.

'So, what can I help you with, Detective?' she asked Holmes.

'We're wondering if you've had any second thoughts about where you were between Trevor Flynn's place in Port Fairy on the day he died and here? You say you came straight home, and that you had your phone with you all day. Unfortunately for you, we have your phone records, and they show your mobile never left Warrnambool at all that Friday.'

Symons feigned bewilderment, shaking her head as though scanning her memory. 'I'm sure I took it with me.'

'You see our dilemma, Bethany,' Larsen said. 'We have no way of proving you weren't still in Port Fairy until late into the evening. We've got no proof of your movements until your partner arrived home from the pub that night.'

Symons shrugged. 'Well, you'll just have to take my word that I came straight back here. I'm not sure why you see it as important anyway.' She stood defiantly. 'Is that it? Can I return to my work? I have a long court document I need to finish by tomorrow.'

Holmes stood, and Larsen followed his lead. Holmes slipped his hands into his pockets. 'Just one other thing. We have your bank records. Your mortgage repayments make interesting reading.' He saw Symons's eyes dart between him and his partner. He had hit a nerve somewhere. 'Can you tell us where you obtained the money for those big cash repayments?'

'Savings,' Symons retorted quickly. 'I save up my wages until I have a decent sum, then pay off a bit of the house.'

Larsen smiled disbelievingly. 'You cash out some of your wages?'

Symons nodded. 'That's right.'

'And store the cash where?' Larsen asked.

'Here, in a drawer, until I've accumulated enough to make it worth doing a repayment.'

Holmes chuckled at the absurdity of her explanation. 'So, you take money away from the security of a bank deposit, stash it at home until you have several thousand dollars and then pay it back into a bank?'

'It's a different bank,' Symons replied, becoming annoyed. 'My wage is paid into the Commonwealth Bank, and my loan is with ANZ.'

Larsen exhaled loudly in frustration. 'Ever heard of bank transfers?'

'Of course I have. I just prefer it this way.'

'To be honest, Ms Symons, that is the greatest cock and bull story I think I've ever come across,' Holmes said aggressively. 'The sums of money we're talking about are in the tens of thousands of dollars, and the cash payments were quite regular prior to the gap before the big one last week. I'd estimate your loan repayments exceed your total salary by many thousands. But we'll check that with your employers.'

'Sometimes I raid my savings at one of the other banks,' Symons replied weakly.

'Well, we'll check those records too,' Holmes said.

Larsen smiled at Symons. 'You see our problem here, Bethany? We are now ninety-nine percent certain that Trevor Flynn's death was tied up with the drugs trade and involved hundreds of thousands of dollars in cash.'

Symons seemed insulted. 'I'd never be involved in something like that,' she shot back.

'Another way one could obtain those amounts of cash would be through blackmail,' Holmes suggested. 'You weren't blackmailing

Flynn over his involvement in drug trafficking and things suddenly went awry?'

'That's ridiculous,' she replied.

'My advice is to have a good think about your options,' Holmes said. 'If things have gone to hell in a handbasket for you, it might be a good time to come clean. We're not far from sorting out this mess.'

Holmes turned and walked towards the front entrance. Symons was quick to follow, hoping her problems may go out the door with the detectives. Larsen held back as she passed the mantlepiece over the fireplace. She stopped and examined a single earring with a silver butterfly.

* * *

'Have you ever heard a greater load of bullshit?' Holmes asked as he snapped home his seatbelt.

Larsen didn't answer until she had backed out of the driveway and was heading out of Dunvegan Court. 'She dug a hole for herself, and the more she tried to explain, the deeper the hole became.'

'Whatever way you look at it, there's dirty money involved. But whether that relates to Flynn's murder is anyone's guess at this stage.' Holmes thought for a moment. 'She has a reputation for spreading herself among the men in the area. Maybe she's turned that into a profitable business.'

Larsen glanced at her partner as she gave way to a tradie's ute at the T intersection with Mahoneys Road. 'For the amounts we're talking about? Come on, Darren, get real.'

Holmes grinned. 'I'd pay that to have my way with you.'

'Well, lucky for you that you get it for free,' Larsen retorted dryly, eyes on the road.

Holmes didn't reply but reached across and placed his hand on her thigh.

'I saw a single earring on her mantlepiece as we were leaving,' Larsen said, changing the subject. 'Silver with a jangly butterfly. Saw an identical one at Katy Flynn's place.'

'Maybe they have similar tastes.' Holmes smiled. 'That seems to be the case in men, anyway.'

'Katy Flynn wears clip-ons. I saw her remove a pair when we interviewed her. And there was only the one butterfly earring at her place as well.'

'You reckon they're a pair?'

'Yeah, I do.'

'And you're thinking Bethany lost one when she was typing at Flynn's house?'

'An earring secured with a stud through the lobe just doesn't drop out while you're typing. If it did, you'd know straight away.' This time, Larsen was the one who patted her partner's thigh. 'And we both know when an earring might be dislodged without the woman noticing.'

Holmes smiled. 'During a red-hot root.'

Larsen burst out laughing. 'In the throes of passion is the term I would use, but the meaning's the same, I guess.' She suddenly became more serious as she turned left onto the Princes Highway and headed back towards central Warrnambool and ultimately Port Fairy. She pulled into the right-hand lane to pass a shiny bulk milk carrier. 'The earring at Flynn's house was in a ceramic dish on a bookshelf with several pairs of clip-ons. There is no way Bethany Symons would have left it there if she knew it had come loose, and there is no way Trevor Flynn would have put it there either if he found it after she'd gone.'

'So Katy Flynn must have found it?'

'Yeah. And my guess is in the bedroom, possibly even the bed itself if it hadn't been remade properly, or if Katy decided on an early night.'

Holmes pondered her theory for a few moments as they passed the funeral home that had once been a McDonalds restaurant. 'Is that sufficient motive to grab a kitchen knife and stick it into your husband?'

'Infidelity and jealousy are powerful forces,' Larsen replied, her eyes never leaving the road.

* * *

Sometimes, in the intricate game of cards that is a murder investigation, serendipity trumps strategy and deft police work. And so it was when the detectives dropped in at the Port Fairy Medical Clinic on their return journey from Warrnambool.

'Just bringing back the crutches,' Holmes informed the receptionist. 'The knee's feeling a bit better, and to be truthful, I'm not really using them. Better that someone more conscientious has them.' He passed the crutches over the counter. 'And I owe you an apology for how I carted away your visiting orthopaedic surgeon last Friday. In the heat of an investigation, we sometimes forget how our actions impact on others just trying to do their own job.'

The receptionist smiled sympathetically. 'No need to apologise.' She moved closer and spoke in a whisper. 'To tell you the truth, he's a bit of a wanker. He tore strips off me one day because I called him Doctor.' She smiled and moved further away. 'Besides, we're getting used to the odd disturbance when he's here. The Friday of *Mister* Matheson's second-last visit, a woman came in late afternoon demanding to see him immediately. I said he had appointments for the rest of the day, so she sat outside on the bonnet of his Porsche until he'd knocked off.'

Holmes was suddenly interested. 'Can you describe this woman?'

The receptionist took a deep breath and looked up at the ceiling, searching her memory. 'I don't know her name. She's not a local, as far as I know, anyway. She was slim, about average in height with short hair, auburn-browny colour. The main thing I noticed was she was only wearing one earring. Pretty little butterfly thing.'

* * *

'So, we have a gap in her cash mortgage repayments for a month leading up to her visit to the clinic here,' Holmes said, looking at the bank statement on his phone. 'Then, bingo, a couple of days later, a big payment is made to the bank.'

'Sounds suss, but there's no guarantee the visit and the money are related. Correlation is not the same as causation.'

'Symons said Matheson treated her for a badly sprained ankle, so the two know each other. But you'd hardly turn up unannounced at a clinic in another town to discuss something she told us she'd recovered from. And if it was about her injury, why the secrecy about her movements that day? No, it was about money. Illicitly obtained money. I'll bet my left…' – he looked at Larsen – '…arm on it. We need to do more digging.'

* * *

It was cooler than the day before, and the early-morning wind whistled in the Norfolk pines outside Gareth Matheson's yet-to-open clinic in Warrnambool. The detectives' car was the only one in the street when the receptionist they had met on a previous visit walked up the footpath and opened the gate to the practice.

'She must put that makeup on with a trowel,' Larsen said snidely as she climbed from their vehicle.

Holmes chuckled as he opened the passenger door and called across the roof of the car. 'Do you have a minute, ma'am?' He stepped across the deep bluestone gutter and limped to where Larsen was already displaying her identification to the late-middle-aged woman immaculately dressed in a navy pantsuit, her dyed-platinum hair coiffured to within an inch of its life.

Holmes removed his ID from his jacket pocket. 'Senior Sergeant Holmes of the homicide squad,' he added to affix more gravitas to their impending discussion. The woman was already on edge, wondering whether the detectives' presence at such an early hour was the manifestation of a decision she had made months before and regretted ever since.

Larsen opened her notebook. 'By the name badge, I assume you're Catherine Price?'

'That's right,' the woman replied, unconsciously touching the badge pinned to her jacket.

Larsen nodded as she scribbled down the name. 'And you're a receptionist here at the clinic?'

'I'm the practice manager,' she said proudly, raising her chin.

'But you work behind the reception desk?' Holmes asked.

'Yes. It's part of my duties.' She nervously feigned a chuckle. 'Keep the younger girls in line.'

'And protect the doctors' backs, I assume,' Holmes added.

Price nodded before her gaze dropped to the footpath.

'Do you remember a patient named Bethany Symons?' Larsen asked.

Price nodded again, then looked up at the detective. 'I thought this would be a professional standards matter. I can't see why the police, especially homicide detectives, would be involved.'

Holmes raised his eyebrows at Larsen, resisting the urge to yell *Bingo!*

'Mr Matheson said he'd fire me if I said anything. He said it wasn't my prerogative to make reports. That was up to the patient.' Price took a deep breath. 'But I knew it was against the rules for doctors to have relationships with patients.' She gave a weak chuckle. 'Having sex with a patient in your consulting room probably counts as a breach of ethics, I'd imagine.' She looked from one officer to another. 'I wish I'd never heard it, or at least not told Mr Matheson I knew what he'd been up to.'

Over the next ten minutes, Price related the details of Matheson's encounter with Bethany Symons, before Holmes advised that the medical practitioners board would no doubt be in touch to hear her revelations. He then asked that their conversation be kept confidential, as Mr Matheson was part of a wider police investigation. Price nodded and walked to the front door, her face betraying an odd combination of worry and relief.

No sooner had she entered the practice than Matheson's Porsche pulled into the parking slot beside the police car.

'This will be interesting,' Holmes said.

Matheson climbed from his silver sportscar and made a point of walking past the officers as if their presence was of no relevance to him. As he opened the gate to his practice, Holmes spoke loudly. 'Got a minute, Mr Matheson?' He smiled. 'We've been here half an hour waiting for you to grace our presence.'

'My practice manager could have told you I don't normally arrive until eight,' Matheson replied.

'She did. So we decided to wait,' Holmes replied, stretching the truth to protect Catherine Price.

'Unless you've got something new to tell me, I'm not interested in further discussions,' Matheson said angrily. He waved a finger in Holmes's face. 'I've told you that I know nothing about Trevor Flynn's murder, and you can't prove otherwise.'

Holmes glanced at Larsen, then stared back at the surgeon. 'The detective sergeant and I struggle to believe that, but we're not here to talk about the murder.' Holmes saw Matheson's face relax. 'Just a courtesy call, really. Yesterday, we were interviewing Bethany Symons–'

Matheson stiffened and interrupted. 'Bethany who?'

'Symons.'

Matheson's brow furrowed, and he shook his head slowly. The pretence of wracking his brain continued for several painful moments. 'I don't know the name,' he said finally.

'She did some typing work for Trevor Flynn,' Larsen replied, allowing the sham to continue. 'She was in Port Fairy the day he was murdered but has found difficulty accounting for her movements later in the day. We were finally able to place her talking to you outside the local medical clinic after you finished work that Friday.'

'Well, she's lying,' Matheson blurted out. 'I've never heard of her.'

'She says she was one of your patients,' Holmes replied. 'We've checked, and she was. A badly sprained ankle, apparently.'

Matheson scoffed disingenuously. 'Well, if she was, I've got no memory of her. I've had hundreds of patients over the years. I can't be expected to remember them all.'

'Do you remember the ones you had sex with during a consultation?' Holmes shot back.

'Did she tell you that?' Matheson asked loudly.

'It's true, isn't it?' Holmes replied without answering the orthopod's question. 'We have corroborating evidence.'

Matheson dropped his head, knowing his career was probably over and mulling whether to take Symons down with him.

'We've contacted the medical practitioners board as a courtesy. That's why we dropped in this morning. To give you a heads up.

Unless it was rape, your conduct has nothing to do with us. But be warned, Mr Matheson, you're still number one on our list of suspects for Flynn's murder. That hasn't gone away.'

The two detectives turned towards their car, confident of what would come next. This confidence was not misplaced.

'Did the bitch tell you she's been blackmailing me?' Matheson blurted out. 'Tens of thousands of dollars I've given her to keep her bloody mouth shut about the slip I made that day. I reckon she probably planned the whole thing. Everyone in Warrnambool knows she's a slut.'

'Where'd you get the money to pay her off?' Larsen asked.

'I'm a wealthy man, Detective,' Matheson replied.

'Too wealthy, according to our calculations,' Larsen said, smiling. 'Ill-gotten gains and all that.'

'Expect a visit from the fraud squad. Homicide doesn't handle blackmail.' Holmes laughed. 'You're going to be a busy man with all these interviews. Your professional standards people, the fraud squad, plus we're only one shred of evidence away from a return visit as well.'

'Have a nice day, Doctor Matheson,' Larsen said with a smile as she slipped behind the wheel of the police car.

This time there was no correction.

CHAPTER 31

Passing the Tower Hill cemetery, Holmes's phone rang and automatically switched to hands-free mode through the car's audio system. Greg Bowker's name flashed on its screen, and Larsen pushed the connect button on her steering wheel. 'Kirsten here, Greg. Darren and I are in the car. You're now on speaker.'

'Where are you off to at this time of morning?'

'We're not off to anywhere, mate,' Holmes replied. 'We're on our way back to Port Fairy. We've just been to see our friend Gareth Matheson. Again.'

Bowker laughed. 'Didn't you catch up with him yesterday?'

'Yeah. I thought you might have rung last night to get the lowdown.'

'I didn't want to push my luck. Yesterday, you sounded a bit shitty that I was sticking my nose into your investigation.'

Holmes raised his eyebrows at Larsen. 'I was a touch put out that someone outside the inquiry was getting information before we were. I'm over it now, though.'

'At the risk of sounding pushy, did anything new come out of yesterday's chat with Matheson?'

Holmes winked at Larsen. 'When confronted with the bloodied fingerprint, he admitted that Flynn was with him on the boat that night.'

Bowker whistled on the other end of the line.

Holmes continued. 'He reckons Flynn went with him to give the boat a run and squashed his finger when they were trying to moor the vessel in the wild weather. Hence the blood. Matheson said he tried to stop the bleeding and that would explain the print.'

'Sounds like bullshit to me,' Bowker replied.

'That's what we thought. In terms of the traces of drugs that were found, he reckons they were probably remnants of gear brought on board by guests at his parties.'

'When we said they matched those found at the bikies' hangout, he just ignored our questions about how that was possible,' Larsen added.

'So, did he explain Flynn's movements after the boat's return?'

'Claimed that when he left, Flynn was on his way back to his Merc,' Holmes replied.

'Which had already been stolen,' Bowker said.

'Matheson claims he knew nothing about that, and assumed Flynn drove home,' Larsen said.

'Did you mention Skeeta Allender's claim that Katy Flynn arrived at the wharf wielding a knife?'

'Yeah. Matheson claims that's just fabricated rubbish.'

A few moments passed before Bowker spoke again. 'What's the purpose of today's visit with the good doctor?'

With a movement of his right hand, Holmes invited Larsen to respond.

'You remember Bethany Symons?'

'Yeah. Flynn's typist and possible mistress. Holes in her alibi, I remember you saying.'

'Well, we've filled those holes,' Larsen replied. 'On the day of the murder, she confronted Matheson at the Port Fairy Clinic.'

'Then why the secrecy?'

'She's blackmailing Matheson about him having sex with her in his consulting rooms during a medical appointment,' Larsen explained. 'She's already fleeced him for tens of thousands.'

'Right now, he knows his career is finished,' Holmes added. 'His professional standards board will most likely strike him off, and we've called in the fraud squad to deal with the extortion. We've hand-balled that whole matter so we can concentrate on the murder.'

'You've put a line through Symons killing Flynn?'

'Yeah. She was well and truly home by the time that boat docked. And we can scratch Petrov as well. Even if he did follow Flynn, that was much earlier in the day, around five o'clock, and there's no suggestion he was anywhere near the wharf when we believe the killing took place.'

'So now it's down to three,' Bowker surmised.

'We think so. Matheson and his sister, plus your old mate Allender. What motive he would have, we're not sure. Unless he was doing some dirty work for his gang. As you know, these drug rings often start off cosy, then they implode. Arguments over who gets what share, that sort of thing.'

'Allender says Flynn was still alive when he left the wharf, as does Matheson,' Larsen said. 'We don't know about Katy, because we can't track her down.'

It was a moment or two before Bowker spoke. 'I'm calling from Melbourne, Sherlock. I packed up last night and headed off. I'm no help to you two, and Rachael was adamant I should come home.'

Holmes and Larsen exchanged looks. 'We'll miss you down here as part of the team,' Holmes replied diplomatically.

Bowker chuckled. 'Yeah, right. Anyway, the assistant commissioner is asking when I'll be back, so she must be convinced I'm in the clear. How much have you guys been feeding back to her?'

'Everything we've got. There hasn't been any need to cover your arse, mate, if that's what you're asking.'

Bowker thanked his colleagues and disconnected. Larsen slowed to 80 kph as they passed through the hamlet of Killarney.

'About bloody time,' Larsen said. 'I love the man like a brother, but him hanging around creates pressure and makes us double-guess ourselves.'

Holmes nodded. 'Agreed. But he has been a help. He got the info out of Allender about Katy Flynn arriving at the wharf with a knife. That's a big breakthrough.'

'It is if it turns out to be accurate. But would you trust that leather-clad turd to tell the truth if his own arse was on the line?'

'Good point,' Holmes replied, knowing his partner's cynicism was justified.

* * *

Wednesday morning's surf was docile and the tide out as Constables Small and Farrell stood over the red towel and beach bag chatting to an elderly man with an ageing fox terrier tethered on a leash.

'And this gear was definitely here when you started your walk?' Small asked.

The old man nodded vigorously. 'Absolutely. One hundred percent sure.'

Farrell stared out to sea. 'When was that?'

'Around seven thirty. It takes me more than an hour to walk down to the mouth of the river and the same to get back.' He pointed to his dog now lying on the sand, puffing loudly. 'Shorty and I are pretty much the same. Just about rooted. Both waiting for the curtain to fall.'

Small nodded towards a vehicle in the carpark. 'And the yellow

Suzuki was here?'

'Yeah. Parked there on its lonesome.'

'And that hound was locked inside it?'

'It was going berserk. Not sure whether it was the sight of my little Shorty here, or he was upset because his owner had disappeared. I went and checked that the car windows were down a bit, so the poor bastard didn't asphyxiate or cook if the weather got too hot. I've never noticed the dog when she's swum here before.'

'And no sign of the woman?' Small asked.

'Nope. But that's not unusual when I set off for my walk. She's often already swimming out to the buoy, and by the time I get back, she's packed up and gone. But today, there's no sign of her and her things are still here. That's why I rang you blokes.'

'Did you see anybody on the beach during your walk?' Farrell asked.

The old man shook his head. 'No. Very quiet this morning. No one walking. No one in the water. Then again, the weather's a bit cooler than the last few days and there's a story going round about a big tiger shark in the river. People might be worried he's the same one that swallowed half of that Flynn bloke a few weeks ago.'

Small pondered the situation for a long moment as a pair of screeching plovers wheeled low overhead. 'I think we better give Marine Rescue a call.'

Farrell frowned. 'Bit early for that, don't you think, mate? She might have changed her mind about a swim and gone for a walk through the gardens or something.'

'She'd take her dog, surely,' Small replied.

Farrell shrugged. 'Maybe she's finished her swim and is up in the dunnies having a shower.'

'Her clothes are still here in her bag, but I will check the toilets before I ring,' Small replied. 'I can't run the risk that she's out there struggling to stay afloat or hanging on to that marker buoy for dear life.'

Farrell slipped his hands in his trouser pockets and shrugged indifferently. 'Your call. That's why you get paid the big bucks. Just don't include me when you're explaining to the rescue team why they needed to leave their paid work and head out on a wild goose chase. As I said, my guess is that she's gone for a walk.'

'We don't act on guesses, mate,' Small replied, his annoyance obvious as he walked away to inspect the changerooms.

* * *

By noon, the old man's concerns had escalated into a full-scale missing person's investigation. With Katy Flynn's close connection to the homicide inquiry, Wilkins thought it wise to involve Holmes and Larsen in her plans going forward. She and the detectives met with Constables Small and Farrell in her office to discuss the apparent disappearance. Small was coy when he first encountered Larsen and looked to her to set the tone of any discussion between them. Larsen established the ground rules immediately.

'Thanks again for the surfing tuition on Saturday, Dale,' she said airily, causing Small to smile and visibly relax, at the same time watching Holmes's face out of the corner of his eye. He saw no hint of reaction and assumed Larsen had not told her partner what had transpired.

'No problems. Perhaps we can give it another go before you head back to Melbourne.'

Larsen caught the innuendo but didn't react. 'Megan told us your sister is down for a visit.'

Small nodded. 'Only for a few days.'

'She's a nurse, we've been told,' Holmes said cheerily.

'Yeah,' Small said with a smile, now sure Larsen had kept the events of the weekend to herself. 'She works in A&E, accident and emergency.' He chuckled. 'Pretty full-on in there, from what she tells me.'

'I can imagine,' Holmes replied, po-faced. 'She must see a lot of busted noses and broken jaws, that sort of thing, you'd think.'

Small was suddenly unsure how much Holmes knew. Was the detective warning him off, or was he reading too much into Holmes's comment about painful injuries? He wasn't about to find out. For the moment, Detective Larsen was off the radar, at least until his sister had returned to Geelong. He would reassess then.

When the four officers were comfortably seated opposite, Wilkins brought them all up to date with the hunt for Katy Flynn. 'The Marine Rescue crew found nothing in the search of the water around the buoy and between there and the beach. That doesn't mean she didn't find trouble. The tide was going out and the currents could have taken her… or her body further out to sea. If she did drown, maybe her body has sunken below the surface and we'll have to wait to see if she washes up.' She shrugged. 'And we can't discount the remote chance she's been taken by a shark.'

'We also need to consider whether she even intended to return to the beach, or just to keep swimming out to sea until she was exhausted,' Small suggested. 'That would take her out of the search area.'

Farrell frowned at the thought. 'What, she punched her own ticket, you mean?'

'Yeah,' Small replied. 'Look what she's been going through. Her husband's been murdered, and her brother appears central to the whole inquiry.'

Wilkins leaned back in her chair. 'I know she's being treated for a cancer of some kind. There's a possibility it's all become too much, and she's decided to end it.'

'Or that she never went into the water in the first place,' Holmes replied.

Farrell tapped his temple. 'Great minds think alike,' he said, smiling at the detective.

God, I hope I never think like Farrell, Holmes thought.

'Yep,' Farrell continued. 'My bet is she's strolling around town and will return to her car wondering what all the fuss is about.'

'I was thinking more about her faking her own death,' Holmes shot back. 'Right now, she's one of the prime suspects for her husband's murder. We've received new evidence that ties her to the wharf that night, so it would be very convenient for her if we rubbed her name off our slate.'

'There are a lot of possibilities,' Wilkins replied, 'but right now, I have to treat her as a missing person.'

Holmes folded his arms and nodded. 'Agreed. But I want her beach gear and her car impounded pending forensic examination. And I'd like to see inside her house as well. Maybe Forensics should look at that too.'

'Her house will be locked up like a church, I'd imagine,' Wilkins said. 'We'll probably need to break in.'

'If you knock on the door, she'll probably let you in,' Farrell replied with a smart-arsed grin. No one reacted.

'Flynn's Mercedes is still in the carpark outside,' Larsen reminded them, 'so I presume we have the keys. Surely there's one to the house among them.'

* * *

Donning gloves and shoe covers, Wilkins and the detectives entered the Flynn home via the main door. The first thing that struck them all was a feeling that the house had been abandoned, although there was nothing overt to suggest Katy had moved out. In the living area, the spectacular views over Bass Strait had been reduced to a blurred mosaic by the salt and sand that the southerlies had hammered against the window glass.

Larsen picked up the butterfly earring from a dish on a bookshelf and showed it to her partner. Holmes nodded. 'Two women, two earrings, one man.' He returned the earring to Larsen, who dropped it into an evidence bag.

In the master bedroom, the king-sized bed was only roughly made.

'A woman didn't make this bed,' Larsen said. 'The sheets haven't been tucked under the mattress, and the doona is the wrong way around. And these decorative pillows are all wrong. The open end of the pillowslips should face the same way, not one out, one in, like this arrangement here.'

'So you reckon a male made this?'

Larsen put her hand on his shoulder and nodded sympathetically. 'Yeah, I do. Sorry for the generalisations.'

'And here I was thinking I do a pretty good job making our bed.'

Larsen squeezed his shoulder and smiled. 'Your long suit is messing it up.' She immediately dropped her hand when she spotted Wilkins exit a second bedroom and wander up the passage towards them.

'I think Katy might be sleeping in that next room,' Wilkins suggested. 'The bed is beautifully made, but there's a pair of women's pyjamas under the pillow.'

The moment the trio walked into the kitchen, Larsen pointed to the knife block on the bench. 'One knife's missing,' she said. 'The same size as the one found in the river.' She lifted one of the other knives out of its slot and perused the pattern on the handle. She passed it to Holmes with a gloved hand. 'Exactly the same embossing as the knife found in the Moyne. Same pattern, same metal.'

Holmes placed the knife on the bench and photographed it with his phone. He then returned it to its slot and photographed the whole block from an angle that highlighted the empty space.

A trail of ants traversed the kitchen bench, their destination a plate with the dried-out remains of honey on toast. Beside the plate was a glass containing a centimetre of curdled milk. Larsen picked up the glass. 'Looks like she hasn't been around for a while.'

A search of the rest of the house produced nothing of immediate interest, and the building was locked awaiting forensic examination later in the afternoon.

Holmes and Larsen walked back to their vehicle parked on the side of the road opposite the Flynn house. Holmes stood with hands on hips surveying the rocky outcrops that were the feature of this south-facing coastline. Called South Beach, it was more a long collection of bluestone rockpools at low tide, with the only swimmable section a small cove known as Pea Soup. This was a popular spot for parents of small children, with its shelly beach, shallow, flat water and sheltered outlook. Holmes removed his mobile phone from his pocket and rang a number from his call history list.

'Who are you after?' Larsen asked.

'Our medical friend, Mr Matheson. I wouldn't mind tracking his sister's movements. Obviously, she hasn't been living here for a few days.'

The phone call was terse, with Holmes reminding the surgeon that a murder investigation took precedence over a patient's tennis elbow. When the call ended, Holmes rolled his eyes and exhaled loudly. 'What a wanker! The bottom line is that his sister has been staying with him and his wife in Warrnambool to get away from' –

he used his index fingers to make quotation marks – '*all the shit* in Port Fairy. The office is closed here, and she's sick of having locals continually asking whether the killer has been found, or overdoing the whole sympathy bit. But apparently, she came back early this morning and planned on having a swim on her way home.'

'What did he say when you told him we'd found her stuff on East Beach but no sign of her?'

'He seemed pretty worried, actually. He said she was a strong swimmer and had done that swim out to the buoy hundreds of times. And in a lot worse weather than today. He asked to be kept posted, and if she doesn't turn up, he'll come down after work.'

'So where to now?'

'I'd like our own chat with Allender. He's the only one who places Katy Flynn on the wharf.'

'One of the dickheads who stole the Mercedes said he saw the yellow Suzuki arrive as he was leaving the carpark.'

'Yeah, saw *a* yellow Suzuki and couldn't identify the driver.' Holmes climbed in the passenger side. 'Let's see what else Allender might be able to tell us.'

CHAPTER 32

There was a hive of activity at the Ocean View Apartments. A late-middle-aged man stood on a stepladder removing the screws that attached the *For Sale* sign to a pair of steel pickets at the front of the complex. A greying, skeletal woman stabilised the ladder, though there was little chance of it toppling, and even less chance the male would be injured if he fell the few inches to the ground.

The police vehicle slowed as it approached the couple. Holmes wound down his window as the car rolled to a stop. 'Finally sold the place, mate?'

Ladder Man smiled and shook his head. 'She's off the market.' He pointed towards the old Birdwatchers Club further up the street. 'Those shitheads have done a runner, so we're gonna give this place another go.'

The woman's narrow face was beaming. 'The *For Sale* boards are coming down on the houses around here as well.'

'I dunno who killed that Trevor Flynn,' the man on the ladder said, 'but if that's who's ultimately responsible for arseholing those bikie pricks, then they deserve a bloody medal as far as people up this end of town are concerned.'

That's an interesting take on things, Holmes thought before smiling back. 'Best of luck with rebuilding your business,' he said, before winding up his window and gesturing to Larsen to continue up the street.

* * *

The only living things within the Barbarian compound were a dozen seagulls picking at scraps on the ground under one of the windows of the clubhouse.

'We're too late to interview Allender, by the looks of it,' Larsen said as she stopped the car.

Holmes nodded but said nothing.

The wire gate was wide open, the chain and locks removed and the door into the building ajar. Holmes gingerly climbed the side steps, his knee protesting this particular challenge. He entered the building warily, followed closely by his partner. He surveyed detritus inside. 'Fucking pigs, if you'll excuse my French. Look at the rotten food and garbage they've left lying around.'

'It's a wonder they made the effort to use the toilets,' Larsen replied in disgust.

'Don't assume anything, so watch where you step. Greg said they were packing up, but I didn't expect them to abandon ship altogether. Not sure what they think they'll achieve by moving out. Most of them will end up inside anyway.'

'They know their Port Fairy operation is dead in the water, so why hang around?'

Holmes nodded. 'Yeah.' He rubbed his chin as he thought about the next move. 'I might ask Forensics to run another eye over this mess tomorrow when they've finished the Suzuki and Flynn's house. They only went through the place a few nights ago, and I don't expect they'll find anything new. But you never know.'

'I don't envy their job,' Larsen said, pointing towards a used condom on the floor with the toe of her shoe.

Holmes shook his head, a pained look on his face. 'Fuck me,' he said wearily.

'I hope they didn't,' Larsen shot back with a smirk.

* * *

Given that Katy Flynn was still missing despite further searches on land and sea, the analysis of material gleaned from her house and car was fast-tracked. The results were conveyed to Holmes by phone early Thursday afternoon.

'I'm not sure we'll be much help solving the disappearance, Darren, but we might have struck gold with your murder inquiry,' O'Meara said in her gravelly voice.

'You're beautiful,' Holmes replied enthusiastically.

'Yeah, all the men tell me that,' O'Meara shot back before laughing and descending into a fit of coughing. Holmes waited patiently for her to regain her breath. 'There are two sets of prints in the car that we can identify. Mostly Katy Flynn's, obviously, but a couple of stray prints that match the victim, Trevor Flynn.'

'So no prints that would surprise us?'

'Nope. And the owner of two tiny lines of blood on the carpet just under the driver's side door probably won't surprise you, either,' O'Meara said with a lilt.

'Trevor Flynn?' Holmes asked with a smile.

'Spot on, Darren. The blood is virtually imperceptible to the human eye because it is so diluted. Our techs reckon it almost certainly came into the car on a shoe, likely a woman's by the size and shape of the deposit. The level of dilution would indicate it was left during wet weather.'

'Like the night Flynn was stabbed.'

'Yeah,' O'Meara replied. 'Weather just like that night.' She coughed loudly, but only for a few seconds this time. 'And just to put a little cherry on the top, soil samples found in the car, including a few grains of sand, match the specimens taken at the wharf where you first found Flynn's blood.'

Holmes delivered a short whistle. 'Katy Flynn is looking more and more like our killer.'

'Don't get ahead of yourself, Detective. I think we are pretty close to proving she was at the scene of the crime, but proving she stabbed the victim is a bit more problematic.'

'She's at least an accessory,' Holmes said.

'Probably. We also matched samples of fibre from the Suzuki's driver's seat to the parka used to wrap the knife you recovered from the river. But once again, that doesn't prove she stuck the knife in her husband.'

'Shit, Erin, you know how to build a man up then cut him off at the knees,' Holmes replied. 'But you're moving us closer to knowing the whole story.' He laughed. 'You should have been a detective.'

'Nah,' O'Meara replied. 'I'd prefer to work for a living.' Her laughter again degenerated into a bout of uncontrolled coughing and retching.

'You alright?'

'Yeah, mate. Just need a smoke.' Holmes heard the clacking of computer keys. 'Now, the Flynn house. Plenty of prints, mostly those matching Flynn and his missus. There's another set that we can't match to anything on our database. Mainly found in the master bedroom, but there's a few in the kitchen as well. Two spots of semen on the bed sheets match the DNA of the victim. Human hair with follicles attached found in the same room have three different owners, Mr and Mrs Flynn and an unknown woman, most likely the person who has left the unidentified prints. A pubic hair found cohered in the before-mentioned semen belongs to this unknown woman. So, without jumping to hasty conclusions, my professional opinion is that Flynn was shagging another woman in his marital bed. If the missus found out, who knows how she would have reacted. She'd certainly have a strong motive to kill the bastard.'

'We're singing from the same hymnbook, Erin,' Holmes finally said. 'Anything else in the house?'

'A bloody big dog lives there, I can tell you that,' O'Meara replied with a chuckle. 'And the food on the bench is probably a week or more old, but you would have guessed that anyway.' She was quiet for a moment, and Holmes could hear her using her keyboard. 'Oh, yeah. There was an earring on the shelves. One of those ones you need pierced ears to wear. There was a tiny fragment of skin on the stud. DNA matches the mystery woman from the bedroom.'

* * *

Bowker felt good to be officially back in harness at the Spencer Street Vicpol headquarters. His Homicide colleagues were happy to see him at work, and it took him less than an hour to become au fait with cases he had been obliged to leave behind when taking his enforced sabbatical. A few new investigations were also underway, including a tragic murder-suicide in the far north of the state and the mysterious death of an organised crime figure who had fallen from a tenth-storey apartment in the city.

As Bowker began reading the crime scene summaries of the latter, a call came through from the police centre's reception desk advising that he had a visitor. A rough-looking woman of indeterminable age was asking to see him and no one else. She was carrying a small cardboard package that had been cleared by security.

When Bowker arrived on the ground floor, the officer behind the desk nodded towards a woman in a leather jacket sitting alone in the lounge area with her back to them, staring out into Spencer Street. Bowker wandered across to where she sat nursing the cardboard box. Her face was familiar but never in this environment. When she looked up and saw Bowker in front of her, she instinctively stood. Dressed in a dirty white tee-shirt and jeans beneath her leather jacket, she also wore heavy boots and a brown leather studded choker.

Without the bikie backdrop and others of her ilk around her, she looked like an elderly woman on her way to a costume party. Bowker felt sorry for her. A teenage runaway, picked up by a young Skeeta Allender when the gang passed through a country town, she was now eating the fruits of her wasted life. In their later years, people often ask themselves if the world was a better place for them being in it. It was hard to know if keeping Skeeta company pushed her life to the positive side of that ledger.

'No, sit down, Janine,' Bowker said. 'It is Janine, isn't it? Skeeta's girlfriend?' He sat down in the chair opposite as the woman dropped back into her seat.

'I'm his partner, not his girlfriend,' Janine quietly corrected. 'And he's Rooter now. Nobody calls him Skeeta anymore, except you and that other detective.'

'Let's call him Daryl, for today,' Bowker said gently. 'You don't like Skeeta, and there's no way I can come at Rooter.'

Janine nodded.

'Where's Daryl now?' Bowker asked.

'He's in custody. All the men have been charged with drug and firearms stuff. There's no bail, cos the police reckon they might shoot through.'

'That would be normal procedure,' Bowker said. 'This all flows from the raid down at Port Fairy, I take it?'

Janine nodded again. 'All us girls have been charged with minor offences and given bail. I guess they feel that without our men, we've got nowhere to go anyway.' She dropped her head. 'They're probably right.'

'What did you want to see me about, Janine?'

She looked at the floor. 'Rooter is going to jail because of the drugs business. But he's more scared that the murder down at Port Fairy might be pinned on him because he was there on the wharf when it happened.'

'OK,' Bowker replied, uncertain of where she was heading.

'Rooter said the only policeman he trusted to do the honest thing was you. He said he'd been in trouble with you before, but it was his fault and you did right by him. He told me you even cleared him of a crime when he was young, even though it would have been easy to just close the case and let him rot in prison.'

Bowker was gobsmacked that Allender could have harboured a positive picture of him when the bikie had such a combative attitude every time they crossed paths.

Janine lifted the cardboard box from her lap and proffered it to him. 'He said to give you this. He said you'd know what to do with it.'

'What's in it?' Bowker asked, taking the box.

'Some stuff he took off his Harley after the man was murdered in Port Fairy. He told me to keep it safe and give it to you if he got taken into custody.'

Janine then stood and walked out through the glass doors into a world Bowker knew would not be kind to her. But that was nothing new for a person of her ilk.

* * *

Bowker didn't open the box until he was back at his desk and had donned rubber gloves. Inside was a motorcycle dash cam system, complete with its various components, including front and rear cameras, a display screen and an assortment of connecting cables. He picked up the display unit, activated it and was relieved on seeing its charge level was high.

Bowker navigated to the control panel and quickly learnt how to reverse, fast forward and play the recorded and date-stamped vision. The system was activated by the motorcycle ignition and automatically turned itself off three minutes after the engine had been shut down. It was a top-end model with high-resolution cameras, large storage capacity, GPS logging and night light enhancement.

It took fifteen minutes of scrolling until Bowker found vision of the time and date he was after. Things must have been quiet that day, since no vision was recorded until after night had fallen, when Allender's bike was started in the Barbarians' compound. As Bowker expected, the weather was diabolical and Allender's journey to the wharf was along empty streets until he passed the Mini Moke departing the carpark. In keeping with the vision Holmes had related seeing on the squid boat's security system, Allender parked his bike under the eaves at the corner of the restaurant. When he dismounted and leaned the bike on its kick stand, the front wheel and handlebars turned slightly, focussing the forward camera on an area between the empty berth where *Hippocrates* would shortly dock and a few metres opposite, under the eaves of the restaurant building. Unfortunately, the camera turned itself off before the vessel had arrived, and the three minutes of vision showed an empty wharf except for Allender as he huddled under the eaves of the building.

When the vision resumed nineteen minutes later, there was a slight shaking of the camera, presumably as Allender was stowing the backpack he'd received from the vessel that was now visible moored against the wharf. Bowker allowed the footage to roll forward, then suddenly lurched back in his chair.

'Fuck me!' he blurted.

CHAPTER 33

The beach was deserted except for the odd sun-lover taking advantage of the ideal weather and warm sand. No one dared venture into the water. Word had quickly circulated that Katy Flynn, a well-known surf club identity and strong swimmer, had disappeared off East Beach. This, combined with the shark mauling her husband's body a few weeks earlier, was enough to evoke images from Spielberg's classic *Jaws*, and no one wanted to offer themselves up as shark bait, not when there was an indoor pool in the town. Tomorrow would be the swimmers' real test of avoiding the cool waves, the day already having total fire ban status across Victoria. Blistering temperatures and rising winds were forecast to make conditions in the tinder-dry state catastrophic.

Holmes and Larsen were seated at a concrete picnic table overlooking the beach and Bass Strait beyond when Bowker's call arrived. Holmes's eyes remained focussed on the line of puffy white clouds dividing the sky from the sea as he put the phone to his ear. 'Holmes,' he said without looking at the screen.

'It's Greg, Sherlock,' Bowker replied. 'I've just sent you an email. It's got twenty seconds of vision attached. Ring me back when you've watched it.' He disconnected immediately, leaving Holmes intrigued.

The email was already in his inbox when Holmes checked. He downloaded the mp4 file and moved closer to Larsen so the two could view the film together. They instantly recognised the wharf area in the teeming rain with the *Hippocrates* moored in her berth. The first few seconds showed Trevor Flynn facing the camera, in deep conversation with his brother-in-law Gareth Matheson under the shelter of the restaurant eaves. Suddenly, over Flynn's shoulder, Matheson caught sight of a figure approaching in the mist and gesticulated in that direction. By the time Flynn had turned one-eighty degrees, Katy Flynn had leapt towards him, driving the kitchen knife into his chest. As Flynn fell to the wharf, she removed the knife from his wound and attempted to thrust it in a second time. Matheson grabbed her hand and wrestled the knife away as the picture shook and swept to the right before focussing on the road as the camera left the scene. The vision ended at the exit to the carpark.

'Fuck me!' Holmes said, his eyes not leaving the screen.

'Ditto for me as well,' Larsen agreed, looking up and staring out towards the horizon.

Holmes played the vision again, this time knowing what was coming and scanning for other information. 'It's obviously dash cam footage. From the position of the camera, I'd say it was on Allender's motorcycle.'

'How did we miss that?'

'I don't think we did. I would have noticed it when I saw his Harley parked in the compound.'

Holmes called Bowker, putting him on loudspeaker so Larsen could hear. 'Where'd you get your greasy hands on that little nugget?' he asked appreciatively.

Bowker explained the visit from Allender's partner and her motives in delivering the breakthrough evidence. Holmes breathed a long sigh of relief when Bowker clarified that the dash cam had been removed immediately after the murder, meaning its presence had not been missed during the investigation.

'Looks to me like a crime of passion?' Holmes suggested. 'And to his credit, Matheson appears to be trying to stop further stabbing.'

'That's the way I read it too, Sherlock. But he's obviously become involved in dumping the body into the river. Flynn would be way too heavy for the wife to get over the edge of the wharf on her own. You'd have to suspect he helped get rid of the murder weapon and her bloodied parka as well.'

'If Allender had sat on his bike for another five minutes, we could have nailed everyone's roles in this,' Larsen suggested with a smile.

'I think we have to be thankful for what we have, Kirsten,' Bowker warned. 'You had Katy pretty well nailed as the killer via the circumstantial evidence, but proving she used the knife would have been difficult without this vision.' He sighed loudly. 'Who would have thought a good deed I did for Skeeta as a kid would bear fruit thirty years later?'

'There was a bit of self-interest there, just the same,' Holmes suggested.

'Yeah, I s'pose,' Bowker replied wistfully.

'So, we now have our killer, but no idea where she's got to,' Larsen said, returning to practicalities. 'No sightings, either dead or alive.'

'You're not ruling out her faking her own death?' Bowker asked.

'Absolutely not, especially now we know she killed Flynn,' Holmes replied. 'But if she did fake her death, where the hell is she? She hasn't been home, and the Warrnambool coppers have checked her brother's place over there. If she drove to Port Fairy and left the Suzuki and dog in the carpark and her gear on the beach, where'd she go to then? Did someone from out of town pick her up? Did she even drive her car at all? Did someone else bring it here and then get a lift somewhere else? The only prints in the car belong to her and her dead husband.' He was silent for a moment as he stared out to sea. 'Maybe the most logical explanation is that she really did go for a swim and either cashed her own chips or was taken by a shark.'

'Where to from here?' Bowker asked.

'To Warrnambool this afternoon. Charge Matheson with being an accessory to murder and see if that shakes out anything about his sister's disappearance. And then I suppose we'll just have to be patient and see if anything surfaces about her one way or another. A yarn to Allender would be handy as well if we don't make progress down here.'

Larsen had her notebook open. 'If we've got nothing extra by tomorrow morning, I reckon we should go for a run up to…' – she consulted her notes – 'Nowhere Creek, would you believe? Matheson told us the only asset his parents had left was the rundown and worthless family home they owned up there. Sounds like a good spot for a hideout.'

Bowker burst into laughter. 'Nowhere Creek! Isn't that the pub in *Crocodile Dundee*?'

'That's *Walkabout* Creek, Greg,' Larsen said, in a faux-mocking tone. 'And looking at the images on Google Earth, there sure ain't no pub at Nowhere Creek.'

* * *

It was exactly twelve noon the next day when the detectives drove into Elmhurst, a small village on the Pyrenees Highway between Ararat and Maryborough. Like so many tiny rural towns, it had long passed its glory days, but evidence remained of a once-thriving centre, with the odd old stately building and a number of long-closed shops. The hotel appeared on its last legs, and a modern primary school in one of the backstreets had a recently installed *Closed* sign across its front fence. The one-officer police station provided the only service left in the town.

On a different day, this would have been an idyllic setting. The village, with its tree-lined service roads on each side of the highway, was set in a valley in the shadows of the Pyrenees Ranges, close to the headwaters of the Wimmera River. But in today's conditions, the location was terrifying. The temperatures were extreme, and the hot wind roared through the gap in the hills. The further north Holmes and Larsen had travelled, the more they regretted making such a speculative expedition on a day like this. However, they'd come this far, so when Holmes spotted the fingerboard indicating Nowhere Creek was just another ten kilometres down a side road, they made the commitment to finish the trip they'd started.

The previous night had been a long one. Matheson continued to deny all knowledge of Flynn's murder until shown Allender's dash cam footage. At that point, all resistance crumbled. He admitted to helping drag Flynn's body into the Moyne River and aiding in the disposal of the murder weapon. He denied being party to the murder and cited the footage he'd been shown as evidence he had attempted to prevent his sister from stabbing Flynn a second time. He claimed that Katy had acted in a fit of rage on finding evidence that her husband had again been unfaithful. All this on top of his regular physical abuse had finally proved too much. In answer to the key question concerning the whereabouts of his sister, he said he was hoping for a miracle but feared she had drowned. She had departed his house in Warrnambool in a depressed state on news that her cancer was not responding to treatment and that her prognosis was unfavourable in the long term. This report, paired with the murder investigation, may have pushed her over the edge, Matheson feared.

At the conclusion of this long interview, the surgeon was charged with being an accessory to murder, obstructing a police investigation and a string of lessor offences. With charges still pending from the drug squad, he was held in custody, awaiting an application for bail.

* * *

Nowhere Creek was little more than a sparse collection of farmhouses in a cleared valley between two wooded spurs of the Pyrenees Range. Finding the Matheson house was a nightmare, particularly on a windy and dusty day like this. The only sign of life, besides a small mob of sheep milling in the shade of a large gum tree, was an old Holden ute approaching on the dirt road ahead. Larsen wound down her window and, after being mugged by the stifling heat, was able to wave down the vehicle, which stopped alongside so that the drivers could speak face to face in the middle of the otherwise deserted road. An elderly bearded man with a red weatherworn face stared across at Larsen, assessing the stranger without saying a word.

'We're looking for the Matheson place,' she said, the hot wind stinging her eyes.

'Picked a day for it,' the elderly man said. 'A fire comes up this valley and there's no way out except the road behind you.'

'So, the Matheson place?' Larsen persisted.

'You family?' the man asked. 'Coming up to check on your asset before it's sold?'

Holmes stretched across from his seat. 'It's for sale?'

The old man shrugged. 'That's the rumour from a tradie who's been up there checking the power and the rainwater situation. I wouldn't buy it. Hasn't been lived in for decades. End of the world up here, mate. They don't call it Nowhere Creek for nothing.'

Following the man's directions, the police officers finally found the cottage hidden in overgrown scrub. The house had once been a reasonable dwelling, better than Matheson had described, anyway, but years of neglect had taken their toll. There were signs a little work was being done on the place, but much more would be needed to make it comfortably liveable and even more to make it saleable. There was no sign of a vehicle and no suggestion anyone had lived there for many years. The back door, sheltered by a dirt-floored veranda, was unlocked, allowing Holmes to make his way through the dwelling. Except for the dust and a strong musty smell, the interior was more presentable than he expected, but a long way from being inhabitable except by possums.

Larsen inspected an old shed to the rear of the house and found it contained nothing but junk. Around the back were old building materials stacked in heaps that Larsen felt sure housed a nest of snakes. Further into the block was dense bush, which she guessed ran down to Nowhere Creek itself.

As she turned to make her way back to the house, her phone pinged with an incoming message. It was from Dale Small. *We still good?* it asked, followed by a fingers-crossed emoji.

Larsen thought for a moment before replying. *Yeah. Still good*, she keyed in. She added a smiley face before sending.

'She's not here, and there's no sign she has been, either,' Holmes yelled from the back step, sweat running off his brow.

The wind buffeted the cottage, and a loose piece of roofing iron slapped somewhere above.

'I say we get out of here before a fire races up this valley,' Larsen said, trudging back towards the house.

Holmes nodded his agreement as he used his shirt to wipe the sweat from his eyes.

CHAPTER 34

It was difficult to keep people back from the edge once news flashed around town about what had washed up among the bluestone rocks lining the shore. But at least the growing crowd respected the exclusion tape that Constable Farrell had hastily rolled out to prevent onlookers descending from the grassed area beside the road and onto the rocky outcrop below.

'If there's a positive side, I s'pose it explains the disappearance,' Senior Sergeant Megan Wilkins said as she crouched on her haunches, using a gloved hand to scrape away sand from a half-buried left foot carrying the lifesavers club tattoo. 'Saves expanding the search.' She stood up and snapped off her latex gloves. 'Not a great way to leave this world, though, is it? Bloody shark bait.'

Farrell shrugged. 'Worms or fish, once you're dead there's not a lot of difference, I suppose.'

'Once you're dead, yeah,' Wilkins replied, not looking at the older but junior officer. 'Getting to the dead stage is where I'd prefer a shark not to be involved.'

* * *

Holmes and Larsen were a few kilometres south of Ararat when the call came through.

'And it's definitely her?' Holmes asked.

'What's left of her, anyway,' Wilkins replied. 'Lower leg. It's got her lifesavers club tatt on the ankle. DNA will confirm it's her, but to me there's no doubt.'

'What condition is the leg in?' Larsen asked. 'It's been in the water for a few days.'

'What you'd expect. Crabs have been into it a fair bit. Lot of loose flesh where the leg has been torn away. I'll send a photo to your phone.'

Holmes looked at Larsen and exhaled loudly, relieved that this tricky investigation had reached a conclusion.

'Where were the remains found in relation to where she went in for the swim?' Larsen asked.

'Around the other side of the town, near the Old Passage. There's half a dozen mates who go surfing there most mornings. The tide was running out, and they found the remains snagged between two bluestone boulders in the shallows.'

'What's your plan from here?' Holmes asked.

'A forensic team should arrive in the next few minutes,' Wilkins replied. 'We're just guarding the scene until they get here. I'm thinking of closing the beaches until we get our head around things.' She chuckled. 'I don't think anybody will be too keen for a swim once news about this gets out properly. The surfers here decided they might leave it for another day, in spite of the big swell that's coming in.'

'Too bloody hot to be out and about anyway,' Holmes said.

'You're telling me,' Wilkins replied. 'I'm standing on the edge of the Southern Ocean and I'm about to melt. The wind's coming in from the north and bringing that inland heat with it. I'd hate to be in a seaside place like Anglesea on a day like today. A fire would rip down from the Otways and turn all that tea tree into an inferno.' She hesitated for a moment. 'Look, a forensic van from

Warrnambool has just pulled up, so I'll have to catch you later.' She disconnected the call.

Larsen looked at Holmes. 'So, we started with a shark and we finish with a shark.'

Holmes nodded slowly. 'Who would have thunk it, eh?' He chuckled. 'We've spent nearly a month down here and uncovered a drug importing racket, dodgy land deals and blackmail, and what do we find is the motive for the murder we set out to investigate? A husband shagging another woman. You could write a book about it and no one would believe you.'

'Time to head home, you reckon?'

'Yeah. Mission accomplished, as the saying goes. We'll pack our gear this arvo and piss off in the morning.' Holmes looked across at Larsen. 'How about we take the locals out to The Stump in appreciation for their support?'

He immediately regretted making the suggestion. Providing a final opportunity for Kirsten and Small to socialise was the last thing he wanted when he and his partner could quietly slip out of town now the case was solved.

'Yeah, good idea,' Larsen replied enthusiastically. 'After all, we couldn't have done it without Grant Farrell.'

They both laughed, Holmes covering his annoyance with himself.

CHAPTER 35

The cold wind whistled down Spencer Street on Tuesday morning. Showers of sleety rain had started before dawn, and the city had that colourless appearance usually associated with the depths of winter. The traffic splashed through puddles, and pedestrians hurried from the shelter of the railway bridge to the shopfront verandas further down the street.

High above the roadway sat the headquarters for the homicide squad in the Vicpol centre. It was mid-morning when Erin O'Meara rang Holmes with the forensic results on Katy Flynn's remains. Bowker and Larsen gathered around their colleague's desk as he switched his phone to loudspeaker.

'DNA analysis confirms the remains are those of Katherine Flynn, or Katy, as she is known to you,' O'Meara announced, stopping every few words to clear her throat. 'Tests show the leg had been in the water for two or three days by the time it was delivered to us. Tissue around the knee area was severely torn, the bones sliced cleanly, in keeping with an attack by a large predator. Almost certainly a shark, and a big fucker at that.'

Holmes smiled. 'Is that a technical term, Erin?'

'Bloody oath,' she replied, before continuing with her summary. 'Since the initial attack, the remaining tissue displays damage from smaller animals, most probably crabs or other crustaceans.'

'Nothing goes to waste in the ocean, by the sounds of it,' Bowker said.

'I know she committed murder, but you can't help but feel some sympathy for the way it's all panned out,' Larsen said sadly.

'She had a tough row to hoe even if the Noah's ark didn't get her. Her leg contained a leiomyosarcoma, so her future would have been problematic anyway.'

Larsen frowned. 'Leiomyosarcoma? I presume that's a fancy name for cancer? We know she was being treated.'

'Yeah,' O'Meara replied. 'Cancer of the soft tissues. Nasty stuff. Her calf was full of it.' She was quiet for a moment. 'Maybe having a big shark go whack is preferable to fading away in palliative care. Scare the shit out of you for about five seconds, then it's all over.' Her mood lightened suddenly. 'Listen, gotta go. Chris Pullen, one of my top operators, is standing at the door.' She lowered her voice. 'If I was thirty years younger, I'd make a play for this guy.' She exhaled loudly with a slight cough. 'But I think that ship might have sailed. Catch ya.' She hung up before the detectives could thank her.

Bowker gently placed his hands on his colleagues' backs. 'Well done, you two. A difficult case with a lot of distractions.' He raised his eyebrows. 'Not least of which was yours truly.' He nodded and walked back to his desk.

'I'll start the paperwork,' Larsen said, wandering away.

Holmes stared at his sleeping computer screen, unsure what still worried him. He opened his internet browser and started typing. After twenty minutes reading, he climbed to his feet and walked to Larsen's desk, tapping her on the shoulder as he passed. 'Grab your jacket. You can drive.'

CHAPTER 36

Today, Nowhere Creek looked a different world to the Friday before. Misty cloud hung low over the Pyrenees. The dirt road was sloppy and carried puddles where dustbowls had sat just days prior. Larsen was dubious about Holmes's theory until she spotted Matheson's silver Porsche parked in the long grass beside the old family house.

'Matheson is locked up, so what's his car doing here?' Larsen asked as she quietly pulled their vehicle up behind the sports car.

'My money's on his wife driving it up,' Holmes said.

They climbed from their vehicle and made their way to the rear of the cottage. There, under the verandah and out of the rain, sat a middle-aged woman neither detective recognised. Opposite, across an old garden table, sat Katy Flynn, the stump of her left leg propped up on another chair.

When she saw the detectives, her head dropped, acknowledging that their elaborate plan had fallen at the last hurdle. 'How did you know?' she asked quietly.

'The results of the autopsy on your leg came back this morning,' Holmes replied. 'You had a leiomyosarcoma. I looked up Doctor Google, and it seems that amputation of the affected area is often the only successful treatment, particularly if the cancer is yet to metastasise. Get rid of it before it invades the rest of your body.

And in most cases, you don't need follow-up chemo.' Holmes smiled. 'Combine that with the fact you knew we were close to proving you murdered your husband, and a fabricated shark attack becomes an attractive strategy to disappear off the face of the earth.'

Flynn looked away and stared absently into the bush, where water dripped off sagging foliage.

Holmes shook his head and chuckled. 'I have to give it to you. It was an ingenious plan, and one not available to just anyone, of course. The average murderer doesn't have a brother who's an orthopaedic surgeon and a sister-in-law who does anaesthetics. And your brother keeping a few craypots where he can put your amputated leg on the bottom of the ocean for a few days is another lucky break.'

Larsen looked at the second woman. 'I presume you're Gareth Matheson's wife?'

The woman nodded but didn't look up. 'Doctor Helen Abbott.'

'I assume you planted the leg in the rocks in Port Fairy, unless this scam involves more people than we think?' Larsen asked.

Abbott nodded again, tears welling in her eyes. 'Gareth was supposed to do it, but you went and arrested him, didn't you? He told me where to put it so the early-morning surfers were sure to find it. Just in case, I had to wait up the street to check it was discovered. If the surfers didn't turn up, I was to collect the leg and move it to a more noticeable spot on East Beach. But that was a last resort. We didn't want it to be found too close to where Katy had been reported missing.'

'A bit too obvious, you reckon?' Holmes suggested.

Abbott nodded. 'And if we placed it in a remote location, no one would find it.' She began to cry. 'I agreed to do the anaesthetic because the leg needed to come off anyway. I never intended to get in this deep. Gareth was supposed to place the leg in the rocks and bring Katy up here.' She stared up at Holmes, looking for sympathy. 'I've been left holding the baby.'

'You drove Katy's Suzuki to Port Fairy and left it in the carpark with the dog, though, didn't you?' Holmes asked aggressively. 'You wore gloves, so you're no babe in the woods here. I presume your husband drove you back to Warrnambool after you deposited Katy's gear on the beach?'

Abbott nodded as she sobbed out loud.

'And you were happy to live the life of luxury that the drug money bought you,' Larsen added.

Abbott stared at the ground and sniffed loudly. 'The whole thing just spun out of control.'

'Indeed it did, Doctor Abbott,' Holmes replied. 'Where'd you do the operation? I assume you couldn't use the hospital. Too many people would know about it for your scheme to work.'

'There's a small theatre for outpatients at the back of my GP clinic. It's mainly used by the practice nurse for wounds, injections, ECGs, that sort of thing. Gareth and I did the operation there one night last week.'

'So where did you stash Katy before she came up here?' Larsen asked.

'We have friends who are overseas at present, and they gave us a key so we could keep an eye on the place while they were away. Katy stayed there while she recovered enough to travel. Either Gareth or I were with her every night. Once the bleeding is under control, it's pretty plain sailing if you keep up the antibiotics.'

Holmes walked up the steps and looked through the back door, into the kitchen. 'Wow! Improvement since Friday. Cleaners must have been here all weekend.'

Katy Flynn was puzzled. 'You were here Friday?'

'Yeah,' Holmes replied. 'Your brother mentioned it in one of his rants about being a self-made man. When you first went missing, we suspected this place would make a good hideout if you had faked your own disappearance. When the leg was found, that theory went down the gurgler. But now we know that you two were smarter than we thought.'

'But not smart enough,' Flynn replied. 'The fuckin' cancer. Even when it's cut out, it comes back to get me.' She looked at the ground and spoke quietly. 'Probably come back anyway.'

'I'm sure you'll get decent treatment in prison,' Larsen said. 'So look on the bright side.'

Flynn didn't reply. She took the sobbing Abbott's hand across the table, wondering how this has spiralled so far out of control.

Holmes turned to his partner. 'Can you ring Port Fairy and let Megan Wilkins know the shark attack was a hoax? Time to let people back into the water, although with weather like this, only the hardy will want to get wet.' He laughed. 'Won't stop the surfers, though. They'll go out in a bloody hurricane.'

'Bigger waves,' Larsen said with a smile before walking to their vehicle and retrieving her phone. She had Wilkins on the line within seconds. 'Good news, Megan,' she said, standing inside the open door, elbows on the roof of the car. 'Katy Flynn is right here beside us. Her disappearance was an elaborate sham. You can all relax down there. You haven't got a killer shark.'

There was silence from Wilkins before she finally spoke. 'I wish that were true, Kirsten. A surfer was attacked at the Passage Break this morning. He died before the others could get him to the hospital.' She hesitated as her voice caught. 'It was Dale Small.'

Larsen let the phone slip from her hand and bounce onto the seat of the car. She stared out vacantly towards the cloud-topped hills.

www.ingramcontent.com/pod-product-compliance
Lightning Source LLC
Chambersburg PA
CBHW070827020826
48982CB00015B/721

* 9 7 8 1 7 6 3 8 6 9 5 2 3 *